A Woman Unknown

Also by Frances Brody

Dying in the Wool
A Medal for Murder
Murder in the Afternoon

A Woman Unknown

A Kate Shackleton Mystery

Frances BRODY

Minotaur Books
A Thomas Dunne Book
New York

A THOMAS DUNNE BOOK FOR MINOTAUR BOOKS.
An imprint of St. Martin's Publishing Group.

A WOMAN UNKNOWN. Copyright © 2012 by Frances McNeil. All rights reserved. Printed in the United States of America. For information, address St. Martin's Press, 175 Fifth Avenue, New York, N.Y. 10010.

www.thomasdunnebooks.com
www.minotaurbooks.com

The Library of Congress has cataloged the hardcover edition as follows:

Brody, Frances.
    A woman unknown / Frances Brody. — First U.S. edition.
        p. cm. — (A Kate Shackleton mystery ; 4)
    ISBN 978-1-250-03704-6 (hardcover)
    ISBN 978-1-250-03705-3 (e-book)
    1. Women private investigators—England—Fiction.   2. Murder—
Investigation—Fiction.   I. Title.
    PR6113.C577W66 2015
    823'.92—dc23   2014040120

ISBN 978-1-250-08717-1 (trade paperback)

Our books may be purchased in bulk for promotional, educational, or business use. Please contact your local bookseller or the Macmillan Corporate and Premium Sales Department at (800) 221-7945, extension 5442, or by e-mail at MacmillanSpecialMarkets@macmillan.com.

First published in Great Britain by Piatkus, an imprint of Little, Brown Book Group, an Hachette UK company

First Minotaur Books Paperback Edition: January 2016

10 9 8 7 6 5 4 3 2 1

'Most men were gentlemen enough to go through the farce of adultery with "a woman unknown" and thus give their wives grounds for divorcing them.'

The Long Weekend, Robert Graves and Alan Hodge

Prologue

The Times

Monday, September 3, 1923

Mr Everett Roderick Runcie has died at the age of forty-seven. Mr Runcie, younger brother of the third Baron Kirkley and a director of Kirkley Bank, had returned to Yorkshire for the start of the grouse shooting season.

A well-known, convivial figure, Mr Runcie was seen in public last Wednesday, at the Ebor Handicap, where he appeared to be in rude health and good spirits, though not enjoying a winning streak.

A charismatic and energetic character, and a patron of the arts, Mr Runcie was unafraid of adventurous schemes. He recently excited enthusiasm among certain investors with his championing of the Big G mine, Tasmania, and the Bechuanaland Peanut Farm Company.

Mr Runcie married Miss Philippa Emerson, only daughter of the American chain store magnate, in 1918. They divided their time between Cavendish Square, London, and Kirkley Hall, Yorkshire.

The Coroner has ordered an inquest.

Ten days earlier

My name is Kate Shackleton. I am a private investigator, drawn to the work almost accidentally through trying to discover what happened to my husband, Gerald, last seen towards the end of the Great War. I received the usual telegram: missing presumed dead. Part of me has gone on hoping he will still be alive. After five years, hopes dim, but occasionally some odd story from the newspapers, or a Chinese whisper of survival, wafts hope to life.

At half past six on an August evening, I was picking out a new tune on the piano, and deciding it was time to send for the tuner, when I heard a familiar rat-a-tat-tat at the backdoor. I closed the piano lid. My ex-policeman assistant does not usually sidle up to the back door in his size tens. He is a front door person.

Walking along the hall, I wondered what brought him here at a time when he would usually be at home with his wife, Rosie, and their children.

Mr Sykes pressed his nose against the kitchen window. I opened the door and stood aside to let him in.

He whipped off his trilby. 'Sorry to call out of the

blue, Mrs Shackleton. I'd just sat down for my tea when someone turned up on my doorstep in a right state of agitation, asking for our help. Told him I couldn't make any promises till I'd talked to you.'

'Who is he?'

'Mr Cyril Fitzpatrick.' He spoke the name meaningfully in his this-could-spell-trouble voice.

'And what have you done with Mr Fitzpatrick?'

'He's sitting on your front wall. I told him to wait there while I spoke to you.'

'What does Mr Fitzpatrick want?' I led the way into the dining room that doubles as my office.

'He's concerned about his wife. What she might be up to behind his back.' Sykes parked his trilby on top of the Remington typewriter. 'I'll feel responsible if Mrs Fitzpatrick has gone dancing down the wrong path. You remember how we got her out of trouble last year?'

I liked his royal 'we'. Sykes had been on store detective duty in Marshalls when he spotted Mrs Fitzpatrick slipping a bottle of perfume into her shopping bag. He challenged her. She burst into tears. He led the distressed damsel to the manager's office. She explained that only the day before she had called the doctor to her mother and learned that there was no hope. The tissue paper-wrapped bought-and-paid-for length of flannelette was to make a nightdress for her mother. Mrs Fitzpatrick had been preoccupied by bad news, leading her to be absent-minded about the expensive perfume.

Sykes had felt sure she was honest. I guessed that she must be young and good looking.

'Let me guess. Mr Fitzpatrick suspects his wife is shoplifting again?'

2

Sykes sighed. 'He claims she's up to something, and he doesn't know what. Says he's at his wits' end.'

'If every wits-end husband and wife came a-calling, they'd queue all the way to Woodhouse Moor.'

'That's as may be. But if she is shoplifting, letting her off won't do my reputation any good.'

'You sit down. I'll let Mr Fitzpatrick in.' I turned back at the dining room door. 'Is there anything I need to know before we see him?'

Sykes shook his head. 'He'll have plenty to say for himself.'

Sykes had met both Mr and Mrs Fitzpatrick. I had met neither.

As I looked at the man who stood inches from my front step, gazing at me expectantly, a frisson of uneasiness made me wish he had found his way to someone else's door. He looked at me from desolate brown eyes, whipping off a brown trilby to reveal thick dark-brown hair, tinged with grey, glistening with hair oil, and combed straight back from a low forehead. He smoothed a nervous finger over his neatly trimmed moustache. In the lapel of his brown striped suit, he wore a Sacred Heart pin. Over his arm he carried a brown overcoat, in spite of the warmth of the August evening. His brown boots shone from spit and polish. The image that came to me was of a wounded seal, washed up and losing its gloss.

'Mr Fitzpatrick? Please come in. I'm Mrs Shackleton.'

His damp handshake strengthened my notion of his likeness to a seal.

Sykes had been gazing out of the dining room window and turned as we came in.

Sitting at the top of the table, my back to the window,

I felt the warmth of the last rays of the evening sun on my head and neck. Shafts of light played across the table. Fitzpatrick took the seat to my right, opposite Sykes.

'It's about my wife,' Fitzpatrick said, without waiting to be asked. 'As I explained to Mr Sykes, Deirdre disappears for days at a time. She has me frantic with worry. I want to know what she's up to.'

I groaned inwardly. This was the kind of request I dreaded.

'Mr Sykes may have explained that we do not take on matrimonial cases.'

'This is not what they call a matrimonial case, Mrs Shackleton. There's nothing wrong between us. I only want to know where she is going, what she is doing.' He flashed an appealing glance at Sykes. 'She could be up to her old tricks. If she's caught again, she won't get off so lightly. It will be prison, shame, disgrace.'

Sykes could not have shut his trap more tightly if he had uncorked and swallowed a bottle of glue, but his concern was obvious.

'Can you be more precise, Mr Fitzpatrick, about what gives you cause for concern?'

I almost said 'suspicion', but chose my words carefully so as not to fuel his anxieties.

He placed his big hands flat on the table. 'Sometimes I wonder has a person got a hold over her, to make her do things she wouldn't do, or is getting money out of her.'

'You speak as though you believe there is extortion of some kind, or that your wife is being blackmailed. Do you have grounds for such fears?'

'The word blackmail has come to me but I don't know

4

from where. I just know she's up to something. I feel it in my bones.'

I resisted the urge to ask which bones, knee bones, funny bones, skull, but nodded encouragement. 'How long have you been married?'

Be careful, Kate, I told myself. Next I would be saying they should talk it over, and spend a weekend at Blackpool, just the two of them, while the weather held.

'Six years. We married at St Anne's in 1917.' He produced a wedding photograph from an inside pocket and pushed it across the table towards me.

The photograph had been removed from a frame. The bride looked happy and confident. She was petite, with wavy hair, high cheek bones and an infectious smile. The groom looked as though he had bet on the wrong horse and lost his wages. 'What age was she when you married?'

'Eighteen.' He shifted uncomfortably in his chair. 'I'm going on forty-five. She has twenty-four summers but looks like spring. Why wouldn't she? I've given her an easy life. She doesn't work. We have no children.' His lower lip quivered. 'And now she's off all hours.'

Fitzpatrick seemed a kindly man. His uneasiness was palpable. 'Have you asked your wife where she goes?'

He frowned. 'She tells lies. Short of locking her in the house what am I to do? I have to work. I did try locking the door once, when we'd had words, but she climbed out of the window. And there's always a plausible story. Her mother is ill. Her aunt at the convent has invited her on a retreat. Another man would beat her over it, but she is so …' He turned to Sykes. 'You know how exquisite she is. I could never raise a hand to her.'

He spoke as if we had suggested such a thing. 'Perhaps she is telling the truth,' I said.

'Oh she is always partly telling the truth. Since she found out last year that her mother is not long for this world, she's there all the time, at the house she grew up in, on the Bank, and you know what sort of area that is.'

I knew the Bank only by reputation. A poor area of the city, situated between the railway line and the river. It was said that the police rarely ventured there.

The sun on the back of my head made me feel a little dizzy. I moved my chair.

He sighed. 'I'm a compositor on the local paper. When I married, I was earning four pounds, one shilling a week. Since then, we've had nothing but wage cuts. I'm down to three pounds, eight and six.'

Sykes raised an eyebrow. This was still a good wage, given the hardship of our times.

Fitzpatrick drummed his fingers on the table. 'I've borne a wage reduction of twelve shillings and sixpence, but have I cut her housekeeping? No, I have not. I took her out of poverty. Now she wants more than I can afford. Is she giving someone money?' He leaned forward, making fists of his hands. 'When I refused her a guinea, she said she didn't care, and it would come from somewhere else. That is what made me wonder, is she out stealing?'

I had the impression that he was stressing the possibility of shoplifting only because this was what most disturbed Sykes.

He coughed, and said apologetically, 'Sorry. Weak chest.'

When he had recovered, I asked, 'Regarding your suspicions about your wife stealing, have you noticed any items in the house that you have reason to believe were obtained dishonestly?'

'I came home a month ago to find her dancing like a dervish to the latest music. She had this gramophone, and no explanation of where it came from. And now it's gone. She says it's being repaired, but she's sold it, or pawned it. Well where did it come from? Who carried it for her? She has an old sweetheart who hangs about, making himself useful to her mother.'

'I don't see how we can help, Mr Fitzpatrick.'

He touched the Sacred Heart badge in his lapel. 'She could have got in with some shoplifting gang.'

Sykes's jaw tightened. He said nothing. For a moment, the three of us sat in uneasy silence. Was Fitzpatrick here to admit that his rage was about to explode, that he might do who knows what if he did not find some explanation that satisfied his doubts, and jealousy?

Fitzpatrick hunched, drawing his arms into his body. 'I have a house that was my parents. They are both gone to their eternal rest. I promised Deirdre that she would want for nothing. And I kept my promise. But I think she was disappointed that I did not agree to bring her mother to live with us. Perhaps I should have, only ...'

'Only what?' I prompted.

'When I first said no, she said that I would say that wouldn't I, because people would think her mother was my wife, and she was our daughter. She can be very cruel. Last year, when I knew how ill my mother-in-law was, I said to invite her. But then she wouldn't come, said she knew when she wasn't wanted.'

Sykes finally spoke. 'Would it hurt,' he said, looking at me, 'to see that Mrs Fitzpatrick is coming to no harm?

7

After all, I was the one who ensured no charge was brought against her.'

'I'll pay, of course,' Fitzpatrick said, hand to his inside pocket, ready to bring out his wallet then and there.

I told him our daily rate, and that if we took on the case, he would be billed in the usual way.

His lip twitched. 'Please don't send an invoice to me at home. If Deirdre sees it, she'll wonder what I'm up to.'

I glanced again at the wedding photograph. This seemed such an unlikely coupling.

It was against my better judgement, but looking from Fitzpatrick to Sykes, I decided that it would not hurt to take a closer look at this young woman who aroused such strong emotions.

Two

Deirdre sat next to her mother's bed in the small white-washed room, with its familiar damp amber patterns on ceiling and walls. The room smelled of camphor, essence of violets and boiled cabbage from last night's supper. She smoothed the familiar tufts of the counterpane.

Mam had dozed off. In her sleep she murmured. Her eyelids twitched dreams. She would be back in the misty Ireland of her childhood, a place about which Deirdre heard endless stories but had never visited.

What convinced Deirdre that her mother must leave this house was the time the rat came down the chimney. Now she spotted another bloody flea on the bed sheet. She snapped it between expert fingers, and then dropped it in the chamber pot, the only way to deal with the little devils. They lurked in cracks in the walls, planning torments. You could murder half a dozen in a minute; there would still be a small army waiting to drop from the ceiling. There'd be none of that in the nursing home.

Sometimes Deirdre transported a flea or two home in the seams of her dress. Fitz would complain that she came back stinking of poverty and trailing disease. He worried about his health and his weak chest.

Her mother opened her eyes and gave a gummy smile. 'I thought you'd gone home.' Her body might be wasted, but her mind was sharp as ever. 'What time is it?'

'It's twelve o'clock. I've brought you calves foot jelly. While you eat it, I've summat to tell you.'

A spark of hope lit her mother's eyes. 'You've heard from Anthony?'

'No.' It took a few moments for Deirdre to raise her mother up and prop her with pillows. She placed a towel under her mother's chin, and handed her the spoon and dish.

Her mam swallowed a mouthful of the jelly. Then she said, 'I dreamed Anthony came. I'm sure he's on his way.'

She wanted to see her son once more, before she died. She had dictated a touching note to the little boy who had left for New York twenty-three years ago. The words had made Deirdre squirm.

'Don't get your hopes up, Mam. He hasn't written.'

'In the dream he was just the age as when he left. His locks hadn't been shorn. Your uncle did that, took the scissors to make a big boy of him.'

Deirdre said nothing. She had written to her brother Anthony every year since she was ten, and in a decade and a half had received two brief replies. Two months before marrying Fitz she developed cold feet and wrote to Anthony. Would he send the fare for herself and Mam to go to New York? Answer came there none. She married Fitz.

'Mam, I'm making an arrangement for you to be more comfortable.'

Her mother dug the spoon into the jelly and left it there. 'I'll accept nothing from Fitzpatrick.'

'There's this lovely place, run by a woman whose grandmother came from Kilkenny. You'll build up your strength. There's a garden to look out on.'

'I won't accept that man's charity.'

'I'm paying for it. I have a job, working for a solicitor.'

Even before she reached Leeds Bridge, Deirdre caught the tang of the River Aire, a sharp, foggy, back of the throat smell. Lucky river, winding to sea. On this hot August Friday afternoon, wouldn't she love to be flowing in that direction herself? She ran her hand along the ironwork bridge, and for her pains muckied the creamy fingers of her glove.

Below, two bargemen called to each other. Looking along the riverbank, she saw Calls Landing, its name painted in glory-of-God-size lettering on the side of the building. It was grand to be in the town with its hustle and bustle. In the distance, the protestant parish church stood smug and certain, sharp against the sky.

A used-up creature shuffled towards her. He caught her eye, as though one person with no legitimate business would always recognise another. The sole of his left shoe flapping, he sidled out a little to give way. He was a man down on his luck, passing the time until nightfall when he would be let in to some lodging house, or the Salvation Army hostel. Deirdre dipped her hand in her pocket and slipped him a coin.

And then she saw the man: Giuseppe Barnardini, lithe, lean and looking not a day over thirty. There was something comical and unmistakeable about him as he lolled over the bridge, bantering with the bargemen.

This man was different from her previous two encounters. The first boy-o had been a will-o'-the-wisp fellow with a shocking cough. The second, a stout chap of few words, half-heartedly asked her to name her price for something extra. He did not take it amiss when she declined.

And now Barnardini, who was gazing at her, in something like wonder.

She heard herself say, 'Are you the man himself?'

He raised his hat, and gave a slight but stately bow. 'If you are the lady herself, then yes, I am he.' He reached to take her bag. 'May I?'

She did not release her grip on the overnight bag. 'No need.'

For a moment, he looked ready to argue his gallant point, and then he shrugged. 'You know the rules. I abide. Shall we begin our adventure, Mrs Fitzpatrick?'

'Why not?' She looked beyond, along the bridge. Their destination, the Adelphi Hotel, lurked just out of view. 'If we are to do this properly we had better call each other by our Christian names.'

'Of course. I'm Joseph Barnard. Call me Joe. Giuseppe Barnardini is my stage name.'

Before she had time to say her Christian name, a tallish man in a raincoat appeared out of nowhere. He whipped out a small camera which he pointed towards the river, but she unaccountably felt the camera's eye on her. She knew this man, with his trademark check cap and sandy moustache. He was the newspaper photographer who took a photograph of children paddling in the river by Kirkstall Abbey earlier in the summer. Fitz had proudly introduced her. She glared at the photographer. He had better not show her picture to Fitz.

Deirdre turned away. Joe was onto the man in an instant. 'I say, you took our picture.'

'Oh no, sir.' The photographer held his camera aloft. 'I'm capturing the bridge and the river. You saw which way my lens pointed. But if you want your picture taken . . .' The photographer held out his hand. 'Diamond, Len Diamond, at your service. I recognise you, sir. It's Mr Barnardini, isn't it? I'm a great admirer of yours. No one sings light opera better. I always say you should be singing at Covent Garden.'

Deirdre took a few slow steps towards the far side of the bridge, hearing Joe blithely accepting the photographer's reassurance.

The vain eejit posed for his photograph. Diamond produced a different camera from his bag. Sure you had to be strong to carry that much stuff around with you, but Deirdre knew someone who was stronger. Let Diamond try and get her into bother with Fitz and he'd rue the day.

Joe caught up with her. He once again reached for her bag. 'I can't let you carry that. It looks bad.' He crooked his arm for her to link him. 'Don't worry about the photographer. If he took our picture, what of it? We weren't holding hands. We mustn't be on edge.'

Deirdre took his arm. This was all too close to home. She should have reckoned on that. Next time she was home, she would casually say, 'Fitz, when I walked across Leeds Bridge the other afternoon, a fellow asked me for directions.'

The wondrous sight of the Adelphi Hotel sent her worries packing. The hotel curved around the corner, like an elegant mermaid flapping its tail and grabbing space for its ornate self on both Dock Street and Hunslet Road. Look at me and marvel, it would call, if mermaids could truly sing. Stepping through the pillared doorway, she breathed deep to catch the magnificent whirl of tobacco smoke, ale and grandeur. Pale green leaf-like shapes decorated shining cream tiles. Brass handles gleamed on the wooden doors. The opaque glass of the first bar was etched with the words *Smoke Room 1*.

Joe led the way along the corridor, between the tap room on the left, and the broad staircase on the right, to a lounge at the back, empty at this time of day. She took this to be the best room, all plush seats, dark wood tables, ornate fireplace and aspidistras.

Moments later the waiter came, his sparse hair white as his apron.

'We are to be resident,' her man said, 'Mr and Mrs Joseph Barnard.'

'Ah yes, sir.' The waiter tilted his head, as if all the better to hear. 'What will you have?'

'A pint of your best bitter for me, and darling? Gin and tonic?'

She nodded. You wouldn't want the waiter to think a husband didn't know his wife's tipple.

When the waiter had gone, Deirdre said, 'From your stage name, I expected an Italian.'

He laughed. 'Barnardini. Good, eh? I stole it from a handsome Italian magician entertaining tourists in Cairo. I didn't know then that I would pursue a career in the most English of operettas.'

Cairo. The name conjured all that was wonderful, kasbahs and hookahs and snakes from a basket.

He looked down at his right knee that was moving

rapidly up and down of its own accord as if it had been wound with a small key. 'Excuse my leg. Nerves.' He placed his palm on it to keep it still. 'This never happens when I'm on stage.'

'Tell me about your travels.'

Over drinks, Joe obliged her request. He spoke of pyramids, the River Nile that flowed from south to north, the dhows, of men in turbans, coffee that made your hair curl, tired donkeys, bolts of silk, and perfumes fit for Cleopatra, until she felt half dizzy with wonder.

Half an hour later, warmed by gin and the heat of the afternoon seeping into the attic room, Deirdre stood by the large oval window, looking down at the street. A tram glided to a halt. The conductor helped a tiny old woman up the high step.

Joe tapped on the door and entered. 'I've done the deed and signed the hotel register.'

He was looking at her. It was that look. She placed the folded navy blouse in the drawer, setting its ties neatly, and then sat down on the straight-back chair.

'There's something you should be clear about.'

'Oh?' He sat on the bed and gazed at her solemnly.

'Mr Barnard, we're here for one reason, to provide your wife with the evidence she needs to divorce you, no less than that and certainly no more. So I'll say this sooner rather than later. I find it a good idea to have a bolster between us ...'

He opened his mouth to speak. She raised her hand. This being her third time, there would be no difficulty about putting him straight. 'Two nights here will be sufficient, and physical ...'

'You've done this before?'

'Yes, but I'll say nothing about the previous gentlemen, just as I'll say nothing about you. Physical intimacy is not necessary or desirable. All that is needed is for you to have the Mr and Mrs hotel bill, and the added assurance of the chambermaid's willingness to testify.'

Having said her piece, she stood and looked down at him, drawing back her shoulders and taking a breath.

He looked up at her in a way that was disconcerting. 'I see.'

Bloody man. Just because he was a singer on the stage. Just because over one beer and one gin he had tried to spell-bind her with tall tales. Well he could get this through his doh-re-mi skull. 'I'm a married woman, Joe. I'm Catholic. I have never committed adultery.'

Those big dark eyes looked into her heart and soul.

She did not say, I have never committed adultery because I have never committed anything. I could teach the mermaids a thing or two.

He smiled. 'I'm sorry. I must have had half a tale. Those legal chaps are all the same.'

And suddenly he was not like the double-jointed creature leaning over the bridge, or the boaster in the lounge bar, but solemn and straight as an elm as he came to his feet. He touched the crown of her head with his lips, more blessing than kiss. Hand on his heart, his face a mixture of adoration and doziness meant to pass as love, he burst into the old song Uncle Jimmy murdered at every party: 'The Ring My Mother Wore'.

'The earth holds many treasures rare in gems and
   golden ore;

My heart holds one more precious far — the ring my
  mother wore.
I saw it first when I, a child, was playing by her side;
She told me then 'twas father's gift when she became
  his bride.'

When he began she thought of Uncle Jimmy and wanted
to laugh. But Joe sang with such feeling that by the time
the last note trembled into the faded wallpaper, she was
wiping the back of her hand across her cheek.

He reached into his pocket and produced a large white
hanky. 'Was I that bad?'

'You were grand. What a marvellous thing to be an
opera singer.'

'I'm sure it must be,' he smiled, did a little dance, twisting his legs as if they were of India rubber, and executing
a deep bow.

And she thought, Why should I live like a mermaid? I
am sick of being as I am. This man is not like the others.

When she handed back his hanky, their fingers touched.

As a parting gift, Joseph Barnard had given Deirdre
Fitzpatrick complimentary tickets for the Grand Theatre.

She and Fitz sat in the third row of the front stalls, middle
seats. Fitz had swallowed the story that the theatre tickets
came to her from her aunt, given by a workmate whose son
painted scenery.

Fitz shuffled in his seat. He brought his brown sleeve
to his nose as he sneezed, not quick enough to pull out his
hanky. He wanted her to look at him and worry that he
sneezed. He found his hanky and his Rowntree's Pastilles.
'The cigar smoke gets to me.'

Poor Fitz, with his weak chest.

She would miss Fitz if he died, his rasping breath, the smell of printer's ink and solvents he brought home on his clothes, the snuff, the heavy tread of his feet on the stairs, the regular wage packet. Some morning she would wake to find that Fitz had died in his sleep. Why shouldn't that happen? After all, you spent most of your childhood praying for a good death. Prayers might as well be answered sooner rather than later.

For herself, Deirdre had long ago giving up praying for a good death in favour of a more lively life.

Something made her look up to the box on her right, the royal box, in which King George and Queen Mary would sit in the unlikely event they came to Leeds Grand Theatre to enjoy Gilbert and Sullivan.

There were two couples in the box. The man who looked back at her, catching her glance but giving no sign of recognition, was the chap who had nabbed her in Marshalls, and nearly had her prosecuted over that bottle of perfume.

Three

Sykes tried out his ventriloquist skills, whispering without moving his lips. 'Don't look now. Middle of the third row, Cyril and Deirdre Fitzpatrick.'

Fitzpatrick had told Sykes that he and his wife would be coming to the theatre to see *The Pirates of Penzance*. Since I was the one who would have the dubious pleasure of tailing Mrs Fitzpatrick, here was my opportunity to take a look at her. The conductor waved his baton. The orchestra struck up the overture. As the auditorium lights dimmed, I raised my opera glasses without enthusiasm and glanced at the top of Mrs Fitzpatrick's head.

She was not my main reason for being at the theatre. There were four of us in the royal box: Sykes, his wife Rosie, me, and my former beau, Marcus Charles. Marcus had unexpectedly telephoned to say he would be in my neck of the woods and was I free this evening. Suggesting an outing for four meant that I did not have to be alone with Marcus. He is a chief inspector at Scotland Yard. We first met last year, both investigating the same cases. To say we became close is one way of putting it. We fell for each other, but on my part not deeply enough. I desperately hoped he had not come to renew his proposal of marriage. He possesses some good qualities, but can be pompous and secretive. That could perhaps be ironed out, but being married to a rising star of Scotland Yard would mean giving up on all that I most enjoy – sleuthing on my own behalf.

The rousing overture reached its conclusion, and the performance began. By the time the pirates sang the sherry-pouring song, I had all but forgotten my client in the third row. As the first act drew to a close, I gazed down at the Fitzpatricks. They were leaning towards each other, as if exchanging a word, not looking in the least like jealous husband and errant wife. I wished now that I had refused Mr Fitzpatrick's request, and certainly felt no sense of urgency about following Mrs Fitzpatrick.

The applause for the first act was so loud that Sykes and Rosie had to make a dumb show of saying they were off to stretch their legs. A tactical move if ever there was one. Marcus and I were left alone, to pore over a box of chocolates and be a little awkward with each other.

Then of course we both spoke at once. I insisted he go first, feeling reasonably confident that he would not renew his proposal of marriage during the interval. All the same, my eyes must have narrowed.

He said, 'It's not what you think. I won't raise that question again. I respect your answer, and I understand. But I'm glad we can be friends. I know that we can trust each other.'

A policeman, when he reaches Marcus's rank, has spent a great deal of time working out how best to talk to people to achieve his required ends. What was he after?

'You're here on an investigation?'

Marcus smiled. He was solid and handsome when he smiled, the kind of man a woman could rely on — if he were ever there and not off sifting evidence, or laying a hand on a scoundrel's shoulder.

'Kate, you know I can't say.'

'And if we had married? If I were your wife, would you tell me then?'

'Of course not.'

Just as I thought. It would not have worked.

Opportunely, Sykes and Rosie came back into the box. The lights dimmed for the second act.

When the chorus of policemen danced and trilled 'A Policeman's Lot is Not a Happy One,' Sykes, Rosie and I practically fell off our seats with laughing. I nudged Marcus and whispered, 'Don't you think it's funny?'

If voices could scowl, his did. 'The rot sets in when audiences are encouraged to laugh at policemen.'

'You're being pompous again, Marcus.'

He laughed, in an unpompous but rather false manner.

It was not until we all sat down to supper that he asked me would I be free to go with him to York races for the Ebor Handicap.

I agreed, curious about what he was up to, and more than willing to put off following Deirdre Fitzpatrick.

Four

Naturally, I needed a new hat for the races. My favourite milliner has a shop that is part of our top hotel: the Metropole, where Marcus was staying, and where I had arranged to meet him.

Madam Estelle, High Class Milliner, beamed a greeting as she stubbed her Sobranie and picked up *The Times*, waving it about, to disperse smoke. She is a tiny, slender creature with lined olive skin, her white hair knotted in a bun at the nape of her neck so as not to discommode her hat.

I explained my predicament of being invited to the races at short notice.

She tilted her sparrow-like head and surveyed my outfit. 'I have just the hat for you.' She swooped across the shop, opened a curtain and delved, emerging triumphant with a small, dark red hat box.

The hat she held out was an elegant cloche with a swirling pattern in the old suffragette colours of green and violet; its only decoration, a white rosebud. Perhaps it was the rosebud. I loved it in an instant.

Like the perfect saleswoman, she did not reveal the price until the love affair was sealed with a hatpin.

Madam Estelle opened the inner door for me to enter the hotel corridor. Turning left took me to the lobby.

I was a few minutes early, and found a seat that gave me a good vantage point. Marcus and I were not the only ones heading for the races. A woman in flowing silks and spanking new picture hat stepped from the lift, followed by a chap in top hat and tails. In that regalia, they must be going to the Knavesmire too.

An odd pair came down the broad staircase. Two men walked side by side, chatting amiably. The younger man was about thirty years old, slight, with a sweet, boyish face. He wore dark trousers, a beautifully tailored grey jacket and a grey silk top hat. His stout companion, a weather-beaten man in his fifties, wore full highland regalia, with a kilt that could have been the Stewart tartan. Around his neck he carried a brown leather binocular case.

Curious, I made as if to stretch my legs, and to pick up a magazine. I watched the men climb into a chauffeur-driven Rolls-Royce. When I turned back, magazine in hand, Marcus had appeared from the direction of the hotel's telephone booth with the speed of a mouse catching the whiff of chocolate. I felt sure that he must have been there all along.

He looked splendid. There is not a huge difference between the dress of a well-to-do racegoer and that of a handsome bridegroom. For a fleeting second, I thought I must have been mad to turn down his proposal.

'Kate! Sorry to keep you waiting. You look wonderful. Green suits you.'

'It's the nearest I could find to camouflage.'

He offered his arm. 'Are you all right to set off straight away?'

'I am.'

If I were not mistaken, he would want to keep the Rolls-Royce and its odd couple in view.

As we left the hotel, a porter stood by a black Alvis saloon. Marcus gave him a nod and slipped him a coin.

I slid into the passenger seat.

The porter cranked the motor to life.

'Scotland Yard have done you proud. Staying at the Metropole, an Alvis at your disposal. I'm only surprised you don't have a driver.'

'Keeps it more discreet this way. Just you and me, enjoying a day at the races.'

'Marcus, I know you're working.' He could be extremely irritating, as if I would give the game way, whatever the game was. 'I'm surprised that someone who has reached your great heights is on an assignment like this. Isn't it usually detective constables who are given the task of keeping an eye on suspected wrong 'uns?'

He thought for a moment, calculating what he would and would not say, before deciding to throw me a crumb.

'Our American cousins have an interest. We need to appear helpful. Now no more fishing.'

Eventually, we joined the racecourse traffic – a long line of cars, charabancs and coaches, a solitary old-fashioned carriage, ponies and traps, and a few riders on horseback, all heading for the Knavesmire.

As we drew closer to the racecourse, a small group of anti-gambling protestors held up posters: Prepare to Meet Thy Doom; The Wages of Sin is Death; All Race Tracks Lead to Hell.

'Whether it leads to hell depends who's on the track and what they're doing,' Marcus muttered.

At the entry to the motoring enclosure, he handed over a half crown to the steward who waved us through. A second steward directed us into a spot next to a Morris.

For a couple of moments, we stayed put. Marcus picked up his binocular case and studied the clasp, as if it would give him inspiration.

The racecourse would be teeming with plain-clothes men looking out for pickpockets, three-card tricksters and bookmakers with fast little cars that would enable them to speed away after a race and welsh on paying out. Some of the plain-clothes men may have been alerted to be the extra eyes and ears for the investigation branch.

I took out a mirror and checked my hat.

Marcus hung the binoculars around his neck.

As I stepped out of the car, my heels sank a little into the grassy ground. Marcus put on his hat. 'The owners' and trainers' enclosure will be a good starting point. Did you really pick your horse with your eyes closed and a pin in your hand?'

'Of course. His name is Flint Jack.' Marcus need not know that the tip was given to me by my neighbour, the professor, who studies racing form.

He laughed. 'I'll wager you were poring over the *Sporting Pink* last night. Admit it! You were checking form, weight carried, jockey . . .'

'Marcus, I didn't know you were such an expert race-goer. Your work doesn't keep you as busy as you pretend.'

The day already had a festive atmosphere. We followed the top hats and posh frocks to the owners' and trainers' enclosure where the steward checked our badges. The first race was about to begin.

'Let's watch this one from the rail,' I said.

It is not such a great view, but I like the atmosphere. We leaned into the rail, watching the horses thundering towards us, and practically feeling the breeze as they charged by, hooves pounding

When the first race ended, lads led sleek horses into the ring, to stretch their legs in the half-hour lull between races.

Marcus fell into conversation with a race card seller. (Probably a plain-clothes policeman).

That was when I saw the two men from the hotel, the ones who had attracted Marcus's interest. They were admiring a rich chestnut horse that bore Flint Jack's number.

'There's my horse. Back in a sec, Marcus.'

If he would not give me any clues about whom he was following and why, it would amuse me to work it out for myself.

A weather-beaten old ex-jockey led Flint Jack into the pre-parade ring. When the Scot from Marcus's hotel spoke to him, he replied that Flint Jack was 'ready for his big day'.

The Scot, definitely a Highlander, was now commenting on the course. He had never been to York before. His companion in the grey silk top hat spoke softly. His favourite race course was in Virginia, he said. The man spoke with a touch of a New York accent, but he was English, and local. He intrigued me. His clothing, shoes and manner were top drawer. His voice was not.

By the time I worked my way back round the ring to join Marcus, my eavesdropping on this talkative pair prompted a slightly Sherlockian jump. It was not enough information to come to a conclusion, but at a guess I would say that the Highlander was selling something. His bluff, confident manner gave that impression. What did I associate with the Highlands? Haggis, bagpipes, Highland Games, Bonnie Prince Charlie, and whisky.

Marcus had said, 'Our American cousins have an interest.'

America had laws against the importation and sale of liquor. Those prohibition laws were being flouted on the grandest possible scale. The man in the grey top hat favoured a Virginian race course; so he was from America. By the cut of his jib, he had called at Savile Row to be tailored; a man with money.

'Well?' Marcus asked when I joined him. 'Is it still to be Flint Jack?'

'Definitely, having seen him.'

We explored, winding our way through the busy throng of small-time punters and York factory workers whose firms had closed for the day.

Band music played in the distance. From one of the food stalls floated the tempting whiff of sausages. A man by a small tent held up a sign that said 'Gentlemen's Convenience, one penny'.

When Marcus suggested we go to the grandstand, I said, 'I'm going to place my own bet, Marcus, for luck. Let me catch you up.'

I had spotted a photographer friend, one of those people who know Absolutely Everything and Everyone.

Marcus sighed. 'If you insist.' He put his hand in his pocket. 'Put two bob on the favourite for me. I'll see you in the grandstand.'

I chose a bookmaker called Willie Price, a rotund, cheerful fellow with a face the colour of a strawberry. A tall, well-built young man, his clerk, stood on an upturned box beside him, signalling to someone further along the course. Boldly, I wagered a guinea to win, with a shilling each way on Little Marten for Marcus.

'Kate!' The voice came from behind me. Good. I had allowed my newspaper photographer friend to spot me first.

'Len, hello!'

Len Diamond and I have been on good terms since he came to talk to my local photographic society about his work. He is the most talented photographer I know, and I suppose that is why I snootily put him in the category of friend rather than acquaintance. 'Shouldn't you be down by the course, waiting to snap the winner?'

He winked, which I was never sure was intentional or a nervous twitch. 'Oh I will be. But you know my love for taking candid pictures. We have a minor royal here today as well as the usual creamy crop.' Even as he talked to me, his eyes flitted about. When he gave his talk at the society, he said how he liked to capture his subject unawares. I supposed that a great coup for him would be to snap a pickpocket in action.

'Who do you have your eye on today?'

'You know me, Kate. Can't keep away from the great, the good and the bad, especially the bad. We've a fellow from New York here today, fits the last category nicely, a so-called businessman.'

'Not the man in the grey top hat?'

'That's what I like about you. We're two of a kind. Never miss a trick.'

'Who is he?'

'His name is Hartigan. He's a Leeds chap from Irish stock, taken to New York by an aunt and uncle as a child. He's supposedly here to visit family whom he hasn't seen since he wore short pants, doubtless with his bum hanging out. Meet me in the Lloyds one day and I'll tell you all about him.'

'Tell me now. He's a good-looking fellow. Nice to hear he's all heart.'

With a frown of concern, Len said, 'Don't even think about it, Kate. Word from my chum on Fleet Street is that Hartigan was arrested for a vicious murder, in broad daylight, on a New York streetcar. Shot a love rival through the heart. But the police and the courts couldn't make it stick. Not a single witness stayed around to tell the tale.'

'And who is the man with him, the Scot?'

Len smiled broadly. 'Oh he's all right. Produces the second best malt whisky in Scotland. What's the betting he'll be travelling home with a big order to ship to Canada, and it will mysteriously find its way across the border into America.'

So my Sherlockian deduction had been right. I smiled indulgently, and ventured a change of tack. 'Hartigan and his chum are putting their money on the same horse as me.'

Len raised an eyebrow. 'Go on then.'

'Flint Jack.'

'Thanks for the tip. Given that money finds its way home, I shall put my tanner on Flint Jack. Now can I give you a tip?'

'I'm all ears.'

'There's a sculptor in the grandstand, Rupert Cromer.'

'I've seen his work. He had an exhibition last year.'

As he moved away, Len called, 'If you come up trumps on your horse, buy something from him. It'll be the best investment you ever make.'

I caught up with Marcus in the grandstand. As he handed me a glass of champagne, he whispered, 'I can relax now, Kate, and pay you the attention you deserve.'

From that I understood that he had handed over the observations to someone else, probably the race card seller. I whispered in reply. 'Your man in the grey top hat and his distiller friend completed their deal then?'

Marcus frowned. 'Who? What deal?'

I took a sip of champagne and lowered my voice to a whisper that an onlooker might mistake for a lover's intimacies. 'Hartigan and the distiller. I assume that's why the Americans want you to watch him, to prevent the importation of naughty drinks.'

Marcus tensed. 'How did you work that out?'

I tapped my lips. 'Don't worry. Sealed.'

He sighed. 'This is very sensitive. We have members of both Houses of Parliament with strong interests in distilleries who don't want to discourage sales. The message we want to send back across the Atlantic is that the gentleman in question came here solely to visit his family.'

'And has he visited them?'

'Not yet.'

And of course, no police force in the country would want Hartigan back on British soil permanently.

We wandered to the balcony, and that was where I spotted a familiar face, Philippa Runcie. I caught her off guard in a look of such sadness that it brought me up short. Philippa is an American, a golden girl, who was sponsored by my aunt for her London season in 1913. She made what was supposed to be a dream match: American money and British aristocracy. She married the most eligible man in London, some said in England, the suave and charming Everett Runcie.

And there he was, but not beside his wife. Everett Runcie, still good-looking as he approached fifty, stood a little way off from Philippa. He was chatting to his long-term mistress, Caroline Windham, universally known as the Viking Queen because of her impressive height and bearing. They were with Rupert Cromer, the sculptor, whom I knew only from his photograph. Runcie and Caroline Windham were laughing at something Cromer said.

The thick-set young man who acted as Philippa's private secretary was trying to make conversation with Philippa, to distract her from being so studiously ignored by her husband. With his broad flat head, thick neck and compact body, the secretary perfectly fitted my mental image of Attila the Hun.

Philippa saw me and waved.

I waved back. 'Marcus, are you all right for properly socialising?'

'Proper socialising sounds just the ticket.'

In that moment, some movement disturbed the private secretary. He turned, in time to see Len Diamond raise his camera and point it at Philippa, with Runcie and the Viking Queen behind her. It was well known that Philippa and Runcie were to divorce. At that moment, I could have cheerfully hit Len over the head with his Thornton-Pickard Reflex. His own paper would never print such a picture. He must be selling to a London-based scandal rag.

Philippa's secretary, King, moved quickly for such a lump

of a fellow. He took Diamond by the arm and propelled the taller man to one side.

Philippa steadfastly ignored the scene. I introduced Marcus as a London friend, in Yorkshire for a couple of days. At the sound of a new voice, Everett Runcie pricked up his ears. Runcie is the kind of man you could not help but like, on first meeting: affable and witty. He is always on the look-out for some new investor to inveigle into one of his schemes. He collared Marcus while Philippa and I talked.

'Don't let your friend be drawn in,' she said, making no attempt to lower her voice.

'Into what?'

'A peanut farm, that's Everett's latest money pit.'

I smiled. 'I don't think that would be up Marcus's street at all.'

She and I moved towards the balcony as the voice came over the loudspeaker that the horses were being led out.

'Have you backed anything?' I asked Philippa.

She said softly, 'I don't bet. But I've bought a horse to ship back home to the States to stud.'

So it would not be long now till the golden couple parted. I had first heard the rumour of divorce a month or so ago.

'Which horse are you cheering?' I asked.

'Not telling yet.' She raised her binoculars in the direction of the starting gate.

'My money is on Flint Jack.'

'You better have these then. I'm not a betting man.'

I turned to see who had spoken. It was Rupert Cromer, the sculptor. He was a giant of a man with a fine head of fair hair and a beard in need of trimming. He held out his binoculars.

'Thank you.'

He smiled. 'That's all right. It's all one to me who passes the finishing line, so good luck.'

They were off to a clean start, Little Marten and Flint Jack running neck and neck. Everett Runcie called for Little Marten, I for Flint Jack.

I kept the binoculars trained on Little Marten and Flint Jack. Come on Flint Jack. And just as if he had heard me, he pulled ahead and was suddenly leading by a length.

From behind, Marcus asked, 'Did you put my two bob on Flint Jack?'

'No! You said you wanted me to back the favourite.'

The race ended to cheers and groans.

The viciousness in Everett Runcie's voice sent a shiver through me. He tore his betting slip and dropped it to the floor. Staring at Philippa with something like hatred, he said, 'I backed the wrong horse. Again.'

She coloured up, and turned away. I was grateful to Marcus for starting a conversation with Philippa. He grabbed the waiter's attention and passed her a drink.

I returned the binoculars to Cromer. 'Thanks. They brought me luck.'

He smiled. 'Always happy to oblige.' He offered his hand. 'Rupert Cromer.'

'Kate Shackleton. I came to your exhibition last year.' Perhaps the thought of scooping winnings turned me giddy. I had never thought of buying paintings or sculpture.

'What did you like best in the exhibition?'

Now I'd done it. I muttered something about his mother and child and tried to remember my impressions. The piece that caused the greatest stir was an abstract nude, rumoured to be modelled on the Viking Queen.

Whatever I said must have either been satisfactory or given the impression of solvency.

He said, 'Come out to my studio sometime.'

'Thanks, I'd like to.'

'Bring your friend.' He nodded in the direction of Marcus who was still engrossed with Philippa.

Poor Philippa. And poor Everett. What would he do without Philippa's money?

Philippa and Everett. Fitzpatrick and Deirdre. Perhaps one day an enterprising insurance company would come up with a policy to cover fire, theft and marital break-down.

Five

There could be no more putting it off. I had agreed to tail
Deirdre Fitzpatrick and that was what I must do.

Sykes and I sat in the parked motor on Abbey Road,
a hundred yards or so above Norman View, where the
Fitzpatricks lived. Now it was just a matter of waiting;
waiting in the morning fog.

For almost an hour, we watched the up and down trams,
the rag and bone man's horse and cart, a coal wagon, and
a window cleaner, his ladders on a bogey. We agreed to
meet, around midday, in the lounge bar of the Lloyds
Arms. If I had not finished my surveillance by one o'clock,
our comparing of notes would have to wait until this
evening. Just as I began to think the surveillance would
not happen at all, Sykes nudged me. 'There she is.'

As if recognising a greater force than itself, swirls of
fog parted for the figure in the silver-grey dust coat.

She wore black heeled shoes and carried a dolly bag.
That was reassuring. With such a small bag, she would be
unlikely to travel far, or elope with her fancy man.

'Just the coat for a shoplifter,' Sykes murmured. 'Loose

and with big pockets. She'd easily leave a shop wearing three frocks under that.'

The long wait had done nothing for my patience. 'For heaven's sake, it's a coat, not a weapon for destroying the retail trade.'

Deirdre walked briskly, making a bee-line for the tram stop. A woman with a shopping basket waited there already and spoke a word or two, looking up Abbey Road, as if she might make the tram appear.

'Drive to the next stop, Mr Sykes. I'll board before her. That way she won't notice me.'

Within a couple of minutes, we were at the previous stop. I hopped out of the motor just in time to catch the town centre tram.

I settled for a seat midway on the left of the lower deck, facing the rear. At the next stop Deirdre Fitzpatrick climbed aboard. She was slim, with a good figure, a pale, heart-shaped face, high cheek bones, and a wide mouth. Black curls escaped from under her cloche. She laughed at something the conductor said, before trotting up to the open deck.

An earlier occupant of my seat had enlivened the journey by squashing tiny insects with a tram ticket. The window was decorated with slaughtered baby flies. I looked through them at row after row of terraced houses, dye works, factories, and a tannery that gave off a powerful stench. As we neared the town centre, I moved closer to the tram stairs. The conductor coughed deeply, caught something interesting in his hanky and took a good look. We passed the tramway depot, and Wellington Foundry. A little way along, the tramline curved.

Mrs Fitzpatrick got off at St Paul's Street. So did I.

She crossed the street.

Another tram, travelling in the opposite direction, hid her from view. When the tram disappeared, she was no longer in sight. I did not know which office building had swallowed her.

I crossed, and looked at the nameplates. Each of the buildings she could have entered housed solicitors, accountants and commercial organisations. There was nothing for it but to wait.

On a street of offices there is really nowhere to tuck oneself away, except in a doorway. Two men in striped trousers and black frock coats talked animatedly as they walked towards City Square. I took refuge in the entrance of a building, where heavy wooden outer doors stood open and the second set of doors stayed shut. My wait lasted fifteen minutes.

Unfortunately, she appeared on the street during the seconds I had to move to let someone pass, so I was no wiser as to whom she had visited.

Along Boar Lane, she did not so much as glance in shop windows. From there, she cut through streets and alleys. I wished I had worn flat shoes. She tap-tapped in her heels and I tap-tapped after her, Mistress Echo. But she did not appear to notice. Everywhere, women walked with baskets, men trundled along with carts and carried boxes into shops. On The Calls, an old soldier played a haunting tune on a flute. She dropped a coin in his hat, and spoke a few words to him. His face lit with delight.

She walked along East Street, passing an iron works and a saw mill. The noise of the factories played a discordant symphony in the smoky choking atmosphere.

After the saw mill, she turned left. A small group of unemployed men sat on the pavement, playing a game of toss. As she approached, an athletic type leapt to his feet to speak with her. There was an easy familiarity in how close together they stood. I slowed my steps so as not to get ahead of her. By the time she set off again, I had overdone my caution by exploring a yard that led only to middens, and found myself far enough behind to lose sight of her.

As I came from the alley, I took a good sideways glance at the chap she had spoken to: shabbily dressed, a broken nose, ruddy complexion, fair hair. His amiable, lived-in face held an expression both vacant and suffering. Perhaps he was the world's worst villain, yet there was something about his look and manner that might make a person want to say, Oh bless the poor fellow, without quite knowing why.

Hurrying, trying to hazard a guess as to which street she had turned into, I spotted her by Steanders Iron and Steel Foundry. After that, the streets narrowed, making me feel even more self-conscious and ill-at-ease.

A couple of half-naked toddlers sat on the pavement edge, poking fingers into the black, sticky gas tar that had begun to melt. The women here, on their doorsteps and pavements, talking to neighbours, were poorly dressed, in dark serviceable clothes and large pinafores. One woman was scouring a window sill. Another swept the street outside her house. Conscious of my short sleeves, good shoes and the plain satchel that now looked exceedingly flamboyant, only dogged determination kept me on Mrs Fitzpatrick's trail. It struck me that we were the only women on these streets who wore shoes. Regulation footwear appeared to be down-at-heel slippers with holes in the toes.

Between every group of eight houses yawned a dismal alley. The slightly sweet and sickly stench of human excrement from the infrequently emptied earth closets made me want to hold my breath. It was Thursday, and so not wash day, but a couple of lines of washing stretched across the street. Patched sheets, worn towels and grey undergarments billowed gently in the soot-filled air.

The footsteps stopped. Deirdre entered a house on the right, but which one? A swaying sheet obscured my view. I felt a sneaking regard for anyone who could properly tail a person.

Slowly, I walked to the end of the street, drawing the attention of gossiping neighbours, a curtain twitcher and a step scourer.

No brilliant thought came to me as to what I should do next. Trying to look as if I had business to transact, I walked briskly to the end of Cotton Street and into the corner house shop. This at least would give me time to think. I bought a packet of Black Cat cigarettes from a stout woman with tight grey curls who wore a flowered pinafore.

Slowly, I made my way back. Having followed Mrs Fitzpatrick's rapid strides, I was uncertain as to how I would find my way out of this maze of back streets.

And then something happened that had doors opening, and women and children falling over each other to look.

A motor ambulance entered the street. It stopped at the first big sheet. A man wearing a navy serge uniform climbed from the vehicle and attempted to raise the sheet for the driver to pass, but this was not a one-man job. Here was my opportunity to perform the day's good deed. 'May I help you?'

The man readily agreed that I may help him. We took either end of the sheet, raised it, and in this way, the ambulance slowly bumped its way along the cobbles until it reached number sixteen.

Only then did the ambulance attendant give me a curious look and a thank you. The driver got out. Several women stood nearby in small groups. I stepped a little way off, watching as the ambulance driver knocked on the door. Once the door was open, the driver and his companion lifted a stretcher from the back of the vehicle and entered the house.

We all waited.

The watching group of women exchanged remarks in low, sympathetic voices.

The two ambulance men carried out the stretcher. The sympathetic voices became louder as they wished the invalid well and called down blessings.

Deirdre Fitzpatrick followed. She waited until the stretcher was placed carefully in the back of the ambulance, and then she squeezed in alongside.

The vehicle set off. My sheet-raising skills were no longer needed as neighbours took on that task, lifting and lowering laundry to let the ambulance pass.

'Where is she going?' I asked an old woman who stood in her doorway.

'The daughter's tekin her to a nursing home, for what good it'll do the poor soul.'

There was nothing more for me here. Following the direction of the ambulance, I made my way to the end of Cotton Street. The roar of a passing train gave me my bearings.

Following the line of the railway, I felt sure of my directions because the railway viaduct runs across the back of the Lloyds Arms, where I had arranged to meet Sykes.

In the pub's best room, Sykes was already cosily ensconced in a window seat, a pint on the brass-topped table. He stood up and budged along. 'You all right, Mrs Shackleton?'

'Yes and no.' I sat down, glad to take the weight off my feet. 'I followed Deirdre Fitzpatrick to Cotton Street, on the Bank, to her mother's house.' I took the packet of Black Cats from my bag. 'It's a dispiriting area, Mr Sykes.' He lit my cigarette. 'An ambulance came and picked up Mrs Fitzpatrick's mother, to take her to a nursing home. Deirdre travelled with her. From the glimpse I caught of the mother, and what the neighbours say, I would guess that the poor woman is on her last legs.'

Sam, our favourite waiter, came across and exchanged a few words before taking our order.

When he had gone, I gave Sykes a brief account of the visit Deirdre had made to an office on St Paul's Street, and the injunction that we would keep that to ourselves.

Sykes drained his glass. 'I wonder where Mrs Fitzpatrick got the money for a nursing home?'

'That's none of our business. As far as we know, she's not shoplifting. Think about it, Mr Sykes. She was foolish and inept enough for you to nab her last year. I don't think she'd hone her skills to such a degree that twelve months on she is a mistress of the art. Say nothing to

Fitzpatrick about the ambulance. All he needs to know is that Deirdre went to visit her mother.'

'That won't satisfy him. What else do we say?'

'Not we, *you*. Damp him down. The man worries me.'

Six

Deirdre recognised Mr Everett Runcie from his photograph. He was waiting for her at the entrance to the Hotel Metropole. Where else? This was the best. Grim humour came to her aid. I'm going up in the world, she told herself.

'Mrs Fitzpatrick?' He spoke her name softly, so as not to be overheard by the uniformed doorman, all gold braid, swagger and flapping lugs.

She smiled acknowledgement, wishing she had chosen another name. But the solicitor liked the name Fitzpatrick. He said it sounded just the right note, and that she would only be Fitzpatrick until the gentleman signed the register.

At the desk, she stood beside Runcie as he signed. Deirdre watched the look of dismay spread over the clerk's face as he saw Mr Runcie write Mr and Mrs. She turned away, so as not to be scrutinised, pretending absorption in her surroundings. From nearby came the strains of an orchestra. The place was all marble tiles, polished wood, palm plants and money.

They walked arm in arm through the hotel foyer, the

page boy already ahead of them, walking up the stairs, carrying her bag that looked suddenly shabby.

She did not like Runcie. He was undressing her with his eyes. He was too confident. This one could be trouble.

In the room, he tipped the page who set down their bags. She opened hers and took out her sponge bag, night-gown and dress for tomorrow. Stop staring at me.

'Will I meet you downstairs in ten minutes?' she asked.

He sat on the bed. 'Oh no. I shall wait with you until you're ready. It wouldn't do to abandon you when we are so devoted, my dear.'

She washed her hands in the basin, and combed her hair, all the while conscious of Runcie's eyes on her.

'I always have this suite,' he said. 'There's the bathroom that connects to the room next door. That other room is ours, too, but we shan't need it.'

He came up behind her, too close.

'Will we be dancing?' she asked, moving away from him.

'Do you know, I'm not in the mood for dancing.'

The meal went slowly. She had chosen cod, in a sauce of some kind. He ate carefully, cutting his lamb into small pieces.

'Tell me about yourself,' she said sweetly. 'I believe you're a banker.'

He laughed. 'Was a banker. Was lots of things, but not any more. I shall shortly be retiring to Italy.'

'You look too young to be retiring.'

She hated herself for this inability to keep from flat-tering.

The waiter filled Runcie's glass. Deirdre put a hand over hers, but Runcie took her hand, and kissed it, and indicated to the waiter to pour. It would be her third glass, and she had no head for drink. It will knock me out, she thought. I won't have to deal with him.

Having set down his knife, Runcie put his hand on her thigh.

'Don't do that, Mr Runcie.'

'Call me Everett, my dear.'

Something in Deirdre snapped, but no sign showed on her face. She lifted his hand and presented it back to him. 'Mr Runcie, I am utterly reliable. The grand inquisitor himself wouldn't winkle out a confession of collusion when your wife cites adultery and files for divorce. You could have asked your mistress or a streetwalker, but I am the perfect "woman unknown", who passes as your wife and disappears again, without further demands or expectations.'

And he could like it or lump it.

This was the role as described to her by the solicitor on St Paul's Street who gave her the assignations. Deirdre liked the matter-of-factness of the explanation. She took another drink, saying to herself, I could develop a taste for this.

'How much do you want?' he asked.

She felt sick. 'I am not for sale.'

He laughed.

It was ridiculous. She knew herself it was ridiculous, but he repulsed her, this handsome man.

'I can tell you like me,' he said. 'Say you do.'

She refused to argue. There was no point. 'Do you want your divorce, or not?'

'Not, as it happens. I did my best by my wife. She did not keep her part of the bargain. I think you understand me.'

She concentrated on squashing peas against her fork.

He took her silence for assent, and said, 'We should have had an heir by now, an heir and a spare as they say. Do you have children?'

It was such a simple question. She ought to be able to say no without some storm brewing up inside her. He wanted children, and so did she. Don't pity him, she told herself.

He waited for her answer.

'No, I don't have children.' Something in the way she spoke closed the subject.

They laboured through the rest of the meal, both choosing a milk pudding. Deirdre thought she must be losing her touch that she could not summon careless chat. It was all the fault of Joe, Joseph Barnard. She had let the singer get under her skin, and now he was gone, and she had no patience left for any other man, not Fitz, and certainly not for this conceited toff who tried to make her feel for him because he had no son. It made her want to scream.

But something happened to keep her from screaming. As the waiter gathered up their desert dishes, Runcie waved to a man at the bar.

He said to the waiter, 'Ask the gentleman from New York to join us.'

'Very well, sir.'

'Be nice to this fellow, my dear. I met him at the Knavesmire this week and I plan to let him in on a little project of mine.'

Here was Deirdre's escape. She felt that her guardian angel had intervened. 'I'm sorry.' She stood. 'I'd be bad company. My head aches. I'll go to the room and leave you gentlemen to talk.'

Looking neither left nor right, doing her very best to walk in a straight line, Deirdre made for the stairs. She held onto the banister. No one would guess I'm tipsy. In the room, she undressed and struggled into her nightgown. By force of habit, she hung up her gown. Take good care of your clothes. Put the bolster between you, the voice in her head commanded. The wine did the trick. Within moments of lying down, she was out for the count.

Deirdre woke with a start. Early morning light filtered through the gap in the curtains. She must sit this out until the chambermaid knocked on the door with morning tea. She raised herself up and looked at Runcie, gratified that the bolster was still in place between them. He must have come up late, thank God, and had not disturbed her.

Her head throbbed. Her mouth felt dry. She went to the bathroom and filled the glass to quench her thirst. Well, she had come safely through the night.

Runcie was lying on his back, sleeping soundlessly, still as an effigy. She stared for a long moment. Something was wrong, strange. There was no rise and fall at his chest. His skin was taut and ghastly pale. The man looked repulsive. Deirdre knelt up on the bed. She did not want to touch him, but made herself lift his hand. One of the nuns at school had taught her how to feel for a pulse. Nothing.

47

She pulled a feather from the eiderdown and held it below his nostrils. The feather did not stir.

There was a knock on the door, a gentle tapping. A young voice said, 'Your morning call, sir. Madam.'

The door knob turned.

Deirdre flung herself from the bed and across the room. No one must see her, in bed with a dead man.

Seven

As I walked up to the old stables that I use as a garage, I wondered why Marcus had suddenly summoned me to the Hotel Metropole.

'It's work,' he had said tersely. 'I would appreciate your help.'

I wondered did it concern the 'businessman' visitor from New York, here to buy vast quantities of liquor. If my photographer friend, Len Diamond, knew the man's reputation, perhaps the hotel management had also found out and grown uneasy about their gangster guest.

But Marcus was giving nothing away. There was an edge to his voice that I had not heard before. Usually, regardless of events, nothing mars his telephone air of professional politeness. Something had rattled him.

No point in speculating. I drove onto Headingley Lane and headed towards the town. Within ten minutes, I turned into King Street.

Two official-looking black cars were parked close to the hotel. I drew up behind the second one. A uniformed policeman stood at the entrance. As I climbed out of the motor, the officer pounced.

Before he had time to ask me to move the car, I said, 'Mr Marcus Charles is expecting me.'

Moments later, I walked along the third-floor corridor. Coming towards me was Mr Nettleton, the police surgeon. He tipped his hat and wished me good morning. 'How is your father, Mrs Shackleton?'

'Very well, thank you.'

'Do give him my regards.'

'I will.'

My adoptive father is superintendent of West Riding Constabulary, which I suppose just may have influenced my choice of occupation.

Marcus had left the door ajar.

'Kate. Thank you for coming at such short notice.'

He did not smile.

The room was done out as a sitting room, with bucket chairs, cocktail cabinet and occasional tables.

'What's happened, Marcus?'

'You'd better sit down. I'll explain.'

I took a seat in one of the bucket chairs.

'I'm afraid that it is bad news concerning someone you know. Mr Everett Runcie was found dead in his room here this morning.'

He gave me a moment to take in this information. I found it hard to believe. 'Everett Runcie?'

'The chambermaid found him.'

'Has Philippa been told?' It crossed my mind that Marcus must want me to break the bad news.

'A detective inspector is on his way to speak to Mrs Runcie.' He looked at his watch. 'He'll be with her round about now I should think.'

'Poor woman. What a shock.'

Marcus nodded. 'I don't envy the inspector, having to break that kind of news.'

'I don't understand. Everett only lives a few miles away. Why was he staying here?'

'The manager tells me that he stays here when he has female company. Someone was with him but has disappeared. Usually the pretence is that his lady friend has a separate room and is signed in under her own name, all very discreet.'

'Caroline Windham?'

'Yes. You know her?'

'She was at the races. You will have noticed her, a tall, aristocratic-looking woman, nicknamed the Viking Queen. She's been Runcie's mistress for years, long before he met Philippa. I can't see her running out on him.'

'The hotel staff know Miss Windham. Last night Mr Runcie was here with a different woman, passing as his wife.'

My thoughts raced. A new mistress, or was this liaison to provide Philippa with grounds for divorce?

'How did he die?'

Marcus took a deep breath. 'He was murdered, strangled in his bed. The local police surgeon just gave me his report.'

'That's horrible.'

'I think we can say he probably did not suffer. It would have been quick. He had been drinking heavily. My guess is that he was sound asleep. There was no sign of a struggle. Whoever killed him knew what they were doing.'

Marcus raised his hands to his throat and touched his thumbs to his shirt collar. 'He or she put pressure on the carotid arteries, enough force to kill him and no more. The bruising was either side of the windpipe.'

The news shocked me, but what surprised me was Marcus's frankness in giving me details of the death.

'Poor Everett.'

'The manager reported the death to the local CID and they knew I was here.'

'You're taking over the investigation?'

'Yes. Leeds CID put in a call to the Yard. I've spoken to my boss. The paperwork is on its way. The local men are going over the scene now. Photographs, prints, inch by inch inspection. It's a room on the second floor.'

At the races, I had resented the fact that Marcus did not confide in me. Now he was doing so, and I could think of nothing to say.

Marcus looked at me steadily, as if judging whether to say more. 'I'm hoping you might help me. You're friends with Mrs Runcie. You knew the pair of them, and perhaps their friends and associates. Do you have any thoughts, however wild, as to who may have done this?'

Now I understood why Marcus had given me details of the murder. He was asking me if I knew anyone who might be an enemy of Runcie, and a competent strangler.

My mind went blank. I felt slightly sick and was glad to have stuck to toast for breakfast.

I shook my head. 'There must be people who hated him for losing them money, with his schemes. He sold shares in an abandoned mine, abandoned because it was worked out. I'm not sure whether it was intentional, or whether he was duped himself. But surely someone who wanted revenge, or was angry, would want to confront Everett Runcie, not kill the man while he slept.'

'That would seem logical.'

'So, not a crime of passion?'

'Before I do any theorising, I have a lot of information to gather.'

'But Marcus . . .'

'What?'

'You have a once-suspected murderer staying in the hotel, the New Yorker. Could there be some connection? Isn't it too much of a coincidence that Hartigan chose this hotel? Perhaps there were American investors who lost money in one of Everett's schemes.'

Marcus frowned. 'How do you know Hartigan was suspected of murder?'

I felt my cheeks redden. 'I didn't ask anyone, someone at the racecourse saw him and told me, a friend who works on a newspaper. They get to know everything.'

Marcus nodded. 'I've thought about Hartigan. He would not have known that Mr Runcie would stay here.'

'But Everett Runcie stays here if he stays anywhere. You said so yourself.'

'Because it is the best hotel. The same reason that Hartigan chose it.'

There was a tap and the door opened.

Marcus called to the person to wait.

I took that as my cue to leave and stood. 'Is that it, Marcus? Sorry not to be more help, but if I think of anything I'll be in touch.'

'That isn't it, Kate. There are a couple of things. Leeds constabulary have one woman police constable, presently otherwise engaged. Will you talk to the chambermaid who found Mr Runcie?'

'Of course.'

'Her name is Mildred. She's seventeen. The manager has her in his office now. No one has been able to get a word out of her. She's in a state of shock. If you could calm her down and get a straight story, I'd be very grateful.'

Mr Naylor, the manager, a short spoon-faced man with rimless spectacles, spoke as if the chambermaid was not there. 'Forced a drink of tea down her. She stops shaking for a minute, and then she's off again.'

Mildred sat in the corner of the office, arms folded across her chest. She was chubby, with a country girl's apple-shaped face, now pale. The poor child could not stop shivering.

I went over to her. 'Hello, Mildred, I'm Mrs Shackleton. Shall we go to your room, and you can perhaps have a lie down, get over your shock?'

She nodded, throwing a nervous glance at the manager.

He seemed relieved to be rid of her. 'The lady's right. You do that, Mildred.'

I reached out to give her a hand up. 'Come on then. Let's go to the lift.'

The manager cleared his throat. 'She's on the top floor. Staff use the back stairs.'

I smiled at Mildred. 'Well then, let's not be staff. Take your pinny off.'

She fumbled, and I helped loosen the bow. Once she had unclipped her headpiece, she was no longer a chambermaid, just a pale young woman in a black dress.

Mr Naylor opened his mouth to object, and then thought better of it. I took advantage of his silence to ask him for hot sweet tea and a bed warmer to be sent up.

The lift attendant opened the door to let us step inside, giving Mildred a sympathetic smile.

Leaving the lift, we walked along a corridor to the back stairs, and up to an altogether shabbier world.

It was a plain room: two narrow beds, neatly made with dark blankets, a washstand, and a wardrobe that had seen better days. On the small table between the beds lay a penny dreadful novel, and a magazine.

I helped Mildred onto the bed and unlaced and removed her shoes. 'How old are you, Mildred?'

She did not answer straight away, and then through chattering teeth, she said, 'Sixteen.'

'Coming up sixteen?'

'Yes.'

'When is your birthday?'

'July 20th.'

So Mildred was just over fifteen, and not averse to telling the odd fib. Marcus would not have pulled 'age seventeen' out of the air.

I tucked the blanket over her. She had stopped shaking.

After a few moments, a plump young woman arrived, carrying a tea tray and a silver slipper, filled with boiling water and wrapped in red flannel.

'Excuse me, madam, I'm ordered to fetch this.'

'Thank you.' I took the bed warmer and slid it into the bed by Mildred's feet.

The chambermaid set the tea tray on the washstand. 'Oh Mildred! What a horrible thing to happen.' Mildred brightened, as if suddenly realising the drama of her situation. Her friend continued, turning to me. 'We share this room. I'm Jenny. You've put her on my bed but I don't mind.' At the door, Jenny turned to her roommate. 'Mrs McT says you're not to worry about work today, Mildred.'

I did not interrupt Mildred's tea-drinking or foot-warming, but flicked through her magazine as she began to revive.

The magazine was a few months old; one that published the doings of society people. A picture of Everett and Philippa Runcie took me by surprise. The Runcies, according to the article, were taking part in an Easter egg hunt on their estate, to which the children of estate workers and bank staff had been invited. If Everett and Philippa Runcie had decided to divorce as long ago as April, it did not show in their smiling faces.

Soft footsteps creaked on the landing. I stepped outside. The man, a waiter, had the same country complexion as Mildred would have when she regained her colour, and the same straw-coloured hair.

'I'm Mildred's uncle, madam. I want to see her.'

'You shall see her, but not yet. I believe this area is out of bounds for male staff.'

It was a guess, but it did the trick. He raised his voice. 'I'm her uncle I told you.'

'I appreciate that, Mr . . .?'

'Heppelthwaite, Archie Heppelthwaite.'

'Well, Mr Heppelthwaite, I'm appointed to take care of Mildred, until she recovers from her shock.'

He looked beyond me, to the end of the corridor. For a moment, I thought he might try to rush past me. He said, 'She's not up to interrogations. She's a child.'

'I know that, Mr Heppelthwaite. I'm not a police-woman, I'm a trained nurse. You'll be the first to speak to her when she's ready.'

That was a lie, but he was not to know that.

He nodded, turned and walked away. Something more than avuncular interest was at stake here, of that I felt sure.

Mildred had been listening. 'Was that Uncle Archie?'

'Yes.'

'What did he say?'

'He wanted to know how you are. I told him you are doing well.' I made a guess. 'I expect he got you the job here.'

'Yes.'

Spots of colour had returned to her cheeks. She struck me as much recovered.

'Was today the first time you saw a body, Mildred?'

She shook her head. 'I saw my grandma, and a neighbour, and the farmer's son when he had a bad accident.'

So death was not new to her. 'All the same, it's a shock. But perhaps you can tell me about it now.'

I hoped she would, before the uncle came trotting along the corridor again.

Her face clouded. 'I want to go home. I want to go away from here. I never wanted to be a chambermaid.'

'What did you want to be?'

'A waitress. That's what I wanted to come as, but I was too clumsy.'

'In another year or so, who knows what you will be able to tackle? If you show what you are made of by telling me what happened, you'll be well thought of.'

She considered. 'I want to talk to my uncle.'

57

'Later, after you've told me what happened this morning.'

After a long time, she said, 'I took the morning tea tray to the door at about six. There was a newspaper as well, for Mr Runcie, *The Times*.'

'Go on.'

'When I knocked, the lady said to leave the tray by the door. I waited a minute because I thought Mr Runcie might call out for me to bring it in and put it on the wash-stand, and I'd get a tip.'

'Did you see her, the person who called out to you?'

She shook her head. 'As I got to the end of the corridor, I heard the door open. She drew the tray inside. I only saw her hand.'

'What did you think?'

'I thought that's goodbye to my tip. I went back later, about eight o'clock, and knocked. When there was no answer, I opened the door. There was just one person in bed. I said, "Shall I come back, sir?" He didn't answer.'

'And then?'

'He was lying on his back, but there was a stillness about him, summat not right. I took one look and ran for the housekeeper.'

'Had you seen Mr Runcie before?'

Mildred's lower lip began to tremble. Her throat and neck turned pink. She clasped her arms tightly to her body. 'I saw him last November, when it was too foggy for him to go home, and then he was up early in the morning and going to his office.'

'And has he stayed between last November and this month?'

'I think so, but not on my floor.'

58

'Which is your usual floor, Mildred?'

'The third floor.'

I took a guess. 'So, you had swapped with Jenny?'

'Yes.'

'Was there a particular reason?'

'I just felt like a change.'

'Was it because your uncle suggested it?'

She said nothing.

'It will come out if he did, and there would be no harm in it. I expect he wanted you to have a good tip.'

She gulped. 'Yes. That was it.'

'When I picked up your magazine just now, it fell open at the photograph of Mr and Mrs Runcie.'

'I was too tired to read it.'

'So you just looked at the pictures?'

'Yes.'

'You didn't see the lady in the room, only heard her voice. If you had seen her, you would have known she was not Mrs Runcie.'

'I don't know who she was.'

'What did your Uncle Archie tell you about Mrs Runcie?'

'That she was an American, and well off.'

'The person who said to leave the tray by the door, what sort of voice did she have?'

'Ordinary, not posh.'

'And not American?'

She shook her head. 'From round here.'

'You've done nothing wrong, Mildred, but you must tell the truth because a dreadful thing has happened. A man is dead. Not telling the whole truth counts as a crime.'

She began to cry. 'Uncle Archie said I would get a good

tip, because I might be asked what I saw when I brought the tea.'

'What did you expect to see?'

'Mr Runcie, sitting up in bed with a woman who was not his wife.'

'Which you knew, because you had seen her picture in the magazine your uncle gave you.'

After writing Mildred's statement, I walked slowly down the stairs and along the third floor corridor to the room Marcus occupied. From inside, I heard voices, tapped on the door, opened it and popped my head round. The furniture had been shifted to turn the suite into an interview room. I caught a glimpse of a constable at a table, conducting an interview.

Marcus stepped into the corridor, where I told him what Mildred had said and handed him her statement. 'You need to talk to Archie Heppelthwaite, one of the waiters. He is Mildred's uncle. He told her to swap floors with another chambermaid, so that Mildred would earn a decent tip from Runcie, for seeing him with his co-respondent.'

Marcus almost hid his surprise, only the slight parting of his lips gave him away, but he kept his jaw from dropping. 'The Runcies are divorcing?'

'It's common knowledge.'

I handed him the key to Mildred's room. 'Somebody ought to keep an eye on Mildred, until you've interviewed the uncle.'

'Wait here a sec, will you?' He went back inside and returned a moment later. 'It's in hand. Someone will be by her door. I've sent for Heppelthwaite. We've spoken to him once. He was on duty last night in the dining room. That man has some explaining to do.'

'You said there was something else I might help with?'

As we walked down one flight of stairs, he said, 'I need to find the woman who was with Runcie last night.'

'Lots of people must have seen her.'

'She was slim, dark-haired and petite. I'd like you to take a look at what she left behind. There's a gown and shoes still in the wardrobe.'

A uniformed man opened the door to the room on the second floor. I looked at the bed where Runcie had lain. It seemed so strange to think that we saw him alive on Wednesday, fed up about not backing a winner, and being rude to his wife.

Small things can sometimes be the most disconcerting. There was a dent in the pillow where Runcie had rested his head. The other pillow was plumped up. A bolster lay on the floor.

'What is it?' Marcus asked.

'Why is the bolster on the floor?'

'Perhaps he didn't like a thick pillow.'

Marcus went to the wardrobe. Carefully, he lifted out a green satin evening gown and hooked it over the wardrobe door for my inspection. 'Take a look at this. What do you make of it?'

There was something familiar about the sleeveless green dress with its round neck and a matching tie ribbon. 'Am I allowed to touch it?'

'Yes.'

'It's elegant. There's no label.' I looked at the hand stitching on the hem and seams. 'My guess is that she made this herself, or a friend did.'

'Didn't have it made for her by a dressmaker?'

'If it had been done professionally I would have expected a label, and the stitching would be more uniform. The side seams are neat. When she got to the hem she was in a hurry, or impatient to have done with it. My old sewing teacher would have said you'd see these stitches from the school gate.'

I looked at a pair of low-heeled strapped shoes. 'They look expensive without being expensive I'd say.'

He nodded. 'You're probably right. I'm having the maker's name checked, and the local outlets.'

'Wait a minute.' I looked again at the dress, trying to think why it was familiar. 'Mrs Sugden pores over the patterns that are syndicated in the local paper. This was one she had sent for, and offered to make up for me.'

'Thanks, Kate. Every little helps at this stage.'

But we both knew that did not take us very far.

Marcus hung the dress back in the wardrobe. We left the room. I did not feel that I had been of much use, apart from taking Mildred's statement.

At the top of the stairs, he said, 'Thanks again. I'll walk you to the door.'

Dismissed.

'I don't suppose you want me to interview the waiter, given that I've talked to his niece?'

Marcus laughed. 'No! Absolutely not.'

'Pity. He'll lie.'

I felt a pang of disappointment. In spite of everything I have achieved, about which Marcus is very well aware, I was surplus to requirements. In Marcus's eyes, solving a murder is boys' work.

We were almost at the door when Marcus said, 'I'm

going to interview Anthony Hartigan myself. That means I have to break my cover. I'll need someone else to keep an eye on him.'

My spirits rose. 'I can do that. I have my car outside, and I'm good at sitting in hotel lobbies, sipping a cocktail. It's my speciality.'

'No, Kate. He's dangerous. And he'd be onto you in a flash.'

'So someone else will take over from you?'

'We're at full stretch. But it occurs to me that your Jim Sykes might step in, if you can spare him. He's trustworthy and knows the area. If you agree, I could have him sworn in as a special constable.'

'I'm sure he'd be glad to help.'

That put me in my place. Good enough to interview a nervy chambermaid and comment on a frock. Something rose up inside me. Cold fury. We'll see, Marcus. You didn't even know the Runcies were divorcing. You pooh-poohed my thoughts about Hartigan, and the waiter fooled whichever of your minions interviewed him. We'll see how you get on.

Eight

Sykes was delighted to be in demand as a special constable. I hid my fury at being entirely sidelined, and slung my hook. There was plenty for me to do. I should cocoa. Let the boys get on with it. I had a report to type, a letter to write, an envelope to address, a stamp to lick. Not to mention checking through the past few weeks' newspapers for interesting items.

My cat Sookie came to greet me. She rubbed herself against my legs, leaving hairs on my stockings, threatening to trip me.

'You'll have to wait until Mrs Sugden gets back from the market with fish scraps.'

I opened the back door. She bounded out.

Right. I would type my report to the insurance company on our investigation of the fraud case. If I got on with it now, it would be finished before Mrs Sugden returned, and I would avoid having an audience watching to see how it was done.

I was so furious that my fingers thumped the typewriter keys too hard. Every single o and every p lost its centre.

The report ran to two pages. I typed the date at the

bottom, and a line for my signature, then released the platen. I typed a short covering letter, and the job was done. I keep envelopes in the dresser drawer, along with table mats, not an ideal arrangement for the efficient office, but it works.

Plenty to do. Envelope. Stamp.

Mrs Sugden returned. She watched me put the cover on the typewriter. 'I could do that sort of thing. If I learned to typewrite, you could concentrate on your brainwork.'

Mrs Sugden likes to keep busy. She is easily bored. No skill is too tricky. She is cook, dressmaker, knitter extraordinaire, gardener and maker of chutney. We agreed that she should look for a typewriting class.

When back from the market, she wants to talk, about who she saw, what she bought, and for how much.

I escaped. Plenty to do. Sort out August's newspapers. They were in a pile on top of the piano. I remembered something I had meant to cut out at the time, to send to my aunt. Where was that newspaper? It was easy to date because it had appeared the day after grouse shooting began. And then I found it. There was a photograph, with the caption: LORD FOTHERINGHAM'S SHOOTING PARTY – STRAY SHOT AT SHOOT.

The photograph showed Caroline Windham, clutching her arm, while still holding her gun, unaware of the camera, a look of surprise on her broad, handsome face. Everett Runcie stood beside her, his head level with her shoulder. The article read:

The first day of grouse shooting was this year postponed to Monday the 13th, due to the Glorious Twelfth falling on Sunday. Renowned shot, Miss Caroline Windham, shown here in the butts at Somersgill, prepared to enjoy her day as guest of Lord Fotheringham. Soon afterwards, Miss Windham suffered a grazed arm from stray shot. She was promptly assisted by her nearest fellow guests, Mr and Mrs Everett Runcie. Thankfully, Miss Windham suffered no lasting harm. After a brief respite for first aid, Miss Windham continued shooting. She bagged seven grouse by lunch – out-shooting even Lord Fotheringham.

Well she would. Caroline Windham, impeccable aristocratic connections, best seat in the county, archery champion, unrivalled on the tennis court, swimmer in wild places, extraordinary swordswoman. It was said she had inherited all the characteristics of her military ancestors, and none of their wealth. What was left of the family lands and money had gone to her timid younger brother who resented her accomplishments and disapproved of her adventures. He kept to his Derbyshire estate and allowed her nothing. Caroline Windham dazzled, she impressed. It was not just her height, her broad cheeks and her flaxen hair that had earned her the sobriquet the Viking Queen. In spite of her lack of money, she could have married well. But Miss Windham's downfall was her love for Everett Runcie, and his for her. When she was nineteen, it was said she and Runcie were about to become engaged. At age twenty-one, she had travelled the continent with him, with no sign of a ring. At twenty-five, they shared his London home. When she was twenty-six, he married wealthy Philippa. Now, people spoke of Caroline as having ruined herself. No one would have her now. She and Runcie were unable to keep away from each other. Everyone knew it, including Philippa.

The article set me thinking. Was that 'stray shot' truly an accident? It did not surprise me that the culprit had not been shamed in the newspaper, as a bad shot and a worse sport. I wondered who fired, and whether the shot had not been accidental at all, but meant for Runcie? If that shot was intentional, and failed, then the culprit might be the murderer.

Had Marcus not put my back up, I may have immediately set off for the Metropole and taken this newspaper article to him, with my thoughts. But he was pursuing his own lines of enquiry, and had made quite clear the extent of my involvement.

Well then, I would explore these possibilities before presenting him with ideas that may appear outlandish or half-baked. I should in any case visit Philippa. Was it too soon? Was I going to express my condolences, or to steal a march on Marcus?

Both.

The Runcie home, Kirkley Hall, is a twenty minute walk for me. A stroll would allow me to calm down. I could barely imagine how Philippa must feel, having heard that Everett had been murdered.

Nine

I walked through the still afternoon towards Kirkley Hall.

Odds on that Philippa Runcie would not want to see me, or anyone. I remembered back to when I received the wartime telegram about Gerald. Had someone called on me in the hours following, I would not have had the wit to hear a knock on the door. But there were a couple of differences. I had not been in the throes of divorce from Gerald. Philippa Runcie knew nothing of answering her own door. Her staff would be well-trained in the practice of sending unwanted visitors packing.

As I walked along the broad wooded approach that led to the house, the trees cast late afternoon shadows. Through the spaces between the trees, I could see Kirkley Hall, in all its grandeur.

One needed only a glimpse of the place to understand why Everett Runcie had to marry an heiress. Everett's much older bachelor brother held the family title. He transferred the house to his younger brother when Everett married Philippa. A clever move: Congratulations. Please accept this fine house, along

68

with its mortgage and all the repair and restoration bills that come with it.

It is a Georgian building, on land that once belonged to the monks of Kirkstall Abbey. The Runcie family acquired the property a century ago, and made extensive alterations when they were in the money. Little by little, with the ebb and flow of fortunes, they sold off the adjacent farmland. Even so, extensive grounds still surrounded the house. It was said that the magnificent beech trees had been planted to represent the layout of troops at the Battle of Waterloo. Wellington himself held pride of place, in the shape of an oak tree. Over a hundred years on from the planting, the beech tree troops, officers and men, threatened to dwarf the old oak leader, Wellington.

Emerging from the cover of trees, I approached the house. Pillars framed the entrance, and on either side of the pillars stood plinths that held two magnificent Chinese lanterns, looted at the time of the Boxer Rebellion.

I lifted and dropped the heavy knocker. After a moment, the butler appeared. He remembered me from this summer's garden party, and ushered me into the panelled drawing room, all gold leaf and brocade-covered furniture. I stood by the bay window, looking out onto the garden, waiting to receive a message thanking me for my call and saying that Mrs Runcie was indisposed.

When I first saw Philippa, we were on a visit to the opera. She was enjoying her first season, having been presented at court thanks to Aunt Berta's machinations. There is always one indelible picture we carry of a person we know. For me the picture of Philippa was of a golden girl, glowing with health and vitality, wearing a copper-coloured gown and diamonds, leaning forward eagerly, as if to swallow every note that floated from the Covent Garden stage.

Slow footsteps approached along the hall. I turned. There was Philippa in the doorway. Although I had seen her only days ago at the races, a little shock ran through me, a memory of that evening at Covent Garden. And now here we were, both widows.

'Hello, Kate. Thank you for coming.'

'I didn't know whether this was too soon. Throw me out if I'm intruding.' We were not on intimate terms, certainly not hugging terms, but I couldn't help myself. I went to her, and kissed her cheek. 'I'm so sorry, Philippa.'

For a moment we were very still, and then she released me, saying, 'Let's sit down.'

I waited to take my lead from her as to where in this barn of a room, to sit. She went to a Queen Anne chair in the window alcove that had a partner, and there we sat. She leaned back in her chair, as if the slightest movement would be too much trouble. She wore an empire line mourning dress of softest crepe, square neck and long, loose sleeves. Her only jewellery was her wedding ring.

She spoke thoughtfully, as though from a long way off. 'I've had to send for the dressmaker. Black was not something I expected to wear this September.'

It is not a good idea to put in your own two pennyworth when on a visit of condolence, but it just came out. 'I didn't wear black, because I expected Gerald was only missing and would come back. I fell out with his parents about it.'

She gave a sad smile. 'You can be very stubborn. Unfortunately for me, the discovery of Everett's body leaves no room for doubt. Though it still has not sunk in. I can't believe that anything happening today is real.'

'Have they let you see Everett?'

She bit her lip. 'The hotel manager identified him. Apparently it's not necessary for me to see him. I telephoned to Harold. He should be here from London by tonight.'

Harold is Baron Kirkley, Everett's elder brother. In the normal scheme of things, he would have died first and the title passed to Everett.

'Is it a relief that he will come?'

'I suppose so,' Philippa crossed her ankles. 'Harold has already spoken to everyone who matters. There won't be a formal announcement until Monday, thank God. Harold hopes to be able to hush up what happened, but I don't see how he can. You can't hide murder. I believe it was shock made him say that.'

'But at least you won't be dealing with this alone. That should be helpful.'

'It ought to be, but Harold was not pleased about the divorce and he will not be glad to have this house back in his ownership, not without my cheque book to pay for the upkeep and running.' She managed a small smile. 'Who knows, he might have to marry and produce his own heir.'

She shivered, and picked up a shawl from a nearby stool. 'This room is always cold, even in summer. Let's go outside, unless you're desperate for a drink.'

I followed her into the hall. She led the way down the steps from the terrace into the garden. To the side of the house, beyond the fountain, was the maze, created by some earlier Runcies from yew hedges.

Philippa looked across at the maze and began to stroll towards it, as if drawn by a magnet. 'When I first came here, I imagined the day when our children would explore it with me. But of course we have no children, thank God.'

We walked in silence to the maze's entrance. Philippa drew her shawl around her. 'Now I come here to lose myself, and pretend that I'll find a secret corner, a way into a different life.'

A man's voice called, 'Mrs Runcie!'

We both turned to see Philippa's private secretary, the man I mistakenly christened Attila the Hun. I saw now that he was Genghis Khan, hurrying to catch up. He was a little out of breath, panting as he reached us, nodding a greeting to me, but clearly concerned about Philippa. 'Would you like me to show Mrs Shackleton the garden, Philippa? Are you all right?'

'Don't fuss, Gideon.'

He hesitated for a moment, and then turned back towards the house.

'Gideon's very protective of me. I don't know what I would do without him just now.'

'I'm glad you have someone you can rely on. I can't remember how long he's been with you.'

'Forever in a way, but here at the hall for about two years. He was at school with my brother, and then studied theology, intending to enter the church. When he lost his vocation, he drifted a little. It's easy to find oneself frowned upon in Boston. It was my brother who suggested he come and take care of my interests.'

We had entered the maze. I guessed that Everett had not minded very much that Philippa had no head for business. That might have suited him very well.

Inside the maze, the stunted yew trees gave off a feeling of menace. Philippa waved a hand for me to go first. 'See if you can find the bench at the centre. I'll give you a start.'

I had only ever once before entered a maze, when I was child, with my younger twin brothers, and cousins. I could still hear my mother calling me, not to hurry ahead, and then the disembodied cries. Where are you? Stay there! Wait for me!

I did not know where I was then, or where I was now. Whatever I might imagine as Philippa's mood, or her reaction to Everett's death, it was not this. Was this her way of dealing with unwanted visitors, I wondered. I would be sent to the heart of the maze and deserted.

The Runcies had not economised on gardening. It was strange to walk alone among the perfectly trimmed ancient yew hedges. Round and round I walked, coming to dead ends, until I felt dizzy and had no notion of whether I was near the edge of the maze or the centre. When I spied an unexpected oblong of evening sunshine, I thought that must be the middle, but it was a little escape gap, just high enough for a frightened child. I retraced my steps, feeling foolish, not wanting to call out.

And then I came to the bench. Philippa was sitting there calmly, as though she had forgotten all about me. She looked up in something like surprise.

But when she spoke, I knew why she had brought me to the centre of the maze.

'Your Scotland Yard friend is staying at the Metropole isn't he?'

'Yes.'

'Did he come up here because he thought Everett was in danger? Is that why you were keeping an eye on us at the races?'

Her question shocked me. Perhaps I was wrong, and her guess was right.

'Marcus doesn't tell me what he does or why, but I don't believe his visit is connected with Everett. I believe it is something else entirely.'

'That's what he told you?'

'As I said, he doesn't tell me.'

'Then you don't know for sure.'

'No.'

I wondered whether Marcus had chosen to let me get the wrong idea about the reason for his visit. But I did not think so, and I believed that Everett's death had shocked him to the core.

Philippa sat with intertwined fingers, hands resting on her stomach. 'I don't know what to think about who could have murdered Everett. Gideon said that the inspector this morning asked some odd questions, as if he thought it might be someone in the Runcie family, or on the board of the bank.'

'Why would they want to do such a thing?'

'Perhaps the police think it would be to avoid the scandal of a divorce, or the disgrace of the financial mess Everett has made.'

'What twisted mind would see murder as a lesser scandal than divorce or financial shenanigans?'

'No, I suppose not.' She looked up at the yew hedge, as if it were the bars of a prison. 'I feel blamed.'

'No one could blame you.'

'I blame myself. I was so starry-eyed about marrying into the English aristocracy, a Boston girl's dream. Everett would succeed to the title. My son would sit in the House of Lords. No one had said, Bring your own tiara, we've sold the family jewels.'

'Your family must have known about Everett's financial situation.'

'Not really. Bankers are very good at sleight-of-hand. Besides, I wouldn't have listened. I did not want to hear that my part would be to play the saving grace, redeem the mortgage on this pile, produce an heir, turn a blind eye to infidelity and bail out Everett when he made foolish investments. Patient Griselda would have buckled under the strain.'

It struck me that at first glance, the yew hedge was very sterile, but it probably teemed with all sorts of tiny insects and entire worlds that we could not see.

'I want to know who killed him, Kate. I want them brought to justice, for my own sake, for everything I've been through. For the dream I once had.'

'It's horrible. No one deserves to have their life cut short.' A ladybird landed on the bench beside me, such a perfect insect, in an imperfect world. 'I'm sure Marcus will do everything he can.'

'Is he good?'

'Yes.'

'It was the local inspector I saw this morning. Later he telephoned to say that Scotland Yard has taken over.'

'Did the local chap have much else to say?'

'Not to me. I don't believe he would have told me how Everett died if I hadn't insisted.' She shuddered. 'It's horrible. Horrible.'

Philippa took a cigarette case from her pocket and offered it to me. We both lit up. 'It just seems so strange that this had to happen when we were about to divorce. I can't help feeling there's a connection.'

'What makes you think that?'

'Why else would it happen now, when Everett was at the hotel to give me evidence, grounds to plead for a divorce?'

The ladybird flew away. 'Perhaps there is no connection. Had you come to an amicable arrangement?'

She laughed, but without mirth. 'I suppose so. It was my turn, Kate. I met someone else and it opened my eyes. I thought a better life, a different life is possible. Oh, my little fling didn't last long. He was just another penniless man who thought himself onto a good thing, but it made me realise that it's not beyond the bounds of possibility that somewhere there is someone who could love me for myself.' She sighed. 'As Everett loved Caroline Windham.'

'He was an idiot to go back to her after he married you.'

'Go back to her?' She blew a smoke ring. 'How naïve I was. He never left her, never gave her up. Oh he swore that he had.' She smoothed a non-existent crease from her dress. 'When we were on our honeymoon in Florence, he arranged for me to have singing lessons, painting lessons,

Italian conversation. And I was glad to do all this, because I was trying to be the most accomplished wife in the world. It was years after that I discovered she was in Florence at the same time, and he was going to her. I'm surprised she let someone strangle him. She's built like the prow of a ship. Why didn't she throttle them, whoever it was?'

This was awkward. No one had told Philippa who was with Everett at the hotel. She was assuming it had been Caroline.

The ash on Philippa's cigarette lengthened. She let it fall to the ground, and then turned to look at me, picking up on my silence.

'He was with her?'

'Probably I shouldn't be saying anything about this. I shouldn't have come.'

'What? You can't hold something like that back from me. I've a right to know.'

'The woman he was with didn't answer Caroline's description.'

'How do you know?'

'The chambermaid was in a state of shock. The one woman PC not being available, Marcus asked me to talk to her. I was at the hotel this morning, and I picked up the description of the woman, not at all matching Caroline.'

'Then I hate Caroline Windham even more than I did before. Who was he with? Someone she fixed him up with probably. I might have known she would not be named as co-respondent. Unless . . .'

'Unless what?'

'Unless he was being unfaithful to her. She would have killed him for that. I put up with his cheating and his lies. She wouldn't.' She became flushed with a kind of wild excitement. 'It was her. I bet she wanted to marry him as soon as he was free. If he said no, or put her off, or betrayed her . . . My God, Kate, it was her. A crime of passion.'

In a maze, it is not always possible to know where a call comes from. A deep voice shouted Philippa's name.

'Go away. Leave me alone,' she said, half to herself, but stood up, and began to lead us out of the maze, with the slow step of a person taking in her surroundings as if for the last time.

I wondered whether she would shut up this house immediately after the funeral and leave for home. Here was someone who, financially at least, would be better off with a dead husband than a living one.

The voice called again.

Gideon King entered the maze, a worried frown on his face.

'Philippa!'

'What is it, Gideon?'

'There's a chief inspector here to see you.'

Philippa touched my arm. 'They've got someone. Would they be this quick?'

'I don't know.'

King said softly, 'He has some questions, for you, and then for me.'

'All right.' She moved away with a sigh. 'Kate, come again soon.'

We watched her walk away. King said, 'How did you come here, Mrs Shackleton?'

'By shanks's pony.'

'I'll walk with you to the gate.'

There was no need, but something in his manner told

me this was more for his benefit than mine. He took slow steps, looking at the ground and then suddenly at me, as if about to speak. He did not.

I considered whether I should wait, prompt him, or start a conversation. The latter might put him at his ease.

'It's good that Philippa has you to rely on at this time.'

'Yes. But it's horrible that this has happened, when everything was going to be dealt with in a civilised way. Now the police will comb through all Everett's dealings. It will be a great embarrassment to the family.'

'I'm sure they'll be discreet. They're looking for a killer, not skeletons in the attics.' We wended our way through an avenue of high tress that turned the world dark. He was taking me a long way round to the gate. 'You're not looking forward to being questioned, Mr King. Nobody does.'

'I don't want to say anything about their private life. It's no one's business. What are they going to ask me?'

He was acting like a person about to take a test and wanting to know the gist of the questions in advance. They would ask him where he was last night and this morning, that much must be obvious even to him. As Philippa's secretary, he had also appointed himself her watchdog and guardian angel. 'I expect they'll ask general questions, to try and build a complete picture of Everett's life in recent days, and to find out about his associates, and any enemies.'

'Do they think Everett was being blackmailed?'

His question took me by surprise. 'Why would they? I'd say it is too early for theories. Do you believe he was being blackmailed?'

'It crossed my mind.'

'If you think there is any possibility of that, you must mention it to the chief inspector.'

He nodded. 'I studied theology. Perhaps law would have stood me in better stead. What I knew of Everett's enterprises I judged in terms of right and wrong, not lawful and unlawful. But say he had some dealings that broke the law, something that might land him in court, even in prison.'

'How would that connect with murder, Mr King?'

'If he refused to pay a blackmailer.'

'If a person being blackmailed refuses to pay, then the blackmailer's bluff is called. He either makes public what he knows or crawls away with his tail between his legs.'

Had King been blackmailing Runcie? He stopped. I went on walking and had to turn back to look at him.

He thrust his hands in his pockets. 'Anyway, it was just a thought, something that struck me. If he was being blackmailed, and threatened to expose the man, or woman, then that could have signed his death warrant.'

'I suppose that is possible.'

'Which is worse in the law here, blackmail or some other crime?'

'Blackmail is a heinous crime everywhere. It must be the same in your country also.' We left the avenue of trees. I saw the gate a few yards off. 'Mr King, is there something you want to tell me?'

He gave a small smile. 'No. Just thinking aloud. Puts the wind up me, the thought of being interviewed by the police. They're a different breed. I don't speak their language.'

'If it is Chief Inspector Charles, you'll find him impeccably proper, and keen to listen.'

'I wasn't a good student of theology because the concepts of evil and damnation gave me considerable difficulty.'

This was the first time I had talked to King. He was an interesting man and my judgement of him as looking like Attila the Hun now seemed shallow and unkind. He was a complex person and I hoped I might get to know him a little better. 'Thanks for walking me, Mr King. Better not keep the law waiting.'

He smiled. 'I won't.' He made a helpless gesture. 'We were so on course, to go back to Boston. Now that we've been thrown off course, I suddenly realise that I never gave myself the opportunity to consider whether I do want to return. Goodbye, Mrs Shackleton.'

'Goodbye, Mr King.'

I walked slowly back to the road, wondering whether Marcus would fathom King, and elicit from him the actions that would have left Everett open to blackmail.

I had come here with the intention of asking Philippa about the shooting party incident, and had found no tactful way to do so. There was one person who would be able to answer my question on that score: Caroline Windham herself.

As I walked home, I thought about Philippa, and about Caroline Windham. Philippa had been shaken by the news of her husband's death but remained calm, almost unruffled. Caroline had not yet learned of her lover's death. If the Runcie family were keeping quiet about it, she would be in the dark all weekend. Would that be a blessing, or would she rather know?

According to my Aunt Berta, who is the fount of all social wisdom, Caroline Windham had loved Everett

Runcie since she was twelve years old. It did not seem fair for her to be left out.

If Marcus arranged for Miss Windham to be interviewed today or tomorrow, then she would hear the news from the police. Otherwise, she would learn of the death on Monday, at the breakfast table. Doubtless there would be something in *The Times*.

That would be cruel. She should be told before the whole world knew.

Shortly after I arrived home, I placed a call to Marcus at the hotel. Unsurprisingly, he was not available. Nor did he return my call.

By the time my head hit the pillow, I had decided that tomorrow I would visit the Viking Queen in her lair.

Ten

Lacking genuine connections and the ability to talk long and lucidly about horses and dogs, I usually stay clear of grand country houses. Now here I was, the morning after visiting Philippa Runcie at Kirkley Hall, driving along the broad approach towards Somersgill. This was the seat of Lord and Lady Fotheringham whose noblesse oblige obliged them to give penniless but well-bred Caroline Windham house room.

A group of young deer looked up from their grazing as my car wheels scattered gravel. Grand and solid, Somersgill occupies a dip in the valley, east of the town, a situation that gives the estate protection from the worst of the elements. Imagine a capital L, put an extra tail on top, and turn it on its side, then you will have the shape of three-storey Somersgill. The front of the house faces south, towards extensive parklands and hunting grounds. Eastward and westward lie farmland and the moor.

As befits a policeman's daughter, I approached from the side.

Had I attended finishing school, or paid more attention to Aunt Berta, I should have known the protocol for paying a visit not to Lady Fortheringham but to one of her houseguests. The last thing I wanted was to explain myself to a Fotheringham. Even facing Caroline Windham struck me as a daunting prospect. But I felt I was right. It was only fair that she should be told about Runcie's death before it became common knowledge.

I circled round to the back of the house and drew up near the stable block. No groom or stable lad sprang into action, or came to enquire who I was and what I wanted.

Searching my bag, I found a card that mercifully had just my name and not my occupation. It would be too alarming to send up a card announcing me as a private investigator. Given the size of the house, there must be some nook or cranny where I could be hidden until Caroline Windham put in an appearance. Sheer boredom and curiosity must ensure that she would come to see what I wanted.

As I knocked on the door, it struck me as absurd that I should be the one to break the news of her lover's death. But I did have the ulterior motive of hoping to slip in an enquiry about the injury she sustained on the first day of grouse shooting, and whether there was a possibility that the shot had been intended for Runcie.

A butler opened the door. Entering, I handed him my card and glimpsed the interior, feeling a slight shock at the shabby appearance of the place. Like Kirkley Hall, Somersgill had been requisitioned as a hospital during the war. Unlike Kirkley Hall, which thanks to Philippa's coffers had been restored to more than its former glory, Somersgill still showed the signs of requisitioning, and of subsequent neglect. Floor tiles were cracked. Paint peeled from the walls. A rail had been added to the wall by the broad staircase, and one of its attachments had become loose.

The butler showed no surprise when I asked for Miss Windham.

'Miss Windham is out riding.'

Why didn't I think of that? Of course the Viking Queen would be out riding in the mornings. Later, she would be casting lines, setting mantraps for poachers and nailing their carcasses to the stable door. 'What time does she usually return?'

He looked at the cracked face of the ancient grandfather clock that had not given the correct time since 1912. 'I should say at about eleven o'clock, madam.'

'It's such a fine day. I'll walk in the grounds and come back later.' I retrieved my card.

'Very well, madam.'

The butler limped me to the door. Like the house, he was worse for wear.

A stone seat had been placed on the terrace, to give a view over the parkland. I sat there for a while, taking in the blue sky, cotton wool clouds and the changing shadows across the broad undulating stretch of green.

It was a good hour before Caroline Windham appeared on the horizon, and she was not alone. As her black stallion trotted closer, I understood why her riding was so highly praised. Side saddle, she sat tall, as though born to ride. She wore a dark skirt, jacket and hat, with a white silk muffler at her throat. I walked round the house, towards the stable block, arriving just in time to watch her dismount. The groom came out, but she led the horse into the stable herself, and was there for several moments before reappearing, hat in hand, a long strand of flaxen hair falling to her shoulder.

Another rider, a man, arrived moments later, calling to her in a bantering tone. Needing to move quickly and speak to Caroline Windham alone, I paid him little attention as he rode to the stable door.

And here she came, stately as the royal coach. 'Miss Windham?'

We had been in the same company on more than one occasion but she is a person who chooses not to notice anyone socially unimportant to her. She turned to look at me, cautiously, as though I might have come from the butcher to ask her to pay for the crown of lamb. Not having riding clothes and height put me at a disadvantage.

She brimmed with life and energy after her ride. 'Do I know you?' She stared at me.

'We've met, through my aunt, Lady Rodpen.'

'Oh, so you are one of us?' She meant the establishment, an old family, the aristocracy, the charmed circle.

'Not really. My mother uses her title only occasionally. She married a police officer.'

She need not know that I am adopted.

She relaxed. 'Of course. Now I know exactly who you are, but not why you're here.'

I dreaded speaking what must be said. 'I have some news for you.'

'From Lady Rodpen? Will you come inside?'

'I'd rather not. Is there somewhere else we can talk?' It seemed absurd, given the size of the house, to want to remain outdoors. But I disliked the thought of bumping into other people and being introduced, or explained.

'How mysterious you are.' She looked around as though deciding where we might park ourselves, then set off at a march.

I fell into step, and saw that she was walking towards a domed bandstand. 'How is your arm, after the shooting accident, Miss Windham?'

'Oh that. Wish I could have found the chump who misfired. It's still a bit sore when I throw things or cast a line. How is Lady Rodpen?'

'My aunt's very well, thank you. She may be coming up this way before too long.' I did not say that it would be for Runcie's funeral.

'Good. I'd be glad to see her.'

Don't give up on the injury, I told myself. 'I read about your mishap in the paper. The newspaper article said that Mr and Mrs Runcie came to your assistance. There was a photograph.'

She looked down at me, and there was suspicion in her voice when she said, 'Newspapers never trouble to get their facts right.'

'What were the facts?'

She did not answer. So much for my on-the-hoof interviewing technique.

We reached the bandstand. She entered first, taking off her hat and flinging it onto the stone seat that circled the inside of the structure. We sat down, a little way apart. She pulled a couple of loose cigarettes from her pocket and put one on the seat between us. I searched for my lighter.

She said. 'What can I do for you?'

I lit her cigarette and gave her time to inhale. 'I'm sorry, but there's bad news concerning Mr Runcie.'

She tensed. 'What is it?'

'He stayed in a hotel in Leeds on Friday night . . .'

She showed no surprise at this information. No doubt she knew about the divorce, and what evidence would be required by the courts. 'I'm sorry to tell you that he was found dead in his hotel room on Saturday morning.'

'No. Oh no.' She closed her eyes. 'That can't be true.'

'The police informed Mrs Runcie yesterday morning.'

'Yesterday morning?'

'It was decided by his family, and the directors of the bank, not to make an announcement until tomorrow.'

Her eyes narrowed with disbelief. 'And you, how do you know?'

Good question. If I knew, who else knew, she must wonder.

'I was at the hotel. I know the investigating officer, but believe me the death is not widely known about.'

'Investigating officer?' She ran a hand through her hair. 'What can you mean? He was so well. What was it? How did he die?'

Having told her of the death, I could not say nothing, and have her beating her brains out with imaginings. 'The death is suspicious.'

She sat very still. 'Suspicious?'

'There will be an inquest.' I did not have either Philippa's or Marcus's permission to give out more information.

'What do you mean, suspicious?' She stared at me in disbelief. 'He would never top himself.'

'He did not take his own life.'

The enormity of what I was saying hit her slowly. She gave a low anguished cry, like the yelp of a hurt animal.

88

Her eyes brimmed with tears. She turned away from me with a shudder. It was distressing to see her. As if she read my thoughts, she flung out a hand, ordering me to keep away from her.

After a long time, she turned to me, her voice unnaturally steady by force of will. 'You mean he was murdered?'

Having come this far, I could not go back. 'Yes.'

'They did for him. The bastards. They did for him.'

'Who?'

'Precious Philippa and her private secretary, Gideon King. They killed him.'

'There's no reason to suppose . . .'

Her lower lip trembled. 'There's every reason. How was the deed done?'

'He would not have felt anything. He died while sleeping.'

'How? Gun, dagger, poison? What did the bastards do to him?'

'He was strangled.'

'Then it was King, under her orders.'

'Why would they? Mr Runcie was doing what Mrs Runcie wanted, agreeing to a divorce, giving her grounds.'

'At a price. She didn't like his price. She's had grounds for years, if she wanted to make use of them.' She took a deep drag on her almost burned-out cigarette before letting it fall to the ground. One arm crossed her middle. She lifted the other hand to her brow and rubbed at the slight frown mark on her forehead.

She looked at me, her bright blue eyes large with horror. 'Is that why you were asking me about the shoot? You think someone may have tried to take a pot shot at

Everett that day? If they had hit him in the face at that range, they would almost certainly have blinded him.'

The clouds flitted across the sky with such speed that I felt half dizzy. She was so quick to pick up on my suspicion. She did not shift her gaze, but waited for my answer.

'I saw the photograph of the two of you together at the shoot. I was merely . . .'

'You were not merely doing anything. I know you now. You're a policeman's daughter and you do investigations and things. I've heard about it. And now you think Philippa killed Everett.'

'No!'

She was nodding rapidly. 'That's it. That's what happened. Everett and I were standing together in the gill bottom when I was shot. He was loading for me. I made a joke about it at the time. I said Philippa had me in her sights. She had someone hiding on top of the gill in that rocky outcrop.'

It seemed ironic that the first person Miss Windham accused was Philippa Runcie, and that Philippa Runcie had accused Caroline Windham.

She rested her elbows on her thighs and put her head in her hands. 'I can't believe it. I can't believe it's true. How dare someone kill him?' She looked up quickly. 'Who, apart from me, knew he was at the Metropole?'

'I don't know.'

'She knew.' She made a bitter sound, like a catch in her throat. 'Everett was finally giving her what she wanted, but it wasn't enough.'

'Miss Windham, do you know whom Mr Runcie was with at the hotel on Friday night?'

She shrugged. 'Someone of no importance. Was the woman there? Did she see anything?'

Now it really was time for me to shut up, but I said, 'So you have no idea who might have been with him?'

She shook her head. 'I wish it had been me. If anyone had tried to hurt him, I'd have killed them myself.'

I looked at her hands. She would have been capable of that, I felt sure.

'Do you know how he came to meet the woman he was with in the hotel? Might she be part of your circle?'

She shook her head. 'I have no idea.'

'Is there anything I can do?' I had a sudden thought that the news could be all around Yorkshire within the hour. 'Will you confide in Lady Fotheringham?'

'Certainly not!'

I stood up. 'I'm very sorry, Miss Windham.'

She did not answer. I had walked a hundred yards or so from the bandstand when she called to me to wait.

With the stride of a colossus, she caught up. 'Where are you going now?'

'Home.'

'Did you come in a carriage?'

'A motor.'

'I saw it. A blue affair.'

'Yes.'

'Take me somewhere will you? You'll have to wait until I change, and make my excuses for Sunday dinner.'

As the clock on the stable block touched half past noon, a harassed young maid appeared, viciously swinging a carpet bag.

'Mrs Shackleton?'

'Yes.'

'Miss Windham asks will you come to the front of the house.'

The cheek of the woman! I did her a service and now she chose to treat me like a chauffeur.

I hid my annoyance, politely thanked the maid and opened the car door for her to put the bag in.

'Would you like a lift?' I asked.

She laughed. 'I'm not allowed to go in the front door, madam.'

I drove to the front of the house and parked opposite the door.

Moments later, Caroline Windham appeared.

Without a word, she clambered in, showing none of the grace of her earlier horseback riding. I glanced at her. In the short time it had taken her to change and pack a bag, she had grown heavier and forlorn with bereavement.

'Which way?' I asked, softening a little towards her.

She waved an arm. 'Just out of here, and then I'll give you directions.'

I drove back the way I had come, and through the gates.

She sighed. 'Sorry about that, but I wanted them to see me leaving. Said I'd been called away. Couldn't face them.'

'Which way now?'

'Left, then straight along.'

'Are we going far?'

'No. Staying on the estate. Hence the subterfuge. Let them think I'm miles away when the news comes.'

We drove in silence for a mile, along a leafy lane. Following her directions, I slowed.

'Right here.' She pointed to a dusty track. Around a bend in the track appeared a fenced off area the size of a field, filled with strangely shaped figures. Nearest was a circle of tall, slender human shapes that cast long shadows. It was as though a magician had cast a spell on Stone Henge and turned the circle of stones into human beings.

'Keep going, and then you can hide the motor behind the barn. There's another way out.'

Following her directions, I stopped the motor between a barn and a disused pig sty.

For a long moment, we sat in the afternoon sun, listening to a thrush. Finally, she sighed. 'It was good of you to come and tell me. Will you come and meet someone? He'll have to know. He'll ask questions, and I can't . . .' She turned those blue eyes on me. I wondered if her Civil War ancestor had looked at his enemies with such sadness before he ran them through.

Curiosity made me follow her from the car. At the side of the barn were more sculptures. Two seated Roman figures formed a bench, their spread togas offering space, and gracefully touching the ground.

'This looks like Rupert Cromer's work.'

She nodded. 'Lord Fotheringham lets Rupert have these outbuildings and the cottage, grace-and-favour.'

My footsteps slowed as I looked about me at a strange collection, some of which I had seen at Cromer's exhibition last year. His pieces looked so different in the open air. Some were miniature. A creature half horse, half human reared up before me, but pint-sized, like the offspring of a Shetland pony and a dwarf.

At the front of the building, huge doors stood open to a space that was both barn and studio. We negotiated our way in, avoiding a square block of stone, tree trunk, a motorbike and strips of metal.

The tap of a hammer and chisel punctuated the humming silence.

The man wore a leather apron, like a shoemaker. He was standing back from a nymph-like figure, his head tilted to one side.

She called, 'Rupert, darling!'

He turned, wiped his hands on baggy trousers, and stared at us. 'I wondered where you'd got to, Caroline.'

So he had been the man out riding with her. Had I seen him dismount, I would have recognised him.

Caroline said, 'I had to come. I couldn't face the Fotheringhams and their sherry after what I've just found out.'

So she was going to tell him. But at least he seemed remote here. With luck, the news of Runcie's death would go no farther.

'What's the matter, Caroline?' He came closer.

She half fell into his arms. 'Oh Rupert, Rupert.'

He closed his eyes as he held her. It was time for me to go. The two of them were in a world of their own. Suddenly he opened his eyes, looked at me in surprise and across Miss Windham's right shoulder said, 'What has happened?'

'I brought Miss Windham some bad news.'

She broke away from his embrace and said in a choked voice, 'Everett is dead.'

'No! No.'

As I walked away, he called, 'Wait!' Keeping an arm around Miss Windham, he came across to me. 'Come inside. Please.'

I did not want to be cross-questioned, but he placed a friendly arm around me also, leaving me with the alternative of an undignified wriggle out of his grasp or acceptance of his invitation. The three of us walked together to the ramshackle house.

A boss-eyed housekeeper glared as we emerged into the shabby hallway from a dilapidated porch. Rupert Cromer left dusty white footprints on the tiles. He opened a door into a dimly lit parlour. The first thing that caught my eye was the bust that stood on a plinth in the corner of the room, lit by a shaft of sunlight. It was Caroline Windham.

I remembered it from his exhibition. It was the piece that had caused a stir, and allowed the connection of Caroline to the abstract nude. It was executed with great delicacy and subtlety. I looked from it to her, and back.

'That's beautiful, and such a good likeness.'

Cromer bowed and then kissed Caroline's cheek. 'Great things are possible with such a regal sitter.' He said quietly, 'Everett commissioned the bust'

She sank into a chair. 'You can't let anyone else take it, Rupert.'

'I won't.'

He glanced at the piece with admiration, which could have been for his own handiwork, or for his sitter.

Caroline said, 'I'm staying the night, Rupert. Is that all right?'

'I'll have a bed made up.'

'I don't want to be at Somersgill tomorrow when they hear about Everett's death, I couldn't bear their pity.'

He knelt before her, put his arms around her waist and his head in her lap. 'You've lost the love of your life. I've lost the best friend a man could have.'

I paid attention to a sketch pad pinned to an easel. It was covered in tiny drawings that may have been ideas for larger pieces of work. One was the sculptor himself, an odd little self-portrait of man and motorbike. Another was drawings from different angles of a Venus figure.

The strange thing about this figure was that it had Deirdre Fitzpatrick's face. Or was I, like Sykes and Fitzpatrick, becoming obsessed with the woman?

I was about to turn away and slip from the room unnoticed, when Cromer came over to me. 'I'm so sorry. It was kind of you to come.'

'Not at all, but I'll go now. Goodbye, Mr Cromer. Goodbye, Miss Windham. I'm very sorry.'

A moment later, I was walking back to my car.

My visit had not gone as intended. Had the same person who shot Caroline strangled Everett Runcie? It was possible. The perpetrator may have preferred a gun, but that would not be a very good method in a hotel.

There would be a list of guests who were here on the estate on Monday 13th August. Where? And how would I get my hands on it?

Eleven

Newly commissioned Special Constable Sykes felt a mounting excitement as he waited in the alley at the side of the Metropole, admiring the Clyno motorbike, checking its tyres. Hardly anyone walked up the alley on Sunday, when the hat shop and tobacconist that adjoined the hotel were closed. It was the perfect spot to wait for the signal to tail his quarry. Dapper Hartigan, Leeds Irish lad turned New Yorker, was probably still pomading his hair.

When he was in the force, Sykes had always wanted to go undercover. Once upon a time, he fancied himself as a lamplighter, or a knife grinder, pushing a cart, knocking on doors, looking through windows. The motorbike knocked those ideas into a cocked hat.

The chief inspector had asked Mrs Shackleton's permission to swear in Sykes as a special constable. He knew the area, could ride a motorbike, would be able to follow Hartigan and report on his movements.

Sykes did not know why the man was being followed. He was a person of interest before the murder. There was no obvious motive for Hartigan to have murdered Runcie, but there was opportunity and proximity. He could be the killer.

Just when the motorbike tyres would stand no more checking, a constable came out of the hotel's back door and gave him the nod. Sykes climbed on the motorbike and fired the engine into life. He edged towards King Street, holding back as he glanced to his right. Hartigan's hired Rolls-Royce stood at the kerb, motor running. Nattily dressed in dark suit, felt hat and bow tie, Hartigan tipped the commissionaire who opened the car door for him. They were off. Sykes kept a discreet distance. He risked dodging up a side street once the car entered Briggate. He zigged and zagged, to come out further along the road and not make himself obvious. The street was less busy on a Sunday, with strolling pedestrians and the traffic more sparse than on weekdays.

It was a twisting journey, with several wrong turns, and a stop while the driver leaned out and asked directions. When they crossed Richmond Road, Sykes did a little detour, and fell back. He rode along a parallel street, just in time to see the Rolls cross Church Road. The car came to a halt by a Roman Catholic church. Sykes waited by the school building, which offered cover. He watched through the railings, keeping his distance. Since boyhood, he had disliked being too near a Catholic church. It was some-thing bred in him that he could never shake, as if dreaded idolatry and superstition would ooze from the forbidding edifice and overpower him.

Hartigan did not go into the church. He went to the presbytery and knocked on the door. The priest must have been waiting. He emerged in his long black cassock, funny little hat on his head, and wearing a narrow scarf around his neck. The clergyman carried a small bag. It would not in the least surprise Sykes to find that they were in cahoots over some deadly deed.

Hartigan held the car door open for the priest, and then climbed in beside him.

Sykes followed, beginning to worry that he would be spotted. The driver showed fewer hesitations now. They picked up speed.

The journey led out of the city, into the leafy suburbs where trees grew in large gardens and on the broad pavements. They passed Roundhay Park, and then turned left. Sykes kept the length of the street between them.

The Rolls entered the grounds of a nursing home. Sykes glanced at the sign: Ashville Nursing Home. He cycled past and parked his bike in the ginnel that bordered the nursing home grounds. There was a side gate that creaked as he opened it.

The gardens blazed with colour. If the nursing staff's capabilities matched that of the gardeners, the patients would be fortunate indeed.

Who are you visiting, Mr Hartigan? Sykes asked silently.

Sykes watched from the shrubbery as Hartigan and the priest went inside. The driver lumbered out of the car, stretched, and lit a cigarette. He began to plod about the grounds. For a moment, Sykes wondered had he been spotted. The man found his way to a bench in the shade of an ash tree. The fellow might look a little on the dopey side, but he knew how to choose a vantage point that gave him a view of the path and the house while keeping an eye on his precious motor.

Like a man with legitimate business, Sykes strode to the front door that was open to the sunshine. A table in the tiled entry hall held a huge vase of roses. Beyond the wide oak staircase was a goods lift, large enough to carry wheelchairs. He looked up. At the top of the stairs, the two visitors were with a uniformed man who Sykes guessed had left the entry desk to escort them. They disappeared into a corridor.

Sykes quickly nipped behind the tall counter. A visitors' book lay open, its neat column headings conveniently recording, date, time, name of visitor and person visited. Mr Hartigan and Father Daley were visiting Mrs Hartigan.

The man was visiting his mother. Sykes felt a twinge of disappointment. But he had done his job. He checked his watch, so as to be able to report how long the visitors stayed.

Sykes left by the side gate, back into the ginnel, out of sight. After about forty minutes, he heard the purr of the Rolls-Royce engine. He mounted his bike and followed.

The car returned the way it had come, back towards the park.

By the tram stop nearest the park, Sykes stopped, to avoid running down a child who had jumped off the tram ahead of his parents and dashed into the road. People were teeming off the tram, children hurrying towards the gates, a woman carrying a picnic basket. I should come here with Rosie and the kids on the next free Sunday, Sykes decided. And then he saw them.

Cyril Fitzpatrick stepped off the tram. He held out his hand and helped his wife alight. When they stepped onto the pavement, Fitzpatrick did not let go of Deirdre's hand. She was looking up at him, smiling and talking. He smiled back.

Typical, Sykes thought. After all Fitzpatrick's moans and

complaints, he and his wife had turned completely lovey-dovey. It was only five days ago that Fitzpatrick wanted a twenty-four watch kept on her. Mrs Shackleton was right. Leave them to sort out their own troubles. Deirdre Fitzpatrick was looking at her husband with something like adoration, as if he were the most handsome of film stars. He looked back at her with a doting gaze.

Damn! Sykes had let himself be diverted. The motor carrying Hartigan and the priest was well out of view.

It was with relief that Sykes caught up with the Rolls and watched it enter King Street. He did not wait to see whether Hartigan's burly driver left it in the road or in the charge of a porter to be taken to the hotel's garage. Sykes drove past the hotel and into the deserted alley where he secured the motorbike.

Moments later he was in the suite on the third floor that the Scotland Yard men had taken over. The bed and wardrobe had been moved out to make way for trestle tables. Sykes reported to the sergeant who kept the log book. The man was a dead ringer for the dentist Sykes visited last year. His wavy hair was the colour of a ginger nut, his skin ruddy and his eyes a washed-out blue. It was the none-too-clean hands and nicotine-stained fingers that most reminded Sykes of the dentist. He could feel the taste of the fat fingers in his mouth even now. Sergeant Wilson at least had the benefit of knowing his stuff, unlike the dentist whose only certificates, framed and placed prominently on the walls, were for tidiest allotment of 1920, and special mentions for marrows and carrots.

Sergeant Wilson greeted Sykes and pushed the log book across to him. Sykes sat down, took out his pen, and in his meticulous hand wrote a brief account of Hartigan's doings, up to seeing him return to the hotel.

Wilson was in charge of both the Hartigan and murder log books. The entry ahead of Sykes's read, Car and chauffeur booked for six p.m.

Sykes tapped the entry. 'Am I stood down till then?'

Wilson nodded. 'As long as you're back in good time, in case our man gets ahead of himself.'

'Good. I'm off home for my dinner.'

Sykes looked forward to his Yorkshire pudding and roast lamb. He took the steps like a lad let out of school.

In the hotel lobby, he glanced at a shapely pair of legs, a woman with a newspaper hiding her face.

She lowered the newspaper.

He stared. 'Mrs Shackleton, what are you doing here?'

Wrong thing to say. She glared at him. 'Sit down a minute. There's something I want you to do.'

Sykes thought about his dinner. He was too loyal to wish he had used the other door.

Mrs Shackleton handed him an envelope. 'See this gets to the chief inspector. It's a cutting about an incident at the Fotheringham shoot. I've put a note in. He'll want to investigate a connection to Runcie's death.'

Why didn't she give it to him herself, he wanted to ask. But his not to reason why. He took the envelope. 'Right you are, boss.' He stood up.

'Not so fast, Mr Sykes. Marcus is bound to get hold of a list of who was at the shoot on 13th August. When he does, I'd like a copy, and I don't believe he will be inclined to give it to me personally. He'll think I'm sticking my nose in and interfering with his investigation.'

Sykes sat down again. 'I can't do that. I'm sworn in as a special constable.'

'Thanks to me.' She smiled sweetly. 'Remember who you work for, Mr Sykes. When the circus has left town, you and I will be on the high wire together again.'

Sykes knew when he was beaten.

Twelve

Sykes is an excellent chap in a crisis, but very grumpy if he misses his meals. He came out of the hotel onto King Street, where I was waiting for him.

'Come on, Mr Sykes. I'll give you a lift home.'

'That's all right. I have use of the motorbike.'

'Then sit with me for five minutes. I want to talk to you.'

He climbed into the car.

'Did you give the envelope to Marcus?'

'The chief inspector is up at CID offices. He'll get it as soon as he comes back.'

'I'm curious. What happened to McFarlane, the Scot who was staying here and went to York races with Hartigan?'

'Word is he took a train back north of the border, directly after the races, with his order for whisky, no doubt.'

Canny fellow. And since Marcus had told me that people in high places with connections to distilleries would not want to see a slump in sales, I guessed that any activity by Customs and Excise would bear a light touch.

'Are you enjoying tracking Mr Hartigan?'

Sykes grinned. 'Money for old rope. If I'd had this kind of job on the force, I would have stayed put. Now can I go home for my dinner?'

'You said earlier that you spotted Hartigan in Roundhay? Was he admiring Roundhay Park Lake?'

'Oddly enough, he has been doing exactly what he said he would – visiting relatives. He went to Ashville Nursing Home, to see his mother, and took a priest with him.'

'So he really does have a good reason for being here.'

Sykes nodded. 'And you'll like this. I saw a couple we know, on their Sunday outing, nice as ninepence, stepping from the tram hand in hand.'

'Who?'

'One guess.'

'The Fitzpatricks?'

'None other.'

Something clicked. Deirdre Fitzpatrick had taken her mother to a nursing home. Where? And when would she visit her? On Sunday afternoon.

'What was Mrs Fitzpatrick's maiden name?'

Sykes gave me a puzzled look. 'I don't know.'

'Where else has Hartigan been?'

He shrugged. 'I only started following him yesterday dinnertime, remember. He went to a boxing gym on York Road.'

'Before that?'

'There were a few hours when nobody followed him, when the chief inspector was starting up the murder enquiry.'

'And where else? What about Thursday, Friday?'

'Nothing's written down. It's in the chief inspector's head I expect.'

It was entirely possible that Cyril and Deirdre Fitzpatrick were stepping out to feed the ducks on Roundhay Park Lake, but I doubted that. Nursing homes allow no more than two visitors at a time. Sykes had watched Hartigan leave. Shortly after, the Fitzpatricks arrive in Roundhay; to visit her mother in the nursing home?

'Did you see which direction the Fitzpatricks took when they got off the tram?'

Sykes shook his head. 'I assumed they were going to the park.' His eyes widened as he picked up my unspoken suggestion.

'You think they were going to the nursing home that Hartigan and the priest had just left?'

I nodded. 'And if I'm right, and there's a connection, and they had arranged to share the visiting hours, what else might they have coordinated?'

Sykes said, 'I could try and find out Mrs Fitzpatrick's maiden name.'

'That might take too long. There is a quicker way.' I got out of the car. 'You wait here. I'll make a telephone call, and then I want you to tell me exactly what Fitzpatrick said when you reported to him on the day I followed Deirdre.'

I went back into the hotel. Someone was ahead of me in the telephone booth, having a long conversation, and refusing to catch my eye.

I crossed the lobby and tapped on the manager's door. He surprised me by being delighted to see me.

'Mr Naylor, would you oblige me greatly by letting me make a private telephone call from your office? The booth is occupied.'

'Of course.'

He hovered.

'Private.'

'Yes, yes. I'll wait outside.'

The operator connected me to Ashville Nursing Home before I had properly formulated what I might say. Thinking quickly, I claimed to be a neighbour of Mr and Mrs Fitzpatrick. I would be passing by shortly, and able to give them a lift. Were they still visiting Mrs Fitzpatrick's mother?

The reply was not long in coming. Mr Fitzpatrick had left. Mrs Fitzpatrick was still with her mother.

Knowing the answer but wanting to confirm the connection, I asked, 'What about Mrs Hartigan's son? Is he still there?'

'Oh he left some good while ago.'

I thanked my helpful informant and rang off.

As Marcus rightly said, the description of the woman who had shared Runcie's bed could fit a thousand women, including Deirdre Fitzpatrick.

I thanked the manager, who was standing very close to the door.

He leaned close. 'Mrs Shackleton, I wonder if I might impose for a moment, a quiet word?'

A quiet word was the last thing I wanted, but he was barring my exit, and perhaps he had something important to say.

We slid back into his office, but I refused a seat. Just as well, as he merely wanted to get off his chest complaints about how much space CID took up and how the sergeant went into the kitchen in the middle of the night, fried an egg and made a mess.

I managed to make a sympathetic comment and tore myself away.

Finally, I was onto something.

Deirdre and Hartigan, in the hotel at the same time: a murderer and a mystery woman.

When I went outside, Sykes was no longer in the car. I looked about and saw him on the corner, beckoning me towards the alley.

He said, 'I didn't want to draw attention to myself by sitting in the car like a show-off. Did you make your telephone call?'

'I did. The Fitzpatricks went to the same nursing home. She is still there, with her mother. It was Deirdre in the hotel with Everett Runcie, I feel sure of it. And Hartigan is her brother.'

Sykes stared at me. 'If you're right . . .'

'I am.'

'. . . what's the significance?'

'I don't know yet.'

'It must have been convenient for Hartigan to be called back to his dying mother. He used it as cover for buying whisky. Wilson hinted that while Hartigan was in London, he ordered thousands of gallons of gin.'

'So he killed two birds with one stone.'

'Two birds or three?' Sykes said thoughtfully. 'Did he kill Runcie?'

Somehow that seemed too neat. What connection could there be between Hartigan and Runcie, I wondered. 'Does he look like a strangler to you, Mr Sykes?'

'No. He's bantam weight. But I've learned a bit about his relatives over the past twenty-four hours. There are cousins, aunts and uncles, some in the church and some involved with the boxing club I told you about, and with market stalls. Heavyweights. Hands for hire. Leeds police supplied the chief inspector with names. They must have missed Mrs Fitzpatrick off the list of known relations because of her change of name.'

She was the one who interested me most.

'Tell me, Mr Sykes, on the day I followed Deirdre, when you went to see Fitzpatrick and gave him my report. How did he take it?'

Sykes stared at a pigeon that alighted on the cobbles and pecked at a crack. 'He did go on a bit. To tell you the truth, I whisked him up to the Chemic for a pint. He wanted chapter and verse, and yet he was terrified of being seen with me by some of his fellow printers in a city centre pub, or by some neighbour in Kirkstall, as if they might earwig, or recognise me as ex job.'

'What else passed between you?'

'He seemed to have dropped his worries about shop-lifting.'

'Those were for our benefit, I think, to make sure we took up his grievances. Anything else?'

Sykes's long pause told me there certainly was something else.

'I didn't tell you because I knew you wanted an end of it, and as you said, what she gets up to is not our business.'

'Go on.'

'Two things. You know Fitzpatrick works on the local paper as a compositor?'

'Yes, he said.'

'There's a photographer on the paper who had a word in Fitzpatrick's shell-like.'

'Don't tell me. Len Diamond?'

'How did you know?'

'He's a brilliant photographer. I've learned a lot from looking at his work and listening to him talk about technique. But if he were a woman, he'd be called the world's worst gossip.'

Sykes lit a cigarette. 'That fits. Diamond told Fitzpatrick that he'd bumped into Mrs Fitzpatrick on Leeds Bridge. Diamond recognised her from seeing her last year at Kirkstall Abbey. I suppose she is the kind of woman a man would remember.'

'So Len Diamond saw Deirdre out and about. That doesn't sound very significant.'

'It was to Fitzpatrick. Because it turned out that this was on one of the Fridays when his wife didn't come home. He could not decide whether the photographer was hinting that she was meeting another man.'

'You said there were two things. What else?'

'Apparently, Deirdre brought something home and forgot about it. Fitzpatrick seized on it, and he had it in his pocket – a table napkin, embroidered with a letter *A*. He asked me to find out where it might have come from and whether she was eating out in restaurants. I refused.'

I felt a sudden chill. The sun did not reach this alley. Even the pigeon had flown. A terrible stillness settled around us.

'Are you all right?' Sykes asked.

'Yes. Someone walked over my grave. Did you ever see *Othello*?'

'I know the story, but I never saw it.'

'Iago produces Desdemona's handkerchief, as proof of her infidelity. Othello is so convinced of Desdemona's guilt that he strangles her.'

Sykes's matter-of-factness can be very reassuring. 'I think the napkin's from the Adelphi. That's just across Leeds Bridge. Maybe Diamond took her to supper and was having a laugh at Fitzpatrick's expense.'

'Do you still have a note of the occasions when Fitzpatrick said she spent nights away from home?'

Sykes tapped the notebook in his breast pocket.

'Good. Here's what we're going to do. I want you to call at the Adelphi and make a few discreet enquiries.' I delved into my satchel. 'Take this photograph of the Fitzpatricks' wedding, but make sure you only show Deirdre's picture. Find out if she stayed there.'

'When? I've to be back at the Metropole for six.'

'Plenty of time. I'll meet you back here just before six. I'm going to pay Mr Fitzpatrick a visit. Since his wife was still at the nursing home, I can be there before she gets back. We're missing something, and I'm not sure what.'

'I know what I'm missing. My Yorkshire pudding.'

'Have it cold later. Sprinkle it with sugar.'

Thirteen

I drove across to Kirkstall, parking the car on Abbey Road
so as not to draw attention to myself. Norman View is a
steep street, with well-tended gardens. I did not have to
knock. Fitzpatrick was in the garden, emptying a teapot.
He was wearing a dark blue striped apron.

He stared at me. 'Mrs Shackleton.'

'Hello, Mr Fitzpatrick. What a pretty garden.'

Fitzpatrick tipped the contents of the teapot onto the
soil.

Sykes would have sniggered at the sight of Fitzpatrick
in his apron.

'What brings you to Kirkstall, Mrs Shackleton?'

Good question. What did I hope to achieve? I had a
sudden mental picture of the evening gown that hung in
the wardrobe of Runcie's hotel suite, and of the dainty
shoes. I should have brought one for Deirdre to try. It
would be a great relief to see that they did not fit.

'Is Mrs Fitzpatrick at home?'

Fitzpatrick froze. His heavy face turned pale. 'Is something wrong?'

I had thought up a story on the way over, and now

it sounded ridiculous: that my sister was about to be married (true) and had heard of a house to rent in one of these streets (false). She had asked me to take a look (whopper). Houses round here would be snapped up in an instant, and we both knew that.

He held the teapot close to his chest.

'I had a question, for you or for Mrs Fitzpatrick.'

'Deirdre isn't here. We both went to see her mother at the nursing home. Deirdre was anxious that her mother see us together and know that everything's all right. Be reassured you know.'

As though he suddenly remembered his manners, Fitzpatrick went to the already open door and held it steady. 'Will you come in?'

'Thank you.'

We stepped into a square kitchen, with the usual range, table and chairs, and the refinement of a curtain to cover the sink set in the recess. A giant picture of a sad-faced Jesus, his delicate hands exposing the bleeding heart on his chest, looked down from the wall. Beside it was the Virgin Mary, immaculately dressed in blue and white, wearing a sorrowful expression, head tilted to one side.

The table was set for tea, with three good China plates, cups and saucers. A dish of lettuce and a plate of tomatoes lay under a mesh cover. A snowy white cloth covered what must be slices of bread and butter. Under a glass cover lay slices of boiled ham surrounded by a boiled egg, neatly sliced. A cake stand held small, square iced creations. There would be a trifle somewhere, keeping cool.

'You're obviously expecting company. That's a grand spread you've put on.'

'The wife's brother, over from America.' He enjoyed saying this. The visit brought a touch of excitement. I imagined him letting the news drop in the composing room at the newspaper. The New York businessman brother-in-law, here on a visit.

'He'll have a lot of stories to tell I expect. You don't have that kind of visitor every day.'

'He went to see his mother earlier, and do you know, the nurse told us that the poor old soul thought it was her husband at the bottom of the bed. Gave her quite a turn.'

'A turn for the good I hope?'

'Oh no. She made all sorts of upset noises, until the nurse explained that it was her son who she hadn't seen since his boyhood.'

'What time are you expecting him?'

'Six o'clock.' He looked at the miniature grandmother clock on the mantelshelf. 'Deirdre should be back by now. She said she'd stay just another hour. Poor Deirdre. It'll hit her hard when her mother goes.' This thought seemed to cheer him.

'Everything's all right between you and Deirdre then?'

He ran his tongue over dry lips. 'What makes you ask?'

'Mr Fitzpatrick, I don't want to alarm you, but if you are still concerned about Deirdre, will you please let me take a quick look around the house? Only some information came to me, and I think it's nothing to do with her, and nothing to be alarmed about, but if I could see her room, where she might keep things?'

He froze. 'There's nothing here that doesn't belong here.'

'Not even a bottle of perfume?'

It was a low blow and he flinched. 'Take a look, if you must.' He glanced out of the window. 'She'll be back any minute. Please be quick.'

A small fire blazed in the speckless front room with its sideboard and moquette sofa and chairs. Fitzpatrick took a cloth from his apron and wiped at a spot of dust.

'May I see your wife's dresses?'

He hesitated. 'You think she stole a dress?'

'Mr Fitzpatrick, I want to eliminate a doubt. You wanted to know the truth about your wife. Now so do I.'

'Go up.'

One bedroom was a little untidy, with a dress flung onto the bed. Fitzpatrick followed me into the room. He took a hanger from the wardrobe, carefully placed the dress on it and hung it on the rail. As he did so, I picked up a shoe and checked the size. It was the same as the shoes in the room at the Hotel Metropole, but it was also the same size as mine.

'Does your wife make her own clothes?'

'She does.' He picked up a perfume bottle from the dressing table. 'I bought her this.'

I nodded, feeling mean, hating the thought that she might arrive home at any moment and find me snooping. She and her brother. They would not be so easily taken in as Fitzpatrick.

'What is it you expect to find?' he asked.

He had left the wardrobe door open.

I looked quickly at the dresses. Every one was handmade, with carefully sewn seams. One had a quickly-stitched careless hem, like the dress left behind in the wardrobe at the hotel. If some skilful seamstress examined the outfits, she might come up with a clever conclusion regarding stitches. I saw only a superficial similarity. I closed the wardrobe door.

'There's another room, across the landing.'

The second room had a single bed, with the same white candlewick counterpane as the first. Fitzpatrick's brown overcoat hung behind the door. His hairbrushes and hair oil stood on the washstand, next to a male plaster saint dressed in brown robes and carrying a lily.

'There's nothing belonging to Deirdre in here. Have you seen enough?'

'Yes. I'm sorry to have troubled you. I'm glad that you and Deirdre have made up.'

'Oh yes. It came from her. I'd prayed about it, said special prayers, and it was like a miracle, and so sudden. Friday night, she was to stay with her mother. But she came back, after I'd gone to bed.'

He led the way back downstairs.

'What time did she get home?'

'I don't know. I was asleep. But on Saturday morning, there she was. She had the kettle on the gas ring, and made my sandwich to take to work.'

Still behind him, as he stepped into the kitchen, I asked, 'What time do you go to work on Saturday morning?'

'I'm up at seven. I leave to catch the half past seven tram.' He forced a smile, but his suspicions were well and truly aroused.

I thought about the timings. The chambermaid had knocked on the hotel door at six. If I were right, and it was Deirdre in the room, there was time for her to make her escape from the hotel, jump on a tram, and be home in time to put a match to the gas ring and boil the kettle.

Fitzpatrick's shoulders stiffened.

He suddenly clutched his stomach. 'I'm going to be sick.' He hurried across the room, pulling back the concealing curtain, grabbing for an enamel bucket beneath the sink.

He vomited. 'I'm so sorry.'

'Don't worry, Mr Fitzpatrick. It's an emotional time for you, with your worries about your mother-in-law, and a visitor coming.'

I ran water into a cup and held it out to him.

Fitzpatrick took a sip. He rinsed his mouth, and spat into the sink. His face was pale. 'What is it you're not telling me, about Deirdre?'

'Sit down.'

Fitzpatrick slumped into a kitchen chair.

'Take some deep breaths.'

He folded his arms around his chest.

'Can I get you anything? Do you need a doctor?'

'You could pass me the milk of magnesia. It's in the cupboard.'

I opened the door above the sink, took down the bottle and handed it to Fitzpatrick.

He took a swig. 'I'll be all right. Please go. I don't want you to be here when Deirdre comes back. She'll guess. She'll think I've been spying on her.'

'And have you?' Were his the hands that squeezed life from Everett Runcie? 'Did you follow her on Friday night?'

'No of course not. I knew where she was. She was staying at the nursing home with her mother.'

The clock chimed, quarter to six. If Deirdre was to be here for tea, she would be getting off the tram any moment now.

'I'd better go, before Deirdre returns and your guest arrives.'

'But what is it? Why did you come?'

'Try not to worry. I hope it will turn out to be nothing. Goodbye, Mr Fitzpatrick.'

He followed me to the gate, carrying the bucket of vomit.

I waved, and he waved back, probably for the benefit of the neighbours.

I needed to meet Sykes and see what, if anything, he had learned at the Adelphi Hotel.

Fortunately, the Sunday evening streets were quiet. I put my foot down and urged the Jowett to hurry.

When I reached King Street, I saw Sykes waiting in the alley, near the tobacconist's doorway.

He looked a little out of sorts.

I parked by the alley and got out. 'Well, Mr Sykes?'

Close up, I saw how glum he looked, as he returned the Fitzpatricks' photograph to me.

He said, 'I was right. The linen napkin did come from the Adelphi. And I showed the photograph to a waiter I know there.'

Sykes's contacts across the city never fail to surprise me. Had he once given the waiter a pair of stockings for his wife, or sat next to him at some long-ago cricket match and ended up doing the man a favour? I was not to know. He avoided background explanations.

'The waiter recognised her photograph. Mrs Fitzpatrick spent the weekend of 24th August at the Adelphi Hotel, with a singer from the Gilbert and Sullivan opera, Joseph Barnard, professionally known as Giuseppe Barnardini.'

'We saw him in *The Mikado*. The Fitzpatricks were in the audience.'

'Yes.'

So Deirdre Fitzpatrick had hidden depths, and secrets. I felt a sneaking admiration that she had the nerve to drag her husband to the stalls of the Grand to see her lover cut his capers and sing his heart out. I played devil's advocate. 'The waiter could have been mistaken.'

'He was quite certain. Apparently Barnard treated the bar staff, and he was a generous tipper, so they all remembered him. A lot of theatre people splash money about. They want to be liked, that's why they're up there, strutting for the rest of us. The most insecure profession and most of them spit in the eye of the future and never put anything by for a rainy day.' There he was again, judging everyone, although often he was spot on in his judgements. Sykes continued, 'The waiter said what a lovely couple they were, and so taken with each other. He felt sure they weren't married.' He pricked up his ears, and then looked round the corner into King Street. 'That's Hartigan getting into the Rolls. Better dash.'

'You'll be following him to Kirkstall, for tea with his brother-in-law and sister.'

'Yes. I've worked that out. I feel sorry for Fitzpatrick.'

'Don't feel so sorry for him that you forget to tell Marcus Deirdre is Hartigan's sister.'

Sykes sighed. 'I don't "tell Marcus" anything. I write my findings in Sergeant Wilson's log book, and I can't do that now because I'm on my bike!'

With that he jumped on the motorbike, kicked it into action and veered dangerously out of the alley, to follow Hartigan's car.

I went back into the hotel and took the lift to the third floor where the investigating officers took up two and a half rooms of Mr Naylor's precious space.

Marcus was in one of them, talking to a freckled chap, introduced to me as Sergeant Wilson. I wondered if this was the man who fried eggs in the middle of the night.

'Did you get the cutting, Mr Charles?' I asked, keeping our exchange formal because of Sergeant Wilson.

He frowned absent-mindedly before saying, somewhat dismissively, 'Oh, the newspaper article about the shooting incident? Yes, I did, Mrs Shackleton. Thank you for your interest.'

Pompous prig! He was trying to dismiss me. They had both stood up as I entered, but I had not been offered a seat.

'There is something else you might like to know.'

They looked at me, indulgently.

'Mr Hartigan has a sister, Mrs Cyril Fitzpatrick, Deirdre, who lives in Kirkstall. It may be worth asking her where she was on Friday night and early Saturday morning. It's possible that she was Mr Runcie's companion.'

Marcus kept his composure, but the sergeant's jaw dropped ever so slightly. 'How do you know about the sister?'

'Mr Wilson, I am a private investigator. I know things. That is my job.'

Marcus attempted graciousness. 'Mrs Shackleton has helped me before in enquiries.'

This gave me the opening to ask, 'Who will interview Mrs Fitzpatrick?' I wondered whether the solitary woman police constable who had not been available to interview the chambermaid might be recruited.

To give Marcus credit, he showed just the slightest discomfort. 'The sergeant is organising interviews.'

Sergeant Wilson gave a satisfied smile. 'Mr Charles

usually entrusts the interviewing of the fair sex to me. He believes I do it well.'

I turned to go. 'Well then, good luck.'

Part of me hoped that Deirdre Fitzpatrick would run rings around him. Her story to Fitzpatrick that she had spent the night at the nursing home was a lot of hot air, and would soon be disproved.

'I'll take a few more details from you if I may, Mrs Shackleton,' Wilson said.

I rattled off the two addresses: Deirdre's mother's on Cotton Street, and the house on Norman View, made my excuses, and left.

Not that I felt peeved about being left out of the investigation. Not much.

Fourteen

Deirdre sat by her mother's bed. Rays of evening sun pierced the window and streamed onto her mammy's face. She should draw the curtains. But Deirdre could not bring herself to shut out the light that would soon turn itself inside out forever.

The pale eyes flickered. 'Who was that?'

'Earlier? Fitz was here.'

'The others, at the foot of the bed.'

Deirdre stroked her mother's hand. 'Your son Anthony came, and Father Daley.'

'At the foot of the bed. A baker, a butcher, a woman with a basket.'

'I didn't see them, Mam. Was her basket full?'

She closed her eyes.

Her mother spoke just twice more. The first time, she did not open her eyes. She said, 'What if he's there? What if he's waiting?'

Deirdre knew who she meant. 'St Peter will deal with him. Don't worry your head.'

The last time she spoke, her voice was light as air and deep as a gravel pit. She opened her eyes sufficiently to catch a flicker of blue, the blue of Deirdre's cardigan.

'Am I still in this world?'

Her mam thought she was catching sight of Our Lady's robes.

'You're still here.'

And then she slept, and slipped so quietly from this world to the next that Deirdre was not sure of the moment of going, or for how long afterwards she sat.

After a long time, someone came into the room, a nurse. She led Deirdre out and said something that she did not hear, and asked her to sit a moment, and wait. But Deirdre went outside.

The garden of the nursing home mocked her with its summer beauty. Mam, you should have seen more of this. You should have come here sooner, to sit outside, to see grass, trees, flowers, a sky with some blue and white, not leaden and laden with fumes of factories and foundries. You lived all your life in a miasma, and here, just to the edge of it, was something else. Now it's too late. You wouldn't have wanted me to do what I did, to earn the money to bring you here. In your heart did you want to die where you lived, not pass your last few days with starched strangers.

The matron came to find her. The doctor must come. They were waiting for the doctor. Deirdre turned back and looked at the window. It felt so cruel to leave her mammy alone at the last.

'How will you get home?' the matron asked. 'I could arrange for you to be taken.'

A pounds, shillings and pence sign flashed in the matron's eyes. It would be added to the bill.

Deirdre did not know what the word meant. Home. She had said goodbye to home the night she lay on the bed in the old room, on her mother's bed, a room full of memories, and struggles not spoken of, just faced, just won or lost, all the tiny battles to hold your head high, not be overcome by the inability to make a shilling stretch, to be always surrounded by want and sickness and small defeats and people who put on a brave face. Cut out the cardboard insoles for your shoes and never heed the holes. Go to the market as it closed to see what was to be had. Pick up a cabbage that had fallen from a cart. But everyone was in the same boat. Then along came the big brown bear, Cyril Fitzpatrick, courting her in the boating lake café with fancy cakes.

The matron looked at her, waiting for an answer. 'I don't need a ride,' Deirdre said.

That would be too strange, and not her at all, to ride in a motor car when her mother would never again feel the air on her skin or see her own shadow on the wall by candlelight. 'I'll take the tram.'

The matron touched her arm with long thin fingers. 'I will walk you to the tram stop.'

'No. Thank you.' She would walk herself.

The matron kept her fingers so lightly on Deirdre's arm. Deirdre felt light-headed, and unreal, as if she might float away.

'Your husband and brother should come tomorrow, to make the arrangements.'

The arrangements.

Deirdre nodded.

Arrangements. Such a strange word and what it meant was, we will begin the long, slow goodbye to your mam.

Who will remember the way you combed your hair?

Deirdre walked.

There was the tram and people getting on, as if nothing had happened.

She turned into the park through the big gates. As others left the park, she went deeper, against the flow, as usual.

At the boating lake, the man in charge called across the water, 'Come in, your time is up.'

She walked back to the nursing home. She hesitated, seeing a big car by the gates. But there was only the driver, waiting, smoking a cigarette.

She passed the motor on the other side of the street, making herself invisible, then crossed and entered the ginnel that ran alongside the nursing home grounds. Overhanging branches formed a shady tent.

She saw Fitz, the man she called husband, the lumbering stranger she had coaxed to more than kiss her but who did not like to be too close, or to touch her breasts or her thighs or any part of her. When she had enticed him, he had acted as if she burned his fingertips, as if to touch her was to feel the flames of hell.

With the man she had called husband was the one who called himself her brother, who had appeared out of nowhere, demanding to be paid attention, frightened her mother to death by his likeness to their dad, and expected to be praised for it.

The resentment rose. Tiny knots of fury made her skin feel too tight to contain her feelings. All those years when Anthony was an ocean away, Mam carried him in her heart, his name on her lips and in her prayers. And he never bothered, never cared. If he did care now, it was in that showy way, all mouth and trousers, and too late. Well let him get on with it.

When Fitz and Anthony finally left, Deirdre opened the nursing home's side gate, a creaking gate, and stepped into the grounds, keeping out of sight behind the trees.

She followed a winding path to the rear of the garden, to a greenhouse, and opened its door.

After the evening chill, it was like entering an oven, but this oven smelled of the jungle, of vines and sharp, sweet vegetation. Potted plants stood on shelves. At the back, on sacking, lay uprooted flowers that had come to the end of their days.

Deirdre carefully folded a rough sack, took off her shoes, and knelt in the centre aisle of the greenhouse. She whispered the 'De profundis', for her mother.

She would spend the night here.

She slept, and dreamed of men: of a husband who was no husband at all; of her brother, who arrived too late; of a dad she did not know but who would drink and hit out. When he tumbled down the cellar steps, it was a blessing, and in answer to a prayer made by her mother to St Rita.

In her dream, the three men perched on clouds, posing as the Father, the Son, and the Holy Ghost.

Her mammy's voice echoed through the greenhouse. Am I still on this earth?

Deirdre slept soundly in the nursing home greenhouse, on the sacking that smelled of earth, mould and eternity, quite unaware of how many people very much wanted to talk with her.

Fifteen

After my brief meeting with Marcus and Sergeant Wilson, I drove home rather fast, and somewhat recklessly, which is not like me at all. Perhaps Marcus did not need my help. Perhaps Wilson really was very good at interviewing women, and I should not have let his attitude annoy me.

I had found out so much, and yet so little. The collusion of Archie the waiter in the matter of Runcie's proof of adultery for the purpose of his divorce; the reasons for Anthony Hartigan's first visit home; the connection between Deirdre and Anthony; Philippa's suspicions of Caroline Windham; Caroline's suspicions of Philippa and her secretary, Gideon King; the nagging feeling I had about the incident at the shoot – the near-miss. And that person who seemed to pop up everywhere, Len Diamond, with his camera on Leeds Bridge; whispering insinuations to Cyril Fitzpatrick; showing off his insider knowledge to me at the racecourse; being jostled by Gideon King, in the grandstand after Diamond attempted to photograph the Runcies and Caroline.

In not asking for my help on the case, Marcus must have uncovered so much more. I wished I knew what.

When I turned into my street, I caught sight of an upright, slender figure wearing stout shoes and a gabardine raincoat. As I drew level, I saw that it was Philippa Runcie, and waved. She waved back and called, 'I'll catch you up.'

I would normally have gone up to the garage, but stopped at my gate and got out, waiting for Philippa.

As she drew level, she looked behind her. 'I wouldn't put it past Gideon to follow me. But I don't think he saw me leave.'

'Why would Gideon follow you?'

'I told you. He's so protective. I had to come out for air. I feel I'm going mad in that house.'

'Would you like to come in?'

'I'd rather walk, if you don't mind coming with me. I want to talk to you.'

'I could do with a walk myself. I'll just put my satchel in the house and change my shoes.'

Five minutes later, we were walking up my road, past the big house whose stable I use as a garage. The wood beyond was quiet at this time of evening, with only the distant bark of a dog. Some leaves had fallen early and crunched underfoot.

Philippa thrust her hands into her pockets. For a person who said she wanted to talk, she seemed reluctant to begin. We followed the path through the wood. Suddenly, she said, 'While you were changing your shoes, I put an envelope on top of your filing cabinet.'

'Oh?'

'I wrote you a letter, in case you weren't in.'

'What does it say, or do you want me to wait and read it?'

A squirrel raced across our path and up a tree.

'It's a letter and a cheque, a retainer. When we were talking in the maze, I told you I want to find out who killed Everett. I meant it. Will you help me?'

'I'll help in any way I can.'

'Not help. I shouldn't have said help. I mean investigate, properly.'

'But Scotland Yard is on the case, and were from the first moment.'

'Huh! I know that the chief inspector is a friend of yours, but if you'd heard the questions his sergeant asked me today, you would be appalled. Meanwhile the perpetrator is out there and I do not feel safe.'

'What makes you think the police are on the wrong track?'

'Their line of questioning. The sergeant did not say this in so many words, but he thinks my family have ordered Everett's murder, to save money, and to protect my honour.'

I guessed that this was because of the arrival at the hotel of Anthony Hartigan. Now that I had handed them Deirdre Fitzpatrick on a plate, Anthony Hartigan might well and truly be suspect number one. 'That's upsetting, but they'll have to look at every possibility, every angle, while keeping an open mind.'

'But they're not keeping an open mind. My brother-in-law, Harold, he felt the same, that they are pointing a finger at us. My family would not do that. They have not stopped liking Everett. Honestly, Kate, if it came to choosing, they would have backed him over me. The thought of them having a contract put on his life is ludicrous.'

I wondered if this was really so ludicrous, given

129

that Gideon had been dispatched from Boston to act as Philippa's private secretary, and to protect her interests.

'That won't be the only line of enquiry the police are following.'

She kicked a stone. 'No, you're right. According to Harold, they're raking through every loan Everett authorised at the bank, every financial misdeed he committed. Harold's furious. It could damage the bank's reputation, not that I care any more but I do feel sorry for Harold. He'd only just got used to the idea of the divorce and having to take back his stately home.'

'Were Everett's connections to the bank to be severed?'

'Yes. They wanted rid of him. That's why he was planning to go to Italy. But Harold has this outrageous suspicion that the police think the bank may have paid for Everett's demise because Everett was demanding money to go quietly after making a mess of things.'

'Then it sounds like a very thorough investigation.'

'Yes! Exactly. Very thorough and very wrong. I know my family. I know bankers. They have cleverer ways of dealing with troublesome individuals than bumping them off. Everett was going to be out in the cold, and he knew it. He was making the best of it and he could have started again. He even hinted there was some Italian countess who would have him, though that may have been to make me jealous. If so, it didn't work.'

That information may not have made Philippa jealous, but it would have enraged Caroline Windham.

I held a branch aside for Philippa as we walked along a narrow section of path.

She said, 'There would have been no advantage for me, my family, or the bank to kill him. It was over, done and dusted. So who did strangle him? Don't you see, Kate? If it's not properly investigated soon, someone will get away with murder.'

We walked and talked for an hour or more.

Finally, she said, 'Will you take on the investigation? There's nothing to stop you making some enquiries of your own. Please don't tear up my cheque. Say you'll do it.'

'All right, I will. But you might have to put up with some awkward questions from me too.'

'Fire away.'

'Gideon King, you said how protective he is.'

'Yes. You saw it yourself at the races when that photographer was trying to take a picture of the not-so-eternal triangle, me, Everett and Caroline. Gideon feels humiliated on my behalf because of Everett's behaviour. But I've told him that I've risen above it. I saw an end to it and I had truly stopped caring what Everett did. That was a great relief, because when he saw that he could not hurt me any more, when I told him it was all over, he was all for trying again, swearing he would stop seeing her. Even at the races, he swore he had not invited her.'

'Does Gideon have an alibi for the night or morning of Everett's murder?'

'We had dinner together at the house, which might seem odd, but I told you he was at school with my brother. We have a long history.'

'And after dinner? I'm sorry to ask but I must try and see a clear picture.'

She shook her head. 'Neither of us has an alibi.'

'Where is Mr King now?'

'I believe he's ensconced with my brother-in-law, Harold. Do you want to see him?'

'Another time, perhaps.'

'I hope that you'll ask Caroline Windham what she was doing that night.'

By the gates of Kirkley Hall, we parted company. I made my slow way home, thinking over everything we had talked about.

It was way past dusk when I reached home. Sykes was there, waiting for me. He knows where I keep the spare key, and that Mrs Sugden would let him in, but he was sitting on the front wall, looking down the street towards Headingley Lane. He walked to meet me.

'Is something wrong, Mr Sykes?'

He nodded. 'Deirdre Fitzpatrick is missing.'

Sixteen

Nothing gets me up so early in the morning as knowing I have a case to solve.

Something puzzled me just a little about Philippa's request. After coming back from our walk yesterday evening, I had read her letter carefully. It was short, and to the point, requesting me to investigate Everett's death. But there was one additional remark, something she had not mentioned on our walk. She wrote, "I have not been feeling very well lately, even before this happened. I want to go home to the States as soon as possible."

It did not surprise me that she wanted to turn her back on everything that had happened. But she is the picture of health. Still in all, it was not surprising that the disappointment of a failed marriage had left her feeling out of sorts. I hoped I would be able to help. Her retaining cheque certainly made the case worth my while.

It was a challenge, too. Who would find Runcie's killer, me or Marcus? Marcus had the disadvantage of not knowing he was in a race. I had the advantage of having Sykes on the inside; I intended to use every card in the pack. I would start by talking to that source of all information, the omnipresent Len Diamond. He was the one person I could be sure had not been interviewed by Marcus's Scotland Yard detectives or Leeds CID. Diamond clearly knew about the divorce, hence his attempt at taking a photograph of the banker, his wife and the mistress. What else did he know?

I breakfasted early and was upstairs, combing my hair, when I heard Mrs Sugden answer the door.

She appeared moments later in the bedroom doorway. 'There's a trio of desperadoes on the back doorstep, asking to see you. What am I to do?'

I looked out of the bedroom window. Parked outside my house was a white Rolls-Royce, a chauffeur in a peaked cap at the wheel. 'Come and look at this, Mrs Sugden.'

She blew out her lips. 'Highly placed desperadoes.'

I looked at my watch. 'Ask them in and offer them a cup of tea. I'll be down in a moment.'

'I won't take them in the dining room. They could be rifling through your private papers.'

A few moments later, I came into the kitchen. Mrs Sugden was placing a pot of tea on the table, and ordering, 'Let it stand a minute.'

Cyril Fitzpatrick, Anthony Hartigan and a fair-haired man with a guileless, open face and a broken nose all lumbered to their feet. I had seen the fair-haired man before, but for the moment could not think where.

Fitzpatrick and Hartigan said hello and good morning. The other man looked from them to me with something like defiance, as if expecting to be told that he had no right to be here. 'I'm Eddie, missis. Eddie Flanagan. Me and Deirdre is good friends.'

'Please sit down all of you.'

The well-mannered desperadoes scraped their chairs again. Mrs Sugden took up a position on a high buffet near the kitchen door, presumably ready to run for assistance if things turned nasty.

Fitzpatrick said to his companions, 'This is the lady I told you about. If anyone can find Deirdre, she will. You know something already don't you, Mrs Shackleton?'

'About what, Mr Fitzpatrick?'

Having given Fitzpatrick the opening gambit and not being satisfied with his throw, the others began to join in, all speaking at once. The upshot of their babble was that Deirdre was missing, which I already knew. She had not come home last night. Mrs Hartigan had died. Anthony was anxious to return to New York as soon as possible.

'Please, gentlemen. One at a time.'

Being close to these three made me feel edgy. Their anxieties burst like lead shot at the ceiling and rained back down.

'She knows I have my passage booked to New York. What is she playing at?'

Eddie said, 'What if she's lying somewhere, hurt? It were brass monkeys last night.'

'Who is the saint of missing persons, is it Anthony?' Fitzpatrick demanded of his brother-in-law. 'You should know, he's your patron saint.'

Hartigan glared at Fitzpatrick. 'St Anthony and me haven't had a lot to do with each other.' He turned to me. 'She could have had the nursing home matron telephone me at the hotel. I would have picked her up and taken her home.'

I held up a hand. 'Stop! One at a time. Mr Fitzpatrick,

you come through with me to the dining room. I'll talk to each of you gentlemen individually.'

This helped bring a sense of calm. Mrs Sugden crossed to the table to take the seat vacated by Fitzpatrick. 'I'll pour now.'

Fitzpatrick followed me into the dining room where I took pen and paper. I quickly noted that Deirdre had left the nursing home at about 5.30 and had not been seen since.

'Have you reported her missing to the police?'

'I have, when she didn't come back last night. Anthony came for tea, just after you left. It went untouched. We set off for the nursing home to bring her home. I left a note, in case she returned while we were gone. The matron couldn't understand it. Said Deirdre had gone to catch a tram. We went to Cotton Street to check with her aunts, and then to Millgarth police station.'

'Do you have any thoughts as to where she might be, however unlikely?'

He shook his head. 'Between us, we've tried every-where and everyone.'

'You're not at work today. Is that because Deirdre has gone missing?'

'I'm on nights this week, though how I'll get through the night if she hasn't come back, I don't know.'

'You said to Mr Sykes that a photographer from the local paper saw her near Leeds Bridge.'

He gulped and nodded.

'Has your wife been downhearted? Might she have thought of taking her own life? Is that why the photog-rapher mentioned her?'

'No! She wouldn't jump off the bridge. If she did, with

her luck, there'd be twenty bargemen fighting to pull her out. She loves life. I wonder if she was with someone, and that's what Diamond was trying to tell me. I wish I'd listened to him, to what he had to say.'

'He could have been mistaken.'

'Oh no. She made a point of telling me that she'd walked across Leeds Bridge and some fellow had asked her for directions. Are she and Diamond teasing me, tormenting me? Is there something between Len Diamond and Deirdre?'

'It's natural that you should be a little jealous about your wife, but try and trust her. It's you she married.'

'I think she wishes she hadn't.'

'With your permission, I'll talk to Mr Diamond. I know him. He'll be discreet.'

There was as much likelihood of Diamond's discretion as of the king and queen washing their own bed socks.

'If you think it will help, talk to him by all means.'

'Do you know what time he starts work?'

'He's a law unto himself that man. Who knows what time he starts? He doesn't clock in, that much I know.'

'Well try not to worry. Send Mr Hartigan in to talk to me.'

'What about your fees? Is it the same daily rate you mentioned when I came before? Only you didn't charge me.'

'It would be the same. But it may be that your wife will turn up of her own accord, and soon. Let us hope so.'

Fitzpatrick nodded. He pushed himself up from the table with a deep weariness. I guessed he had not slept.

Anthony Hartigan strutted in, chin forward, reminding me of a cockerel in a farmyard.

He did not waste time. 'It's worth a lot to me to see everything settled before I go. I didn't expect to have to arrange a funeral for my ma, but Deirdre's left me no choice. If you ask me, it's her way of getting back at me for not coming sooner.'

'Your family must have been very pleased to see you.'

'It was meant to be a surprise. Some surprise. My sister took against me, and my ma took fright.'

'I'm sorry. It is a pity you had so little time with her.'

'She wasn't the ma I remembered. Deirdre must have been a baby when I left. But I didn't remember her at all. She started sending me annual begging letters as soon as she could write.'

'When did you first see your sister, on this visit?'

A sudden wariness came over him.

I added quickly, 'I'm wondering whether she said anything, dropped a hint about being unhappy, or having other plans.'

He darted a quick look at me. 'You were at the races last Wednesday.'

'I was, and backed the winner.' Had he seen me with Marcus, I wondered. Marcus had broken his cover to interview Hartigan. I best tread carefully.

'Me too,' he smiled. 'Good old Flint Jack.'

'I was trying to think where I had seen you before. You were with a chap in a kilt.'

'Not the cheeriest of companions, but he went home happy.'

That was probably an understatement. With an order to supply prohibition New York with alcohol, he would have gone home cock-a-hoop. If Hartigan had seen me with Marcus, he was covering it well. Perhaps my flitting about alone, trying to gather my own information, had paid off.

I might squeeze a little information from Hartigan that would help me in the murder investigation.

'Did you and your sister get on well, Mr Hartigan? Once you met I mean.'

'I hardly got to know her. And she wasn't exactly delighted to see me.'

'Was that after or before the races?'

'I travelled from London on Tuesday, and went to the races Wednesday and Thursday. Friday, I went to Cotton Street to see my mother. She wasn't there. Neighbours told me she'd been taken into a nursing home and no one had the address, except Deirdre, and no one had Deirdre's address, except that she lived in Kirkstall. So I tracked down half a dozen other relations. It was Friday night when I finally spoke to my aunts and got the addresses. They'd been working all day, see. Didn't see my ma till Saturday, and she was asleep. Deirdre just bawled me out for not coming sooner, and not writing.' He warmed to this injustice. 'I could have stayed in London, done my business there.'

'What a shame,' I said, mustering fake sympathy. 'To come all this way. Where are you staying?'

'The Metropole, the best hotel, recommended by the tailor in London. And that's turned out a disaster. Just because I had a brandy with a hotel guest who ends up dead, I'm questioned a first time politely and a second time as if I did it.'

'Do you know, I had heard there was a death at one of the hotels. Who was it?'

'Some banker. *He* made the running. Guy saw me at the

races and had me down as a soft touch. I'm sorry that he died, but if I topped every chancer who tried to fleece me, there'd be a lot of mourning widows.'

Sometimes I can tell when a person is lying. This man was so accomplished that he had probably convinced himself of the truth of any and every lie he uttered. If he had not met Deirdre until Saturday, that eliminated her as the 'unknown woman' who spent the night with Runcie. Or did it?

'How awful for you. So were you the last person to see him alive?'

'No! He was with some broad. She went upstairs before I joined him.'

'Well that's all right then. No one could reasonably suspect you.'

He grinned, and relaxed a little. 'That's exactly what I told them, only not so polite.'

But he might suspect me if I did not stop probing. I wrote down his name and the name of the hotel. 'I hope I'll be able to help. If I find out anything at all about your sister, I will telephone you at the hotel, and send a telegram to Mr Fitzpatrick.'

'Thanks.' He took out his wallet. 'I'll stay for the funeral, but after that I need to get back to New York fast. Deirdre oughta to be home where she belongs. Her husband speaks highly of you.'

I waved his wallet away. 'Let's see how I get on.'

Hartigan raised an eyebrow. 'Not often people turn down my money.'

'I'll do what I can. Will you send in the other gentleman please?'

Eddie Flanagan stepped into the room as if springing from the corner of the boxing ring, but once he sat down, his energy evaporated. Weariness rose from him in waves. His face was smudged, his eyes puffy with lack of sleep. Now I remembered him. On the day I followed Deirdre, he was part of the group of men playing toss on the corner. He had stood to talk to her.

He said, 'It was so cold last night. It rained. I looked everywhere.'

'Where exactly?'

'Everywhere.' He waved his arm. 'I tried to find Roundhay. I don't know where it is. I'll go there now. Deirdre is so sad. She must be lost.'

Somehow I did not think Eddie would be a great help in this enterprise. 'Were you out all night?'

He nodded. 'I looked round the town. I looked round the Bank. I got people out of bed to ask had they seen her. I went to the Little Sisters convent where she stayed once.'

'The Little Sisters?'

'They're the nuns who teach in the school we all went to. And Deirdre has been there on retreat. But they haven't seen her. I think she's hiding.'

'Why would she hide?'

'Because she's sad. Because her heart hurts.'

We sat in silence for a moment. I made a note that he had been to the neighbours' houses, and to the convent.

'Have you known Deirdre a long time?'

He nodded. 'Always. I think we was almost sweethearts once, before I lost my brains.'

His eyes darted around the room and came to rest on Gerald's photograph on the sideboard. 'Who is that?'

'My husband. He didn't come back from the war.'

He nodded. He did not have to tell me that he was an old soldier. I could see it in his eyes.

'Come on then, Mr Flanagan. The sooner I get started the better.'

'Call me Eddie. Everyone calls me Eddie.'

I led Eddie into the kitchen.

Mrs Sugden said, 'They've gone without you, Eddie. Never you mind. I'm going to make you some breakfast.'

'I have to go to Roundhay,' he said, as if he had not heard her. 'To the nursing home, to see if I can find out where Deirdre went.'

'You listen to Mrs Sugden, Eddie. She'll look after you, and then explain how to get to Roundhay.'

He was the one with least claim to find Deirdre, but I had the feeling he was the one who loved her best, and most unselfishly.

His guess as to where Deirdre might be would be better than mine.

Seventeen

Len Diamond had not arrived at the newspaper offices by the time I got there, at about half past nine. I hovered near the entrance, waiting for him.

When he did turn up, about twenty minutes later, he looked genuinely pleased to see me. 'Kate, hello! Bumping into you twice in a week, the heavens must be smiling on me.'

'Hello, Len. I was hoping you might be able to help me with an enquiry.'

He pulled a mock fearful face. 'Sounds worrying.'

'Do you have a moment? I can wait until you've put in your appearance.'

'Let me see what the editor has in store for me. I'll be with you in a flash.'

Twenty minutes later, we were sitting in Schofields over coffee and toast. I felt guilty about detaining him from his work but he assured me it was a treat to have breakfast. 'So what's this enquiry of yours, Kate?'

I wanted to ask him about the altercation he had with Philippa's secretary at the races, and about the photographs he had taken at the shoot. But if Diamond got a whiff that I was investigating on behalf of Philippa Runcie, he would dine out on the story for a decade.

By starting with my search for Mrs Fitzpatrick, I would be able to lead into the questions concerning Runcie in a more roundabout way.

'It concerns one of your fellow employees at the newspaper.'

He looked suddenly interested. 'Are you going to tell me who?'

'One of the compositors, Cyril Fitzpatrick, came to see me. I have his permission to talk to you.'

Diamond spread strawberry jam on his toast. 'Is something wrong?'

Len and I usually converse in a light-hearted banter, even where our shared passion of photography is concerned but I resisted the urge to say that Mr Fitzpatrick had mislaid his wife.

'His wife is missing. He is concerned for her welfare because her mother died yesterday.'

'How sad for her, and what a worry for him. But I haven't got her, Scout's honour.'

'I tried to reassure Mr Fitzpatrick. Said that perhaps she just didn't feel like going home and visited a friend, or booked in somewhere.'

'Does he want a missing person piece in the paper? If it comes to a major search, there's a photograph of her in the files. I took it last summer at Kirkstall Abbey.'

'Then I would certainly like a copy, today if possible.'

He nodded. 'Consider it done.'

'Mr Fitzpatrick said you saw her not long ago. He got the strong impression she must have been with a man.'

Diamond pulled his reluctant-to-tell face. 'She was

talking to someone, but not a person who would have run off with her. Look, if she doesn't come home soon, I'll break all my rules and tell you the man's name. Then you can don your deerstalker and track him down, just in case.'

'Anything else you know about her?'

He swallowed a mouthful of toast. 'No. Sorry. He has reported her missing I take it?'

'Yes, last night, which isn't long ago but I'm not sure how urgently it will be treated.'

'Well it ought to be.'

Now for my change of tack. 'I agree. But the police are at full stretch.'

'You mean because of the murder? Now there's a shocker.'

'It seems unbelievable, Len, given that we both saw Mr Runcie only on Wednesday at the Ebor.'

'I nearly got what would have been the last photograph of him. I would have, too, if that hanger-on of Mrs Runcie's hadn't intervened, I would have got a good shot. When the Runcie divorce hit the headlines, it would have sold to the *Illustrated London News*, and half of Fleet Street. Of course as things have turned out, no one would buy it now, out of respect for the dead and bereaved.'

'I'm glad I'm just an amateur, Len. I wouldn't have the heart to do that sort of thing.'

'Yes you would, if your rent depended on it. The printers moan about their wage cuts. I wish my wages were on a level with theirs. I'd be a happy man.'

'I can't imagine you ever being happy, Len. You always want the photograph you didn't take, or the job you never applied for, or the roll of film you left in a drawer some-where.'

He laughed. 'You're probably right.'

'I liked your photograph of Runcie and Caroline Windham at Lord Fotheringham's shoot, moments after she was wounded.'

'Thanks. That was one of my right-place-at-the-right-time moments.'

'Did you take many pictures that day?'

'A few.'

'May I see them, not to take away, just to look?'

He drawled out a long, 'Why?'

The waitress brought the bill. We stopped talking while he put a coin on the tray, waving away my offer to pay.

I had planned to say that I wanted to study the compos-ition of the photograph, but he would not believe that, so I said, 'It's just a wild thought, regarding Runcie's death. What if that stray shot was not a stray shot at all, but attempted murder?'

He let out a low whistle. 'Now there's a thought. Have you told the police?'

Something made me lie. 'They'd think I was mad, coming up with an idea like that.'

He laughed. 'It does sound rather far-fetched. I'll look out the photographs, and the one of Mrs Fitzpatrick at Kirkstall. Believe me, if there had been any such drama at the shoot, I would have spotted it.'

As we left the café, I said in what I hoped was a casual tone, 'What time would be good for me to call?'

'Around six. I can't promise. But if I don't dig them out today, I shall be onto it first thing tomorrow.'

'Thanks.'

'Don't mention it. And if I succeed in helping you track down the elusive Mrs Fitzpatrick, I shall tell her husband I'd like her to sit for me.'

We parted by the door. I made my way back to the car. His words made a little connection in my memory. Deirdre Fitzpatrick was the sort of woman that a photographer would like to capture, or that a sculptor would like as his model.

I remembered the sketch on Rupert Cromer's drawing pad, and the startling resemblance between the Venus figure on the bottom of the page and Deirdre Fitzpatrick. Modelling was a tried and tested way for a person to make a little extra cash. It seemed unlikely, and yet the resemblance had been uncanny.

I would pay a visit to Rupert Cromer, and make another double-edged enquiry.

If Cromer had been at the shoot, he might be able to tell me who else was there, and perhaps let slip who may have accidentally on purpose discharged a shot in the direction of Caroline Windham and Everett Runcie.

Eighteen

On this bright September morning, Lord Fotheringham's estate was at its green and glowing best. My sturdy Jowett, 'the little engine with the big pull', bounced along the bumpy track towards the cottage and outbuildings occupied by Rupert Cromer. This was a tucked-away place. I wondered how many more such spots the Fotheringhams had on their vast estate. A few sheep scattered at my approach. A deer looked up from its leisurely grazing. I could not help but picture the overcrowded streets of the Bank, and the lack of amenities and sanitation. Sometimes it amazed me that we came through the war without a revolution.

As I came closer, it occurred to me that Cromer may be in the middle of some hugely important job and would not wish to be disturbed. That of course would not stop me, but he was a man who took his art with high seriousness.

As I reached the end of the track, his sculptures loomed into view, as if growing from the landscape. One piece cried out to be photographed: the tiny centaur. I stopped the car short of the house and took out my camera. Coming close, I looked for the best way to frame the piece. Taken from below, the creature had a menacing appearance, from above it looked lonely. I could imagine the centaur finding a shady nook in Batswing Wood behind my house. In the wood there is a natural stage where children play. Sometimes a theatre company will put on a performance of Shakespeare. *A Midsummer Night's Dream* works best. The stone bench formed by the figures in togas would make a fitting seat. Being Headingley, we have a residents' committee that oversees the well-being of the wood. Next time the committee met, I would raise the question of acquiring a piece of sculpture.

I put off my interview with Rupert Cromer by spending a little while getting just the right angle for my photographs, and checking the light. The Romanesque figures cast satisfyingly strange shadows.

Putting the camera back in the car, I walked towards the cottage. Sounds came from the barn that Cromer used as a studio, but I decided to knock on the cottage door, so as to announce my arrival in the usual way.

The housekeeper was slow in answering. If she would let me in, I could take another look at the pad on the easel, and satisfy myself whether Cromer's sketch of a woman's head really did bear a likeness to Deirdre Fitzpatrick.

This estate would be a perfect bolt hole for someone avoiding the world's gaze.

'Yes?' Cromer's housekeeper snapped at me. There were traces of dough on her fingers. She did not appreciate being torn from her baking. 'What do you want?'

'I'm here to see Mr Cromer.'

'He's over yon.'

'Shall I come in and wait?'

'You'll have a long wait.'

'Right. I'll go across then.'

'You do that.' She gave a toothless grin. 'He won't thank you for disturbing him.'

She shut the door.

I could see why this particular employee of the great and good was exiled to a far-flung corner of the estate.

Retracing my steps, I approached the barn. One of the big doors stood slightly ajar, giving me a view of the interior. At first sight it was one great disorder of work benches, tools, buffets and pieces of wood and stone waiting their turn for the Cromer treatment. There was a stove, a pile of logs beside it, and a kettle on the hob. Oil lamps hung from the ceiling. Cromer wore a brown smock, like a workman. He did not hear my approach, intent as he was on chiselling at a large rock.

Nearby, a young assistant was busy at a bench. The assistant turned, looked at me, and then at Cromer, uncertain what to do. I took a few steps forward. Cromer looked up. I expected a frown, but he seemed pleased to see me.

'Hello, Mrs Shackleton.'

Something about his look told me instantly that he expected to make a sale. Oh dear. Well at least I could truthfully say that I would suggest one of his sculptures for our wood.

He came across, beaming.

'Mr Cromer, I'm sorry to disturb you while you're working.'

'Don't worry about it. We were just about to have coffee, weren't we, Bernard?'

The young assistant nodded and made off in the direction of the stove.

Cromer led me outside to a stone bench that stood against the wall of the barn. We sat down companionably, side by side.

'How is Miss Windham?' I asked.

He spread his hands on his knees. 'She went back to the house this morning. Sent me a note that there's a piece in *The Times* about Everett's death.'

'Yes I saw it. I expect there'll be a lot more.'

'Caroline's devastated. I don't think she'll ever get over it.'

'They were going to Italy I believe.'

'Yes. Runcie has a villa there. I hope he had the decency to leave it to Caroline in his will. If he managed to hang onto it.'

'You think he may not have?'

'Who knows? Everett's financial affairs were convoluted to say the least.'

'Yet he was a patron of the arts.'

He gave a short laugh. 'True, he commissioned work. He was inspirational in that regard. But he was a good friend to me and I'll hear nothing said against him.'

From the rueful tone, I guessed that Runcie enthusiastically commissioned work, and then failed to pay for it. That would fit the Runcie approach to life and art.

I changed the subject at that point, owning up to photographing his work.

'So you're a photographer?'

'When I have time, and after my fashion.'

It would be immodest to say I won second prize in the *Amateur Photographer* magazine competition last year.

'What sort of camera do you have?'

I listed my cameras.

'I'd like to see the pictures you took of my work. I'm hoping for an exhibition and it's always difficult to get good material for the catalogue.'

'I'd be happy for you to see them. If they're up to scratch you must let me know if you want me to do more sometime. But I took them because I intend to show them to my neighbours. I want to suggest we buy one of your pieces for the woodland we jointly take care of.'

He brightened. 'Thanks, Mrs Shackleton. That's jolly decent of you.'

'I would like to have one of your pieces for myself but my house is small, my garden smaller, and I don't put myself in the collector bracket.'

He smiled. 'You should. It's not as daunting as people think. Make an offer, if there's something you like.'

'Thanks. I'll bear that in mind.' With my cheque from Philippa, such a purchase might not be out of the question. Of course I would need to succeed and find Everett's killer if I were to earn my fee. So I must raise the topic of grouse shooting, in a roundabout way.

'Talking of photography, you had an excellent photographer on the estate not long ago, taking pictures of the shoot.'

'Oh, who was that?'

'Probably no one you would know. Len Diamond from the local paper, never without his cap. You might have spotted him.'

'Now that you mention it, a journalist came to interview me last year and brought a photographer in a check cap.'

'That will have been him. He came to speak to our photographic club and was as eloquent as he is artistic.'

Being an artist, Cromer was likely to shift the conversation back to himself and his work at any moment, so I pressed my point.

'Mr Diamond was up here for the first day of grouse shooting. I saw one of his photographs in the paper, the one of Miss Windham, nursing her arm.'

'For which she'll never forgive him. She doesn't like to be shown in a weak moment.'

'No I suppose not. Were you at the shoot yourself?'

He gave me an emphatic no. 'There's no thrill for me in shooting such stupid birds. I would rather get on with my work.'

So much for my tactful broaching of the subject. At this rate, Scotland Yard would have an arrest, a conviction and a hanging before I found a single clue as to what had happened to Everett Runcie.

The apprentice, a pale serious young chap, brought our coffee. We edged away from each other so that the mugs could be set down on the bench between us.

Cromer said, 'Thanks, Bernard. Take a break yourself.'

When we had sipped our coffee, I took the photograph of Deirdre Fitzpatrick from my satchel.

There was still hope. If I could find Deirdre, not only would I earn Fitpatrick's undying gratitude, but if my strong suspicions were confirmed, she would turn out to have been at the hotel, and could have valuable information.

'Mr Cromer, there's an ulterior motive to my visit. Would you take a look at this photograph, please? Just the bride, not the groom. I'm searching for someone who's gone missing. She may have worked as an artist's model.'

He took the photograph from me, looked at it carefully,

and shook his head. 'I can see why she might work as a model, but no. She's not familiar.'

I took the photograph back. 'Thanks.'

'Who is she?'

'She's married to a compositor on the local paper. He is very worried at her disappearance.'

'Poor fellow. She looks the kind of woman to drive men mad. If you find her, and she does want to pose, let me know.'

'I doubt if her husband will let her out of his sight once he finds her. She is in enough trouble.'

'What kind of trouble?'

'I'll know the answer to that when I find her. Only what made me ask, when I was here last, I looked at the sketch pad in your parlour, and I thought the face on it so much resembled Mrs Fitzpatrick.'

'Oh? Now you've intrigued me.' He stood up. 'Come on, we'll take a look.'

We carried the mugs with us and walked towards the cottage. As he opened the door, the smell of baking filled my nostrils. The housekeeper may lack social graces, but her buns smelled good.

In the parlour, he went to the sketch pad. 'Turn the pages. Show me the one you mean.'

The top page was full of recent sketches of the house-keeper, half human, half gnarled tree. There was a drawing of Caroline Windham. She sat in the battered armchair, right leg tucked under, her head tilted to one side, a picture of grief and loss.

The page below was the one I had seen, with man and motorbike, and a Venus figure, the one I thought had

Deirdre's face. Now I saw that it did not. There was a similarity but seen side by side with the photograph, it was not her.

'Sorry. It's me. I'm seeing her everywhere.'

Cromer was by the window. 'It's all right. It happens to me all the time. Our eyes and hearts play tricks, thank God.'

I left shortly after, and was glad I did. From the bend in the track, I saw Caroline Windham riding across the parkland towards the cottage.

Stopping the car, I called good morning.

She spoke to her horse, and veered over to exchange a word with me, an honour indeed. I wondered did she want a lift to Edinburgh, or the loan of a fiver.

From the great height of her mount on the stallion, she looked down. 'I have something for you, Mrs Shackleton.' She put her hand in her pocket. 'I shall want it back. It's my lucky cartridge. I found it inside that rocky outcrop on top of the gill. One of Philippa's minions was hiding there.' She placed the cartridge in my outstretched palm. 'While I was out riding, Lord Fotheringham had a visit from the police, asking who was in the shooting party. They seem to be chasing the idea that someone shot me deliberately. I wonder where they might have got that from.'

'I can't imagine.'

'Naturally, Lord Fotheringham is furious. He personally vouches for every guest.'

'But you are not so sure?'

She shrugged her magnificent shoulders. 'I'm sure of nothing, Mrs Shackleton. But you were the one who thought of it first, so I'm passing this to you for safe transit. I believe the police can do very clever things regarding matching guns and cartridges. Tell them they might want to start with Philippa Runcie's secretary.'

Nineteen

It had been twenty-four hours since Philippa asked for my help. So far my only gain was the spent cartridge given to me by Caroline Windham, and the knowledge that both she and Marcus took seriously my theory that the so-called "stray shot" could have been meant for Runcie.

At going on six o'clock, I arrived at the newspaper offices, hoping that Len Diamond might have left me photographs he had taken on the day of the shoot, along with his picture of Deirdre from last year.

It is very useful to have good contacts on the local newspaper, and this included old George, the porter who sits on the front desk. I keep on his right side, and exchanged a few words before asking him whether Len Diamond had left an envelope for me.

George checked through the papers and envelopes in his tray. 'No, sorry, Mrs Shackleton. Mr Diamond left nothing for you.'

It is infuriating when you have something to do that feels really urgent, but urgent to no one except oneself. It was too much to hope that Len Diamond should have troubled to dig out photographs when he was busy with what mattered to him today. Len was a man always looking around the next corner.

'Thanks for checking, George. I'll call again in the morning.'

'I'll tell him you were in, if he turns up before I go home.'

When I first met George, I thought him surly and uncooperative, but it is surprising what a little bribery can achieve. A couple of tickets to the cricket, a packet of smokes before pay day ('Someone gave me these and I don't smoke them'), and he is my friend for life. He hated to see me go away disappointed.

'Can't Mr Duffield help you today?'

'I wish he could.'

And then I had a brilliant idea. It was because the thought of bribery had entered my head: small offerings, sweeteners, generous tipping.

Both Sykes and I had at first assumed that Joseph Barnard and Deirdre Fitzpatrick were lovers, or out for a fling. Sykes had reported that Mr Barnard was remembered at the Adelphi as a good tipper, which he attributed to the singer wanting to be liked. What if there was a different interpretation? He had tipped to be remembered. If I could discover whether he was there to gain evidence for a divorce, the next step might become clearer.

If Deirdre was meeting men for the particular purpose of being a co-respondent, someone must be behind it. It was hardly the kind of service to advertise in a shop window.

Without some brilliant lead, like a finger pointing from

the sky at a guilty party, I would concentrate on something small, a re-tracing of steps.

'George, you've just given me a good idea. Mr Duffield may be able to help. What time does he finish work?'

'Six o'clock.'

I looked at my watch. Five minutes to go. 'Is it all right if I telephone up to him?'

'I'll do it for you.'

He made the connection and handed me the receiver. 'Mr Duffield, Kate Shackleton. Are you rushing straight home?'

He was not, and would meet me by the entrance in five minutes.

Mr Duffield is a gentleman in his sixties. I first met him when I was looking into the disappearance of a mill owner, and wanted to read back copies of newspapers. He was most helpful, then and since. Some people always spark off ideas, and he is one of them. The perfect escort to take a lady into a lounge bar.

He is tentatively courting a friend of my mother's. This was a good opportunity to be brought up to date on the courtship dance.

It surprised me to see him looking so smart. He is always reasonably well turned out, but slightly shabby; a worn-cuffs look about him. That had vanished under the influence of my mother's friend, Martha Graham.

He readily agreed to come with me for a glass of sherry, and we set off walking, rightly thinking that at this time of the evening it would be quicker to go on foot.

I asked about his bridge lessons from Mrs Graham.

'I am doing very well indeed,' he said. 'Mrs Graham kindly calls me a natural.'

My mother always discouraged me from playing bridge, saying it got in the way of life, and people took it too seriously.

The narrow pavement was busy with people hurrying home from work. For a moment we were separated as an office boy, running for a tram, charged between us.

As we crossed Leeds Bridge, Mr Duffield said, 'Excuse my suspicions, Mrs Shackleton, but is there an investigative motive behind our visit to the Adelphi Hotel?'

'What if I said that the sole purpose of our visit is to imbibe sherry, Mr Duffield?'

'I would be most flattered to hear that, and somewhat disbelieving. I hear your friend, the chief inspector, is investigating Mr Runcie's murder.

'He is.'

'So am I helping in an investigation?'

'You could say that.'

'Good.'

I had not minded talking to Len Diamond about Deirdre's disappearance, but Mr Duffield is such an old Victorian. Something told me that Cyril Fitzpatrick would not want him to know.

Once inside the Adelphi, I had sudden misgivings. We walked the corridor, looking into the different bars. The key person would be a chambermaid. In a large hotel, chambermaids would clean rooms, make beds in the morning, turn down sheets in the afternoon, and then do I knew not what. I hoped that in a small hotel, there would be a doubling up of tasks.

'Which room?' Mr Duffield murmured.

'One with a barmaid.'

In the first room, a confident middle-aged couple held forth with a couple of regulars.

'The landlord and his wife,' Mr Duffield murmured.

In the busy tap room, a barman presided.

Smoke Room 1 seemed to be the likeliest choice. It had the advantage of quiet. The woman behind the bar had a round, friendly face, and looked up from polishing a glass as we entered.

We sauntered up to the bar together, with the excuse that I wanted to look at the names on the sherry bottles. I lingered while Mr Duffield placed our order for amontillado.

'Isn't this the place where the Gilbert and Sullivan singer stayed the other week?' I asked.

The barmaid smiled as she poured the sherry. 'He did and gave me a signed photo.'

'How marvellous.'

She produced the photograph, signed *To Gloria*.

I sighed with envy.

Mr Duffield rallied. 'You could have that framed.'

'Oh I shall. I wish I could have gone to see him, but I was working all day and all night that week.'

This sounded promising. 'Well I'm a great admirer of his.' I lowered my voice. 'My firm acts for him now and then, in legal matters.'

Mr Duffield cleared his throat.

Gloria said, 'Such a lovely man, didn't have show business written all over him like some of them do. I'll fetch your drinks across.'

I nudged Mr Duffield. He took the hint. 'One for yourself, Gloria.'

'Thank you, sir.'

We took our seats at a corner table. Mr Duffield tried to give off a wave of disapproval. 'Don't you ever feel guilty at being underhand with people, Mrs Shackleton?'

'Mr Duffield, stop pretending you would have been better off at home with a cup of tea and a boiled egg.'

When the barmaid brought the tray across, I waited until she had placed our glasses on the table and then lightly touched her arm. 'Gloria?'

'Yes?'

'Don't look alarmed, but we have a question regarding Mr Barnard's stay at the hotel. You would be willing to vouch for his and Mrs Barnard's stay, I believe, and that they were in all respects man and wife?'

She glanced over her shoulder, and answered most impressively as if she were half-expecting the question. 'Yes I would. I took their tea in two mornings running.' She perhaps may have said more, but a glance at Mr Duffield prevented what might have been some saucy elaboration.

I reached for my purse. 'Thank you.'

She leaned towards me. 'Might I have to go to the court in London?'

'It's a possibility. If you are summonsed, you would have your fare and expenses paid.'

She nodded.

'Did one of my colleagues see you beforehand about that?'

I put a half crown on the table.

She slid the coin in her pocket. 'Oh no, just what Mr Barnard said, you know.'

Mr Duffield stared studiously into his sherry as she returned to the bar. She looked at herself in the ornately lettered mirror behind the rows of bottles and touched her hair into place.

'She might not have been the chambermaid.'

'Well then, I was lucky.'

It was about time something I did turned out lucky.

'What is all this about?'

'Scout's honour on your silence, Mr Duffield?'

'My lips are sealed, only my ears are open.'

'You'll know all about the new Matrimonial Causes Act.'

He did. Mr Duffield keeps a closer eye on newspapers than he does on the weather. He knew that the act had come into force on the 18th of July this year. 'Which particular part are we thinking of here?' he asked.

'The part that allows women uncontested divorces on the grounds of a husband's adultery, without the additional cause of cruelty or desertion.'

Mr Duffield sipped his sherry. 'And from what you say, a certain amount of collusion may be involved.'

'Yes, which I suppose could invalidate proceedings. But I'm not interested in putting a spanner in the works of Mr Barnard's divorce. I want to find a woman who is missing, and see what connection there might be to the murder.'

'Do you suspect the woman has come to harm?'

'It's smoke and mirrors, Mr Duffield. I don't know what to think.'

I was now convinced that Deirdre Fitzpatrick had not only spent a weekend with Joseph Barnard, but a night with Everett Runcie. What I did not know was how to confirm this conviction. Nor did I know who paired her up with these two very different men, and was that person involved in Everett Runcie's death?

I would have liked one more glass of sherry, but thought it better to make this a fleeting visit and hope that Gloria would not have time to reflect that Mr Duffield and I made an unlikely pair of solicitors.

He was of the same mind.

Five minutes later, we crossed the bridge, walking towards Mr Duffield's tram stop.

'Mr Duffield, you have extensive connections.'

'I do.'

'You worked on a national newspaper in your youth.'

'I did.'

'Might you be able to discover what chambers acts in the matter of Barnard v Barnard and Runcie v Runcie?'

'I suppose that might be possible, though not in good taste.'

'Murder has a nasty taste, Mr Duffield.'

We had reached his tram stop.

He hesitated.

'I could come back to the library with you, if a telephone call might help.'

'It might.'

'And I could give you a lift home afterwards.'

'Is this bribery, Mrs Shackleton?'

'Mr Duffield, what a shocking thing to say.'

By seeking snippets of detail from different people, one keeps the whole package of information discrete. When I arrived home after dropping off Mr Duffield, I telephoned my Aunt Berta in London. She is my mother's elder sister, Lady Rodpen. Aunt Berta has sons but no daughters. She and I have always got on.

Like everyone else, she had read the piece in *The Times* about Everett's death.

'Has there been news?' she asked.

'Not yet, but Aunt, I'd be grateful if you might find out the tiniest little thing for me.'

A pause. 'What is it, dear?'

I gave her the name of the Lincoln's Inn chambers Mr Duffield had written down for me. 'Might the chamber's clerk be prevailed upon to recommend a reliable legal person in my neck of the woods, someone a man might consult if he required matrimonial advice?'

'What sort of advice?'

Her thoughts would fly to property rather than separation. I needed to be more precise. 'Advice regarding an irrevocable, insoluble, difficulty. One that involves a dissolution.'

'I'll see what I can do.'

'Thank you, Aunt.'

'How is your mother?'

Aunt Berta's younger sister, Virginia Hood, known as Ginny, adopted me at birth. 'Mother is very well, thank you.'

'And how is Philippa bearing up? You have seen her?'

'It's hard to say. Fortunately she has an excellent secretary, and Harold is with her.'

'Good. Is there a date for the funeral?'

Early the next morning, I stood in the hall with the telephone receiver in one hand and my hairbrush in the other.

'Kate, good morning. Did I wake you?'

'Hello, Marcus. No. I've been up for ages.'

'Can you spare the time to call in at the hotel and have a word?'

'This word I'm to have. Is it with you, or with Sergeant Wilson?'

'With me.'

'Only I hear that Sergeant Wilson is very good at interviewing females.'

The non-pompous Marcus would have made light of my remark, but he said, 'Yes he does have a good approach.'

'How nice for him. Well, I'll be there soon. I was coming to town anyway.'

'Oh and Kate.'

'Yes?'

'I believe you have a photograph I would like to see, of a woman who may have stayed at the hotel.'

'I'll see if I can lay my hands on it.'

'Do try.'

I hung up the receiver. That man could be so exasperating. Now he wanted the wedding photograph of Fitzpatrick and Deirdre. Well perhaps his explorations into the machinations of Philippa's family and Kirkley Bank skulduggery had led him up a blind alley.

Of course when I saw him, in the busy room on the third floor of the hotel, the pomposity had vanished. Perhaps it was his protective coating since I had turned him down. He was his usual polite self and I could not help liking him again, just a little.

'Kate! Thanks for coming in.'

'Never one to ignore a summons from the constabulary, Marcus.'

'You have the photograph?'

I took it from my satchel. 'It's six years old. Mr and Mrs Cyril Fitzpatrick. Deirdre. It's possible I'll have a more up-to-date one later today.'

'That would be good.' He looked at the likeness. 'Do you have any idea where she might have got to?'

'No. But I am looking for her, on behalf of her husband. He came to see me with his brother-in-law, Mr Hartigan.'

He frowned. 'She has been reported missing to the police?'

'On Sunday.'

'You will let me know if you find her first.'

'Marcus, it is Mr Sykes you have as your special constable, not I. But you know how willing I am to cooperate.'

'I've talked to Hartigan. He sticks to the story that he did not meet his sister until Saturday.' He paused, waiting for me to comment. I did not. Marcus continued, 'Is there anything else you can tell me about Mrs Fitzpatrick that might help?'

Trust him to ask such a thorough question. I could have told him about the shoplifting incident, and chapter and verse on Fitzpatrick's suspicions, but I did not.

'She was not at home on Friday night. I believe she was here, in the hotel, and bolted straight after Mildred knocked on the door with the morning tea. She was home putting the kettle on when her husband came down on Saturday morning. Also, she stayed at the Adelphi Hotel on the weekend of 24th August with a man whose wife was petitioning for a divorce.'

Marcus tapped his pencil on the blotter. 'You've done well, to say you are not on the case.'

'Anything else?'

I had not yet heard from Aunt Berta regarding a solicitor in Leeds who may have made the arrangement for Deirdre to be with Joseph Barnard and, possibly, Everett Runcie.

'Nothing else just now. Will that be all, Marcus?'

'Not quite. I had a man out to interview Mr Runcie's long-term companion yesterday afternoon'

'His mistress?'

Marcus nodded. 'I understand you have already spoken to her. Twice.'

'Marcus, someone had to tell her that Runcie was dead. I knew she would be discreet. She had a right to know.'

'Then you should have informed me.'

'I tried, if you remember. You did not return my call. I'm not blaming you. You were busy, naturally. But I have to make my own judgements.'

There was a brief and heavy pause. We both knew now

that the intimacy there had been between us was a thing of the past, gone but not forgotten.

Marcus said, gently, 'I know. And you're right. Miss Windham said nothing to the Fotheringhams. Lord Fotheringham was as shocked by the piece in *The Times* as anyone else. But you saw her again yesterday.'

I took the cartridge from the inside pocket of my satchel. 'She has a theory about where the person who shot her may have been standing.'

He waved away the cartridge. 'Lord Fotheringham has a good idea who fired the shot. The man is so inept that he was unaware of causing an injury.'

'Will that be all, Marcus?'

'Do you have something planned? You said you were coming into town.'

The cheek of the man. He wanted to know would I step on his toes.

'You know me and my hobbies. I always have something planned.'

We were interrupted by Sergeant Wilson, and I took the opportunity to bid Marcus goodbye and be on my way.

I hurried to the offices of the *Herald*, where I had parked the motor. With a little luck, I would catch Len Diamond before he set off for his assignments and ensure he remembered his promise to show me his photographs of the shoot, and of Deirdre.

George was on the desk, taking possession of an advertisement from an anxious-looking gentleman who wished to announce soothing pills for sale at a shilling a box. I hung back, waiting patiently.

When the man had gone, George said, 'Sorry, Mrs

Shackleton. No sight nor light of Mr Diamond this morning.'

'That's too bad.'

'But Mr Duffield asked if you would go up.'

'Thank you.'

I took the lift up to Mr Duffield's domain, his library with its high windows and gentle light. Mr Duffield nodded a greeting. 'You'll have heard that Mr Diamond hasn't come to work.'

'Yes. Is he often late?'

'I'm afraid so, especially recently.'

That was a relief, because I had wondered whether Len Diamond had been and gone, having come in early so as to avoid me.

Mr Duffield offered me a seat.

'I expect he'll roll in shortly.'

I did not sit down. 'He said he would let me have copies of some of his photographs.'

'I have some on file, if that would help. Do you want to take a look?'

'Yes please.'

'They're not top secret. I don't see why not.'

Mr Duffield led me to a corner of the room shielded from view by tall stacks of shelving. From a drawer, he took a cardboard document case, tied with red tape, set it on the desk and began to untie it carefully. The case was labelled, "August, 1923, L Diamond."

Len had been busy. I sifted through the photographs until I came to two of Leeds Bridge, and of Joseph Barnard on the bridge. There were no photographs of Deirdre.

Mr Duffield was explaining how, within a day or two,

the month's pictures would be filed according to subject. He watched as I picked out the photographs of the first day of grouse shooting. There was the picture that had appeared in the paper: a surprised Caroline Windham, clutching her arm, Everett Runcie beside her.

There were photographs of Philippa with Lord Fotheringham, and Lady Fotheringham, sitting at an outdoor luncheon table between two men I did not recognise.

'You're looking for something in particular, aren't you?' Mr Duffield asked.

I picked up the photographs of the bridge, and of the singer. 'I thought there may be another figure on the bridge.'

Mr Duffield looked at the clock. 'I left a message for Mr Diamond to kindly call up here. Let me go see whether anyone has sighted him. Between you and me, he had better buck his ideas up. He is a good photographer but he puts people's backs up. A little too intrusive, and not reliable.'

I looked at another photograph of the shooting party, half a dozen guns striding out. Len had caught a sense of purpose and anticipation. The picture was clear and clean.

It was a good ten minutes before Mr Duffield returned, frowning.

'No sign of him. We have a mole in the cellar who develops the photographs. He does remember one of a couple on the bridge recently.'

So Diamond had chosen what to put on file in the library, and what to retain. Nothing unusual in that, but I wondered what lay behind his selection process.

Mr Duffield sat down. Together we began to gather up the photographs, which had been of no help whatsoever.

Mr Duffield said, 'I would hate to see Diamond sacked. The editor has brought in a young chap as an assistant. Anyone else would see the writing on the wall.'

'Do you think Mr Diamond may be ill?'

'No. I think he may have been drinking. He had several assignments yesterday, one featuring the lord mayor. He did not turn up for any of them.'

'Has someone telephoned his house?'

'We do not have a telephone number for him. He lives alone in lodgings, in Harehills. I know because I once walked that way with him on a foggy night and saw him to his door.' He looked at the clock high on the wall, and then scratched his neck beneath the stiff collar.

'I have my motor outside, Mr Duffield. Shall we go to Harehills?'

Following Mr Duffield's directions, I took the route of the tram along Roundhay Road. We made for Bank Side Street and came to a halt by a group of three-storey houses. Mr Duffield walked through a ginnel between the houses. Halfway, he paused, and knocked on a door within the ginnel.

'I know he lives in the basement because he told me. There's this entrance and one down the steps at the back.'

We walked to the rear of the house and down the steps. Once again, Mr Duffield knocked. As he pushed the door, it opened. We stepped inside and he called. 'Len!'

It was so unlike Mr Duffield, with his formal manners,

to call a first name that he took me by surprise. 'Len! Leonard!'

The room was in a state of disarray, a chair overturned, crockery smashed. Expensive cameras had been damaged, broken and flung about the room. Most overpowering was the stench of photographic chemicals.

On the far side of the room was a door that fitted its frame exceedingly well. Across the top had been pinned a strip of black sheeting. His dark room.

Stepping carefully, and keeping on my gloves, I crossed the room. The door to the dark room opened when I touched it with my toe.

The slight stir of air caused the hanging figure to sway gently, the toe caps of his boots coming within inches of my chest. I put a hand to my mouth and nose, and forced myself to look up at the distorted face of Leonard Diamond. Chemicals had been spilled across the floor. Under their stink came another smell. I was glad of the dimness of the light but even as I averted my gaze in the half light, I could see that this room, like the other, had been ransacked.

'My God.' Mr Duffield was behind me, his hands on my shoulders. 'What has he done?'

I did not know whether Mr Duffield was trying to move me out of the way for my own sake, or to get to the body.

I turned to him. 'It's too late. Don't touch him. Don't touch anything. We must fetch the police.'

As my eyes grew more accustomed to the gloom, I saw that someone had more than touched this room. Someone had been searching. Photographic plates were scattered across the floor. Drawers had been pulled out.

Yet an expensive camera hung on a hook in the doorway, next to a tripod. It had been opened but was undamaged. Whoever rampaged through Mr Diamond's makeshift studio had not been intent on a random act of robbery. They had been looking for something.

I took one more glance at the scene before we stepped outside. Mr Duffield was pale and trembling. I persuaded him to sit on the low back garden wall, and keep guard.

The nearest police station was Stanley Road, and that was where I headed, and reported what we had found.

'What was your business there, madam?' The sergeant asked as he took my name and address.

Good question.

Mr Duffield and I had given our statements to a constable. Still shaken, we detoured to the Cemetery Tavern on Beckett Street. It is aptly named, being close to the cemetery, and opposite the old workhouse.

I was glad of the smoky atmosphere of the lounge bar, but it did not dispel the stench of chemicals, and death. We chose a seat in the corner. The brass edging on the table felt smooth and reassuring to the touch. The waiter quickly brought our brandy.

'What on earth made him smash up his own rooms?' Mr Duffield gazed into his brandy balloon.

'Do you think that's what happened?'

'It has to be. If someone was bent on robbery, they would have taken his cameras.'

The explanation did not sit well with me. Poor Diamond. The balance of his mind must have been deeply disturbed for him to destroy his own photographs, leave them scattered across the floor. He had seemed so calm, so himself, when I saw him yesterday morning in Schofields café. I could not imagine that, whatever his state of mind, Diamond would destroy his own work.

'It's a shock,' Mr Duffield said, 'a terrible shock to be so close to death. We none of us know when our turn will come.'

We ordered a second brandy.

'It must have been the drink,' Mr Duffield said, staring into his glass. 'He must have drunk himself into a state of hopelessness.'

'I didn't know he drank to excess.'

'Oh yes, and gambled.'

I asked, 'Does Mr Diamond have relatives that you know of?'

Mr Duffield shook his head. 'He never mentioned anyone, only a sister he lost touch with years ago. She migrated to Canada with her husband before the war. I must get back to work and tell the editor about this.' He looked at me steadily. 'What was it that you hoped to find among Mr Diamond's photographs?'

'I'm not sure. Possibly a photograph of the singer Giuseppe Barnardini, and a lady not his wife; photographs of the shoot, showing who in particular Everett Runcie may have hobnobbed with that day.'

I kept my theory about Caroline Windham's injury at the grouse shoot to myself.

Mr Duffield took another sip of brandy. 'Are you interested in Mr Diamond because you suspect he may have been blackmailing someone, to get money for his drink and gambling? He always had his nose in other people's business.'

Up to now, that thought had not occurred to me. But it

made sense. If I were right, and someone had ransacked the room, then I was not the only person interested in Len Diamond's photographs. What did he have that may have cost him his life?

Mr Duffield stared ahead, unseeing, to the bottles arranged so artistically behind the bar. 'He was in trouble, financially, more than usual. He had a winning streak in the spring, and was patting himself on the back over a clever investment. He tried to interest me, but I'm not a betting man and I don't trust stocks and shares.' Mr Duffield stood up. 'Circumstances call for another brandy, and then I must be back to the office.' He caught the attention of the waiter. When he sat down again, he said, 'Do you know, I believe we are being watched. Perhaps the gentleman in the tap room is envying me my charming company. Don't look now.'

I waited until we had finished our drinks and were leaving. Only then did I look across the bar, into the tap room, and glance at the familiar figure staring glumly into his beer. It was Eddie Flanagan, the unemployed ex-boxer, Deirdre's faithful friend.

'I won't be a moment, Mr Duffield.'

I went into the tap room and stood over him. 'Hello, Mr Flanagan. Are you following me?'

Eddie looked at me sullenly, as if he wanted to argue over the word hello. The poor man had a permanently puzzled face, as if the world presented itself to him through a fog. He said, 'Deirdre slept in a glasshouse last night.'

'A glasshouse?'

'I went looking at sunrise. I could tell she'd been there.'

'Where?'

'That place, the place she took her mam. I know

Deirdre, heart and soul. She went to the park, I know. Roundhay Park. I looked. But now she's gone. I could tell she'd been in the glasshouse.'

It struck me that he was probably right, because the man loved her, and he had no hopes for himself where she was concerned. There was something touching about him, like a faithful dog.

'How do you know she was there?'

I expected him to say that he sensed her presence, a lingering trace of her scent.

He put his hand in his pocket and produced a small white handkerchief which he spread on the table, smoothing it carefully. He pointed to a letter *D*, embroidered on the corner. 'It's hers.'

'Thanks, Eddie. I'll do my best, believe me. It might not look like it, but I'm searching for her now and I'll go on searching.'

He looked at me steadily, as if deciding whether to believe me. I passed the test. 'What did they say your name was?'

'Mrs Shackleton.'

He repeated my name softly, as though committing it to memory.

'What brought you here?'

The Cemetery Tavern was a long way from home for him.

'Searching. I thought she mighta been hurt and taken to the Workhouse Infirmary over there.'

'Have you been to ask?'

He nodded. 'She's not there. Not anywhere.'

When I dropped off Mr Duffield at the newspaper offices, I had to ask him a question, even though he was late, and flustered, and upset at the thought of having to break the news to the editor.

'There's no tactful way of saying this, Mr Duffield, but I want to know if one of the compositors was in work last night, Cyril Fitzpatrick.'

He stared at me, and blinked. 'Why?'

'I can't say, but please trust me. It is important that I know.'

He nodded. 'I'll look at the clocking-in cards for the print works.'

Why was it important that I know? I had no idea, except that Diamond had given a hint to Fitzpatrick that he had photographed his wife on Leeds Bridge, and now that photograph had disappeared, and Diamond lay dead among the debris of his craft.

Moments later, Mr Duffield emerged. He leaned into the motor and whispered, 'He was in last night, and the night before. He is on the night shift all this week.'

'What time does the shift end?'

'Seven a.m.'

'Thank you.'

He nodded. 'And now I have to tell the editor that Len Diamond has committed suicide.'

'No, Mr Duffield. We don't know that, and I don't believe it. Len would not have destroyed his work, his cameras. Someone else has had a hand in this.'

Mr Duffield said sadly, 'The outcome is the same. We'll not see such a good photographer on this newspaper again.'

He turned, and I watched him walk away.

Perhaps Diamond's death had no connection whatsoever with the demise of Mr Runcie, but I decided to tell Marcus anyway, and drove the short distance to the Hotel Metropole.

After that, I would visit Philippa. Even though I had little to report, talking to her might give me some new lead.

Twenty-One

Word of my arrival was sent up to Philippa while I waited in the drawing room at Kirkley Hall. I hoped she would not expect me to have worked miracles, and to be here bearing vital news.

I took a seat by the window and looked onto the garden, so green and tranquil. It seemed incongruous that in one morning I could have witnessed a scene of death and destruction in Len Diamond's lodgings, and now looked out on this manicured yet somehow time-less view.

The footsteps in the hall were not Philippa's. I looked up to see a smiling Gideon King.

'Mrs Shackleton, good morning.'

'Good morning, Mr King.'

'Philippa sends her apologies. She is a little unwell this morning.'

'I'm sorry to hear that.'

'But she is glad to hear of your visit. If you have any news, I should be happy to pass it on.' He walked across to join me. 'I have sent for coffee.'

'Coffee would be good.' It might neutralise the brandy I had drunk after finding Len Diamond's body.

Did King know that Philippa had engaged me, I wondered. It seemed likely, given that he was her trusted secretary, but I did not want to assume. After all, Caroline Windham had first accused Philippa and King, and had then said, on learning that Runcie had been strangled, that it must have been King.

I noticed how still and contained he was; no gestures or unnecessary movements. He had a powerful build, and strangler's hands. He talked to me about having had a very pleasant walk that morning.

'Last time we spoke, you said you had not had time to consider whether to return to Boston. It sounds from your love of the walks roundabout that you will miss this place.'

He smiled. 'I shall. But I won't be sorry to leave. And Philippa wants to go home.'

I had seen for myself how protective he was of Philippa. Protective enough to kill for her?

We made polite conversation until King looked up at a noise from the doorway. 'Ah over here, Simpson.'

The elderly butler brought a tray of coffee and set it down between us. I was pleased that Simpson took on the task of pouring. It had been the kind of morning to leave me clumsy and uncoordinated. I would end up spilling coffee over King, and ruining my attempt to get the measure of this odd, self-contained man.

When the butler had left, King said, 'Well, Mrs Shackleton, do you have news for Philippa? It's all right. She did tell me that she had asked for your help. She was a little perturbed by the police lines of questioning.'

'I remember you were somewhat concerned yourself, Mr King.'

He rubbed his chin. 'Yes, that is true. The police want to know so much, whether relevant or not. My title of secretary contains the word secret. One has one's loyalties.'

I took a sip of coffee. 'To Mrs Runcie, of course.'

'Yes, but also to the family she has married into. I have been working with Harold, Baron Kirkley, to try and make sense of Everett's papers. Any disgrace that falls on one member of a family leaves a shadow over the rest.'

'And what about Philippa's family? You are a school friend of her brother's, I believe?'

'Yes. I've known Philippa all my life. We always got on.'

'You are very protective towards her. You would do anything to help her, I think.'

He spooned sugar into his coffee, and laughed. 'Not murder. I told you before that I was a student of theology. I am no longer a very religious man, but the sixth commandment is not one I would break.'

It was time to admit that so far my efforts had come to nought. 'Unfortunately, Mr King, I have nothing definite to report to Philippa.'

He nodded. 'I thought it would be a little soon. Then you must have come with questions. Is there anything you want to ask me?'

'Yes there is, regarding Lord Fotheringham's shoot. You were there I believe?'

He spilled the tiniest drop of coffee into his saucer.

'Yes. Philippa is kind enough to ensure that I am included in such invitations, being a friend of the family as well as an employee.'

'There was an accident that day.'

'Oh the first day, yes that is correct. You mean Miss Windham's drama.'

Was it my imagination, or did he seem relieved at my line of questioning? Perhaps he had expected something quite different.

'Did anyone discover who fired the shot that grazed Miss Windham's arm?'

He shook his head. 'No one owned up to it.'

'Where were you when it happened?'

He put down his cup. 'I don't know. One hears shots all the time, naturally. I was not close enough to see anything. I heard about the accident at lunch. Lord Fotheringham was quite cut up about it.'

'Well thank you. I had meant to ask Philippa about it, but it didn't quite arise. It must be a sensitive subject for her.'

King became suddenly animated. 'I see what you are thinking. Was the shot meant for Everett?'

'It had crossed my mind. But of course I do not know who was there, in the vicinity, or if someone in attendance might have had a motive.'

He leapt from his chair. 'If you wait, I can tell you exactly who was there that day.'

'That would be a help.'

'Excuse me.'

After some little while, King reappeared, carrying a handsome, leather-bound diary. 'Here we are.' He turned the pages. 'Monday, 13th August.'

I took out my notebook.

'I am very impressed, Mr King. Have you kept a diary long?'

'I was brought up to keep a diary. Jot down what's happening in the world, what I have achieved, or not, and any pressing thoughts. I would rather no one sees it, but it interests me to look back year by year and remember whom I met and where, and how my ideas and opinions change.'

From his diary for 13th August, he read the names of Lord Fotheringham's guests.

I jotted the names in my notebook, asking him for comments about each person, and their relation to Runcie.

At the end of the list, I was no wiser as to who might have fired the shot.

'What about the staff?' I asked. 'The beaters and so on. Is there anyone among them who was recently recruited?'

He shook his head. 'Not that I know of. They are all men known to the estate manager.'

So much for my theory.

'Mr King, what do you have for your diary entries over the weekend and in the days before Mr Runcie's murder? Is there anything at all unusual, anything he said that you may have remembered, any visitors?'

'I could tell you that without looking, but I will check. This has not been a very sociable household lately, as you can imagine. That day at the races was the only time we went out, and you were there yourself so you know we were not a large party.' He glanced at a page, and read, 'Friday 31st August. *Supervising inventory all day. Scratch supper.* That was how I spent most of that week, and this weekend just gone. It's a big job, separating out what in each room goes home with Philippa and what stays here as belonging to the house. We have still another dozen rooms to attend to.'

'Yes, quite a time-consuming task. You do not do it alone I suppose?'

'Heavens no,' King said. 'I have Simpson and Withers alongside. My only time off this weekend was to go to church. The vicar came back with us for sherry, and luncheon. That was it for the day.' He flicked through the pages once more. 'According to my diary I have been fagged out almost every night, and went to bed early.'

I had not told King about Leonard Diamond's death. Yet he had given me an alibi for this weekend, when it must have happened. I pictured Diamond and King in the grandstand on the day of the Ebor Handicap. King had chivalrously prevented Diamond from taking a photograph of the Runcies and Miss Windham. But surely he could not have had any other connection with the photographer? All the same, the memory of that event gave me pause for thought.

'You're so busy, Mr King, and I have taken up too much of your time. Please give Philippa my good wishes.'

'I will. And feel free to call on me at any time. I am glad to be of service.'

He walked me to the door.

'Thank you for the coffee.'

'A pleasure.'

In spite of the coffee, my head throbbed as I walked away.

It occurred to me that King had been very prompt to supply me with a list of other people's names. This could have been out of his desire to be helpful, or it could have been because he wanted to point me in the wrong direction.

Having been a theology student, knowing the commandments, did not put him in the ranks of the angels, of that I felt sure.

Twenty-Two

Blame the reaction to the horror of discovering Len Diamond's body, or too much brandy. When I arrived home, I slid onto the chaise longue in the drawing room, and fell asleep.

My dream must have been prompted by hearing about Mrs Hartigan's death, and imagining Deirdre's feelings. I dreamed my own mother died, and I was given the news. In the dream, it was unclear exactly who had died. I tried to find out whether it was the woman I thought of as my real mother: Ginny, who adopted me and brought me up, or my birth mother, she whom I could only ever think of as Mrs Whitaker, who lived in Wakefield, in White Swan Yard, and who gave me up when I was only weeks old. There was a sense of panic when I woke. I had asked the question, but had no answer. Who is it? Who is dead?

My head ached. I was desperate for a glass of water and went into the kitchen, thinking about Deirdre Fitzpatrick, wondering where she had fled.

Mrs Sugden heard me, and appeared. 'I kept quiet. I was going to do the stairs and landing but when I saw you sleeping, I didn't want to disturb you. I've made a stew. You better have some by the look of you.'

As we sat at the kitchen table, I told Mrs Sugden about Len Diamond's death, and about Mrs Hartigan's death, and Deirdre's disappearance.

'No wonder you had to escape into dreamland.' She ladled rabbit stew into a dish. 'Do you think this Deirdre person has run mad and done away with herself?' Mrs Sugden was generous with her helpings. Stories of death always made her hungry. 'With that nursing home being near Roundhay Park, the poor lass could have been drawn to the lake.'

The stew tasted good. 'Something tells me that Deirdre Fitzpatrick is made of stouter stuff than to drown herself.'

Mrs Sugden knew about Sykes's soft spot for Deirdre. 'Aye, well if she can turn Mr Sykes's head, and he with no fondness for left footers, she must have a way with her.'

The remark about left footing reminded me of Deirdre's Catholicism. 'I wonder if she's gone somewhere to say prayers for the dead. Whatever else she may or may not have done, she was devoted to her mother.'

'Search me. And it's no use asking Miss Merton. She doesn't mix with Irish Catholics. They're a different breed altogether, according to her.'

Elizabeth Merton is our neighbour, a single lady, and Catholic convert, who keeps house for her professor brother.

Sookie chose that moment to leap from her spot on the rocking chair and stroll up to us, waving her tail in the air. Perhaps she recognised Miss Merton's name as the person who came to look in on her on the rare occasions that both Mrs Sugden and I were away from home at the same time. Or perhaps she wanted to lick the dishes.

'Happen there's some man in the picture,' Mrs Sugden suggested. 'If Mrs Fitzpatrick is not crying on her husband's shoulder, then maybe there's someone else.'

That brought me back to part two of my plan. For all I knew, Deirdre Fitzpatrick may have a string of gentlemen friends, or none at all. But I knew of only one name, time and place: Joseph Barnard, weekend of 24th August at the Adelphi Hotel. I stroked Sookie, and then went to the dining room drawer where I had tucked away the *Pirates of Penzance* programme. It gave a list of other performances. Tonight's performance, at eight o'clock, would be *HMS Pinafore* at Wakefield Opera House.

'Mrs Sugden, do you fancy seeing a Gilbert & Sullivan opera this evening?'

'Where?' she asked suspiciously.

'Wakefield Opera House.'

'No I do not. You dash about that much, you'll take years off your life.' She forced a piece of seedcake on me. 'The City Varieties and the Empire are good enough for me.'

I bit into the cake. The inevitable seed lodged in a tooth. 'Well I'm going. I want to take another look at Giuseppe Barnardini. He plays the George Grossmith parts so I expect he'll be Sir Joseph, First Lord of the Admiralty.'

'It'll be dark when you come out. You're not driving are you?'

'Don't worry. My trusty Jowett hasn't let me down yet.'

It does not do to tempt fate. My sturdy 1913 motor should be in her prime. Perhaps she disapproved of my mission, mistrusted light opera, or the subversive lyrics of Mr Gilbert.

On a country road, somewhere in the middle of nowhere, the motor began to lose power and choked out a rasp. I pressed on the accelerator. Something rattled. I de-clutched to a lower gear. The rattling increased. Whiffs of smoke rose from under the bonnet, giving off a burning smell. After half a mile of this, I slowed down, thinking a rest might do the trick. I got out and touched the bonnet; hot enough to cook a dinner. I tried to remember when the oil and water were checked.

'Sorry, little Jowett.'

My sweet car looked very sorry for itself.

For a good ten minutes, I sat hopefully by the roadside, in expectation of rescue. A man on a slow horse-drawn cart offered me a lift. After another twenty minutes, I wished I had accepted. There must be an inn, or a house, or a garage nearby from where I could telephone. I tried to remember, from my previous drives in this direction, where the nearest human habitation would be. All I could recall was the pub, passed some miles back.

The engine cooled but came back to life with the same fearful rattle. Just as I was about to set off walking, another Jowett appeared, coming from the opposite direction. The driver stopped. He was a Bradford man with a neat moustache and greying hair. Together we examined the motor.

'Your radiator hose has gone, Miss,' he announced. 'Where are you heading?'

'Wakefield.'

'Have you ever been towed?'

'No.'

'Keep the distance of the rope.'

My eternal gratitude to my fellow Jowetteer and the unnerving experience of being towed into Wakefield need not form part of this story. Suffice to say that *HMS Pinafore* had long set sail when, hungry, thirsty and upset about my poor motor, I gave the stage doorkeeper a note to be passed, urgently, to Giuseppe Barnardini, asking him to meet a lady from Leeds at the stage door after the performance.

By the time Barnardini's rendition of "ruler of the Queen's navee" had the house roaring with laughter, I wondered whether he might link the note to Deirdre, not wish to see her, and find another way out of the theatre.

After the performance, I sat on the hard bench in the stage door area, and waited. Members of the chorus hurried out first, calling their goodnights to the doorman, who studiously ignored me.

It was a good twenty minutes before Joseph Barnard appeared. He looked quite different out of costume and without make-up, but with that presence actors have, the art of filling a space, and of letting you know they are there. His cautious glance gave nothing away.

I stood up. 'Mr Barnard.'

'The lady from Leeds?' If he had expected someone else, whatever disappointment or relief he felt was well hidden.

'Sorry to be so mysterious.' I handed him my card, the one that gives my name and the ominous words 'private investigator'. He ran his tongue across his lips, but said nothing. 'We have a mutual friend.' I glanced, in what I hoped was a meaningful way, at the doorkeeper who was pretending great interest in the evening paper.

The singer nodded. 'Pleased to meet you.' He did not say my name. 'Perhaps you'll ...' He took my arm, gently at the elbow, called good night to the doorman, who now looked up, and gave a cheerful reply.

Once we were outside, I said, 'I'm sorry to be mysterious. And congratulations on the performance tonight. You were wonderful.'

My once upon a time theatre director friend had assured me that these are always the best opening lines to a performer. He thanked me and relaxed a little. 'We had a good audience. That always helps.'

It was a fine night. Outside the pub across the road from the theatre, a small crowd stood in the open air, drinking. I glanced at Barnard in the glow of the gas lamp. Perhaps he was putting on another performance, and Deirdre was finding her way back to his digs, or waiting somewhere for him.

'Is there somewhere we can talk privately?'

'The name of our mutual friend?' he asked.

We were a stone's throw from where my birth mother lived, in White Swan Yard. I wanted to be able to see Mr Barnard's face as we talked. He would be well-versed at dissembling, but I would take that chance. 'The White Swan?'

'Mrs Shackleton, what is this about?'

Once I said her name, he could deny knowledge of Deirdre, and march off into the night.

'A certain person whom you spent time with in Leeds

has gone missing. I'm hoping there might be something you can tell me that would help me find her. It could save a lot of trouble, and police involvement.'

He thought for a moment. 'The first initial of her Christian name?'

'D.'

'I don't believe I can help you.'

I was on the verge of losing him, and for all I knew I might have missed the last train and be stranded, as well as beginning to feel light-headed. 'Look, Mr Barnard, I know this has come out of the blue but I've gone to a lot of trouble to get here. I believe Deirdre found herself in a dire situation recently, and that shortly afterwards, her mother died. The police want to talk to her. If I don't find her first, every inch of her life over the past months will be under the microscope. If I do find her, your name can be kept out of it.'

'I see. But I don't know where we can talk. My gang have already discovered the Swan.'

'The railway station?'

'Not exactly the spot I had in mind for my post-performance tipple, but lead on.'

We strolled the short distance to the railway station, where the buffet was closed. This was not my day. 'The waiting room?'

He nodded.

We sat on a bench in a room deserted except for a man in a mac huddled in the far corner, smoking a pipe.

'Do you know the lady you are seeking?' he asked as we seated ourselves on the leather-covered benches.

'Not personally. As my card says, I am a private investigator.' I felt him tense. 'But this is nothing to do with matrimonial matters. I simply want to find Mrs Fitzpatrick. Her family are concerned about her disappearance.'

'I haven't seen her. Nor have we been in touch. Really, Mrs Shackleton, you are looking in the wrong place. Do you think I have her packed in my trunk?'

'Something happened. I can't say what. She may have information that could help the police.'

He spoke cautiously, not denying, not confirming that they had spent the weekend together. 'Is she in trouble?'

'She may be. I thought she may have come to you.'

'Well you were wrong. She has not.'

'Look, I know you want to be with your friends in the pub, but is there anything that you can think of that might help me find her?'

'What kind of trouble may she be in? Has her husband . . .? If someone has harmed her . . .'

'I have no reason to believe she has come to harm.'

For the first time, it occurred to me that she could have come to harm. Not the self-harm that Mrs Sugden suggested, but from her husband, or her brother. What better way to cover a crime than to ask the police and an investigator to search for the victim?

'I can't help you. I liked Deirdre. We took to each other.'

'Was there anything that happened while you were together, or anything she said that hinted that she might leave her husband, or where she would go, or anything that alarmed her?'

'She wasn't happy with her husband. There's something I could say, but I won't. A gentleman doesn't tell.'

But you will, I thought, if I don't push you too hard. I waited.

'We were on Leeds Bridge,' he said carefully, 'and someone took a photograph. That upset her.'

'I suppose it would. It's not a picture she would want to have seen.'

'She thought she recognised the photographer, as someone who worked for the same newspaper as her husband.

'Why was he photographing you?'

'At first he said he wasn't, and that it was the scene he was taking. I did wonder whether . . .'

'What?'

'No. I'll say no more on that.'

'That her husband was having her followed, or that the photographer may ask a high price for his wares?'

When he stayed silent, I asked, 'Who put you in contact with Deirdre?'

His answer came out so quickly and so pat that I knew it to be false. 'We met in a café and hit it off. She was a good sport.'

'What café?'

'Does that matter? It was a café, that's all. I can't tell you the name.'

'Where was the café?'

'Just a café. We met in a café.'

'That's what the solicitor told you to say?'

He repeated his answer, word for word.

'Thank you.' There would be little more to draw out of him. I stood up.

'Wait!' He touched my sleeve. He let out a sigh and lowered his head. 'If someone has hurt that lovely lady ...'

This seemed an odd way to describe a 'good sport' he met in a café. 'Mr Barnard, what can you tell me?'

'It was her first time, and ... Well I'm sure it was her first time.'

'Do you mean her first time meeting a man in a café and going to a hotel with him?'

He hesitated. 'I can't divulge.'

I sat down again. 'Mr Barnard, if you have any regard for Mrs Fitzpatrick, then please help me. I enjoyed *HMS Pinafore*, but I'll probably be waiting in this station for the milk train, so have a heart, for Deirdre and for me.'

'It was as I said, we met in a café and . . .'

'Oh, spare me! She was with another man, in the same situation as you, and the outcome was rather unfortunate. And now I don't know where she is.'

He had turned red and uncomfortable. He tugged at his collar. 'What kind of husband does she have? What sort of man is he?'

'It's a little late for you to be asking that. You realise that your wife's petition for divorce could be at risk?'

He hesitated, and then said, 'Mrs Fitzpatrick, Deirdre, she needed the money. That was why she did what she did.'

'You can rely on my discretion.'

Could he? I was not so sure, but he nodded. 'I hope so.' He did not look at me, but stared at his feet. He spoke quietly, but his actor's voice allowed every word to come out so very clearly.

'When I said it was her first time, I did not mean her first time meeting someone in a café. We agreed that intimacy need not form part of our arrangement. What you do in a situation requiring a certain sort of proof is not as important as what you are seen to do. What is seen, what can be used as evidence, that is what counts.

We agreed to sleep with a bolster between us, and then we didn't; didn't have the bolster I mean. We liked each other, very much. I wished I had met her years ago, and I believe she felt the same. The next morning . . .'

'The next morning?' I prompted.

'There was blood on the sheets. She was very embarrassed and tried to wash it out. We had a wash basin in the room.'

'She had her bleeding period?'

'No. It wasn't that. It was her first time.'

A silence held between us, and then he spoke again. 'She was lively, and funny, and told me about her mother, and her brother in New York who she thought must have died or moved because he never answered her letters. And now I feel helpless, because to act in any way on her behalf . . . the solicitor stressed . . .'

'The solicitor . . .?'

'That's as much as I can say.'

Barnard stood up, and offered his hand. 'I hope you don't have to wait too long for a train.'

'If there's anything else, you have my card.'

'You might as well know. I thought the photographer might be working for the solicitor, a belt and braces idea of seeing us together on our way to the hotel, but I cannot be sure. Deirdre thought not.'

'Thank you.'

He nodded. 'Goodnight.'

'Goodnight.'

It would have been a better night's work if I had found out the name of the solicitor. But at least I had eliminated the slim possibility that Deirdre would be with Barnard. I gave him time to leave the station, and then went to the platform to study the timetable. I need not have worried about trains. One was due in ten minutes. But if I took a train to Leeds, then I would be abandoning my motor to its fate. Far better to take a tram to my parents' house in Sandal, where I would be better placed to do something about the motor in the morning.

The tram stop was a short walk away. On an impulse, I decided just to look and see if there was a light on at the house in White Swan Yard, where my birth mother lives. Not that I believe in the power of dreams. I had only dreamed of a mother's death because of Deirdre's mother dying. But it would not hurt, just to see.

A gentle glow from the gas mantle formed a golden edge around the blind. I could hear whistling, tapping or stamping, and a child's voice that I recognised: my niece, Harriet.

I peeped through a gap at the side of the blind. There was Mrs Whitaker, the mother whom I didn't know what to call, playing a penny whistle. My parents adopted me from Mrs Whitaker when I was a few weeks old, and I am only just getting to know her. Harriet was clapping and singing. The hearth rug was rolled back. Little Austin wore clogs and stomped a dance.

The dog barked.

Hurriedly, I turned away. It was late. I wanted to knock, but I didn't want to knock. If the children saw my face, I might break the mood and remind them of sadder days, of the loss of their father.

But I was not quick enough. The dog's bark alerted Harriet to someone at the door. She opened it as I was about to turn away, and her face lit up at the sight of me. 'Auntie Kate! How did you know I was here?'

I smiled at her wonderful assumption. 'Just a good guess, Harriet.'

She held open the door for me to step inside.

Austin had stopped dancing. He smiled, but not wanting to be seen smiling, looked at his feet.

Mrs Whitaker said, 'Well you better sit down, our Catherine.'

I pulled out a buffet and sat by the table.

Harriet said, 'Have you remembered it will be my birthday soon?'

'I have.'

'I'll be eleven.'

'I know they should be in bed,' Mrs Whitaker said, as though I had criticized her, 'but the bairns need a bit of enjoyment.'

'Of course they do. I've just been to the theatre myself, to see Gilbert and Sullivan.'

Having called here, I had to stay for at least half an hour; half an hour of cups of tea, bread and dripping.

Harriet said, 'Mam is going to come and stay with you while the banns are read for her and Uncle Bob to marry at Leeds Register office.'

Was she now? First I had heard of it. I tried not to look surprised. It was barely four months since my brother-in-law Ethan's death. But Mary Jane is nothing if not full of surprises. She is my sister, but a sister I only met this year, brought up in this house, part of the Whitaker family, of whom I know only Mary Jane, Harriet, Austin and Mrs Whitaker.

Harriet talked about the proposed move to Helmsley, where her mam and step-father would run the newsagent shop. The children had been taken to see the place. Harriet seemed to be looking forward to the move. Austin gave nothing away.

I felt glad that they were moving to somewhere new, for a fresh start after the loss of their father.

Austin was persuaded to do another dance. When he stopped and we applauded, he asked, 'When we move to Helmsley, how will Dad know where to find us?'

Harriet said nothing. Neither did I. His grand-mother said, 'Your dad will be looking down from heaven. He'll be that pleased to see you getting on right well.'

I waited downstairs with the dog, looking into the fire, while Mrs Whitaker took the children up to bed.

Shortly after she came down, I made a move. I explained about the Jowett. 'I won't go back to Leeds tonight. I'll find a cab to take me out to Sandal.'

Mrs Whitaker is a practical woman. She straight away insisted that her neighbour down the yard would be happy to take me the three miles in his horse and cart.

She left me alone while she went out to ask him.

During the moments she was gone, I wondered how my life would have turned out if Mr Whitaker, a police constable, had not died suddenly while Mrs Whitaker was pregnant with me, and taking care of her already large family. It was hard to imagine a life other than the one I have lived.

Mrs Whitaker returned, all smiles. 'Mr Cutler is getting his boots on. Give him ten minutes to get his pony out of the stable and harnessed.'

'Where is the stable?'

'Down the yard here.'

Ten minutes.

We looked at each other.

She said, 'You tell Mary Jane, if you don't want her to stop. It's not right she should be imposing. She hadn't asked you, had she?'

'No.'

'Just like her. But she regards you as family, you see. Because you are. But you mustn't feel obliged to us.' She poked the fire. 'Are you warm enough?'

'Yes thank you.'

Is this how we would be, Mrs Whitaker and I, polite, not quite knowing what to call each other?

Catherine, she called me.

'Did you name me after someone in your family, Mrs Whitaker?'

Your family; I should have said our family.

'Your father liked the name. Catherine if you were a girl. I can't remember what we would have called a boy.'

So in spite all of their other children, they had thought carefully about my name. It gave me a different feeling towards this woman with the greying hair who looked so much older than her years.

'And what is your Christian name, Mrs Whitaker? I never know what to call you, you see. I call Ginny Hood mother.'

'So you should. And I don't suppose you could say Ma.'

'Ma.' I laughed. 'I've never said ma.'

'Call me whatever you please. Ada, Ma, Mrs W. It makes no odds. You'll always be Catherine to me.'

There was a gentle knock on the door. Mr Cutler had harnessed his pony in quick time.

I said goodnight to Mrs Whitaker, still unsure what to

call her, but with a feeling that I would see her again, and soon.

Mr Cutler helped me onto the cart. I waved to the woman in the doorway, and the pony trotted us out of the yard.

I hoped that by morning, my brief interview with Joseph Barnard would make more sense, and that I would wake with an inkling of what to do next, or whether to withdraw from this business altogether.

Twenty-Three

It was almost midnight when Mr Cutler called whoa to his pony. I paid him and clambered from the cart. My parents' house was in darkness. Fortunately, my mother insists on my keeping a key, 'just in case'. I let myself in as quietly as possible, but not quietly enough.

Dad appeared at the top of the stairs in his dressing gown and slippers. 'I heard the cart. Is something wrong?'

My dream came back to me. 'Is mother asleep?'

'Fast asleep.'

Not dead then. So my anxiety-filled dream had indeed been all about Deirdre Fitzpatrick. I flicked on the hall light.

Dad came down the stairs. 'Wondered when you'd arrive.'

He never ceased to surprise me. 'I didn't say I was coming.'

He tapped the side of his nose. 'Do you want a cup of cocoa?'

'Didn't mean to wake you.' I followed him into the kitchen.

'You know I'm a light sleeper.' He poured milk into the saucepan, turned on the tap and added water.

I sat down at the kitchen table, and watched the match flame bring the gas ring to flickering blue life.

He spooned cocoa and sugar into mugs, adding a drop of milk to each one, mixing to a paste. 'Your mother rang and spoke to Mrs Sugden. She said you had come to Wakefield to see a Gilbert & Sullivan.'

'It was all a bit last minute.'

'That's what I said. She would have liked to go with you.'

'She would have enjoyed it. But I really came because I wanted to talk to one of the singers.'

'I guessed you weren't in Wakefield solely for the love of *HMS Pinafore*.'

'How did you guess?'

'You wouldn't have chosen to go to the Theatre Royal on your lonesome unless you had some ulterior motive.'

He watched the saucepan as I told him about the Jowett having lost heart, and that I had been towed into Wakefield and left the car near police headquarters, where Dad works.

'That was bad luck, but good thinking to leave it by the station. We'll do something about it in the morning, first thing.'

'And I called in to see Mrs Whitaker.'

'How is Mrs Whitaker?' Even he, especially he, did not say, 'your mother'.

'She seems very well. Mary Jane's children are staying with her.'

He poured the milk and water into the first mug, stirring carefully. 'Where's that biscuit barrel?'

'Where it usually is.' I went to the cupboard and took out the biscuit barrel. It is an awkward thing, made of dull steel, dented, and with a lid that never wants to budge. There must be some sentimental reason why my mother keeps it. You have to edge up the lid bit by bit until it gives in.

Ginger nuts. My favourite.

Dad stirred his cocoa and sat down. 'So, your chief inspector is in Leeds, investigating the death of the banker.'

'He's not my chief inspector, Dad, but yes. I would have liked to help but he keeps me on the edge.'

'Perhaps not so on the edge as all that.' He took a sip of cocoa. 'Too hot.' He put down his mug. 'He sent you a message via the station. Mrs Sugden told him you might call here.'

I wish I was not surrounded by people with a sixth sense. It can be unnerving.

Dad pushed the note across to me. 'Bit cryptic, but I expect it makes sense to you.'

The note read: *The C.I. presents his compliments and seeks your help in finding the woman unknown. Urgent. Fingerprints at scene match fingerprints in woman's home.*

I stared at the note.

Dad said, 'Apparently, they found a fingerprint on a shoe she left behind in the room, and on a glass in the bathroom.'

'So I was right.'

'Who is she?' Dad asked.

'Deirdre Fitzpatrick. She was with the banker on the night he was killed. Marcus has already told me to let him know when I find her.'

'He's making it official. He wants you to find her on

behalf of the police, rather than whoever asked you to find her.'

'I suppose that is a compliment to me.'

Dad dunked a ginger nut in his cocoa. 'No one is better at finding people than you. How many widows and mothers did you help after the war?'

'That was different. All I had to do was seek old comrades, and do a little digging around.'

'And there was Braithwaite, and your brother-in-law. Mr Charles knows what he's doing in asking you. You'll find her, Kate, this woman unknown. Just make sure the Yard pay you for your services, as I don't believe you'll be doing it for love.'

So he had understood that Marcus Charles and I had no future together.

He sighed.

It is always a mistake to dunk a ginger nut after you have taken a bite. His biscuit disappeared into the cocoa. He fished for it with the spoon.

'No, Dad, I won't be doing it for love. Marcus and I are friends. That's all. And I wish you wouldn't sigh over me. I'm glad he's asked for my help. I hate being on the edge, the spare part.'

He raised his eyebrows. 'I suppose I couldn't expect anything else but a sleuth for a daughter. If you'd known Mr Whitaker you would have admired him. He never made more than beat bobby, but not much passed him by. He could have had promotion but he liked being out in the open air, keeping an eye on the world. You have his blood in your veins and my example.'

What neither of us said was that I had so far failed in

my search for Gerald. It was now five years since the war ended. I had no answer as to what had happened to him and whether he was alive somewhere, with disfiguring injuries or loss of memory.

'Do you have much to go on regarding the woman?' Dad asked.

'Yes. She is Deirdre Fitzpatrick, daughter of the late Mrs Hartigan, sister of a New York "businessman", Anthony Hartigan, a murderer and bootlegger. She's married to a strange chap who works on the local paper. I'm not sure of the ethics of this situation as I'm already looking for her, on behalf of her husband.'

Best not mention the trio that came a-calling, the husband, the brother and the lovesick swain.

'Any leads?'

I believe she stayed in hotels, with at least two different men, acting as co-respondent. Someone put her in touch with them, probably a solicitor on St Paul's Street. I believe she worked for him. That solicitor could be giving her somewhere to lie low. Or she may have proved an awkward person to have around. I need his name.'

Dad gave his cocoa another stir. 'Tell me about it.'

My parents' neighbour, Arthur, is a Jowett fanatic, with a fully-equipped garage. He and Dad brought my poorly motor back before breakfast. Dad disappeared to work. Arthur, who is in a position to set his own hours, called to me to come and look. We stood in his garage that smelled of oil, rubber and manly competence. Arthur was seriously kitted out in dark blue mechanic's overalls, his moon face showing distress.

'Kate, there were only forty-eight of these motors made up to 1916, and you have this beauty. It's a sacred trust.'

'Well I didn't know she was going to spring a leak.'

'The radiator hose has gone. You've damaged the pistons and the big end.'

'I thought it was topped up.'

In the dim light of the garage, I could not tell what shade of puce he turned. 'Didn't you notice anything amiss?'

'Well yes, obviously, with the smoke and the rattling.'

'Before that?'

'Are you saying I can't drive home?'

'Leave her with me for a couple of days.' He shook his head. 'You were lucky a Jowetteer came along and towed you last night. If you'd driven any further, I dread to think what you might have done to her.'

I looked at the Jowett fondly. Sometimes that motor seems alive. I could have sworn in that moment she transferred her affections to Arthur. I half expected her to speak and warn me to expect a charge of neglect.

It seemed heartless to turn and walk away.

Fortunately, Pamela, my mother's maid, called to me from the garage doorway, giving me an escape route.

'Thanks, Arthur. I'll talk to you about it later.'

I went indoors with Pamela.

'Mrs Sugden telephoned to you, Mrs Shackleton. I wrote down exactly what she said. And your father sent a note from the office. It all happened at once when I was seeing to the kitten.'

I thanked her and picked up the two notes. Mrs Sugden's message was from Aunt Berta, informing me that a solicitor by the name of Walter Lansbury on St Paul's Street might be able to help. What a grand name for a shady man of the law. Well, Mr Lansbury, you can expect another visit, very soon.

Dad's note was more cryptic, that he had sent a message to the chief inspector naming a legal person who would be worth talking to.

This was very good because it gave me a reason to speak to Dad. I picked up the telephone and was soon connected to him.

'Dad?'

'Katie?'

'That legal person, does he begin with an L and end in a Y?'

'Your Aunt Berta beat me to it?'

'She had a start. And, Dad.'

'Yes?'

'May I borrow your Morris, just for a couple of days?'

'I suppose so. But be careful.'

'I will.' I returned the telephone receiver to its cradle.

My mother usually sits in bed reading until ten o'clock. I had taken her an early morning cup of tea.

As I was on my way up the stairs to see her, she called, 'Is that you on the phone, Kate? I'm coming down.'

'It's all right. I'll come up.'

She has a special arrangement of pillows when she reads, and a cushion under her knees.

Smiling, she set her book aside. 'It's the latest Arnold Bennett, very good indeed.'

'I must get around to it.'

'You should. It's about this bookseller and a woman who takes a shop opposite him, and they are both very thrifty. I don't know whether they are going to pair up or whether it will end in tears.'

I sat on the edge of the bed. 'It was all a bit spur of the moment last night, and to do with work, that's why I didn't ask you to see *HMS Pinafore*.

She sighed. 'I didn't like to think of you going alone. Marcus is up on an investigation isn't he?'

'Yes, but we haven't got back together, not in the going out way.'

'I thought not. Are you sure you're doing the right thing in turning him down?'

'Yes.'

'And it's not out of loyalty to Gerald, because I'm sure Gerald would want you to be happy.'

'I am happy. Don't worry. Everything is fine.'

Twenty-Four

When Mrs Shackleton came out from seeing the chief inspector, she asked Sykes to walk up the town with her. She wanted to talk to him about something, she said, but not in the hotel. Straight away, he knew she was up to something.

Like a couple of conspirators, the two of them occupied a corner table in Schofields café.

She said, 'Mr Lansbury on St Paul's Street is the solicitor Deirdre Fitzpatrick has dealings with. His office is where I lost sight of her on that day.'

Jim Sykes stirred his tea, again. 'But he has been interviewed by Sergeant Wilson.'

Mrs Shackleton had that stare-you-out look in her eye. 'Lansbury admitted to Wilson that he spoke to a woman answering Deirdre Fitzpatrick's description.'

'Yes, but that was weeks ago! He said she came to see him to enquire about a separation from her husband. It had gone no further than a brief interview. He made a few notes but when she did not return, he disposed of them.'

'He is lying because what he has done could see him in hot water. He made the arrangement. Now he is afraid.'

Sykes sipped his tea. What did she have in mind? Well he had no intention of asking. Let her come out with it.

She did.

'This is where you come in, Mr Sykes. I want you to visit Mr Lansbury, in the guise of a husband seeking a divorce. Wave money at him. Flush him out. He may be our only link to Deirdre Fitzpatrick.'

Sykes felt himself being manoeuvred into a corner. 'I'm acting as a special constable. I can't go chasing about off my own bat.'

'Marcus agrees with me. You could do it. Not as a special constable.'

'But I'm sworn in.'

'Then you can be sworn out for as long as it takes.'

This was not fair. Sykes had wondered what Mrs Shackleton and the chief had been talking about so furtively. He might have known that there was something not quite pukka, and that the dirty work would fall to him. He waited, not wanting to encourage her.

'Listen, Mr Sykes, Wilson told Marcus that the solicitor seemed afraid. That could be because he is lying, or he may be being blackmailed. There is more going on than we have found out. We have to use any means to get to the bottom of this. Runcie is dead. Diamond is dead. Who will be next? Deirdre Fitzpatrick could prove most inconvenient to someone, and we don't know who.'

Sykes did not like the 'we' in the 'We have to use any means'. He would still have to live here when the Scotland Yard men hightailed it back to London.

'Why me?'

'Because you will be good. You will be convincing.'

There was no way out. Sykes took a gulp of tea. 'What would I have to do?'

'We'll come up with a plausible story. You must persuade Lansbury to arrange a co-respondent for you.'

'You mean Deirdre Fitzpatrick?'

'It doesn't matter whether it is her or not. If Lansbury does it, we'll know he's lying. If it is her, then perhaps we can start to make some headway. She wouldn't have flown without reason, without leaving some trace. '

Sykes knew when he was outnumbered. 'All right. It looks as if you've volunteered me. I'll do my best.'

Mrs Shackleton turned to practicalities, what his story would be, how he would dress. 'Lansbury won't make such arrangements for nothing. You'll need money.'

She had money, in a brown envelope. Sykes looked at it. He knew that it came from a Scotland Yard petty cash fund. No doubt the numbers on the notes had been recorded.

'Lansbury will smell a rat, with me turning up so soon after Wilson interviewed him.'

'No. That's exactly why we have to make a move soon. He won't expect it.'

'Why am I going to him and not to some other solicitor? He'll ask how I got to know about him.'

'He was recommended to you before, by a gentleman on the Chamber of Commerce committee, Mr Gledhill, chairman of Leodis Insurance Company.'

'What if he checks with Mr Gledhill?'

'Mr Gledhill spends every August on Lake Garda.'

'It's September.'

'He travels slowly.'

She had an answer for everything.

*

213

The dapper, bespectacled man who climbed the stairs to Lansbury's solicitor's office carried a silver-topped cane. He wore grey flannels, a flamboyant plum waistcoat, blazer, and cravat. Sykes almost had second thoughts about the cravat. Best not overdo it. But then, a man who did not overdo it would never contemplate allowing his wife to divorce him.

Sykes had once known a man called Paul Sheridan who was a devil of a man for the ladies, and that was the name he assumed.

Mr Lansbury, a diminutive man whose bald pate gave off a healthy glow, rose to shake Sykes's hand, and to introduce himself. 'Please be seated, Mr Sheridan.'

He indicated a straight-back chair, its ample green leather upholstery surrounded by brass tacks. Sykes sat down. His mouth felt dry.

'Now what can we do for you?' Lansbury smiled pleasantly in his best putting-the-client-at-ease manner.

Sykes cleared his throat.

'Would you like a glass of water?' Lansbury asked.

'No, no it's all right.' Sykes took a deep breath. 'I'm very sorry to say that my wife and I have come to a parting of the ways.' He had practised this with Mrs Shackleton, but now had difficulty remembering what came next. The words 'my wife', conjured up Rosie. She would not like this one bit, even though he was not at this moment Jim Sykes and was not, when he said 'my wife', meaning Rosie. 'She tells me that these days a married couple do not have to stay together for life.'

'Perhaps I should take your address first, Mr Sheridan, and a few details.' Mr Lansbury picked up his pen.

This part was not hard. Paul Sheridan, recently having

returned to Yorkshire from Brighton, was lodging with an old friend in Chapeltown. His occupation was engineer. His wife, Isabella, a flighty Brighton belle, had a new love in her life. Out of courtesy, Paul Sheridan had agreed to give her grounds for divorce.

'And what brought you to me?' Mr Lansbury enquired softly.

Good question, thought Sykes. Thank you, Mrs Shackleton. 'The friend who is kindly putting me up gave me a couple of names that he had gleaned from a fellow golfer, a chap in insurance who knows you from the Chamber of Commerce, Mr Gledhall I believe.'

'Gledhill?'

'Yes, that's it. Gledhill. To be honest,' Sykes said sheepishly, 'you were not the first person I contacted, but the first who could fit me in at such short notice. My wife and I have decided that we both wish to make a fresh start, you see, and the sooner this matter can be put into motion, the better.'

He gazed into the pale blue eyes of the man across the desk, hoping that Mr Lansbury would not consider his dress outlandish for an engineer. Mrs Shackleton had suggested that Sykes present himself as some sort of Bohemian literary man. Sykes had agreed, but changed his occupation at the last moment, in case the solicitor was exceedingly well read. Though the only books Sykes saw in the room were legal tomes in a glass-fronted bookcase.

The solicitor proceeded cautiously. He put down his pen and leaned back in his chair.

'Are you and your wife certain that this is not some temporary falling out that can be patched up?'

Sykes looked suitably regretful. 'We are quite certain.

She wants to marry again, though I don't believe I ever shall,' he added sadly.

The solicitor's hand hovered over his pen. 'In that case, let us consider how we should proceed. Have you given the matter thought?'

'I tried not to, but I had a letter from her yesterday and well ...'

'May I see it?'

Sykes handed the letter to him, hoping the man would not expect to look at the envelope or postmark.

The solicitor read the letter, and shook his head sadly. 'A divorce can be a most expensive business. A lot of preliminary work must be undertaken, contacting counsel and so on. I do usually ask for a payment in advance.'

'Of course.' Sykes brought out his fat wallet. 'My wife tells me that if I give her grounds, it should be adultery.'

'She has done her homework. It is very gentlemanly of you to comply with her wishes.'

Sykes warmed to his part. 'Her friend is a lively sort of chap, and not short of a bob or two. Unlike me, he does not have to earn his living and so is able to squire Bella about to amusements, dancing and so on.'

'That is sometimes the way,' the solicitor said sagely, stroking his chin. 'You will want to know what realms of finance we are speaking here. There will be additional costs. The matter will be dealt with in the Probate, Divorce and Admiralty Division and will require the services of a barrister.'

'Yes. My wife advised me that would be the case.'

Sykes took out a notebook. He had bought this specially. It was bound in leather and was the type of thing he imagined an engineer might favour. He made notes.

The solicitor talked pounds, shillings and pence. Sykes handed over the notes, counting them onto the desk.

Mr Lansbury wrote a receipt. 'You are unlikely to have your case heard in the current sessions. It may be next year.'

Sykes said, 'Oh that is all right. Only Bella wants to know that she can begin proceedings as soon as possible. She asks me for a hotel bill.'

'It may be better that you go to a seaside hotel. Would you manage to get away for a weekend by the sea?'

'Getting away would present no difficulty. Only … the thing is … How to put this delicately? My wife is very good at making friends with the opposite sex, the opposite sex to her I mean. I am not, unfortunately. I never thought I should have to start again in that regard.'

Mr Lansbury gave a sorrowful look, accompanied by a sigh. 'Indeed. You have my sympathy. But I may be able to help you.'

Sykes felt his shoulders stiffen. Would he meet Deirdre Fitzpatrick at some sleazy seaside hotel?

'Does it have to be the seaside?'

'My dear chap, I'm not asking you to swim the channel in December, I'm thinking of a night or two in Scarborough.' Mr Lansbury smiled, waiting for his remark to lighten the proceedings and draw a response from his client.

Sykes did his best to muster a small smile. He thought, I know why you choose Scarborough. Too many adulterous liaisons in one town could begin to look suspicious. If it was to be done, let it be quickly. 'Once I take up my appointment my time will be devoted to my work, so the sooner the better.'

The solicitor opened his diary. 'Could you be at an appointed place on Friday evening?'

'Yes.'

'Excellent! By this time tomorrow, I shall send you a message. Or perhaps you would prefer to call back and see me?'

'A message will be satisfactory. Thank you.'

That was probably the wrong answer, Sykes thought. He could have come back with a CID man and nipped this in the bud. Too late.

They shook hands.

And now Mr Lansbury would have to communicate with the lady in question.

Sykes left the building. He went to the boy who had set himself up to polish shoes at the entrance to the alley, and ignored the other boy who cycled by.

The boy began to polish Sykes's shoes. 'Keep your eyes open, Andy. If a messenger comes from this building, you or your pal follow him, depending whether he's on foot or bicycle.'

'What about the shoe cleaning stuff?'

'If you follow on foot, ask your pal to take care of the shoe-shining. One of you must follow any messenger and make a note of where he goes.'

The boy nodded.

When his shoes were well and truly polished, Sykes gave the boy a sixpence.

A sudden thought struck Sykes. Perhaps Mr Lansbury had a whole stable of 'other women' ready to play the adulteress. The thought made him shudder. Surely there wouldn't be the call for this sort of malarkey in Yorkshire. Folk had more sense than to rush to the divorce courts.

As he walked back toward the Metropole, Sykes's elation at accomplishing his task swiftly gave way to melancholy. In the suite given over to the murder investigation, Sykes and his fellow minions occupied the room that would have been the bedroom. He undid his cravat, and ignored the raised eyebrows of the sergeant as he picked up the pen to note his visit to Mr Lansbury in the log book.

The sergeant moved the book out of reach. 'No need for that, Mr Sykes. I believe you just made a private visit.'

Twenty-Five

Fitzpatrick's telegram was waiting for me when I arrived home.

COME URGENTLY STOP HAVE NEWS
FITZPATRICK

I wasted no time in driving to Kirkstall. Fitzpatrick must have been looking out of the window because he opened the door on my first knock.

The sight of him shocked me; his face was grey with grief, hair uncombed. His left foot was bandaged to three times its normal size. He supported himself with one crutch, and a hand on the wall. Hobbling aside, he moved from the door to make room for me to step inside.

'I came as soon as I got your message.'

He took hold of a second crutch, propelled himself across the room and lowered himself gingerly into a chair, waving a crutch at the opposite chair.

'I've not much experience of sending telegrams. That "stop" was unnecessary. You would have understood if I'd said, Come urgently have news.'

'Yes.'

He nodded, as if he had satisfied himself on an important point. 'They charge by the word.'

I sat down. 'What have you done to your foot?'

'I'm no good any more. I can't hold myself together.'

'What happened?'

'I was tidying at work. I dropped a case of type on my foot. I do nothing right. Had to be helped to the dispensary. It's my concentration. I've lost it.'

'That's terrible. As if you don't have enough to worry about.'

In spite of his injury, the room was immaculate. A low fire burned in the grate. Holy figures gazed from their framed position on the wall, looking with compassion at Fitzpatrick and wisely ignoring me.

I took his telegram from my pocket and unfolded it. 'What is the news?'

He stared at the telegram. 'You think Brown at the counter would have told me I didn't need that "stop". Nobody ever tries to save you a penny.'

'Don't worry about it, Mr Fitzpatrick. The "stop" makes a telegram a telegram. It imparts urgency.'

The word urgency struck a chord. He said, 'Deirdre has been here. She's taken her rosary and her lucky pixie.'

'Are you sure she didn't have them with her?'

'No. They were on her dressing table yesterday.'

'Well that's a relief. She's safe and well. Did she take anything else? Any clothing?'

'Her grey coat has gone, a black skirt and two blouses.'

'When do you think she was here?'

'I waited in yesterday, and then went off for the night shift. I have to keep working.'

'Of course you do.'

'I left home at five yesterday evening. It was about three o'clock this morning when I dropped the case of type on my foot.' He stared down at his foot as if it were far away, and belonged to someone else.

'Is it very painful?'

'I don't mind if it is. It's nothing. What's a pain?'

We contemplated this immense question for a moment. 'And what time did you get home?'

'I was in the infirmary until after five. They know how to keep you waiting, so I would have been home by six or half past. I didn't know she'd been. I was that done in, I crawled up to bed, and slept for a few hours. And then I saw that the rosary was gone ...'

'And the pixie.'

'Yes.'

He looked suddenly forlorn, and quite weak. 'Can I get you anything, Mr Fitzpatrick? Cup of tea? Slice of bread and butter?'

He shook his head.

'How are you coping?'

'I'm framing well enough. I know I've to keep my strength up.'

'Mr Fitzpatrick, might any of your neighbours have seen your wife? Is there anyone she is close to?'

'She keeps to herself. We don't like getting over-familiar. You never know where it might lead. All I know is that she hadn't been home when I left for work yesterday evening, and she had been back when I woke up.' He ran his fingers through his hair. 'The question is, did she come in the middle of the night, or while I was sleeping?

Surely she'd have stopped if she looked in on me and saw I had a poorly foot.'

'Yes, I'm sure you're right. Tell me, when you went to the post office to send me the telegram, did you inform the police that she has been home?'

He shook his head. 'No. I want you to find her. The police are useless. First they showed barely an interest. Said they were doing what they could, but short of manpower. Then overnight it was as if they were hunting a criminal. They were here taking fingerprints. How will fingerprints help to find her?'

'You said some of her clothing is gone. May I look in her room?'

He nodded glumly.

'At least now we have something to go on. If you are right about her coming back last night, or early this morning, we know that she is safe, and has some plan.'

I escaped to the stairs and into the front bedroom. Two summer dresses hung in the wardrobe, alongside a wool skirt and a winter coat. I opened the dresser drawers releasing the smell of mothballs. There was a paisley print home-made blouse, a hand-knitted jumper and cardigan. Was the neat folding Fitzpatrick's doing, I wondered. The washstand held towels, a face cloth, along with liniment, aspirins, a curved tortoiseshell comb, an expensive tablet of soap and various odds and ends.

When did you take your underwear and stockings, Deirdre, and your nightdress?

Slowly, I went down the stairs.

His look was hopeful, as though I may have divined some crucial information from the whitewashed walls.

'Is there an overnight bag missing? You'll have noticed that there is no nightdress, underwear or stockings in her room.'

His mouth opened. 'No. I did not open that drawer, where she keeps her . . .' He eased himself up, grabbing the crutches, hobbling towards the cellar head.

'Don't risk that, Mr Fitzpatrick. What is it you have thought of?'

'Her shopping basket and bag. They should be on the slab in the cellar. That's where she keeps them, so as not to untidy this room, you see. They were there on Sunday, when I took the ham back into the cellar.'

'Do you have a light in the cellar?'

'No. Take the candle from the mantelshelf.'

I lit the candle with a taper from the jar.

The chill came instantly as I opened the door to the cellar. I felt a ripple of horror as I descended. What if Fitzpatrick had killed her, and all this concern was an elaborate charade? Yet the cellar had no smell of blood or fear, only coal, and damp. Everything was in order – the cold press, the dolly tub, brooms and mops. There was an overnight bag, an unlocked trunk that contained a valise, but no shopping basket.

When I came back upstairs, I said, 'No shopping basket. So it looks as if she took her few things and carried them in a basket. She probably wore the coat.'

'Where has she gone?' he wailed.

'That's what we shall find out. Think carefully. Tell me everywhere she has been where she may go again: friends, family, anywhere at all.'

He closed his eyes. 'That's just it. I know only what she tells me. Mostly, she goes back to where she came from, to those streets around the Bank, Cotton Street, where her mother lived, Flax Street, where she has a school friend who worked with her at the shoe factory before we married, Holdforth Square where she visits Eddie's mother, so she says.'

'Who else lives in the house on Cotton Street, Deirdre's mother's house?'

'The aunts, Mary and Brenda. They don't like me any more than her mother did.'

I began to suspect plots. Perhaps Deirdre's brother would take her back to America. His having come to me with Fitzpatrick and Deirdre's lovesick childhood sweetheart Eddie was nothing but a smokescreen. 'Anywhere else you can think of? Somewhere she may have been happy and wanted to return to.'

'We had our honeymoon in Scarborough. She loved the sea.'

'Where did you stay?'

'In a boarding house on the front, with a Mrs Redhead. Very smart woman.'

I would pass on that information, but the fact that Deirdre was still in this area three days after she had been last seen, made me think she was closer to home. 'I'll make enquiries,' I said lamely, 'but I wonder if she is somewhere nearby, with some friend in Kirkstall she hasn't mentioned, or an old school friend or a former workmate, someone who would keep her confidence.'

'If she was on the Bank people would know. You can't keep secrets there.' He suddenly became animated. 'You've hit it. She must go to Cotton Street tonight.'

'Why tonight?'

'It's her mother's wake. Deirdre can't not be there.

My brother-in-law made the funeral arrangements. Her mother has been brought home, and later she'll be taken into church. The Requiem Mass will be tomorrow.'

'Then we should go. You're right.'

His animation fled as quickly as it had come. 'Her people don't like me. They won't want me there.'

'But you're the son-in-law. You were getting on famously with Deirdre. You went with her to the nursing home.'

'How can I get there, like this?'

'Get your coat, Mr Fitzpatrick. We're going to the wake.'

He looked at me in alarm, as though I had made a lewd suggestion. 'How will I explain you? My wife gone, and me turning up with a strange woman?'

'Tell the truth. Introduce me. Say I am helping you to look for Deirdre.'

'You're right. I want her to know . . . if she is there . . . or even if she isn't and somebody knows where she is, they can tittle-tattle back to her that I came.' Fitzpatrick struggled to his feet. He nodded at the jacket on the hook behind the door. 'Do you mind?'

I helped him on with his jacket.

He balanced on one crutch, switching it from left to right. 'You're right. What do appearances matter where Deirdre is concerned? I can't miss the wake. And I mustn't go empty-handed, being the son-in-law.'

'I have never been to a wake, Mr Fitzpatrick. You must tell me what to expect.'

'I must buy a bottle of whisky. You'll stop at the outsales?'

'Yes of course.'

'Pass me that tin will you?' He nodded at a toffee tin on the mantelpiece.

When I placed it on the table, he took off the lid and tipped out coins, including a guinea. He began to shake. His grey face crumpled.

'She hasn't taken a penny. She's been back but she's left pay for the milk, coal, insurance, housekeeping. How will she manage?'

'Never mind that now. Is there enough for what you need?'

Given I was the one with two good feet who must buy the whisky, I stopped at the Lloyds Arms where I am known, and would not be stared at.

I gave Fitzpatrick the bottle to nurse.

As we came closer to the Bank, he veered between optimism, convincing himself that Deirdre would be at her mother's to receive condolences, and pessimism, that she wandered lost on some moor or in a wood, with only a rosary and a lucky pixie in her pocket.

As I drove, I asked Fitzpatrick, 'Tell me a little more about who shares the house and who might be able to help us.'

'The two spinster aunts, Mary and Brenda, as I mentioned, and there's the old uncle, Jimmy, who chooses to confine himself to the cellar when he's not out and about on his rounds or attending funerals. You'll recognise him from his similarity to a picture-book gnome.'

'Who is most likely to have useful information?'

'They are. The aunts. And Deirdre has a friend she was at school with, and worked with at the shoe factory on East Street.'

'What's her name?'

'Rita O'Neil. She was our bridesmaid, married to one of the fellows from the factory. You won't miss her if she's there. She takes over any room she enters. You'll know her by her waving ginger hair.'

On Marsh Lane, a train rattled overhead, belching steam and smoke. Everything about these streets looked dull, grey and black.

As the motor bumped across the cobbles, half a dozen thin, dirty children looked up from their listless games of dipping fingers into summer-warmed gas tar and chalking on the pavement with a stone. Two of them were barefoot, all of them poorly dressed. As one, they jumped to their feet and ran after the motor.

When the children saw at which house we drew up, they kept a respectful distance. I parked behind Anthony Hartigan's hired Rolls-Royce. Perhaps never in its history had Cotton Street been host to two motor cars at once.

Fitzpatrick exited awkwardly from the vehicle, holding onto the bonnet while I passed his crutches and the bottle of whisky.

A group of men stood about outside the house, by the window, smoking. Behind them, the curtains were drawn.

Fitzpatrick swung towards the door. He acknowledged someone, with a nod and a murmur of his name, Jimmy. Here then was the ancient gnome, his moth-eaten cap worn at a jaunty angle. He leaned against the window sill, his gaunt cheeks sucked in as he drew on a clay pipe.

I followed Fitzpatrick into the downstairs room, which hushed as we entered. Chairs and buffets must have been brought in by neighbours. There was barely an inch of unoccupied floor space. As we entered, two women stood to leave. I turned sideways to let them pass, and they acknowledged me with nods as they left.

Fitzpatrick set the whisky down on the table. Anthony had been standing with his back to the fire. He leaned across to shake Fitzpatrick's hand, and at the same time gave me a friendly nod. 'Mrs Shackleton, thank you for coming.'

'My condolences,' I said to him and to anyone else who wanted to accept them.

Fitzpatrick turned to the woman nearest the fire. 'I'm sorry for your loss, Aunt Mary. Mona did her best in life, and that's a fact.'

I glanced about the room, wearing my amiable yet slightly sorrowful visitor look. The mirror above the fireplace was turned to the wall. The shelf held a crucifix, statues and little black-edged cards with pictures of saints.

The hum of conversation resumed.

Fitzpatrick was explaining to Aunt Mary how he injured his foot.

A woman seated by the table said, 'You'll have a cup of tea.'

'She will of course,' Hartigan said. 'And Cyril, you'll take a drink. What was it you said you did to your foot?'

While Fitzpatrick explained his accident again, I watched the woman with tight ginger ringlets pour tea. She was about Deirdre's age, and I took a guess. 'You're Rita, a friend of Deirdre's?'

'I am. Or that is to say we were good friends but some people don't like a woman to keep up with old friends.' She stared accusingly at Fitzpatrick.

Fitzpatrick ignored her. To the room in general, he said, 'This is Mrs Shackleton, a family friend.'

He had lost the nerve to introduce me as the person helping him to find his wife.

Rita said, 'Well I've never heard of you.'

There seemed to be no opportunity to ask had anyone seen Deirdre. She simply was not mentioned.

Fitzpatrick turned to me. 'Will you come upstairs, Mrs Shackleton?'

Rita gave the slightest of titters.

Fitzpatrick let me go first and I was glad of that as I did not relish the thought of his toppling backwards down the narrow stone staircase and crushing me to a pulp. But after the first step, he gave up. 'Will you carry up these blessed crutches? I'll manage best under my own steam. I'm used to being on my knees.'

I carried the crutches up the stairs, and then turned to see Fitzpatrick making rapid progress on hands and knees.

Once upright again, Fitzpatrick dipped his fingers in a small font of holy water that was nailed to the wall where in a different house there may have been a light switch. The font was attached to the base of a metal crucifix, about six inches long, the tiny thorn-crowned figure looking sadly down at the water below his feet.

The bedroom window was open a little but gave no breeze. A sheet had been rigged to stretch from the posts at the bed head to its foot, providing a canopy. Candles flickered on the mantelpiece and washstand. I hung back as Fitzpatrick adjusted his crutches and approached the bed, stepping round three women who knelt at the bedside, telling their beads with a low murmur, as if chanting spells.

Fitzpatrick touched the dead woman's forehead. I brought myself to look at Deirdre's mother for the first and last time. Mrs Hartigan's skin had a parchment-like quality, with many small lines, like cracks in old paper. There was a sharpness to her features and the severely parted grey hair and closed, deep set eyes made her look already like an effigy on a tomb.

Fitzpatrick stepped back. 'Say goodbye,' he ordered.

I hesitated. It felt strange to be paying respects to a woman I had not known, and too intrusive to touch her, as Fitzpatrick had. But having come into the room, I could do no other than approach, ignoring the kneeling women on my right.

I almost touched her forehead, sufficiently close to feel a cold tingle in my fingers. This would get me nowhere. Where is your daughter? I asked silently.

You'll be the last to know, came the dead woman's wordless reply.

Fitzpatrick disconcerted the praying women by awkwardly using his crutches as an aid to lowering himself to his knees. He pulled beads from his pocket to join in.

I glanced around the room. There was a flowered dress on the back of the door, carefully placed on a hanger. It did not belong to the dead woman, or the aunts. It was a short-sleeved summer frock. How much time did Deirdre spend here? I wondered. And was she here now? Perhaps she had dashed to hide in the cellar when someone said, Your husband is coming.

It was then that I noticed Eddie in the corner of the room, looking every inch the boxer, dazed from life's punches but waiting to spring into the ring. One look at his unhappy face told me that Deirdre was not here.

When the rosary came to an end, two of the women stood up nimbly enough and after kissing the dead woman's forehead, and touching her cheek and hands, they left. The remaining woman then pushed herself to her feet, using the edge of the bed. Fitzpatrick, forgetting his own infirmity, moved to help her, saying, 'Sorry for your loss, Aunt Brenda. She looks at peace. Her troubles are over.' He then spoke to the dead woman. 'Mona, your life was hard but you saw your son at the last. You died a contented woman.'

Brenda was not unlike her sister Mary, but her hair was still black, and her bright eyes looked altogether more intelligent, and more wary. 'Is that so? Is that so indeed, or did himself downstairs, turning up in the image of his father, push you over the edge altogether, Mona? That and the rattling of the cart they call an ambulance, bumping her over the cobbles all the way to Roundhay until the poor soul's insides must have been shook about and her very bones worked loose.'

Fitzpatrick adjusted his crutches. 'That nursing home was a good clean place,' he protested mildly. 'And sure isn't the matron's family from Kilkenny? Deirdre did what she thought best.'

'I don't hold Deirdre to blame. But where is she?'

Fitzpatrick looked uncomfortable. 'Here's the point. I'm at a loss to know where she could be and I have this lady here helping me to find her.'

'Aye well you're looking in the wrong place. No one has seen her here.'

A heavy silence filled the room. Through the open window came the voices of the men, talking quietly in the street below.

'Do you hear that, Mona?' the aunt addressed the dead woman. 'Your precious son-in-law does not know where your daughter is.' She turned to him. 'What have you done to the lass?'

'I've done nothing. For mercy's sake, Brenda, I'm doing my best to find her. You talk as if it's my fault.'

She stared at him, and then spoke to Mona again. 'Will you listen to the man's excuses? It's not his fault that he can't find his wife.'

I caught Fitzpatrick's eye, to let him know that he must not stand here arguing.

He took the hint and turned to go.

In the doorway, he put down his crutches and lowered himself onto his bottom to descend the stairs.

I offered the aunt my condolences. Eddie sat still in the corner, watching and listening.

When Fitzpatrick had gone, I said to the aunt, 'Last year, Deirdre was in a spot of bother, a misunderstanding in one of the town shops. My partner helped her then and I want to help her now. She came here all the time. She came here when she didn't come here, if you catch my meaning. If there's anything at all you can say that will help me find her, please don't keep it to yourself. I would like to talk to her for just five minutes.'

For a moment, I thought Brenda was about to tell me something.

Eddie cleared his throat.

Brenda walked to the door, saying to me as she left, 'May God forgive you, casting aspersions on the girl in front of her dead mother.'

When she had gone, Eddie said, 'Deirdre keeps her fancy clothes in a trunk under the bed.'

'Has she taken anything?'

'Not a thing.'

Something else was troubling him. I waited, but he did not speak again.

Footsteps on the stairs alerted me to Mona Hartigan's next round of visitors. When they had entered, I left the room and slowly picked my way downstairs.

As I looked into the crowded room, I noticed that even the younger women were all wearing dark clothing. I was wearing light blue, wrongly dressed, a Protestant in a Catholic world.

I leaned over to Deirdre's friend. 'Thank you for the tea, Rita.' I saw from her face that it was no use asking her about Deirdre. If she knew anything, she would go to the stake rather than tell me.

Fitzpatrick was no longer in the room. I said goodnight to the aunts and received a cold, 'Thank you for coming,' from Mary.

Outside, Fitzpatrick leaned against the wall, in the crowd of men. 'Oh, Mrs Shackleton . . .' He reached out and put down a glass on the window sill, moving as if to come towards me, but one of his crutches fell to the pavement. The group of men parted, so that we could speak. 'Thank you for your kindness in fetching me. My brother-in-law will give me a lift home. We're seeing Mrs Hartigan into the church.'

I nodded. 'Then I'll say goodnight.'

'Goodnight.'

Anthony Hartigan's sweet baby face wore a solicitous look. 'Let me see you to your motor.'

This was ridiculous as my car was just a couple of feet away, but he walked beside me.

He took my hand, and looked at me, his bright blue

eyes full of sorrow. 'Thank you for coming. Here I am, home to see my ma, and this . . .'

'A sad occasion.' I climbed into the car.

He leaned towards me and said, quietly, 'Have you found anything out?'

'Not yet, but I will.'

'And only a few days ago, we were at the races and we both backed a winner.'

'Yes,' I said. 'Sometimes outsiders can be surprising.'

The street had suddenly come to life. A man pushed a cart that held a coffin. From another direction came men and women in black, priests and nuns, here to take Mrs Hartigan to the church. Hartigan went to meet them.

Eddie appeared as I was about to drive away. He leaned into the motor and breathed whisky into my face. 'Your name is Mrs Shackleton.'

'Yes.' The poor man must be more punch drunk than I had imagined.

'And you are a war widow.'

'I am.'

'Was your husband in the army?'

'He was a captain in the medical corps.'

He nodded. 'I saw his photograph. God bless you. I can't stop now. I have a coffin to carry.'

I waited until the coffin had been carried into the house, hearing the calls to Watch out, Lend a hand, Mind the door.

Twenty-Six

Anthony Hartigan may have arrived a little too late to give ease to his mother's time on earth, but her send off could not be faulted.

I squeezed in at the back of the packed church, to the whiff of incense, not-so-clean humanity and the scent of lilies and roses. Through the crowds, I glimpsed the high altar, bedecked with blooms.

Marcus's sergeant, Wilson, stood a few feet away from me, hat in hand. We did not acknowledge each other, although he had asked me to take out my hanky if I spotted Deirdre Fitzpatrick. This was not the best of signals because it left me desperately wanting to wipe my nose.

The organ struck up a melancholy hymn with fine dramatic timing as the chief mourners walked into the church, headed by Anthony, the aunts, old Jimmy with his penknife knees, and Fitzpatrick, crutches tapping out a tune on the tiled floor, his bandaged foot looking bigger than ever. No Deirdre.

After the endless service, the mysterious Latin, and the touching pieties from the pulpit, the coffin was carried out. Mourners followed. Those of us who were simply there to pay respects, or to conduct an investigation, politely hung back, watching as people with blood ties and long-standing connections left the church, headed by Anthony Hartigan, who turned to acknowledge the nods, outstretched hands and whispered words. Priests and nuns followed close behind.

Being close to the door, I slid out and watched from the church steps.

Four patient, black-plumed horses waited while the bier was placed on the hearse, ready for the perilous trot along the cobbled streets. The chief mourners were helped into two waiting carriages.

As the carriages set off, some of the congregation stayed to watch, others slipped away, but many began to walk behind in procession.

Marcus's sergeant stood behind me. He prodded me in the back. I ignored this invitation to ride in the car that had been parked nearby for the purpose of taking us to the cemetery. If a thing is worth doing, do it properly. I fell in behind the procession, snaking out of the Bank, towards York Road, keeping clear of the plain-clothes men who stuck out like sore thumbs.

All the way along the route, men and women stood respectfully with bowed heads while the funeral passed, moving only to cross themselves, and the men to remove their hats. After what seemed an endless trek, the cortege passed through the gates of Killingbeck Cemetery.

Proceedings had a brisk, practised quality. I manoeuvred my way around the crowd so that I would have a view of the chief mourners. Behind me, a woman sniffled. A voice with an Irish lilt whispered to comfort her, 'Save your sniffles, Bridie. Isn't she in a better place? And there'll be no shortage of masses said.'

'True enough. I know there's an arrangement for perpetual participation in the Capuchin Seraphic Masses.'

We who were on the edge did not have to observe the same high degree of solemnity as those closer to the graveside. Bridie said, 'Well there you are. Sure with that number of nuns and priests in the family she won't be spending half eternity in Purgatory.'

Time stands still at a funeral, each instant packed with centuries of other similar moments when emotion swells and it is too soon to say goodbye. Time also races, and that is something I can never understand, as if the earth spins faster, determined to move on to whatever comes next. And here's something that always brings me close to tears at a funeral. I think that it might one day be Gerald's, and that I will find him, or his body. He will no longer be a soldier known only to God, he will be known again to me.

The throng of mourners by the graveside began to disperse, and still Deirdre Fitzpatrick was nowhere to be seen. Cyril Fitzpatrick blew his nose loudly.

He hobbled over to speak to me.

'Good morning, Mrs Shackleton. Thank you for coming'

'Good morning, Mr Fitzpatrick.'

He nodded, his lips tight. 'Poor Mona. Rest at last.' He shook his head sadly. 'There's so much I want to say to Deirdre, when I find her.'

'Let's hope there'll be news soon.'

'If she's not here, where could she be?' He shook his

head miserably. 'I was awake all night, hoping she would come, listening for her footsteps along the street.'

'Not everyone reacts to death in a way we might expect. Perhaps she has found a place to hide with her sorrow.'

The tip of his crutch dented the ground as he leaned on it. 'Deirdre came here with me shortly after we first met. My mother had died. She's buried over there, with Dad.' He waved a crutch towards the west wall of the cemetery. 'Deirdre was such a comfort to me then, and now I can't do the same for her.'

'She'll be back in her own good time.'

Now was not the moment to tell him that Marcus had arranged for her photograph to be sent to every police station in the West, North and East Riding, and that the Scarborough police had called on Mrs Redhead to see whether she was giving houseroom to a lady visitor.

'You'd think she would want to say goodbye to her brother. He'll be off back to New York soon. He has business to attend to.'

I guessed Mr Hartigan would need to be back on the other side of the Atlantic to arrange collection of his liquor from a Canadian port.

Said brother was now moving from the graveside. A small group of nuns came towards the grave. 'The Little Sisters,' Fitzpatrick said. 'How people on the Bank would have lived without them I don't know.' He gave one of his heartfelt sighs.

'Will you be going to the funeral breakfast?' I asked, knowing that Marcus wanted to question him again.

'I have to get back to work. I said it was a family funeral, but they won't put up with another day's absence.'

'How will you manage when you can't stand?'

'I shall manage. I . . .'

Fitzpatrick stopped. He stared at the Little Sisters, a faraway look in his eyes, and I guessed he must be remembering his own mother's funeral. Suddenly, he swung his crutch into action, saying, 'Excuse me, Mrs Shackleton.'

I watched him go, mourners considerately making way for him. When he stumbled, it was Eddie, Deirdre's childhood sweetheart, who put an arm around Fitzpatrick and supported him.

There was nothing more for me to do here, but still I lingered, hoping that Deirdre might appear from behind a tree and make her solitary way to her mother's resting place before it was filled in by the gravediggers.

I hoped that when everyone else had gone, she would be here.

I walked slowly along the path towards the chapel. A tram would take me back to town.

'Kate!' Marcus walked towards me. He was frowning. 'Have you seen Cyril Fitzpatrick?'

'He's gone. He was going to work.'

'I had a man on the gate looking out for him.'

'Perhaps they missed him, or there may be another way out.'

'No. He would have gone through the main gates if he intended to go back to work. He must still be here.' Marcus heard a sound, turned, and saw a few people emerging from the chapel. 'That'll be where he is.'

Looking for the big man, he watched the black-clad mourners. Not one of them was tall enough to be Fitzpatrick.

'I have an idea where he might be.'

Marcus called, 'If you see him, bring him to me!' He walked towards the chapel.

I started out on the path where Fitzpatrick had indicated. The poor man was perhaps talking to his dead mother, and had lost all sense of time.

I picked my way across the ground. There is something about cemeteries. I have to look at names, dates, sentiments, as if I am reading a compelling book where every syllable counts. Fitzpatrick had pointed in this direction. I was looking for the name when I saw the man.

Fitzpatrick lay prone across a well-tended patch of earth. A stray dandelion kissed his ear. His crutches lay on the ground on either side of him.

Either grief had laid him low, or he had tripped.

'Mr Fitzpatrick? Are you all right?' Fitzpatrick did not reply. Something about his stillness alarmed me. I bobbed down and took his hand, felt his wrist for a pulse. There was none.

A trickle of blood stained the stone edging that surrounded the grave, where his head rested.

And there were the names on the stone: Aloysius Fitzpatrick, Mary Fitzpatrick, his wife.

Jimmy came hurrying from further up the cemetery. 'Bless us and save us. What's the matter with the man?'

'He's dead.'

'Bejesus. I was just up there praying and talking to my brother.'

*

241

The three of us sat in the cemetery chapel, Marcus, Jimmy, and me.

Marcus had examined the scene, and left a constable to stand over the covered body until the doctor arrived. The ground was dry, and marked only where the pressure of Fitzpatrick's crutches had made small round holes as he propelled himself to his parents' grave by the wall.

'You say you are Mona Hartigan's uncle by marriage?' Marcus asked.

Jimmy perched on the edge of the pew, holding his knees as if they were the most precious part of him. 'I don't just say it, I am. And never a sweeter woman walked God's earth. She married my brother's son and got the worst of the bargain. We Hartigans are saints or sinners, there's no one treads the middle line excepting myself, sir.'

'Why did you stay behind here when the rest of the mourners left for the funeral breakfast?'

'That's just what I was by way of doing. Only I had to go across to my brother's grave and tell him where we all stood now, and how I'd always said she shouldn't have married him.'

'Who shouldn't have married?'

'Why Mona of course. She should never have married my nephew. He led her a dance.'

'You were there a long time, Mr Hartigan.'

'The dead can't be doing with indecent haste.'

'When were you aware of Mr Fitzpatrick's presence?'

'Some sort of rustle made me look up and see him swinging across on them crutches of his. Then he was out of my sight on his knees. I could have heard a small cry, but my attention was on reciting a prayer.'

'Was there anyone else nearby?'

'Not a soul. They were all making their way to the gates and looking forward to the funeral breakfast, which I'll miss completely, unless it lasts longer than you might expect.'

'Did you approach Mr Fitzpatrick?'

'Not at all, not until the lady here was by him.'

'Mr Hartigan, do you know where we can find Mr Fitzpatrick's widow, your great niece, Deirdre?'

He shook his head sadly. 'If I knew where she was, I would go to her like a shot, the poor girl.'

'Does Mr Fitzpatrick have any other relations?'

'None that I know of.'

Marcus looked at me, inviting me to ask another question, but I could think of nothing more to say.

Old Jimmy said, 'I'm weak with the shock of it all. What more can you be wanting from an old man?'

'Thank you, Mr Hartigan. You can go. We'll want a statement from you and you may be asked to give evidence at the inquest.'

'Where will they take him?'

'You will be informed.'

Jimmy grabbed his cap, sniffed and said, 'Well I'll be off on the tram, sir, or I would be if I had the fare.'

Marcus put his hand in his pocket and gave Jimmy a coin.

When he had gone, Marcus said, 'An accident then, if Jimmy Hartigan is to be believed.'

'Poor Fitzpatrick, he was such an unfortunate man.'

We walked in silence out of the chapel. Marcus replaced his trilby. 'All we need now is to find out that Deirdre Fitzpatrick drowned herself. This is turning into a Greek tragedy.'

'Do you think she may be planning to go to America with her brother?'

'She's not going anywhere until I've spoken to her.'

Twenty-Seven

Sykes woke with a powerful idea. He wheeled the Clyno from his downstairs room, where everyone bumped into and tripped over it, and rode from Woodhouse onto Headingley Lane. He was not a man given to wild imaginings, yet could not shift the uneasy feeling that lodged in his guts. He wanted to know if Mrs Shackleton shared his unease.

Some deep instinct told him that Deirdre Fitzpatrick was in danger. The chief inspector and Mrs Shackleton, who were on the spot, might choose to believe that Fitzpatrick's death was an accident. Sykes, who had the disadvantage of not being at the cemetery, imagined the incident differently. In his mind's eye, he saw Fitzpatrick's crutches knocked from under him. When the man fell, big red hands – whose hands Sykes could not say – raised Fitzpatrick's head and gave it that extra crack against the gravestone edging. Were these the same hands that had tightened around Everett Runcie's neck?

Mrs Shackleton was still in her dressing gown. In the few minutes between his resolution and his arrival, Sykes decided against voicing his theory. Instead, he said that it would not hurt to check the house on Norman View.

'It's a feeling,' he said. 'If Mrs Fitzpatrick has heard about her husband's death, she may have gone home.'

To his surprise, Mrs Shackleton agreed. 'It won't hurt to look. Give me ten minutes and we'll go together.'

'Don't trouble yourself, Mrs Shackleton. I'll be very quick and you know she trusts me. If she's there I'll ask her to come back with me.'

'On the motorbike?'

'I thought I'd take the motor.'

'Stick to the Clyno, Mr Sykes. I've borrowed Dad's Morris and I want to be sparing of it.'

'What's the matter with the Jowett?'

'I'll tell you later.'

He would not be long, Sykes told her. He should be back by the time she had finished breakfast.

As he rode, Sykes fleshed out his theories. Anthony Hartigan planned to take his sister back with him to New York. There, she would be safely out of the way of saying what really happened in the hotel room. Hartigan claimed he did nothing more than join Runcie for a drink. Sykes did not believe him.

Hartigan could have told Deirdre to lie low, and meet him in Southampton. Perhaps he would send her on ahead, on a different sailing.

Sykes's theory went entirely against that of Marcus Charles who had put Hartigan in the clear. But Sykes knew well enough that the chief inspector wanted Hartigan out of the country, back where he came from, with a clean bill of health, so that the American authorities would have no cause to refuse him entry. The last thing Scotland Yard wanted was a clever English-born Irishman returning home after a course in New York gang warfare and criminal ways.

On Norman View, Sykes found the door key, under a stone by the roses. He let himself in. Somewhere there would be a clue, something that had been missed. He started in the cellar, where two traps held dead rodents.

Finding nothing of consequence in the cellar or the downstairs rooms, Sykes went upstairs. He opened the bedroom drawers and looked under the lining. He checked under the mattresses, turned back the rugs, lifted the jug and bowl on the washstand.

Mrs Shackleton had said Deirdre had taken some clothes, but some were left behind, including a winter coat. Why take an old black coat to New York when she might be dressed in furs?

He sat down on her bed, and thought where she may have gone. And then he heard a sound downstairs.

Sykes froze. How would he explain being here to some next of kin, or a workmate of Fitzpatrick's, or Deirdre herself?

All was quiet. He waited. After another few moments, he slowly descended the stairs.

No one.

A square white envelope lay on the mat. He had heard the click of the letterbox.

The letter was addressed to Cyril Fitzpatrick, in neat, childlike, writing.

It was from her.

Sykes told himself that his hands did not tremble as he picked it up. It was the envelope that fluttered of its own accord. He felt a wave of relief. She was alive. He should not open it, of course. The postmark was York, and the date, not one bit smudged, was yesterday, a late collection. He should not open a dead man's letter.

Sykes took a knife from the kitchen drawer. He slit the envelope. It was a short note, without endearments.

Fitz, I did all I could for Mam. It was Anthony's turn so I let him get on with the funeral. I could not face everyone saying sorry for your loss and outdoing themselves in the prayers department. I said my goodbyes on Sunday when Mam died and will visit her when she and I can be on our own.

Don't worry about me. We both did our best in our own ways but it cannot go on.

I am going to the n. sea and you will hear.

May God keep you close as I cannot any more.

Your wife, so they say,

Deirdre

Sykes read it again. One line in particular puzzled him. I am going to the North Sea and you will hear. What did she mean? This did not sound like the note of a woman about to flee the country. Unless North Sea meant just that, that she was leaving the country with no sense of geography. She would not leave for America via the North Sea.

He put the note in his pocket, left the house, and replaced the key, no further on than when he had arrived. Intending to show the note to Mrs Shackleton, before handing it in for entry in the murder log, he rode back to Headingley.

Mrs Shackleton was not alone. Rosie was waiting with her. The two of them sat at the kitchen table, drinking Camp coffee.

Sykes passed Deirdre's note to Mrs Shackleton who raised an eyebrow. Sykes knew he should not have gone haring off on his own.

'Where were you?' Rosie asked. 'Alfred's son cycled across from Chapeltown with a message. He said to tell you it was for Paul Sheridan and you'd understand. Paul Sheridan has to speak to his solicitor. That's the message.'

'I know what it's about,' Sykes said. 'It's work.' He shot a quick glance at Mrs Shackleton, hoping for moral support. She appeared to be totally engrossed, reading the label on the Camp Coffee bottle.

Rosie had a right to be put out. He had hardly been home for more than a couple of hours since this business started.

'What's it all about, Jim?'

Sykes took a deep breath. 'It's to do with acting as a special constable. I adopted a nom-de-plume. It's all hush-hush, Rosie, but I might have to go to Scarborough. We'll go back home now and I'll pick up my shaving gear.'

'Why? Are you stopping the night there?'

Two hours later, Sykes was on the train. His small valise in the luggage rack contained hairbrush, comb, shaving gear and a clean shirt.

When the train pulled into York, he hardly dared look about the platform in case he saw Deirdre Fitzpatrick.

Everything fitted. He was to meet the woman in the Peasholm café. She would be slim, in her twenties, wearing a green hat, and carrying a copy of *The Lady*. He imagined her dark hair, spilling down from her hat as it had when he looked at her through opera glasses when she sat in the stalls at the Grand Theatre.

When he alighted at Scarborough station, Sykes risked glancing at the other passengers, to see if Deirdre was among them. She was not. Suitcase in one hand, The Times in the other, he set off walking the mile or so to the café on the corner of Peasholm Gap and the Promenade.

When he saw her, he must put her at her ease, tell her not to be afraid, gain her confidence. He would explain that she must come back to Leeds with him, and answer a few questions. He tried to imagine her state of mind, having lived six years in a marriage where she did not share a room, never mind a bed, and something told him that it was not because Fitzpatrick snored. The compositor could read upside down and inside out; he worshipped his Roman Catholic God and virgins, but not his own good-looking wife. Sykes would have to tell her that Fitzpatrick was dead. She was free. The man must have something put by, an insurance policy. Deirdre would be her own woman. When would he tell her, now, or later?

There it was, the café on the corner.

Sykes checked his watch. Three minutes to go. Would she be early, late, or on time? With a minute to go, he entered the café, chose a table and sat down, laying his copy of The Times on the table.

The waitress delivered a tray of tea to people seated by the window. She returned to the counter. I'll wait, Sykes thought, and order when Deirdre comes. He had begun to call her Deirdre now, no longer Mrs Fitzpatrick.

At a minute past three, the clapper clanged as the door

opened. A tall slender woman in green entered, carrying a bulky tapestry bag and a copy of *The Lady*.

She crossed to his table, glanced at the newspaper, and said cheerfully, 'Hello. It's Mr Sheridan isn't it?'

Her long blonde fringe reached her narrow painted eyebrows.

Twenty-Eight

On Friday night, Marcus arrived at my front door just as I was opening it to go out.

'Marcus, what a surprise!'

'Sorry.' He looked subdued. 'I shouldn't have turned up out of the blue. Just needed to stop for a while and clear my head.'

I noticed his car and driver, parked in the street.

'So are you giving yourself an hour or two's rest and recreation?'

'Something like that.'

'Come round to the Chemic with me, if you don't mind having a drink with your special constable, Mr Sykes.'

He hesitated. I half expected that he would resist fraternising with the troops. He caught my look and laughed. 'Why not?'

'The air will do you good. Tell the driver it's on Johnston Street.'

If I needed confirmation from Marcus that he is never off duty, it came as we rounded the corner, into Headingley Lane. He asked me if I have ever been on one of Lord

Fotheringham's shoots. When I admitted that I had, years ago, he was full of questions about the guns, who I know and what I know.

In the Chemic, the four of us claimed a corner of the snug, Rosie and me on the bench by the wall, Sykes and Marcus on buffets. We played a couple of good-natured games of dominoes, against the background banter of darts players, before giving up seats to the regulars, a knot of pipe-smoking, snuff-taking old fellows who take the dominoes a lot more seriously than we do.

We moved to a table vacated by a group of young chaps who like to crawl pub to pub and were setting off for the White Rose.

In spite of winning at dominoes, Sykes was down in the mouth. It pleased me that Marcus took the trouble to reassure Sykes. Yes, he had failed to find his quarry in Scarborough. But he did give the lie to a certain gentleman's claim that he never would supply a co-respondent. The solicitor had some difficult questions to answer.

I felt sorry for Rosie who had cottoned on that her husband had been to Scarborough on a wild-goose chase, but knew no details. She sipped her port. 'I hope you got some sand between your toes, Jim.'

Sykes stubbed his cigarette into the full ashtray. 'The tide was in.'

'Well don't tell the kids you went, or they'll be asking for their stick of rock.'

Marcus hailed the waiter and ordered one more round as the landlord called last orders.

Rosie suddenly said, 'I do read the papers. I can guess what you're all not saying.'

Sykes gave her a warning nudge. 'Not the time or place, love.'

There was an awkward lull in the conversation. I obligingly changed the subject and talked about *HMS Pinafore*.

The landlord called, Time gentlemen please, and we finished our drinks. Marcus glanced at his watch. I guessed he would not be laying his head on a pillow anytime soon.

To calls of goodnight, we left the pub. Sykes and Rosie set off up Johnston Street. Marcus's driver had returned, and was parked outside.

Marcus said, 'Get in, Kate. We'll give you a ride home.'

But it was a pleasant evening, and I wanted some air after the fug of the pub. 'I'm going to walk.'

The streets were filling up as the pubs emptied. Walking among whistling, singing merrymakers might help my brain function. Something was niggling at me, something I had missed, and I could not quite bring the thought into focus. It was to do with Mrs Hartigan's funeral.

Marcus was not to be put off. 'I'll walk with you.'

He spoke to the driver, and then took my arm. 'The driver will follow us round. I wanted a word with you.'

'I thought so. You didn't expect Rosie to come along tonight?'

He laughed. 'No. I imagined it would be just you and Sykes. Shows what I know about how normal people spend their Friday nights.'

'She'd be discreet.'

'I'm sure. But there are things I can't say.'

'But what can you say to me? Or did you just come for the dominoes?'

Marcus slowed his pace. 'The solicitor, Lansbury, that was a good piece of work, Kate. I left him in a room at CID HQ, telling him I'd be back to continue questioning him. He admits that he supplied co-respondents for the Barnard and Runcie divorce cases. He could hardly wriggle out of that when presented with Sykes's evidence. But he denies knowing the whereabouts of Deirdre Fitzpatrick.'

'What is his attitude, to being found out?'

'He tried to bluff a little at first, but underneath he is afraid. It's left me wondering whether someone else had found out what he does and was blackmailing him.'

I thought for a moment. 'If he is being bled for money, then that would explain why he took the risk of providing a co-respondent to meet Mr Sykes in Scarborough.'

'I can't force the man to talk, but I may have to offer him a way out of his predicament, if he'll tell me the truth.'

'He must know how serious this is.'

In both directions, people were wending their way home. By the light of the streetlamp, an old man searched the gutter for tab ends.

'Have you had confirmation of Mr Fitzpatrick's cause of death?'

Marcus said, 'It was a deeply unfortunate accident. The pathologist found no indication of foul play. Mr Fitzpatrick tripped and hit his head.'

'I feel so sad about the poor man. It's somehow worse because I found him irritating, and that leaves one feeling guilty about not being kind.'

'I'm sure you were kind.'

'Don't be so sure.'

'Kate, you got to know Fitzpatrick.'

'A little.'

'Did he believe that the photographer, Leonard Diamond, was having an affair with his wife?'

His words made me slow my steps. 'I did not get that impression. Mr Fitzpatrick thought Len Diamond may have known something about Deirdre, where she went, whom she saw. Why do you ask?'

He sighed. 'This morning, I had a second pathology report on Diamond. He did not take his own life.'

'I knew it!'

'Yes you did, and you were right. The first examination of Diamond's body was too cursory, assumptions were made because of the way he was found. The local men interpreted the disarray in his rooms as his own doing while drunk. The first report seemed to bear that out. With hanging, the rope marks angle towards the knot, which was true in Mr Diamond's case. But the second pathologist noted horizontal marks, consistent with ligature strangulation.'

'That's horrible. Why didn't you tell me earlier?'

'Sorry. I don't want to give you nightmares. And I didn't want to tell you before we went in the Chemic. I know you liked the chap.'

'I admired him, or his work that is. He was an odd man, always a little reserved about himself, but a gossip about other people.'

A knot of drinkers, reluctant to go home, stood outside the Hyde Park. We manoeuvred our way around them.

'You think the perpetrator was looking for something?'

'I do. Kate, you knew Diamond. Can you think of

anything he could have had that someone would go to such lengths to find? Did find, for all we know.'

'Not money. He gambled, and drank, which I didn't know until my friend Mr Duffield told me.'

'Duffield?'

'He's the librarian on the local paper.'

We turned into my road. 'I'll gladly help if I can. I'm desperately sorry about Everett Runcie, naturally, having known him. But in a different way I find Diamond's death a small tragedy, a loss. He was talented. It seems such a waste.'

'There is a strong possibility that the same man killed both Runcie and Diamond. But what did those two victims have in common, that's what I need to know.'

'They were in the same place at the same time twice this month, once at the shoot, and again on Ebor Day.'

'And they have Deirdre Fitzpatrick in common, one taking her photograph and the other taking her to his bed.'

'Yes. With Fitzpatrick dead, the other man most closely connected to her is Hartigan. He is ruthless, Marcus. He ignored his mother and sister for years, and then used a visit to them as a cover to come here and buy liquor.'

Marcus sighed. 'He's a man I don't want let loose on our streets. If I thought he was involved in murder, I'd see him hang. But Hartigan turns out to have an impeccable alibi. After he had a drink with Runcie in the hotel bar, on Friday night, after the lovely Deirdre had retired, he extricated himself and embarked on an all-night card game with two other guests, respectable professional men. We have to rule him out.'

I thought about the incident in New York, when Hartigan

had allegedly shot a man on a street car and there were no witnesses. 'Can you be absolutely sure?'

'Yes. The waiter, Archie Heppelthwaite, would lie under oath for a half crown, but there were other diners who saw the woman go to her room before Hartigan joined Runcie for a drink. I've given Hartigan the all clear to leave for Southampton. The sooner he's back in the arms of the Statue of Liberty, the better I'll feel.'

We had reached my gate. Like some young courting couple, we lingered, but not for reasons of courtship.

Marcus said, 'I'm glad to be able to report to our American cousins that Anthony Hartigan visited his terminally ill mother, arranged her funeral, and returned in mourning to Southampton.'

'You won't report his dealings with the Scottish distiller?'

Marcus smiled. 'Last time I looked on our statute book, we had no laws against dealing in spirits. I have no intention of giving US immigration an excuse to deport him back here as an undesirable alien. New York made him, New York can have him back.'

I had rarely heard Marcus sound so downhearted. 'You don't think he'll try and take his sister back with him?'

'I'd say there's no love lost between them, and that she could be a nuisance to him, but I just don't know. I'm concerned that she knows something and could have come to harm. The longer this goes on, the harder it will be to get to the truth.'

I glanced down the street. Marcus's driver had turned the corner and was parked under the street lamp.

We said goodnight. Marcus insisted on waiting until I

had gone inside, as though some monster might leap from the shadows.

After the noise and smoke of the pub, and the busy streets, the empty house felt peaceful. Sookie came to greet me, asking to go out. I opened the back door. She spotted something and made a dash for it, perhaps a field mouse or a pipistrelle bat. I could not make out what she saw.

And then it came to me that Fitzpatrick had seen something, or more likely someone, when he parted from me in such haste at the cemetery yesterday.

The deckchair was still in the back garden. I sat down and stared into the darkness, remembering the scene at the funeral, and my conversation with Fitzpatrick. He had been telling me about Deirdre, and how she helped him after his mother's death.

I closed my eyes, to help me recall the scene. He had looked across at the nuns, the Little Sisters of the Poor, and said how good they had been to the people of the Bank. Speech suddenly deserted him, and he left me quickly, which was surprising given that I was the only person at the funeral who spoke to him. Then he had stumbled. Eddie, Deirdre's childhood sweetheart, had grabbed him, to keep him from falling. But now that I pictured the scene again, I wondered, was Eddie catching him, or stopping him? Where or who would Fitzpatrick have got to if Eddie had not intervened?

Had he swung himself on his crutches in the direction of the family, the neighbours, or the nuns?

Fitzpatrick had been looking at the nuns. All wore black, except one. One nun had worn a brown habit. The lenses of her spectacles had caught the sunlight. She must be some novitiate, I thought.

Across the wall, Sookie prowled. She gave one of her giveaway small meows of frustration. Some prey had eluded her.

And then the wild thought came, and those are always the best thoughts though sometimes far too wild to be true. The nun in brown was Deirdre, with a pair of spectacles to aid her disguise. Eddie had recognised her, and so had Fitzpatrick: the two men who loved her.

Eddie had prevented Fitzpatrick from betraying Deirdre. But Fitzpatrick had hoped she would come to him, to his parents' grave by the wall where they had once stood together. Perhaps he caught her eye and sent a pleading glance before turning in that direction.

Once more, I went over the scenes from the funeral. There was the long walk from the church, all the way up York Road to the cemetery, the hearse, followed by carriages carrying family, including Fitzpatrick and his crutches, priests and nuns. None of the nuns in the carriages wore brown. Some of the younger ones walked, all wearing black.

The figure in brown had appeared only at the cemetery. The more I thought about it, the surer I felt.

Cold night air made me shudder. I went inside.

Back in the house, I tapped on my housekeeper's door. Mrs Sugden emerged, spectacles on the end of her nose. She held her thumb in a book to mark her place.

'Sorry to disturb you so late. I saw the light under your door.'

'I heard you come in. I hope you didn't walk home on your own among all them drunks.'

'No, and they're a harmless bunch.'

She gave one of her doubting snorts. 'What's up?'

'I've just had an idea. I've a question concerning nuns' habits.'

She looked blank. 'Don't ask me.'

'I wasn't going to. Miss Merton, will she still be up?'

Miss Merton lives across the street. She and Mrs Sugden exchange books and recipes.

'Oh no. Early to bed, early to rise, that's her motto.' She frowned. 'What kind of nuns' habits do you want to know about? I know the ones up the road by sight. They teach at the school and walk in twos.'

'I mean what sort of apparel do they wear? Which order of nuns wear brown, with a cord belt, and sandals?'

'Isn't that just like them.' Mrs Sugden shook her head in disbelief. 'They'll swelter in summer from the robes and be martyred to chilblains in winter from the sandals.'

'About Miss Merton, how early is early?'

'Rising or retiring?'

'Both.'

'Bed at half past nine, up at five.'

'But she'll know, about habits?'

'Most likely. Converts always take their religion over-seriously. There are certain novels she refuses point blank to read.'

'Well thanks. Goodnight.'

She shook her head. 'I might as well make some cocoa.'

'I'll go across and have a word with her in the morning. And I'll make the cocoa, for disturbing you.'

'Did you see the message by the telephone?'

'No.'

'Mrs Runcie wants you to telephone to her, no matter what time.' She put down her book. 'I'll make the cocoa.'

Philippa must have been waiting downstairs, near the telephone. She answered herself.

'Kate, hello. I'm sorry I wasn't well when you called.'

'How are you now?'

'Much better thank you. Do you have any news for me yet?'

'I hope to have, soon. If my hunch is right, I could find the woman we need to speak to by tomorrow.'

When I knocked on her door at quarter past five the next morning, Miss Merton was already spooning chutney into jars. She showed no surprise at seeing me, but explained that these were windfall apples and we must waste not want not.

She listened as I describe the nun, and how I had seen her at the cemetery, alone and apart from the Little Sisters.

'And she wore sandals?'

'Yes.'

'They're called the sandalled sisters. Their full title is Sisters of the Sacred Candle of St Genevieve. They gather used up candle wax from all the churches across Yorkshire. They melt it down and make new.'

'Where is their convent?'

'It's in York. I forget the name of the little lane, but it's off Bishopsgate.'

I thanked her but she did not straightaway let me go. 'Wait.' She screwed a lid on a jar. 'You might as well take this across with you. I promised Mrs Sugden a jar of chutney.'

'Thank you.'

'And take one for the sandalled sisters while you're at it.' She reached for another lid. 'You say this nun was alone?'

'Yes.'

'Well that's not right. They never travel singly. It's not allowed. They're always in pairs.'

Twenty-Nine

From York railway station, I turned right into Queen Street, along Nunnery Lane and into Bishopsgate. It was with some misgivings that I wended my way through the narrow lane that led to the convent of the sandalled sisters. As a visitor, I should clang the bell on the iron gate, and wait for someone to come, but the bell, with its chain pull, looked powerful enough to wake the Roman and the Viking dead who lay beneath my feet. The gate opened noiselessly. I stepped into a meticulously kept walled garden blooming with flowers, herbs and vegetables.

At the end of the garden, the path led into a courtyard. An atmosphere of perfect tranquillity and joy made me slow my steps. How exquisite it would be sometime to sit here, and forget about the world.

No one appeared by the time I reached the heavy oak door, though I could see along the path into another plot beyond the building, where nuns in brown habits stooped, absorbed in their gardening. I knocked on the door.

Presently, a small, wimple-squeezed face appeared on the other side of the inset iron grille.

'My name is Mrs Shackleton. I wish to speak with the

mother superior, please.' The nun hesitated. I took the impression that nothing here happened in haste. 'It is on a matter of some importance.' She thought for a moment. 'Real importance,' I added.

She nodded, and then turned away. I heard her soft footsteps slap the stone floor as she retreated, and I looked through the grille into a dim corridor.

She was not long in returning, and opened the door. 'Come in.' She looked at my feet as I stepped inside, and I cursed my lack of forward planning. Brown sandals may have furthered my cause.

At the end of the corridor, she led me into a dimly lit whitewashed room that smelled of rosemary, lavender and, overpoweringly, of melting wax. High narrow windows, heavily leaded, let in very little light. Bunches of herbs hung from the ceiling beams.

The nun gave a most economical gesture. 'Be seated.'

On either side of the scrubbed deal table stood a bench. I sat down and placed Miss Merton's offering of chutney on the table.

Presently, a quiet footfall announced that I must gather my wits.

Something about the tall, angular woman in the brown habit was familiar. Perhaps it was the way she moved, the thickness of her straight eyebrows, or the pale blue-grey eyes. 'You asked to see me.'

'Mother Superior, my name is Mrs Catherine Shackleton. Excuse my intrusion. I am here on an errand, and have also brought some chutney from a Catholic neighbour.'

That information told her that I was not of her persuasion.

'Would you care for some refreshment?'

'Thank you.'

A hovering figure emerged from the shadows. The nun who had answered the door went to a cold press by the wall. She had an odd way of slapping her feet on the floor, soles first. She poured something from a jug and placed it on the table in front of me. I took a sip. It was lemonade, bitter, but refreshing.

When she had gone, I said, 'I believe you have someone staying here, someone I am searching for.'

'Oh?'

'Deirdre Fitzpatrick.'

The mother superior opened her mouth. It stayed open just long enough for me to add, 'It is imperative that I speak to her.'

'Who are you?'

'I'm Kate . . .'

'Mrs Shackleton, I know. I mean on whose behalf do you come here?'

'Mrs Fitzpatrick's husband asked me to find her.' The nun's mouth formed a grim line. Deirdre certainly knew how to bring out the protective side in all who met her.

'I really must speak to her.'

'Deirdre is my cousin's niece. She is unwell, and here for retreat and recuperation.'

The relationship explained why the nun looked familiar to me. There was a family resemblance between her and Deirdre's aunts. 'Some things have happened that she should know about, and there are questions.'

The nun fingered her heavy-duty rosary. 'What questions? She has told me everything.'

I doubted that. 'Are you saying she has sanctuary here?'

'She is here for solitude, time to reflect and pray. She was too distraught to go to her own mother's funeral. Went to the Minster, prayed, walked the walls like a soul trying to find its way home.'

So that had been her story. Curiosity got the better of me. 'She went to the Minster on the day of her mother's funeral?'

'Yes, the Minster. It will be ours again one day.'

So while Deirdre had boarded a train, wearing a nun's habit, and attended her mother's funeral, the mother superior thought she had been tripping round York, admiring the walls and praying for the return of the Minster to its rightful owners, the Roman Catholic Church.

Deirdre has style, I thought. I'm very keen to meet her.

'I must see Mrs Fitzpatrick.'

'No.'

I stood up. 'Then I'll go. The police will not be so understanding.'

'The police?'

'They want to question her, as a possible witness to murder.'

'Murder? That's preposterous.'

'A murder in a hotel, where she was present.'

'No. That can't be right.'

'Will you please tell her I am here?'

'She could have nothing to do with any murder. A man enticed her into a hotel when she was going about her business. She was foolish enough to believe some story of his and found herself in his room. When she realised his true intentions she ran for dear life. After that ordeal, she watched her mother die. She must be left in peace.'

'Please ensure she does not leave the premises until the police arrive.'

I left the room and walked along the corridor.

'Wait!'

I turned.

'You said her husband asked you to look for her?'

'With respect, Mother Superior, I have nothing more to say, unless it is to Mrs Fitzpatrick.'

'I would need to sit with her.'

'If she wishes it, yes.'

'I will speak to her.'

'Thank you.'

I went back into the dim room, and waited.

I half expected to see Deirdre wearing the brown habit. She was dressed in dark skirt, blue blouse, navy cardigan, and had purloined a pair of the regulation brown sandals.

Mother Superior said, 'This is the person who wishes to speak with you, Deirdre.'

I offered her my hand, which she took, cautiously.

At last, I was face to face with the woman who broke hearts, who decided on a course of action and stuck to it, who lied, deceived, helped herself in shops, and blundered through life in her own sweet way.

'I'm sorry for the loss of your mother, Mrs Fitzpatrick.'

'How did you know where to find me?'

'I have my sources.' Wanting to let her know that I am an investigator, I said, 'Mr Sykes works with me. You met him one day last year when you were shopping.'

'Ah.'

'You will wish me to stay,' the mother superior said.

'No thank you. I will be all right.'

Deirdre expected me to be as gullible as Sykes had been.

268

'Very well,' the nun sighed. 'This lady has some inkling of what you have gone through, I believe.' This was addressed to Deirdre, but meant for me. I nodded. She walked to the door. 'Ring the bell when you have finished.'

Alone, Deirdre and I faced each other across the table; each of us perched on a hard bench.

'It's almost dark in here, Deirdre, like a twilight world.'

'It's dark in here on the brightest of days. The nuns are very conscious of not overusing candles.'

'I suppose you know everyone has been looking for you.'

'I just want to be left alone.'

'In a way then, you have your wish.'

'What do you mean?'

It was too soon to tell her of her husband's death. Once I said that her husband was dead, she would have a perfect excuse to swoon into silence. 'You sent your husband a note that arrived yesterday morning.'

'You've read it?'

'More than that, I've copied it.' I placed my copy of her note on the table.

An angry flush coloured her cheeks. 'I wanted him not to come looking for me. Fitz showed you my note?'

'He saw you at the cemetery, dressed in a nun's habit.'

'Is that what he told you?'

'Deirdre, what did you mean, in this note, when you said you were going to the North Sea? You had poor Mr Sykes catching a train to Scarborough.'

'That's ridiculous. Fitz would know what I meant.' She reached out and took the note. 'You've copied it wrong.'

'How wrong?'

'Fitz thinks he can't live without me. If I stay away, he'll know he can, and that I'm not coming back.'

'Deirdre, stop being so enigmatic. Mr Sykes got you out of trouble last year. You're in worse trouble now. You left the scene of a murder.'

'A murder?'

'Yes.'

'You're trying to frighten me. That can't be true.'

'Don't deny that you were with Mr Runcie at the Hotel Metropole.'

She lowered her head. 'I don't know anything about a murder.'

'Did your brother tell you to scarper?'

'Anthony? What does he have to do with anything?'

'He was staying at the hotel where you spent the night.'

Marcus had told me that the sister and brother had not met that night, but I wanted to be sure.

'I never saw Anthony. Not until Saturday, when he found his way to Kirkstall. Then he told me where he was staying. Mr Big wouldn't have thought to stay on Cotton Street with his family. We're nothing to him. He doesn't fool me.'

She picked up the note again and began to fold it, smaller and smaller. I wished I had not put it down. When she let it go, I took it back.

'Fitz had no right to show you my note.'

'Why did you say you were going to the North Sea? Did you want him to think you meant to drown yourself?'

'He would know. Fitz would know. Why do you think it's a capital letter? It's not an *N*, it's an *H*, and it's not an *a*, it's an *e*. The See. The Holy See, where annulments are given out. I'm not going back to Fitz.'

'It's the kind of thing a husband might expect to hear in person.'

'He wouldn't listen. My aunt, the mother superior, says it can be done quietly, under the circumstances. But it's none of your business, nor Mr Sykes's business neither. Just because he got me out of bother once.'

I wanted her to stop, but she did not, as if it was a relief for her to talk about last year, and perhaps pretend that she had not been in a hotel room with a murdered man, and seen her mother die, all in the space of a weekend.

We sat in silence for a long moment. She had said so much more than she intended, and knew it.

'I think I understand. You are entitled to an annulment, and after such a long time. How many years have you been married?' I knew this from Fitzpatrick, but wanted her to talk to me, to gain her trust.

'Six years.'

'They must have been very difficult years.'

She nodded. 'Mam knew. She guessed. I didn't tell anyone. I thought it was my fault.'

'Of course it wasn't.'

'I see that now. At first, I thought that Fitz didn't find me attractive, didn't want me in that way. Mam just thought him a cold fish. They all did. She thought he might be a bit more human when we had children. When it didn't happen, she said, there's summat wrong with that man, and he'd no business marrying you. She wanted me to tell the priest, and then she didn't because she said at least I had a roof over my head, and maybe childlessness and comfort were preferable to poverty and a brood of crying kids. But he has no soul. Oh, he is devout, always at Mass, but he has no soul, Mrs Shackleton, and he can't bear to be touched. There was no one I could tell, and then someone guessed.'

She seemed surprised that someone had guessed, but it was to be expected, if she was spending weekends in hotel rooms with strange men. 'Wait.' I reached out and touched her hand to stop her saying more. I had not come to talk about her marriage. I had come to take her back for questioning. But I should have told her straight away about Fitzpatrick's death. And I hesitated to hear about Joseph Barnard, the man who 'guessed'.

'There's something you must know. I have to take you back to Leeds, so that you can give an account to the officer who is investigating Mr Runcie's murder.'

'I told you. I don't know anything about a murder. God's honest truth.'

'Then tell me what you do know.'

At that moment, there was a footfall in the corridor. Deirdre went across to the door and closed it. When she sat down again, she said, 'Mr Runcie was dead when I woke. I didn't realise straight away because I was groggy from drinking too much the night before, which I did because I couldn't face being conscious when he came to bed. I knew what he would be like. In the morning, I went into the bathroom, for a drink of water and to splash my face. I thought I'd stay in the bathroom, dash out when the chambermaid knocked, climb back into bed. I came out of the bathroom because I remembered I'd left the bolster in the middle of the bed and I would have to put it back so we could sit up properly. It was when I picked up the bolster and looked at him that I realised something was wrong.'

I remembered going into the room with Marcus, and

asking him why the bolster was on the floor. She was telling the truth, I felt almost sure.

'Why didn't you call for someone?'

'Why do you think? I didn't know what had happened to him, stroke, heart attack, anything. I just wanted to get out of there.'

'You left your dress and shoes behind.'

'I know. I'd only worn that dress twice.'

I felt a brief pang of despair. Deirdre had no notion of the seriousness of her situation. Marcus, his sergeant, even Sykes, all of them would put her into the category of no better than she ought to be.

We were only a few months on from the hanging of Edith Thompson, not because she was complicit with her lover in the murder of her husband, but because the jury regarded her as immoral, vain and contradictory.

Part of me wanted to leave Deirdre in the convent, tell her to learn how to make candles, and lie low. But she would have to face the consequences of her actions. And I must tell her about Fitzpatrick's death.

'There's something you must know, about your husband.'

She closed her eyes. 'I won't go back to him. I saw that he'd done something to his foot but I still won't go back to him.'

'He had an accident at work, dropped a box of type on his foot. That's why he was using crutches, and I think he hadn't quite got used to them.'

Something in my voice gained her attention. She stared at me, waiting.

'After he saw you at the cemetery, and Eddie stopped him from coming to you, Mr Fitzpatrick hobbled across to his parents' grave. He fell. I found him there, his head bleeding onto the stone. I'm sorry to say he died from that injury.'

'Oh God, poor Fitz, poor, pathetic Fitz.' She rocked back and forth, her arms now crossed over her chest, her eyes closed. 'Isn't that just like him? So neat, so proper, goes to a cemetery to die.'

'Are you allowed brandy in here?' I took Gerald's flask from my satchel, unscrewed the top and handed it to her.

She sniffed and shook her head. 'I can't drink this stuff straight.'

I poured a good measure into what was left of my lemonade and handed it to her.

As I watched her drink, I thought how convenient it was for Fitzpatrick to be gone, and how easy it would have been for her uncle Jimmy, or her swain Eddie, to have knocked Fitzpatrick's crutches from under him, and sent him sprawling into eternity.

She drained the earthenware mug and put it down. 'An annulment would have broken his heart.'

Better a broken heart than a broken head. 'Come on, Mrs Fitzpatrick. We have a train to catch.'

Thirty

We travelled back from York in silence. When we disembarked at Leeds, I still did not know where to take Deirdre. An obvious choice was straight to the incident room at the Metropole. That would be better than marching her up to CID headquarters. In the face of indecision, the railway station buffet is always a good idea. We found a table away from the door, so she could not very easily jump up and make a dash for it.

When the waitress came, I ordered a pot of tea for two, and a slap-up meal of egg and chips.

'Do you have a smoke?' she asked.

I had two Craven As. A man at a nearby table practically fell over himself to light our cigarettes.

She took a deep drag. 'What happens now?'

'That depends on you. If you'll stay put, I'll take you home, and telegram that you'll be at your house, to answer questions. If you're going to try and hop it, I'll ask the waitress to fetch the railway police now.'

'Before I've had my egg and chips?'

'I'm not that heartless.'

'Anyway, where would I go?'

'I'm sure you would think of somewhere. If you go back to the Bank, there'll be a baker's dozen of friends and relations willing to keep you out of the way. Your old flame Eddie would be top of the list.'

'I've made a pig's ear of my life as it is, without going back to throw in my lot with people who love me but haven't two ha'pennies to rub together. I want to go home. I want to sleep in my own bed.'

The tea and bread and butter came first. I left Deirdre to pour, as I spotted a railway policeman on the concourse. I took a business card from my satchel and wrote Marcus's rank and name, and the message that Mrs F would be 'at home' at six o'clock. The officer looked suitably impressed at Marcus's rank and went immediately to his office to make the call.

Six o'clock would give Deirdre time to get used to the idea that she must start telling the truth. Of course it would also allow her to concoct a clever tale, but I would have to risk that.

Deirdre splashed brown sauce on her chips. 'Who sent you to look for me?'

'A question for a question?'

'All right.'

'Your husband, brother and Eddie all came to see me. And there's a police search on for you. I told the chief inspector in charge of the enquiry that I would do my best to find you.'

'Poor Fitz asked you to look for me.' She played with a chip, dipping it into the egg. 'Last Sunday, after Mam died, I couldn't face seeing him. My life would have been so different if I'd married someone else. I just fell into it. I wanted Mam to come and live with us when we married, and Fitz said no. He relented when she got ill, but by then she'd taken against him and she wouldn't come. I was caught between the two of them, pulled apart.'

'But at least he came with you, last Sunday.'

'He insisted on coming, to show her that everything was all right between us.'

'And it wasn't.'

'No. I should never have married him. What's happened to him is a judgement on me, my punishment.'

'It was an accident, a terrible accident.' That may not have happened if he had not been so exhausted as to be clumsy enough to drop something on his foot and hobble about on crutches. She would think that soon enough. 'Why did you marry him?'

She shook her head. 'I'm not sure any more. By then it was over between me and Eddie. Oh, he was a great dancer, top boxer. Poor lad never had much going on in the attic and he went on boxing long after he should have stopped. When they sent him home from the war, he'd lost his stuffing and the lights went out. He couldn't see beyond bedtime. If I'd stuck with Eddie, I'd have had a life like Mam, eight or more kids and living in a place where you can't keep the vermin out, rats down the chimney, bugs in the wall.'

'Eight? I thought there was just you and your brother.'

'Two alive, six dead. And they're the ones I know about. I sometimes think Mam lost count herself.'

We finished our egg and chips. Deirdre wiped round the plate with a crust of bread. 'Fitz hated me doing this, wiping round my plate. He said it smacked of poverty.'

'Weren't you ever happy with him?'

'He was kind. He wanted the best for me.'

That sounded like a no.

'Deirdre, how did you meet Mr Lansbury, the solicitor?'

She chewed and swallowed her crust. 'How do you know about him?'

'I just do. You went to him, for your assignments I suppose we could call them. Some of them are known about, some not.'

'Did Fitz know?'

'No.'

She breathed a sigh of relief. 'Thank God for that. I had to do something. I wanted money, for Mam, and for me when I finally plucked up the courage to leave Fitz.'

'So how did you meet Mr Lansbury?'

'I was with my friend, Rita, sitting in the Varieties bar, and I overheard him talking to another man. We got to chatting. They tried to pick us up, and then Mr Lansbury gave me his card. There was never anything between us, but I asked his advice about the state of things between me and Fitz. It was such a relief to talk to someone who looked at it all so coolly and thought something could be done. He said I could get an annulment, and him a Protestant. But I knew whatever happened, I'd need money. That's when he made the suggestion of how I might earn some. But I won't give the men away. That wouldn't be fair. And I won't give Mr Lansbury away either.'

It touched me that she thought in telling me, she was not giving him away.

'Deirdre, it's struck me during the time I've been looking for you, and talking to people, that there might have been some blackmailing going on.'

'Blackmailing?'

'Yes, when someone is fearful about something becoming known and will pay for silence.'

'I know what blackmail is. Who was doing it?'

'I don't know. That's what I'm asking. Did you ever get any feeling that someone may have been blackmailing,' I wanted to say 'Mr Lansbury', but held back from putting ideas in her head.

'If there was anything like that going on, I didn't know about it.'

The waitress took our plates and cups, leaving an empty wiped-down table and my dilemma of knowing that Deirdre believed she could talk to me and it would go no further, as if I were her friend Rita. Not sure what to do about this, I ordered two cream buns and another pot of tea.

'Tell me what happened at the Metropole, with Mr Runcie.'

'I told you.'

'I meant before, when you met him there.'

She lowered her head and twisted a strand of hair around her finger. 'Oh Jesus, Mary and Joseph, it was like somebody else's dream. First off I took against the man, for his arrogance and for the way he was trying to get me drunk. So I tipped it back anyway, like I told you. Then didn't he want to call over some chap from the bar to join us for drinks.'

'Did you see who this man was?'

'No! I didn't wait to see him. That was my chance to make a dash for it. I kept my head down and went straight for the stairs. I had my back to him. I concentrated on reaching the banister, and keeping my balance after all I'd drunk. And never again. I felt so sick.'

It was the little touches that made me believe her, keeping her balance, aiming for the banister.

'In the morning, there he was dead. Well why would I stay? He was nothing to me, and nothing to do with me. For all I knew, he'd died of his own nastiness. I just wanted to be away from there and I thought even Fitz is better than this. We'll make a go of it, and I went haring back faster than I'd left.'

'It didn't last long then, the feeling that you would stick with Fitz.'

'It lasted till Mammy died. There he was, so neat and trim by the bed in the clinical room, and everything felt so empty. I sent him home, so I could be on my own with her. When you've come up with a life that's messy and noisy and you're in the hands of cruel fate, there's something good about dodging and coming through. And with Fitz, there was nothing. Nothing. Poor Fitz.'

She sat very still and composed. In the convent she had seemed desperately sad, but this was something else, something deeper. This was bereavement.

I asked the waitress to have the cream buns wrapped in tissue paper, to take back to Kirkstall.

On the railway concourse, I hesitated. It would not be Marcus who knocked on the Fitzpatricks' door at six o'clock, but the detective sergeant, bright red hair and a freckled face, Sergeant Wilson, renowned for interviewing females.

I imagined the scene. He would politely identify Mrs Fitzpatrick, offer his condolences, and take her for questioning. Perhaps he would bring one of the shoes from the hotel wardrobe and ask her to try it on like a latter-day Cinderella. He would say, That fits, is it comfortable? And now that she was in talking mode, she would say, Not very comfortable but it's mine. Can I have the shoes back, and the frock? Later I would see Marcus, and he would ask me what she had said.

'What's the matter?' Deirdre asked.

I thought of Edith Thompson, so confidently taking the stand to defend herself against a charge of murder. 'Deirdre, you need a solicitor.'

This was entirely different to Edith's Thompson's case. No one had accused Deirdre of murder. Yet.

'Won't you sit in with me?' she asked.

'That wouldn't be allowed.'

She groaned. 'Don't tell me I have to go through all that again, and telling it to some solicitor.' She brightened suddenly. 'It could be Mr Lansbury.'

'Mr Lansbury would not be the best person. Think about it. What he was doing wasn't exactly above board. He will be watching his own back.'

Either my words or my manner told her that trouble could be just around the corner.

'Then get me a Jewish solicitor. My brother, he'll find someone.'

'I don't see how, when he's only been here a few days. And where do we find a Jewish solicitor on a Saturday. Why Jewish?'

'Because a Catholic would despise me, a Protestant wouldn't care. I think a Jew would have feelings.'

I racked my brains, but could think of no one.

'The gym,' Deirdre said. 'Brasher, the boxing promoter. He knows everyone.'

I looked up at the station clock. It was approaching five. If we were not back in Kirkstall by six, Marcus would send out a search party. 'Come on. We'll take a taxi. Where is this gym?'

I was right in thinking that Detective Sergeant Wilson would come to Norman View to collect Deirdre.

I let him in. 'Mrs Fitzpatrick is in the front room, with her solicitor.'

I did not relish the call I would make to Philippa, to tell her that I had found the woman unknown but that the investigation did not appear to have moved on even an inch.

Thirty-One

'How does she do it?' Sykes joined me on a sofa in the hotel foyer. We were trying to blend in, so as not to upset the real guests by being living, breathing reminders that a murder enquiry was underway. It was easy for me, but Sykes cannot help looking like a plain-clothes policeman, in my eyes anyway.

'How does who do what?'

'Deirdre Fitzpatrick. Not only does she arrive with the fiercest solicitor this side of the Pennines, who presents her as more sinned against than sinning, but in her wake come two priests and six nuns, four in black, two in brown, speaking up for her, offering to act as chaperone, insisting she is in a state of near collapse after her multiple ordeals. Where's the bishop? Why isn't the pope here? Apparently she's planning to take the veil. How soon before she's canonized?'

'Calm down, Mr Sykes. People are looking.' It was time to go outside before we were thrown out. 'Come on, I need some air. And I'd quite like a ride on the back of your motorbike.' I had come into town with Sergeant Wilson, while Deirdre travelled with her solicitor.

'Where do you want to go?' Sykes asked.

'I'll tell you when you calm down.'

Avoiding the main entrance, we walked through the corridor towards the hotel's side door, where there is entry to the tobacconist's and the hat shop, both of which were still open. Sykes muttered something about buying a small cigar and went into the tobacconist's. I decided to tell Madame Estelle how pleased I was with the hat she sold me on race day.

She was packing up for the night, but delighted to see me. 'You were in such a dash when you came in for the hat last week, we didn't have time for a word. Are you pleased with the hat?'

'It's perfect, and brought me luck, too. I backed the winner.'

Madam Estelle clapped her hands. 'There you are, just goes to show! Some people say luck at the racecourse depends on the size of your brim. Obviously that's not true. It's the quality of the hat, whether brimmed or a cloche.' She drew back the curtain that concealed the shelves where she kept her stock, brought out a small hat box and removed the lid with a flourish. She lifted out a cream and brown silk turban hat, decorated with a coffee-coloured flower.

'It's lovely.'

She handed it to me. 'Try it on. I designed it myself. The moment it was finished, I thought, Mrs Shackleton to a t.' Madam Estelle moved to the back of the shop and bolted the doors that led into the hotel. 'I've had no end of hotel guests who would have snapped this up, but I didn't let them clap eyes on it. And believe me, after the expense of this week, I was tempted to give it pride of place in the window.'

I took off my own hat and set it down. 'What expense is that?'

'Of course you don't know. I haven't seen you since race day. I had a new lock to fit.' She nodded at the shop door. 'Two new locks, to be on the safe side.'

'What happened?'

'Well it was a break-in, wasn't it? I joked to the bobby that it must have been a single man, or he'd have helped himself to a hat for his wife. Fortunately, I don't keep money here, though the cash drawer had been pulled out. Go on, let me see you in it!'

I put the turban hat on the counter. 'When did this break-in happen?'

'In the early hours of Saturday morning.' She waited for me to put on the hat. 'I know you'll fall in love with it.' She turned the shop sign to Closed.

'Did you report the break-in?'

'Yes, to my insurance company. Constable Millen secured the premises, sent for a locksmith. It all went in Mr Millen's notebook.' She warmed to her subject. 'You see sometimes, we have vagrants find their way up this side street. They are attracted by the warm air vent from the hotel, and these doorways.'

I was looking at Sykes through the window, smoking his cigar. 'I'm going to ask Mr Sykes to come in.'

'You want him to see the hat?'

'I'd like you to tell him what you've told me, about the break-in.'

'Oh it's all right. I've had no trouble since.'

I opened the door. 'Mr Sykes, Madam Estelle had a break-in, in the early hours of last Saturday morning.'

Sykes stepped into the shop. 'Was anything taken?'

'The cash drawer was pulled out but there was nothing in it.' Madam Estelle pursed her lips. 'I'm sorry, but cigar smoke has a rather penetrating effect on hat materials, felt and straw, you understand.'

Sykes made instant apologies and left the shop.

Madam Estelle resumed her sales talk. 'Well, are you going to try the hat?'

'It's beautiful. Will you keep it for me to try next week?'

She sniffed. 'Of course. I can't promise mind. I do tell my assistant, don't touch this, don't bring out that, but she does. You could put a deposit.'

'I'll come back. There's something I have to attend to. Sorry.'

I joined Sykes in the alley. Moments later, the door blind descended in a very definite manner.

My first motorbike ride would have to wait.

'Mr Sykes, has that break-in found its way into the murder book? Apparently PC Millen reported it and saw to the change of lock.'

Sykes shook his head. 'I didn't see anything about it. Whoever broke in could have gone through to the hotel.'

'Exactly. They would need to draw two bolts, that's all. Pulling out a cash drawer made it look like attempted burglary.'

He stubbed his cigar. 'How could that have been missed?'

'I don't know. You're the special constable with access to Sergeant Wilson and his murder book. You tell me.'

'They're overwhelmed with paperwork up there. And that's not counting everything up at CID headquarters, relating to Mr Runcie's financial affairs at the bank, and all his dubious schemes.'

We went back into the hotel through the tobacconist's shop. 'Mr Sykes, after you've spoken to Wilson, let's try and be one jump ahead on this. See if you can talk to this PC Millen who reported the break-in. Call round this evening and let me know what you find out. It doesn't matter how late.'

Sykes nodded. He strode quickly to the wide staircase, and took the steps at a rapid pace.

It was time for me to tell Anthony Hartigan and Eddie Flanagan that I had found Deirdre. It would not please either of them to know she was now being questioned by the police.

At Reception, I asked when Mr Hartigan would be leaving. Tomorrow morning, came the reply.

I asked for paper and an envelope. In the briefest of notes, I told him that his sister was safe and well, and gave him the name of her solicitor.

The hotel buttons took the letter by hand to Mr Hartigan in his room, no doubt expecting a better tip than my sixpence.

As the buttons disappeared upstairs, I left the hotel. Having promised Deirdre that I would inform her aunts, I now wished I had told her to send a telegram. Abandoning the idea of a lift on Sykes's motorbike, I set off walking towards the Bank, to break the good and bad news. Your niece is safe and well. I debated with myself about mentioning the solicitor, the entourage of clergy, and that she was helping police with their enquiries. I did not know where to find faithful Eddie Flanagan, but felt confident that the aunts would get word to him.

Glad of the lightness of the evening, I tried to remember the labyrinth of streets Deirdre had led me through when I followed her that Thursday morning. Many of the factory chimneys had stopped smoking at noon. The air was clear of the worst of the fog. This part of the town is depressing, but then so much is. People live on nothing, in the most abject surroundings. I kept my eyes front, and marched on towards Cotton Street.

It was only when I began to lose my bearings that I remembered – the police either give this area a wide berth, or walk in twos. On East Street, passing a crowd of ragged men on the corner, I wanted to turn back. There were small public houses, no bigger than a couple of dwellings knocked together, and men standing outside, drinking and making remarks as I passed. But turning back is not in my nature, especially when I have an audience.

From nowhere, someone lunged against me, and grabbed my satchel. I yelled and turned to run after him, but the youth suddenly dropped to the ground as he received a punch, then my satchel was being handed back to me, by Eddie, the once upon a time boxer.

'You shouldn't be round this end on your tod.'

'I know. Stupid of me.'

'I was in the Black Dog. Someone said a posh tart was walking along. I thought it must be you.'

I put my satchel on my shoulder. 'Well you were right.'

'You might be clever but you've no sense. I've no sense left, but I've these.' He clenched and unclenched his fists, looking at them as though they belonged to someone else.

'I was on my way to tell the aunts about Deirdre, and to tell you too, since you asked me to find her.'

His face clouded with anxiety. 'Where is she now?'

'She was in a convent, as you probably guessed. I believe you spotted her at the funeral.'

He nodded.

'She knows about her husband's death, and she wanted to come home.'

'To Norman View?'

'Yes. But at present, she's talking to the police.'

He swayed as if he had taken a hard punch in the solar plexus. He closed his eyes. 'It had to happen, Mr Flanagan. She has a solicitor, a Mr Cohen, arranged through a chap you probably know, Mr Brasher.'

He nodded.

'I've left a note for her brother at the hotel. He will be signing out tomorrow, and on his way to Southampton. I came to find you, to tell you and the aunts not to worry.'

'What will they do to her?'

'Something tells me Deirdre will come out of this unscathed.'

He nodded, and even smiled. 'The aunts can bide awhile. I'll walk you back.'

Thirty-Two

Sykes checked with Wilson. It had taken a week for the information about the hat shop break-in to filter through from uniform, to CID, and from there to the murder enquiry room. Sergeant Wilson went to interview Madam Estelle.

Sykes would not have the motorbike or his special constable position much longer. Once he had seen Anthony Hartigan safely on the train to Southampton tomorrow, his duties would end. It would be over to the railway police and whoever else the chief inspector had appointed.

He decided to make the most of his last hours of officialdom. Sykes knew the City Centre beat, and the shifts. PC Millen would be pounding his beat now. The question was, where would he be? Sykes rode to the top end of town, up by the barracks, and along onto North Street. Slowly he rode through the streets of the town, keeping his eyes peeled for the portly constable. He finally caught up with Millen in City Square, under the watchful eye of the Black Prince.

Sykes hailed him. 'Mr Millen! Jim Sykes.'

The men knew each other by sight and nods. Sykes told him to expect a summons. 'I thought you'd like to be forewarned. Your report on the hat shop break-in has only just come through to the murder enquiry bunch. The sarge will be wanting a word with you.'

After two minutes with him, Sykes knew exactly how the slow progress of details about the hat shop break-in had come about.

Millen seethed. If CID chose to recruit smart Alecks who did not know that Estelle's Hats for the Discerning Lady formed part of the Hotel Metropole premises, then that was their mistake, not his.

'I'll be blowed if I'll take the can. If they'd had me in CID instead of doubling my beat and putting it down to economies, it would've been my business to make that connection straight off and I would've done it.'

'The hat shop owner speaks highly of you. You're a man who does his job.'

Informed sympathy came as a balm to PC Millen. The two men withdrew for a brief chat, into the Post Office doorway.

'People on my beat appreciate me. Can't say the same for the upper echelons.'

'You don't need to tell me,' Sykes sighed. 'My face didn't fit in the force. I admire you for staying put.'

'Well, I've a family to think of.'

They exchanged a few words about their children.

'I'm just on as a special,' Sykes said. 'So I know what it's like to be kept out of the scheme of things. You did your job beyond the call of duty, according to Miss Estelle.'

This gratified the constable. 'She's a nice lady. She'll speak up for me. Some young fellers out to make mischief, that's what I thought. The connecting door into the hotel was bolted. Nothing had been taken, and no damage done.'

'They'll be asking you next who dosses down in which doorways.'

The constable tapped the side of his nose. 'I'll make my own enquiries in that regard.'

'Tell you what,' Sykes said confidentially. 'Let me in on your side. A beat your size, you can't go chasing every vagrant who might have summat to say. If anything comes of it, you'll hear first.'

'Straight up?'

Sykes offered his hand.

The constable took his hand. 'I dunno though. Chap I have in mind, would have nothing to do with attempted burglary, much less murder. These CID fellers, if they get hold of his name and chuck him in the cell under the Town Hall, it'd finish him.'

'Likely he wasn't there, but if he was, and he saw something, or someone, that'd go to your credit. It's up to you where the information goes.'

Millen thought for a moment.

'There's two fellers doss down there sometimes. One of them's in the infirmary on his last legs. The other, I only know a first name. Charley.'

'Age? Appearance?'

'About forty. Tries to keep hisself clean. Has a right bad cough, no lung power to speak of. He's thin, about same height as you, Mr Sykes, but stooped. Doesn't talk local. I think he's from somewhere like Barnsley, bit of a twang.'

'Where am I likely to find him?'

'You could try the Salvation Army, or the hostel on St Peter's Street.'

Sykes drew a blank at the hostel on St Peter's Street. The warden there thought that a man answering Charley's description slept under the arches, which was what Millen had said. Sykes walked there, and looked about, but it was too early for anyone to have settled down for the night.

As he walked through the doors of the Salvation Army Hostel, a rhyme they had recited as children chimed in his head.

> The Salvation Army are a good little lot,
> They all went to heaven in a corn beef pot.
> The corn beef pot was far too small,
> The bottom gave way and the devil got 'em all.

Don't think of that, Sykes said to himself. They're a good bunch. Where else would these poor souls be spending the night? Sykes glanced into the communal room where men sat at long tables, each with a bowl of soup and a hunk of bread.

Sykes knew the warden, Eric Wrigg. It always paid dividends to be nice to people. He had once helped sort out an affray, coming to the aid of an Army trombonist. Ever since then, Eric had always been willing to pass the time of day.

'After some soup, Jim?'

Sykes would not have minded a bowl of soup, but it didn't do to take it from the mouths of them as had no wife to go home to.

'No. I'm after talking to a chap called Charley.'

'We've a couple by that name.'

'About our height, thin, bad cough, stooped.'

Sykes could tell by Wrigg's voice and look that he knew the man. 'What is it you're after him for?'

'Just a bit of information. He's not in any bother.'

'Don't suppose he would be. He's a quiet chap.'

'Is he here?'

It would be too good to be true.

'Aye, he's here, but he's turned in for the night. Poor chap was jiggered.'

'Only it's right important I have a word.'

'I'll go up and ask. But if he says no, he says no.'

'Right.'

Sykes waited. In the room where the soup had been dished up, a little half-hearted singing began.

Eric returned. 'Look sharp. Speak to him before the others go up. He wouldn't want to be spotted talking to the law.'

'I'm not the law.'

'You look like the law, you sound like the law, you're the law. Upstairs, first on your left.'

Sykes half ran up the stairs, glad that he had been the one to find Charley. The CID men, especially the London lot, would scare him into silence. If they took against him because the enquiry was going nowhere fast, heaven help him.

It was a room with eight beds, and only one occupied. Charley was sitting up, a folded coat behind him. Sykes guessed he slept that way, so that he could breathe.

'Charley, I'm Jim Sykes. Thanks for talking to me.'

'I've said nowt.'

'You sometimes go up by the Hotel Metropole.'

'I've done nowt. I go there to flog matches.'

'You haven't been up there for a few days. Why's that?'

'No reason.'

'Could it be you were there when someone broke into the hat shop?'

Charley said nothing.

'I'm hoping you were there. There's a reward for anyone that can help with enquiries and I'd like it to go to you.'

'I'm no nark.'

'The man who was there, it wasn't to steal hats. A man was murdered.'

'I heard about that.'

'And you put two and two together didn't you? Faster than the detectives did.'

Charley gave a hoarse laugh. 'I might've made three with my two and two. I might've made seven.'

'Why haven't you been up there lately?'

'It's too far from here. I don't allus have the puff to drag meself back here for a bed, so I've stopped away.'

'On the nights you're up that end and don't have the puff, you kip down there, in the alley, or the shop doorway.'

'What if I do?'

'Come on, Charley, have a heart. Eric's keeping the poor buggers downstairs singing till we've had our chat. No one will know, and if they did they wouldn't blame you. Were you there that night? Did you see anyone?'

Charley started to cough. It took him a few minutes to recover and get his breath.

'I were there all right. I heard him coming and dodged up t' alley. I've a snout for trouble.'

'Go on.'

'He rode a motorbike. Wheeled it up, outa sight. He went into t' doorway. Had summat with him, mebbe a crowbar. He forced shop door. That were it. I were off, out other end of t' alley. It were too late to find a bed.'

The man started to wheeze. His breath came in short bursts. Sykes opened the window, to give him a little more air.

'Did you get much of a look at him?'

Talking seemed too much for the man now. He shook his head and gave a weak but emphatic, 'No.'

'Pity.'

The breathing steadied a little. 'Only that he were a big chap. His motorbike, it were a two-stroke Enfield.'

'Are you sure of that?'

Charley nodded. It took a great effort for him to speak again. 'I rode despatch on one.'

Sykes put his hand in his pocket. He pulled out a packet of cigarettes and a half crown, his week's spends.

'You should be in the infirmary, old lad.'

The man gave something like a laugh. 'You go there to die. I'm not ready yet.'

He began to cough. He turned red in the face as he tried to shift something that would not come.

Sykes said, 'It's not me who talked to you. It's Constable Millen, and he'll look out for you.'

Charley said, 'No bugger talked to me. I've said nowt.'

Thirty-Three

Mr Duffield was at his desk in the newspaper library, giving instructions to a young clerk. When the clerk retreated behind distant shelves, I approached, wondering why he had asked me to call so urgently.

As usual, his manner was calm and unhurried. Knowing him well, I sensed his deep agitation. His nervousness betrayed itself in the tightness of his smile and the stiffness of his gait as he brought a chair for me.

We had not seen each other since the day we found Len Diamond's body. I hoped there would be other, more social, occasions when we would meet, and soon, so as to overlay that dreadful shared experience.

Mr Duffield took a folder from his drawer. He explained that in the absence of near relations, he had taken on the task of advertising in the Australian newspapers for Leonard Diamond's sister, and in papers here, in case other relatives may be traced.

'What is going to happen about a funeral?' I asked.

'We're waiting on the coroner. He has not yet ordered release of the body.'

The body. The words conjured up that dreadful image of the unfortunate Len.

We sat in silence for a moment.

Mr Duffield gave a slight gulp and there was reluctance in his voice. 'I'd like your advice, Mrs Shackleton. It concerns Leonard Diamond's effects.' He glanced about, to make sure no one was listening, though the young clerk was at the far end of the library.

'Do you mean the belongings in his lodgings?'

'No. The police have taken charge there. This concerns work matters. The part-time chap, young Tom Ashworth, will be taking over Len's work. Naturally, Tom wants a locker for his belongings. Because I have been here longest, I have become storage monitor, by default. Len had a basement locker so that seemed the obvious one for Tom. I have a duplicate key.' Mr Duffield unlocked a large drawer on the bottom left of his desk. 'I went to check that the locker was clear, and it was not. Take a look at what was in it. I'm not sure what to do.'

Mr Duffield reached into the big deep drawer. He brought out a hand-knitted scarf, winter gloves, and a brown paper carrier bag with neat twine handles. He placed the scarf and gloves to one side, and set the carrier bag on my side of the table. 'It's this.' He parted the twine handles to reveal an unsealed envelope, containing several five-pound notes that looked, crisp, white and new. 'I haven't touched them, but I should say there is a hundred pounds here.'

'Perhaps he did not trust banks.'

'They look too neat. I used tweezers to check the numbers. They are sequential, so not savings, not five pounds at a time into the piggy bank and then into the locker.'

There were also loose photographs, at least a dozen.

'Do you have those tweezers to hand?'

He took a pair of tweezers from a cracked coronation mug that held pencils. 'Here.'

One by one, I lifted out the photographs. Mr Duffield pushed the blotter towards me. I set them in two rows. A couple sat on a park bench, a man of about sixty with his arm around a slim, fair-haired young woman. Another showed a different couple in a park, the man white-haired, his companion a girl of about fifteen years old. He had his hand up her skirt. There were two photographs of Deirdre. In one, she sat by the riverbank, with Kirkstall Abbey in the background. In the next, she stood with Joseph Barnard, on Leeds Bridge. Here was Philippa Runcie at the shoot. She was with Lord Fotheringham, who had his hand on her bottom, an action he was well-known for. Another photograph showed Gideon King, Philippa's private secretary, with one of the beaters at the shoot. They appeared to be holding hands.

'What touching pictures,' I said.

'Touching is the word, Mrs Shackleton.' Mr Duffield's nose twitched. 'I would say some of these are compromising photographs.'

I could not make myself say what came into my mind.

Mr Duffield stroked his chin. 'Is there any other explanation than what we are thinking, especially when they are all together, and in a bag stuffed with money?'

It took me a moment or two to readjust my view of Leonard Diamond. This would explain so much about him: his love of the candid shot, which he had perfected; the array of expensive cameras and equipment, not affordable on a newspaper photographer's pay; the penchant for dashing off on photographic expeditions without a thought for the cost. Say the words out loud. 'A blackmailer does not need damning evidence. He needs to be able to drop a hint; to say, "You were seen", or "I have a photograph". Leonard Diamond was a blackmailer.'

Mr Duffield, said, 'I can hardly credit it. The last thing I want to do is besmirch his memory. I am looking for some other explanation, Mrs Shackleton.'

'We'll let the police deal with it, shall we? Do you want to hand over this material, or shall I?'

'I'd rather you did. If I'm to correspond with Len Diamond's sister, there may be matters I could best leave out if I am not too closely involved.'

Slowly, I picked up each photograph with the tweezers and dropped them back into the bag. 'Is there anything else, Mr Duffield?'

'I left something in the locker, too. That was another reason I wanted to see you. Tom will be in later today, seeing whether he has his promised locker. Will you come down to the basement?'

My heart began to beat faster, perhaps at the thought of looking at something Diamond had wanted to keep private.

Mr Duffield locked the brown paper bag in his bottom drawer and slipped the key in his waistcoat pocket.

We walked to the lift in silence. The clang of the doors had never seemed so loud. We stepped out into the dim basement corridor. There was a row of metal lockers against the opposite wall.

Mr Duffield inserted a small key into the third locker. The door swung open. A brown paper package tied with string was marked 'Finished Negatives'.

'They're on newspaper property,' Mr Duffield said, 'so I expect I should take them to the dark room. It's just along here.'

'It's either that or hand them in to the police, but I can't see they will want to be making prints along with everything else they have to do. Why don't you put them in at the dark room, and tell your chap it's urgent.'

He nodded. 'I'll do that.'

'Good. And I'll hand the contents of the bag to the investigating officers.'

Mr Duffield sighed with relief. 'That's why I telephoned to you. Since the old chaps have died, Len was the closest person I had to a friend in this building. I should hate to let him down in any way, even if he has been mixed up in something unsavoury.'

'Ask the dark room assistant to make two copies. Then if there is anything of interest to the police, it can be passed on.'

Mr Duffield nodded. 'I'll do it now, if you don't mind waiting.'

'That's all right.'

'And I expect I should leave the camera for the new chap.'

Mr Duffield walked along to the dark room.

I picked up the camera that had been left in the locker. It was a simple reflex camera, with an Aldis-Butcher lens, but on closer examination I saw that it had been skilfully adapted, with another lens on the side. Shutter and lens appeared to be in the correct place at the front of the camera, but had been moved, and replaced with a dummy lens. Len Diamond had been able to point the camera in one direction, and take a picture of something, or someone, off to the side. A French photographer who liked to take candid shots unobserved had secretly used this method years ago. Len Diamond had copied him.

That explained how, when he came to talk to the photographic club, he had shown such an array of photographs of individuals in unguarded moments. 'How did you do it?' people had asked. But he kept his secret, until now.

Mr Duffield walked with me along Albion Street. He was nervy because of his shock at uncovering Leonard Diamond's blackmailing. I was nervy because of having almost lost my satchel to a rascal on the Bank yesterday.

Mr Duffield hugged the brown paper carrier bag of money and photographs to his chest. Len Diamond's specially adapted camera bulged in my satchel.

Not until the doorman at the Metropole ushered us inside did we come close to relaxing. Mr Duffield handed me the paper bag and took his leave.

The manager provided sanctuary in his office while he went upstairs with my message that I must see the chief inspector in person.

Eventually, Marcus appeared, and glanced at the stuff on the table. He gave me a tired smile. 'What have you got for me, Kate?'

I told him about the photographs, and the new notes. 'Neither Mr Duffield nor I have handled them.'

Marcus carefully took out the envelope of money. He picked up a letter opener from the desk and used it to separate and peer at the crisp white fivers. 'Issued by Becketts Bank. Where is that?'

'Park Row. It's my bank, as it happens.'

'So you'll know the manager.'

'Slightly. But I don't usually rise to such dizzy heights. I deal with the clerks.'

The sight of the notes cheered Marcus enormously. Whether this was because it represented some new line of enquiry, or whether he was one of those people who cannot help being delighted at the sight of cash, I could not tell.

'We're going to note these serial numbers, Kate. I'll write a brief letter to the manager, authorising him to tell us who they were issued to. You can follow this through for me if you will, since it's your bank.'

His confidence and this official responsibility would have made a lesser woman quite giddy. 'Very well,' I said, feigning calm. 'If it will help.'

At last, I was helping Scotland Yard with their enquiries in a through-the-front-door manner.

Five minutes later, we were in the incident room. Marcus's freckled sergeant was carefully noting the serial numbers, and writing them in the log book. I copied the numbers onto a sheet of official, headed notepaper. Had the prime minister telephoned at that moment and appointed me head of CID, I could not have been more pleased. The notes amounted to seventy-five pounds.

When we had finished, Marcus put through a call to the bank manager. He introduced himself and looked at me steadily as he informed the manager that he was sending a trusted emissary with an enquiry connected to an important investigation, which required urgent and confidential cooperation.

Bearing my note to the bank manager, I left the hotel,

feeling relieved not to be carrying the money, which amounted to several months' salary for a press photographer, even one as good as Leonard Diamond.

Becketts Bank stands on the corner of Park Row and Bond Street. It is a palace of a building, immortalised by Atkinson Grimshaw in his painting, *Park Row by Moonlight*, a work of art commissioned by the bank in its own glory.

As I entered the hallowed portals, it was as if the eeriness of the moonlight painting seeped into my flesh. What I was about to find out might shed a moonbeam onto dark and terrible crimes.

The hushed atmosphere permeated the banking hall. An elderly customer stood at a ledge in stooped concentration. Each of the clerks was dealing with someone. No one looked in my direction as I turned towards the holy of holies, the inner sanctum of the manager's office.

I had met Mr Pearson only twice, around the time when Gerald did not return from the front and there were financial matters to be dealt with. Mr Pearson had been efficient, helpful and kind.

As he was then, so he was now.

'Good day, Mrs Shackleton.'

'Good day, Mr Pearson.'

'Please be seated.'

As I sat down, I remembered that when I first came to see him, he had walked round to my side of the desk most solicitously, drew out the chair and stood over me until I sat down. Remembering that time, I guessed that I must have seemed like a lost soul, incapable of finding her way to a chair. I shrugged off the memory, and handed him Marcus's letter containing the serial numbers.

He read the letter quickly, and then rose. 'Excuse me a moment.'

A heavy oak door led to an adjoining office. He disappeared through it. After a couple of moments, he returned. 'Our chief cashier will look into the matter. In the meantime, I have requested tea.'

Wide-ranging small talk took place over a decent cup of tea and digestive biscuits. Mr Pearson asked for my professional private investigator card. I gave him two, believing that working with Scotland Yard would boost my credentials no end.

After about twenty minutes, and a tap on the communicating door, the cashier's salt-and-pepper head appeared. Mr Pearson once again excused himself and vanished into the other room.

When he returned, he looked grave, and carried a piece of paper.

'I have the information.' He took an envelope from the drawer, folded the paper, slid it into the envelope and sealed it. He picked up his pen, dipped it in ink, and wrote: M Charles, Esquire, Chief Inspector.

Charming. All he needed now was sealing wax. So much for my great credentials.

'Mr Pearson, Mr Charles entrusted me with this task while he follows another line of enquiry. Please tell me the information, so that I may assess what action must be taken, and how quickly.'

He paused. The hushed silence in the room turned even the sounds from the street, a clopping horse, the wheels of a cart, the call of a newspaper vendor crying *Sporting Pink*, into one solitary faraway hum while I waited for his decision.

Mr Pearson cleared his throat. 'The money was with-drawn on Tuesday, 28th August by Mr Gideon King.'

Gideon King. Philippa Runcie's private secretary.

I would have expected King to bank with Runcie's Bank rather than Becketts, but perhaps it suited him to keep his affairs separate from the Runcie family.

Mr King would have some explaining to do.

On the day I visited Philippa, King had asked me did I think that Everett Runcie was being blackmailed. Now I wondered whether King was trying to confide in me but lost his nerve.

I wanted to kick myself for not being more perceptive.

Thirty-Four

It was several hours before more information emerged regarding the seventy-five pounds in fivers found in Leonard Diamond's locker. Marcus ordered that finger-prints be checked. He sent his sergeant to interview King.

There were three sets of dabs on the notes: the cashier's, King's and Diamond's. On the envelope that contained the money were two sets of dabs: King's and Diamond's.

I could imagine King's nervousness at being asked to explain how his money came to be in Leonard Diamond's locker. Even with the evidence staring me in the face, I hoped there would be some innocent explanation.

Duffield had voiced his suspicions of his old friend when he produced the photographs of unlikely couples. But several of the photographs were so innocuous as to raise my doubts. I wanted to believe that this was simply part of Len's interest in candid shots, human interest pictures.

I had shared my conclusion with Mr Duffield: black-mailer, but still searched for another explanation, not wanting to believe the worst. Grasping for other possibilities, I came up with the mad hope that Len Diamond was in the process of exposing a wrongdoer. The hope did not last long.

As the minutes and hours ticked by, I saw the photographs again in my mind's eye, especially the ones of people I knew: Deirdre with Joseph Barnard on Leeds Bridge, Philippa Runcie with the groping Lord Fotheringham, and Gideon King with one of the beaters at the shoot. And the anonymous couples caught in unguarded moments.

Some pictures were innocuous, perhaps, but may make a guilty person worry that something worse might be known about them. What I found so difficult to grasp was that a talented, gifted man such as Diamond could have stooped to blackmail.

Given my part in gathering this evidence, I hoped that Marcus might include me in the investigation that followed. Some hopes!

Yet he did have the courtesy to speak to me privately about the outcome of his sergeant's investigation. We were in the hotel room. Marcus sat at his desk, King's statement in front of him. 'Mr King admits to withdrawing the money from his bank on Tuesday, 28th August, the day before the Ebor Handicap. He says the money was in his wallet and was stolen.'

This seemed to me unbelievable. 'Why was it in an envelope?'

'He said he was keeping separate his gambling money and what he wanted to hold onto, what he had withdrawn for his own expenses.'

'Did he report the theft?'

'No. He claims to have felt foolish.' Marcus looked at King's statement, and read part of it to me. 'King says, "What sort of idiot lets himself be pickpocketed? It's not as if there are no warnings. One should be very careful at a racecourse." He says that he did not mention the loss to others in his party because he did not want to spoil the day. Someone jostled him on his way into the grandstand.'

'Did he mention Leonard Diamond?'

'Oh yes, though he pretends not to know the man's name. He says he had a bit of an altercation with a photographer, that he pushed the man away, to try and stop him photographing Mr and Mrs Runcie and Miss Windham.'

It struck me that King could hardly have denied that, given the number of witnesses who saw him elbow Diamond aside. That contact between King and Diamond could have been engineered: the moment when money changed hands.

Marcus pushed the photograph of King and the young beater at the shoot across the desk. It was not a very good photograph, falling short of Diamond's standard in terms of composition and lighting, but then one would hardly have expected the two fellows to pose for him.

I faced up to the fact, and made myself say it aloud: 'Len Diamond was a blackmailer. He was blackmailing King, and King paid up.'

Marcus stared glumly at the photograph. 'So it would seem. And perhaps King did not pay enough, and decided to end your photographer friend's life. He may have done a lot of people a favour, but if that proves to be the case, the noose dangles perilously close for Mrs Runcie's private secretary.'

'Have you arrested him?'

'No. There'll be more digging before we get to that stage. King thinks he will be getting his pickpocketed money back, and that the fingerprinting was for purposes of elimination. He won't be going anywhere. I have his passport, and have put a warning in place for him not to be allowed to leave the country.'

'Then he'll know he's a suspect.'

'I don't think so. My sergeant has a very soothing and plausible way with him. King believes this is to do with the security of ensuring that the money will be returned to its rightful owner.'

I thought back to the film that Mr Duffield had handed in to the newspaper dark room. 'There are more photographs, Marcus. Perhaps King was not the only man being blackmailed.'

Marcus gave me a sympathetic look. 'Sorry, Kate. I know you admired Diamond. And you don't want King to be a murderer because he is Mrs Runcie's secretary.'

'Marcus, surely you don't believe Philippa is involved?'

'I didn't say that. But the very fact that he is part of the household makes it more likely that he should come under suspicion. With Runcie dead, the expensive divorce becomes unnecessary. Mrs Runcie had agreed a settlement on her husband. That is now null and void. Mrs Runcie will be able to keep her money.'

The way he spoke, made me believe that Marcus did not only suspect King; he suspected Philippa. When I put this to him a second time, and more forcibly, he made it clear our chat was at an end.

As I rose to go, he said, 'Does Mr Duffield at the newspaper know I need the other photographs as soon as possible?'

'He's aware of the urgency.'

Marcus did a little packing up motion of the papers on his desk. 'Thank you for your sterling help, Kate.'

He smiled, and I smiled back. 'Bye, Marcus.'

I wondered whether our positions would ever be reversed, and I would thank Marcus for his help.

I could have gone back to the newspaper offices to try and persuade Mr Duffield to come out for a glass of sherry when he finished work. Or, I could have gone home.

Instead, I decided to pay Philippa a visit. She had asked for my help in finding Runcie's killer. All that I had done was to bring suspicion into her house and onto her trusted secretary.

The investigation was moving, but whether that was in the right direction I could not tell. Philippa had given me a generous retainer. It was time to tell her that I should return it to her. After all, I had found Deirdre, and that took the investigation nowhere in particular. I had discovered blackmail, and that seemed to me to be going down a dark alley. For once, I felt up against the wall, without ideas, without a plan.

And then a thought occurred to me. Perhaps King had deliberately planted the idea of blackmail in my head, to send me off on a wrong track. He knew of my friendship with Marcus, and that a word in my ear might find its way to the investigating officer.

What if the money in Diamond's locker was a part-payment towards murder, the murder of Everett Runcie?

And having done the deed, Diamond was too dangerous to be allowed to live?

The search of Diamond's rooms after his death could have been because the killer was looking for money that could be traced back to him.

It could have been to make the murder look like a burglary gone wrong.

Thirty-Five

Nothing felt right, and that was not just because I was driving the wrong car. A fine drizzle spattered the windscreen of Dad's Morris as I turned into the gates of Kirkley Hall. The troops of beech trees took on a mournful aspect. Poor oak Wellington stood his tallest, shrouded by raindrops, as if waiting patiently to vanish into the mists of time.

I wondered what the original occupants of Kirkley Hall would have made of an investigation into the death of a banker and a photographer. They would have understood the trade of banker, but photographer? That would have seemed like so much magic. A gardener, face lined as a furrowed field, looked up and saluted as I passed. He would have made a perfect subject for one of Len Diamond's candid photographs, but would be a useless target for extortion. 'Give me your sunflower seeds and I won't tell anyone you sold a cabbage.'

But was Diamond guilty of murder? Was the victim also a killer? If Len Diamond had blackmailed King, that would bring them together. King could have turned the tables and said, If you really want money, rid us of

Everett Runcie. Diamond would know his way around the Metropole. He killed Runcie. And then King strangled Diamond.

It was an outlandish notion, but plausible. If this idea stood up, Philippa might be involved. Just because I liked her and she had asked for my help did not put her beyond suspicion.

Parking the motor by the stable block, I decided that the best purpose for my visit would be to enquire after Philippa, and see if she needed a sympathetic ear. This was one visit to Kirkley Hall that I did not relish. I told myself she may not be at home. But of course she would be at home. There was too much planning to be done; the planning of a fine funeral for Everett; overseeing the packing of trunks to return to Boston.

The trouble with investigating murder is that one begins to look at people in a different way. On the surface, it is business as usual. When the butler opened the door, I found myself thinking, what do you know? What have you heard, and seen?

Strains of a Schubert sonata floated from the music room, the talented Philippa losing herself in music.

'One moment,' the butler said, and I was left standing in the double-height hall, admiring the grandeur of the winding staircase.

The music stopped.

'This way please.'

I was ushered into the vast space furnished with small sofas and elegant chairs, a harp, a flute on an elaborate stand, grand piano and harpsichord.

Philippa was alone. I felt relieved not to see Gideon King. She turned from the piano and stood to greet me.

In that instant, I caught her in profile. The silk dress floated against her body, revealing her pregnancy.

I stared, and then looked away quickly. She immediately picked up a matching voluminous sleeveless over garment and put it on. But it was too late. Perhaps she wanted me to know.

Philippa walked to the nearest sofa, one of a gold brocade pair that would have looked ridiculous in a less grand room.

Seated on the sofas, we faced each other.

She leaned back. 'I wondered when you'd come.'

'I'm glad to see you recovered.'

'Thank you. And well done on finding the woman. I knew you'd be faster off the mark than the police. Who is she?'

'No one you would know.'

'I should like to know.'

'It was purely a business arrangement.'

'I suppose it would be. Is she a whore?'

'She's a woman who needed money.'

'Well in that respect, it was a good coupling, though she might have had the decency to stay around and report his death. Or is she involved?'

'No sign of that.'

'I suppose she wasn't paid enough to deal with a corpse.'

'Philippa, I may have to return your cheque. Apart from locating the woman, I have done nothing yet to earn it.'

I did not say that my sudden suspicion of King made me feel uneasy about working on her behalf.

She looked at me steadily. 'Don't give up, Kate. I have faith in you. The police could jump to a wrong conclusion, and then I really would need your help.'

Reluctant to be drawn into a discussion of what the police may or may not discover, I looked towards the window, as if light might give me inspiration, or a way out. Something caught my eye. The room was full of works of art. The paintings were few, but striking, including a full-length portrait of Philippa. There were bronze figures and, by the window, a bust of Philippa, beautifully carved. This was very much her room. If I was not mistaken, the bust was carved by Rupert Cromer. Put side by side with the bust of Caroline Windham, the pieces would represent the two important women in Runcie's life.

She saw me looking. 'I'm wondering what to take with me. Gideon started to do the inventory, what belongs in the house and what I brought and bought. But it's all ground to a halt since Gideon took to his room.'

'Why has he taken to his room?'

'Embarrassment and annoyance, I think. Apparently he was pickpocketed at the races, and the money has turned up.'

'Well that's good.'

'Apparently not, if you are Gideon King.'

To fill the awkward silence that followed, I walked across the room to where Philippa's bust stood on a small plinth. 'This is beautiful. It really captures you.'

'Does it? An engagement present from Everett. He commissioned it. I had to sit for Cromer, who I felt sure had taken a dislike to me. Either that or Everett had beaten him down on the price for the job.'

It was several moments before Philippa spoke again. 'What's going on, Kate, regarding Gideon I mean? I don't believe Scotland Yard would take an interest in the victim of a racecourse pickpocket. I hate it that the spotlight is being turned on my own staff. Why are they worrying about pickpockets when they should be looking for Everett's killer?'

'How much do you know about it?'

She shrugged. 'Not much. The money Gideon lost has been recovered, from some petty thief. I said he should have reported it, but he's so careful of my feelings. He didn't want to spoil the day, or upset me by making a song and dance about it.'

So all she knew was that Sergeant Wilson had questioned King about the money he "lost" at the racecourse.

She leaned back and shifted one leg across the other. 'This man, the one who had Gideon's money, was he a gambler?'

'Yes, so I'm told.'

'Gideon got into trouble in Boston through his gambling. That's why he was sent here. I employed him as a favour to my brother and I would swear he's turned over a new leaf.'

She might be covering for King, by providing a reason why his money would be in Diamond's possession.

I said, 'I don't believe there is any suggestion that Gideon was gambling.'

'I'm glad the sergeant spoke to him privately. Gideon values my good opinion. He feels so foolish over that incident.'

Now would be the moment to tell her that the man in whose possession the money was found is dead, strangled. Like Everett. But I felt a sudden dread. She had gone through such a lot, and had been unwell. What if my frankness made her lose the baby?

I tried to make light of the situation. 'Well I hope he

doesn't feel so foolish that he won't be able to help you pack.'

'Oh, he'll come round. He has been a great help to me, though sometimes overbearingly so.'

'In what way?'

'Oh, all sorts of ways. He overheard me arguing with Everett. We had arrived at the stage where Everett never talked to me, not really talked. He addressed me, as if I were the board of directors, or someone he wanted to wheedle money from. Well after he overheard me saying that to Everett, Gideon took to talking to me all the time, chatting incessantly, turning himself into the Malvolio of verbiage. He dotes on me.'

I did not want to ask, but I must. 'The baby . . .'

She placed her hands on her bump, and said, 'Ah yes, the baby.'

'Is Gideon the father?'

She gave a short laugh. 'No. And he would not have killed Everett for me, if that's what you are thinking. To tell you the truth, I think he's otherwise inclined.'

'Oh?'

Well that explained the photographs.

'Letters that come for him are addressed to Gideon King the third. The servants have a nickname for him, Gideon King the last, which leads me to believe they know a little more about his night life than I do. But in his fashion he is faithful and doting, and now I feel guilty about his being caught up in this business.'

Did she feel guilty enough to give him an alibi for the time of Leonard Diamond's murder, I wondered.

She looked down. 'The funeral needs to be on a cold day, so I can wear a big coat.'

I could hear footsteps on the stairs. 'Who does know about the baby, Philippa?'

'My maid and my doctor know. Kate, I want to be on the other side of the Atlantic when this child is born. Just imagine if it's a boy. He'd be in line to inherit the title. Everett's brother will never marry. This millstone of a house and this ridiculous life would come to my son. What kind of curse is that to put on an innocent babe?'

There were sounds from the hall. I heard King's heavy stride and his cultured Boston voice giving chapter and verse about something or other.

He put his head around the door. 'Philippa, Mrs Shackleton. I'm resuming the inventory. Sorry to be such poor company.'

With a Cheshire cat grin, he was gone.

I was glad, because if he had killed Leonard Diamond, I did not want to be in the same room as Gideon King.

'Philippa, do you need any help prior to the funeral? Please tell me if there's anything I can do.'

'Thanks, Kate. But my brother-in-law has most of the arrangements in hand. I shall be sending notes to people whom I regard as friends, including your Aunt Berta and family, and you of course.'

'Don't send me a note, just tell me.'

'A week on Friday, at All Saints, the family church.' She stood up. 'You might give me an opinion, if you'd care to.'

'About what?'

She walked to the window, and lightly touched the marble bust that Cromer had carved. 'I will take this. I'm sure it will have some value some day, and I half-believe that Everett was in love with me when he commissioned it.'

'I'm sure he was. You must keep it. Even if you put it out of sight for a year or two.'

'Or a decade or two. There are all sorts of bits and pieces that Everett bought me. I don't know what to take, and what to leave behind. Part of me wants to ditch everything he ever gave me. It was all such a lie.'

'I'm sure it wasn't. When I think back to that time at the opera, and the way he looked at you. He loved you, Philippa, in his fashion.'

'In his fashion, exactly.'

'Take everything that's yours. You can always pack it in a trunk and look at it in a few years, and perhaps see what the child may want.'

She looked at me sharply.

'There is that, I suppose. Yes, I'll take everything. This family and this house have had enough from me already.' She tapped her belly. 'And you won't say anything … I must change this dress.'

'I won't breathe a word.'

'Come upstairs with me. There is one favour you could do.'

I followed her up the broad staircase. The late afternoon sun shone through the splendid leaded lights of the window that picked out a knight, a page and a fine white steed.

She opened a bedroom door onto a room with old oak furniture, and an Elizabethan bed, draped with canopies. Philippa opened a dresser drawer. She took out a silver cigarette case and a lighter.

'Give these to Caroline. I heard that you went to visit her.'

'That's very generous of you, Philippa.'

'She gave them to Everett, so she can have them back. And perhaps you'll tell her, I have no objection to her coming to the funeral. I expect she'll handle herself impeccably, as usual. And her absence would cause more remark than her presence.'

'I'm not sure I would be so kind if I were you.'

'It's not kindness. It's pity. She's so grand, and so pathetic. What life will she have? No one will ever marry her.'

As we left the room and walked back down the stairs, I asked, 'What was Everett planning to do, after the divorce?'

'His brother had squeezed him out of the bank. He was too much of a liability. His plan was to go to Italy, and live in splendid retirement.'

'With Caroline?'

'Why change the habit of a lifetime?'

She walked me to the door. I took a deep breath. 'Don't think I'm prying for the sake of it. I have to know, because it impinges on events. Who is the baby's father?'

'You really want to know?'

'Yes.'

'Everett.' She sighed. 'It was the night he was pleading with me for a second chance, and I let him plead. That's why I have to leave this country, Kate. Imagine, if I have a boy, and he becomes the future Lord Kirkley. Once, that would have been my dream. Now, the prospect feels like a nightmare. I do not intend to breed an Everett Runcie, a British aristocrat. This child will be an American.'

I left the house and walked back to the car.

So absorbed was I that it gave me a shock to open the car door and see Gideon King sitting there.

'Mr King.'

'I want to talk to you,' he said quietly. When I hesitated, he said, 'Please get in as if there is nothing unusual. We don't know who may be watching from the window.'

I climbed into the car.

'It won't take long.'

We sat side by side, as if considering a destination.

'You'll have guessed I suppose,' he said. 'Because of what I spoke to you about on that Saturday, when you came to talk to Philippa.'

'You mentioned blackmail.'

'Yes.'

'You thought that perhaps Everett Runcie was being blackmailed, but it was you I think.'

'It was. And now I've lied to the police. I didn't have my pocket picked. I gave the money to the photographer by arrangement because he had something over me. I can't tell Philippa and lose her good opinion.'

'Tell the police. They'll find out anyway.'

'Yes I realise that. Diamond was supposed to give me a photograph.'

If it was the photograph I had seen, of King touching hands with a groom, or a beater at the shoot, then he had little to fear; but it would not console him to hear that. 'Did you have anything to do with Diamond's murder?'

'Of course not. I wanted him dead but I would have been too scared. I can't account for my movements, except for part of Sunday when we were at church, and then all together in the house. They'll think I did it.'

'Lying won't help. Make a clean breast of it. I can give you a lift now if you like.'

He thought about this for a moment. 'Oh God, I feel such a fool. Philippa thinks I came to England to work for her because I got into bad ways gambling, and that I'm totally reformed. I never was a gambler. There were other reasons.'

A deer appeared from the trees. We watched it sniff the air, and then begin to graze.

He said, 'I had a friendship with a fellow theology student, Edgar. It was drawn to the attention of the authorities and we were quietly given our marching orders. That was why I left Boston.'

A second deer joined the first.

'Blackmail is an ugly, cruel business. Ask to see the sergeant again, or the chief inspector. If it helps, you can say you talked to me.'

'They'll despise me.'

'Believe me, there is nothing you can say that will shock them. And whatever Leonard Diamond said or wrote to you, I would guess most of it was bluff and exaggeration, pretence of a little knowledge.'

He nodded. 'Will I need my toothbrush?'

'Let us go, Mr King. I hope you won't need a tooth-brush, but if you do, I promise to bring you one, and whatever else you need.'

It was a quiet journey into town, with much of the traffic coming in the opposite direction. I was conscious that now and then, King ran his tongue over his lips, or shifted his posture, unable to be comfortable with himself. I wished that I could say it would be all right.

When we passed the municipal buildings, he said, 'Where are we going? I thought it would be in there.'

'Not to CID headquarters. We'll go to the hotel, where the chief inspector and his sergeant are based.'

'Thank you.'

'Have you ever been in the Metropole?'

He gave a short laugh. 'Interrogating me already? No, I have not. It was Everett's haunt. I kept away, as did Philippa.'

When we reached the hotel, both of us hesitated. Should I go in with him? He did not budge. I got out of the car, and he followed.

Slowly, we entered the hotel and walked up the flights of stairs. It seemed the longest walk of my life, so I could imagine how King felt. He gives off a prickly air, and is not the kind of man whose arm you might touch or give a squeeze for good luck, but all the same, I did. 'Come on, Mr King. You can do it. Be brave.'

Red-haired Sergeant Wilson looked up from his log book. 'Mr King. Mrs Shackleton.'

I nodded, and held back.

King said, 'There's something I'd like to add to my statement.'

Without betraying the least surprise, Wilson said, 'Of course, sir. Come through.'

He led King into the room usually occupied by Marcus. I did not know whether he was in there or not. Wilson popped back, just as I was leaving.

'Mrs Shackleton, the photographs. Have they been printed yet?'

'I don't know. Mr Duffield had it in hand, but I'll check.'

'Thank you, that would be very helpful.'

'Mr Wilson, if Mr King is to stay the night, would you let me know, so that I can bring his toothbrush?'

'Of course.'

I knew he would forget the instant he turned away from me. I was glad to be collecting the photographs myself. I wanted to see the depths to which my once-upon-a-time friend Len Diamond had sunk.

Thirty-Six

As I left the hotel, Mr Sykes caught up with me, to cadge a lift home.

'I saw you fetch King in.' He chuckled. 'What with your lassoing in Mrs Fitzpatrick, and now the private secretary, if I were chief inspector I'd send the rest of us home.'

'Very droll, Mr Sykes.'

'I'm stood down for an hour or two. Now that Anthony Hartigan has left our fair city, I don't believe I shall be needed much longer. The railway police will keep him in view all the way to Southampton.'

'Shame I didn't get to say goodbye. I'll drop you at home, but I have a call to make first.'

'Shall I come in with you?' he asked when I stopped outside the *Herald*'s building.

'No. I'll be two shakes.'

The reception desk was deserted. It was that twilight time between the day and night shifts.

Without anyone stopping me, or asking my business, I found my way to the basement.

The dark room was a huge cellar, the size any amateur photographer might envy, but it was unpleasant, with a nasty smell. As my eyes grew accustomed to the dark, I saw that in one corner lay a mountain of discarded plates, and used film curling into waves. A cat shot from it and through the door. So the dark room doubled as the newspaper cat's lavatory.

A shape appeared. As it came closer, it took on the form of a young man in a brown buttoned-up overall. He was more surprised to see me than I him.

'Hello. You must be the dark room technician?'

'That's right.' He switched on a low light, revealing himself as pale as a pitman.

'What's your name?'

'Terence Kitchen.' He wore a tiny affectation of a beard in the centre of his chin, though whether this was to express his Bohemian character or hide a spot there was no way of knowing. 'No one's supposed to come in here.'

'I'm Mrs Shackleton. You developed some negatives earlier. I'm here to collect them.'

'What negatives?'

'The negatives that Mr Duffield passed to you.'

'Mr Duffield's gone home.'

'I know. That's why I'm asking you. It is important. I believe he stressed that.'

'I take my instructions from the boss. He said nowt about important.'

'Where is your boss?'

'Gone home.'

'Where was he earlier? Didn't he leave instructions?'

'He was out.'

This was getting us nowhere. 'Have you got the photographs or not?'

'No.'

'Can you do them now, while I wait?'

He drew back his head and pursed his lips, 'Oh no, Missis, that won't be possible.'

'Then I shall take them back.'

'I can't hand over newspaper property.'

'Outside in a motor car you will see a plain-clothes inspector from Scotland Yard. If you won't hand them over to me, go tell him why.'

Jim Sykes would be pleased to hear of his meteoric rise.

Terence Kitchen played with a button on his overall. 'I've no printing paper. It's all locked up till tomorrow.'

That I could believe.

He glanced to his left. I saw that the folder of negatives lay on his table. 'Do you give it willingly, or shall I take it?'

He gulped.

'Come with me, Mr Kitchen. The inspector outside will give you a receipt for the folder.'

After dropping off Sykes, I returned to my own dark room, where everything is familiar and to hand. The only strangeness for me was in the thought of developing someone else's prints; the work of someone I had greatly admired. I felt a trembling sort of nervousness. I must do the artist in Diamond justice, by producing an excellent print. It was as if Len Diamond stood at my shoulder, looking at the negatives. I must choose what to print first.

The pictures were all taken at Somersgill, on the first day of grouse shooting. There was a beautifully framed shot of Gideon King and a young man, possibly the same beater from the previous photograph, taken near the stable block. King would not be the only man to be grateful that Diamond would click his shutter no more. Perhaps Diamond thought life owed him more than he had achieved. Perhaps he had some dream of spending his life taking different sorts of photographs, or none at all. His work took him among the rich and almost famous, and his record of those lives was ephemeral. It struck me that as an artist, for that is what he was in his way, he had never been given his due, and so had taken it. But it is easy, when a man is dead, to put a kind gloss on ill deeds.

One by one, I glanced at the more innocuous negatives and set each one aside. There was Philippa, with Lord Fotheringham; Everett Runcie, Caroline Windham beside him. And here was another, taken from an odd perspective, through a gap in rocks. It showed Rupert Cromer, concealed—or so he thought—in an outcrop, shotgun raised. I could almost hear Len Diamond congratulating himself on his ability to take a tricky photograph in difficult surroundings. A second negative, from a slightly different angle, showed that Cromer had Runcie in his sights. Len would not have been satisfied with the photograph's quality but a blackmailer has other priorities.

In the instant when Cromer pulled the trigger, Caroline must have moved. Either that or Rupert Cromer was a bad shot. Cromer had denied being at the shoot. I had his own word for that, and I knew that his name had not been on the guest list because Gideon King had told me who was there.

Living close by, on the estate, and knowing the shoot so well, Cromer could easily have hidden himself amongst the rocks whilst the previous drive was in progress.

These were the negatives I must print. Fortunately, I have several printing frames, two with clear glass suitable for film negatives. I polished the glass of the first frame with a pocket handkerchief and placed the negative in the printing frame, with the printing out paper glossy side downwards on the negative.

I did this twice, and then carried the frames into the light, setting them on the kitchen windowsill where the evening sun obligingly performed its magic. As it did so, I looked out through the window, across my back garden to the wood beyond. This was the place where I had imagined a Rupert Cromer sculpture might stand.

When I had allowed time for the light to do its work, I took the frames back into the dark room, and checked the results. Now it was time for the Hypo, the fixer. But what would I fix? This picture spoke to me of attempted murder. But what would it tell a jury? A clever barrister would sow seeds of doubt, would mock the picture's veracity, and have the case thrown out. Cromer was admired, with friends in the right places. These images could be dismissed as so much jiggery-pokery.

On the other hand, King, whom I had delivered up to Sergeant Wilson, would make an excellent suspect: an outsider, an American, a man whose private life would not bear too much scrutiny.

I put these thoughts from my mind as I diluted the Hypo in the fixing dish and slid in the printing out paper. The print slowly turned brown. Never had the process of fixing and washing taken so long. And then the prints must be hung to dry.

And I thought of King. Someone was going to hang.

While the prints dried, I went to my bathroom. Yes, I had a spare toothbrush. King might need it.

The strange thing about this photograph was that

without other knowledge, one would not know an attempt at murder was about to take place. The man with the gun could have shifted in a second. It was a picture with a narrative, and yet what tale did it tell? The skill of the photographer, the framing of the subjects and the camera angle made it distinctive. It turned me into a witness, and yet that was an illusion. Could the camera lie? Something in the eye of the man with the gun told me that this was no lie of the camera, but an attempt at murder.

When the prints were not quite dry, I picked one up by its edge and took it with me, out to the car.

I needed to get the print to Marcus straight away. But Dad's Morris decided to behave as my own Jowett sometimes did. Unaccountably, it set off in another direction.

If I put my foot down, I would be able to gather up Caroline Windham and take her along to the Metropole. She had stayed there with Runcie. She would know whether Cromer had also stayed there, and whether he knew Runcie would be at the hotel on the fateful night.

Slowly, the realisation dawned. Cromer had failed to kill Runcie at the shoot. He had succeeded at the hotel.

As soon as Diamond heard about Runcie's death, he guessed who was responsible and decided to make a little money from his knowledge.

But why would Cromer kill Everett? He had described the man as his best friend.

I remembered back to the Sunday when I broke the news of Runcie's death to Caroline Windham, and gave her a lift to Cromer's house.

I had thought it a trick of my imagination that the face of the Venus Cromer had sketched on his pad bore an uncanny resemblance to Deirdre Fitzpatrick. Now

I understood: he had seen her lying asleep in the bed beside Runcie. He knew I had seen the picture and he had re-drawn that page, giving the Venus figure a different face.

Lucky for Deirdre that she had not woken. She too may have ended her life in that hotel room.

Thirty-Seven

There is something forbidding about Somersgill House at dusk. Out of habit, I parked by the side of the mansion. I went to the front door and clanged the bell. By good luck, the maid who answered was the one I had met during my previous call here.

'Is Miss Windham at home?'

'She's not, Miss.'

'Do you know where she is?' There was a hesitation. She knew well enough, but did not want to say.

Someone called to the maid from inside the house.

I made a guess. 'Miss Windham is with Mr Cromer, perhaps?'

She nodded.

I thanked her, and went back to the car.

This changed matters. I should not go blundering in. But then I had a good idea. I would give Caroline Windham the cigarette case and lighter, and tell her that Philippa Runcie wanted to see her. Once we were away from Cromer, I would take her, and the photograph, to Marcus.

As I drove from the big house through the grounds, out

of the east gate, trying to remember my way to the sculptor's ramshackle cottage and outbuildings, I went over what I would say: tell Caroline the date of the funeral, that there would be people coming from Boston, casually mention that Philippa would like to see her, now, before relations descended and private conversation became difficult.

Having a perfect plan can be both comforting and pointless. Circumstances dictate.

I knocked on the cottage door, bringing me face to face with the still-angry housekeeper; even without dough on her hands she resented disturbance. Irritation must be her permanent state of being. She informed me that Mr Cromer and Miss Windham were in the barn, working. The word *working* was delivered with sneering contempt.

I walked in the direction of her waving arm, along the well-trodden path that ran by the side of the house.

They were indeed working. I saw that through the crack in the door. The adapted barn was lit by half a dozen oil lamps and a host of candles.

I pushed open the door on a scene of intense concentration and great tranquillity. Caroline lay on a sofa, naked, a trance-like look on her face. A single paraffin heater stood a foot away from her, giving off a faint blue haze.

Cromer had his back to me. He was standing at a table, tapping at a piece of stone that followed the shape of her legs, her hips, breasts and head, but which became something more than the model, with a timeless quality, part landscape, part human.

She saw me but did not react. Even so, he sensed some subtle change in her, and turned to look at me.

'I'm sorry to disturb you. I was looking for you, Miss Windham, I wanted a word, but you're obviously busy.'

I took a step back. That would be best. Go back to my car, then to the house, telephone Marcus.

The two of them exchanged a look. She said, 'I need to move. My left leg's going into cramp.'

He nodded.

She drew a Chinese silk robe around herself, and stood up. 'I'm going inside, Rupert. I need a drink.'

He would be bound to follow. But he did not.

As we went from the barn, she shivered. 'He forgets how cold it gets if you're still for any length of time. Of course he's working and doesn't notice.'

'You're working too,' I said, adopting a casual tone, listening out for him.

'Is there some news?' she asked. 'Has Philippa set the date for the funeral? Am I being given orders to stay clear?'

So she had given me an opening. But I wanted to be well away from the barn, and from Cromer, to put my case for leaving sufficiently forcefully. She would need time to dress. I had not counted on finding her naked.

'You must be cold. Are you planning to go on sitting for him half the night?'

'Oh you know artists. I'm supposed to be grateful to be his muse. And of course it does divert me. Anything is better than the boredom of the big house, though I am expected for supper. What time is it?'

I told her.

'I shall have to dress. I suppose you could give me a lift.'

This was better than I had hoped. 'Of course.'

We were in the porch, and suddenly Cromer was behind us, having made giant strides from the barn.

'I'm packing in, darling,' Caroline said. 'You'll have to carry on without me.'

He put a hand on her shoulder. 'That's all right. Have the rest of the night off.'

She laughed.

Cromer turned to me. 'Stay for a drink, will you?'

Inward groan. That was the last thing I wanted to do, but could hardly refuse.

The three of us went into the shabby parlour.

Cromer made for the decanter on the sideboard. 'Who's for a drop of Lord Fotheringham's finest?'

'Make mine a double. What a miserable fire.' She drew the battered armchair up to the hearth, but made no attempt to put coals on the fire. She would ring the bell for that.

I sat down on the small sofa opposite the fireplace.

Cromer handed us each a glass.

I took a sip and placed my glass on the low side table.

'Now what's all this?' Caroline took a swig. 'I'm getting to know you by now, Mrs Shackleton. You don't come without a reason.'

'You were right, Miss Windham. There is a date for the funeral, and Mrs Runcie asked me to tell you. It's a week on Friday.'

'So I'm not banned?'

'On the contrary. In fact, there's a silver cigarette case that Philippa thinks you gave to Everett.'

A look of deep hurt flashed in her eyes. She turned to look at the fire. 'I might have given him a cigarette case. Is it valuable? Studded with diamonds or something? If so, I definitely gave it him.'

I wanted Cromer to sit down, well away from me. But he did not. He hovered between me and the fire.

'And a lighter,' I added, 'also silver.'

'Why is she being so magnanimous? Doesn't she know we planned to go away together the minute the divorce came through?'

Cromer was looking at me. There was something in his eyes: suspicion. That put me on my guard. Well I could allay his suspicion by producing the cigarette case and the lighter. I took the cigarette case from my satchel. I stood up and handed it to Caroline.

She gave a small, hurt cry. 'He hardly ever used this. Oh he did at first, but then she bought him gold. Just like her to buy him gold. And not even a damn cigarette in the thing.'

I handed her one of mine.

Cromer did not move from his spot, standing on the hearth rug between us. I sat down again.

'Where's the lighter?' Caroline asked. 'I bet it's not even working.'

I delved in the satchel for the lighter but could not find it.

Cromer took a taper from the jug by the fire and lit Caroline's cigarette. He laughed. 'Women's bags! May I help you?'

Before I could stop him, he tipped the contents of my satchel onto the space on the sofa beside me. I straight away knew why. He had seen a corner of the photograph. Fortunately, it had fallen face down. I reached to retrieve it.

Cromer smiled. 'You took such an interest in my work the last time you called, Mrs Shackleton. I almost thought you might be here about a commission.'

My hand was on the photograph; too soon. 'Our residents' committee meets at the end of this month. I shall be showing the photographs of your work.'

Caroline looked at us curiously. She took a long drag on her cigarette. 'Do you have the lighter, Mrs Shackleton? I remember it now. It was a birthday present, and I meant to have it engraved.'

'Here it is.' I handed the lighter to Cromer to pass to Caroline. The moment he shifted his position, I would return the photograph to my satchel. But without passing the lighter to Caroline, he made a sudden movement and reached for the photograph. 'Is this one of the pictures you took of my work?'

Caroline said, 'Give me the lighter.' She leaned forward and took it from his hand, as he stared at the print.

With his back to the fire, he held onto it, without saying a word for the longest time.

Caroline clicked the lighter. 'It works.' She looked up at Cromer. 'Rupert, why do you men always hog the fire?'

At last, Cromer looked at me. 'It's trick photography. I hope you know that, Mrs Shackleton. I wasn't there.'

Caroline stood up. 'What are you looking at? What's trick photography?'

She took the photograph from him.

'It's the shoot. Rupert, you weren't in the shooting party.'

'I told you. It's trick photography. Diamond was known for it.'

I tried to make light of the situation. It was in my favour that Caroline was here, and the angry housekeeper. 'I printed a negative from Leonard Diamond's locker.'

Caroline said, 'Rupert? You're pointing your gun at me.'

She became so still, as if turned into the stone figure Cromer had been carving.

'I told you. It's bloody trick photography.'

I said quickly, too quickly, 'Len Diamond had a great sense of humour.'

'Had?' Caroline looked at me, and then at Rupert.

'He's dead,' I said flatly. It was too late for pretence. 'Mr Cromer isn't pointing the gun at you, Miss Windham. He's aiming at Everett Runcie. You moved, and so did Everett. I expect there was too much of a commotion for him to try a second shot.'

Time stood still.

Cromer said, 'This is ridiculous. You've cooked this up in your dark room.' He turned to Caroline. 'She's a photographer.' And then back to me. 'Admit it. I don't know what your game is.'

'I have no game, unlike Leonard Diamond who I believe wanted rather a lot of money for this print and the other negatives.'

'The man was unstable. He hanged himself didn't he?'

In a small voice, Caroline said, 'How do you know that?'

'It was in the paper.' There was a burst of confidence in his voice.

'I didn't see it.'

'Not in *The Times*, in the local rag.'

'You don't take the local paper.'

'For God's sake, Caroline, it was in the paper. This picture proves nothing.'

I said, 'Leonard Diamond did not commit suicide. You strangled him, and made it look like suicide, because he knew what you had done. You wanted Everett Runcie dead. You went to the hotel. You strangled him in his bed while he slept, knocked out by wine and brandy. It must have seemed so simple.'

Caroline stared at him. Her voice came out in a throaty whisper. 'You bastard. All this time, you've had me being your bloody muse, shivering and naked. And I thought you were on my side. I told myself, Rupert is asking me to pose because he thinks it will help me survive. And it was you. You killed Everett.'

She was still holding the photograph.

He snatched it from her. 'You're wrong.'

'You killed him, didn't you?'

'No!' The big man took a step back. It's not how it looks.' He threw the photograph on the fire. He looked at her beseechingly, shaking his head. His arms fell limply by his sides. I noticed the size of his hands, large enough to put around a man's neck, to choke, to press the life away.

'I did it for you, Caroline. Runcie ruined you. He should have married you when you were young. Now no one will. You'll never have a home, unless it's with me.'

'You? You? We were going to Italy.'

'Where he already had a widow in his sights. A countess.'

'Liar!'

'He told me. He planned to marry her. An old bag with money. You would have been the mistress still.'

'Well then, yes I would. Do you think he would ever have loved anyone but me?'

'He was taking you where he thought I couldn't follow. But I would have followed. Because it would have been the same as before, swearing his love for you, and marrying someone who would pay the bills, and he would have hurt you over and over again.'

They had forgotten I was there. It was not enough that he should confess to killing Everett Runcie. I wanted him to admit killing Diamond.

I stepped between them. 'Leonard Diamond tried to blackmail you,' I said.

'Him!' He gave a dismissive gesture as if to wave away a fly. 'It was easier to put my hands around his neck than to put my hands on fifty pounds. I gave him the chance to return the negatives, but I took a rope with me, just in case.'

Cromer stepped around me, towards Caroline, saying her name, pleading.

That was when she picked up the poker. She struck at him, hitting him on the shoulder. He cried out in pain. She raised the poker again. He grabbed her arm and forced the poker from her hand. He encircled her in his arms, he said, 'I love you, Caroline. I've always loved you. He knew that. He played with both of us.'

'Don't touch me!'

'Just kiss me, Caroline, just kiss me.'

She struggled to free herself and brought up her knee, giving him a sharp knock where it hurt.

He released her, turned and ran from the room.

'Caroline! Let him go. There's nowhere he can hide.'

She ignored me, picking up the poker again, running after him.

I followed her, into the hall, through to the kitchen.

Cromer ran from the house, through the back door.

Caroline, barefoot, chased after him, screeching a war cry, brandishing the poker.

I watched as Cromer jumped on his motorbike and sped off into the night.

Caroline raced after the motorbike.

At the same moment, two police cars, and Sykes on his Clyno motorbike, came bumping along the path.

Cromer did not get far. Haring at a bend, his motorcycle overturned. He was flung through the air, a dark shape against a darkening sky. Die there, I willed, hating the thought of Rupert Cromer with a rope around his neck. But he came stumbling back towards the police car, half carried by two sturdy constables, wildly calling out that he was glad he had finished off Runcie. 'I killed a cheating fraudster, and I killed a blackmailer. Where's my medal?'

The car door slammed shut.

Cromer's head appeared through the window, calling, 'I did it for you, Caroline. He didn't deserve you.'

The car drove away.

Caroline, hair blowing in the wind, marched after the disappearing police car, as if an avenging army fell into step behind her.

Two policemen each took an arm to restrain her. She shook them off.

A third policeman disarmed her of the poker.

Marcus said, 'Why, Kate? You could have left this to me.'

'How did you know I was here?'

'Sykes called at your house to see if you had printed the photographs. He intended to bring them in to us. Good thing he was able to let himself in. He had the foresight to look at the drying print and made the connection.'

Sykes joined us. 'Are you all right, Mrs Shackleton?'

I felt anything but all right, but nodded.

Sykes turned to Marcus. 'Cromer's bike is a two-stroke Enfield, sir, same as the one seen in the alley.' To me, Sykes said, 'Where was Mrs Sugden when we could have done with her to send a message?'

'At night school. She's started a class in typewriting.'

I glanced back towards the cottage. The dour Sergeant Wilson was struggling to make Miss Windham listen to him, to calm down, to dress.

Marcus cleared his throat, drawing my attention. 'Kate, I suppose you know Miss Windham reasonably well and could pacify her and take her statement.'

'No, Marcus. Not this time. I'll leave Miss Windham to you and Sergeant Wilson.'

'She's the one they call the warrior queen?'

'The Viking Queen; beaten but undefeated.'

Thirty-Eight

Night had fallen by the time I drove away from the Fotheringhams' estate. Sykes insisted on giving me a motorbike escort, riding the motorbike a few yards behind me, along the dark, moonlit road, as if he thought I might have some terrible mishap on the way home.

Mrs Sugden, having returned from her typewriting class, had placed a page of letters, mostly f, j, d and k, on the hall table for my perusal. The effort must have exhausted her for she had retired for the night. She had also left a note: *Arthur has fixed the Jowett. He will bring it across first thing.*

Goody, goody. Now I could look forward to a lecture, and would probably have to endure demonstrations involving oil and water, tyres and big ends

Sykes hovered. 'Shall I put the Morris away?'

'No, leave it there. Arthur will be across at the crack of dawn, returning my Jowett and taking the Morris back to Wakefield.'

'Right then, I'll be off.'

'There is one thing you could do for me, Mr Sykes.'

'Of course.'

'Gideon King went into the hotel to add something to his statement. Would you find out if he has been allowed to return home?'

Sykes nodded. 'Yes I'll do that.'

'Please say I ask that he be released. But I'll give you a spare toothbrush to take to him, just in case.'

I went up to the bathroom and took a toothbrush from the cabinet.

Sykes put the toothbrush in his pocket. 'I expect this will be the end of our involvement.'

'Yes.'

'It's been interesting, being a special constable, and having the bike.'

'Come round in the morning, Mr Sykes, not too early. We'll put our heads together about where we go from here.'

I listened until the motorbike engine hummed into life, and then faded as Sykes rode away.

No matter what the hour, Philippa would want to know that Everett's murderer had been apprehended. I picked up the telephone. It was a relief to me when King answered.

'Mr King, I'm glad you're home.'

'So am I, Mrs Shackleton.'

'Would you please tell Philippa I have some news and will come now, if it's not too late.'

'I'll be waiting for you.'

And he was waiting. As I drew up outside the house, he approached the car, and opened the door for me.

'Was it terrible, Mr King?'

'Gideon. And, yes. But thankfully, Philippa did not realise I had been and gone, thanks to her own preoccupations, and because dealing with the inventory takes me into far-flung corners of the house.'

'Well I'm glad you didn't need the toothbrush.'

We walked towards the doorway that was lit by the looted Chinese lanterns. 'I haven't told Philippa, about Diamond and the money, and so on.'

'Then I won't either. You can rely on me.'

'Thank you.' He paused by the steps. 'I'm not going back to Boston with her. I haven't told her that either.'

'What will you do?'

'I thought of Paris, somewhere I can start again.'

'Well that sounds a good idea. There are lots of Americans in Paris. But Philippa will miss you.'

'No she won't. She won't need me any more.'

'What will you do there?'

He shrugged. 'I'm sure someone will want a private secretary, and I daresay I shall have a testimonial from Philippa.' We walked up the steps towards the front door which stood open. 'She knows you are coming. I'm to take you up.'

I followed him up the broad staircase.

He tapped on Philippa's door, and then discreetly vanished.

A fire glowed. Philippa sat at her table, a pile of papers in front of her. She stood and came to greet me. 'Kate, come and sit down. What is it? You look quite pale.'

'It's been quite a day, quite an evening.'

As we sat by the fire, I told her that Cromer had been arrested for Everett's murder, about how the newspaper photograph and the 'accidental' shot at Caroline had roused my suspicions, about the photograph of Rupert Cromer, pointing his gun.

'I didn't even know he was at the shoot.'

'He wasn't supposed to be.'

'What did he have against Everett?'

This was the hardest part, to tell her that Cromer loved Caroline Windham, his muse. He more than loved her, he was protective of her and obsessed by her.

Philippa stared into the fire. 'Do you know, I can see why Cromer would care passionately for Caroline. She would be his type. It's a pity she did not see it that way. It would have saved us all so much heartache.'

'And Everett his life.'

'Yes. Poor Everett. In many ways, he was such a stupid man. He couldn't see where his own true interests lay.' She went back to her table and opened a drawer. 'I'll write you a cheque now, Kate. My brother-in-law will be very relieved that the spotlight has turned from the bank and Everett's business associates.'

It was a more than generous cheque but I did not demur. I had earned this.

She said once again, 'Rupert Cromer. To think he was at the races, and to think some people call him a genius. What a waste, Kate.'

'I know.'

For me that was almost the hardest part, two artists of the highest calibre, Diamond and Cromer, both damned to hell for their crimes.

The next morning, as I ate a late breakfast, a large package arrived, brought by one of the men from Kirkley Hall. I opened the accompanying envelope first.

Dear Kate

I cannot now take this bust with me. It is the one Everett commissioned from Cromer. Although it may be regarded as a work of art and a thing of beauty, I do not want to have it near me, or to know that it is on my side of the ocean. Have it if you wish, as a memento of this strange episode. Or, if you do not want it, give it to some gallery with instructions that they must never let it go in case it finds its way in my direction.

My thanks again. The chief inspector called this morning, to give me the news you gave me last night. I kept quiet, so I suppose he thought me heartless, and that I took the blow most stoically.

Yours truly,
Philippa Runcie

Mrs Sugden said, 'Shall I unwrap this object?'

'Not yet. I'm not quite ready to look at it.'

There was a knock on the door. 'Put it out of the way, or Mr Sykes will be curious to see it, and he can wait.'

Sykes joined me for a cup of tea and a slice of toast.

'I see you've got the Jowett back.'

'Yes, thanks to Arthur. And we have a surprise journey, Mr Sykes. You can map read. I'll drive.'

'Where do I map read to?'

'Five Lane Ends in Idle.'

'Bradford?'

'Yes. You'll see the map on the dining room table.'

'Right-o. I shall peruse it now and commit to memory.'

Half an hour later, we were well on our way in the Jowett, which looked spruce after Arthur's attention, me driving, Sykes navigating. He tapped the map. 'It's a right here.'

I turned right onto a twisting road. 'I've been thinking, Mr Sykes.'

'Oh?'

'Cyril Fitzpatrick earned three pounds eight and six. I'm not paying you enough.'

'If you say so.'

'I do.'

He cannot help but argue, even when it is against his own best interest. 'I have my special constable fee, and a few bob more, here and there.'

'Yes, well the less said about that the better. You shouldn't need to be selling swimsuits and stockings in public houses.'

'It can be a good cover.'

We reached a fork in the road. 'Do you want a rise in pay or not?'

'Turn left, and yes. It wouldn't go amiss.' He looked up from the map and stared ahead. 'Why are we visiting a slag heap?'

'It's not just a slag heap, there's a works here.'

And as we turned, there it stood: the Jowett Motor Manufacturing Company.

Sykes let the map slide to the floor. 'So what are we doing here? Don't tell me someone's nicking their motors?'

'I have an appointment with Mr Benjamin Jowett, to test drive a new car.'

For once, Sykes was shocked into silence.

Such had been Philippa Runcie's generosity that I could pay one hundred and sixty pounds outright for the motor, plus ten pounds extra for the electric starter, and still have enough left to pay Mr Sykes and myself handsomely for another eighteen months.

As we drove into the massive yard, Sykes found his tongue. 'Can we get a black one? I've nothing against pale blue for frocks, but I come in for some funny comments when I drive this.'

'Keep your voice down. Don't offend her.'

He tapped the dashboard. 'She's not listening. She's looking at her cousins.' By the far wall, standing elegantly in a row, were half a dozen gleaming motors.

'So what sort of comments do you get when you're driving?'

'Unrepeatable.'

'Oh go on.'

'I couldn't possibly.'

'Can't be worse than what I have to put up with. Tell me or I'll get blue again.' I stopped the motor by the factory's big doors.

'Oh, all right. Last time I was out in this, some stupid bloke shouted, Do you pee sitting down?'

I started to laugh. Sykes climbed out, in one of his huffs. I slid out after him. 'Well I don't want to drive a black car, Mr Sykes. But you can have this one painted any colour you like.'

'What? I'm to have this one?'

'Unless you'd prefer a motorbike?'

He picked up the map from the passenger seat and started to fold it carefully, to hide his emotion. 'This one will be just grand, once she's painted black. I'll do it myself.'

'You will not. They'll do it here for you.'

A smiling man in a good suit emerged, walking towards us. 'Mrs Shackleton?'

We shook hands. I introduced Mr Sykes, who gladly

agreed to have a senior mechanic give him a tour of the works while Mr Jowett and I went across to the dark blue Short-Two, with black mudguards, that we had discussed on the telephone.

'You're testing a popular motor, Mrs Shackleton. We made five hundred of these last year and we're set to double production this year.'

'Lots of Jowetteers on the road then?' I remembered my kindly rescuer, and all the salutes I had given and returned over the years.

'Yes indeed. And what's going to happen to your present motor?' he asked.

'Mr Sykes will have it.'

'That's the ticket. Old Jowetts never wear out, they're inherited.'

He opened the door. I slid into the driver's seat, my coat squeaking across the new leather.

'I say, if you don't mind my asking, are you the Mrs Shackleton who solved the murder of the banker?'

'Well, it was really Scotland Yard.'

'That's not what I heard.'

At this rate, I would be as famous as the Jowett.

Thirty-Nine

Sykes surprised me by announcing that he would attend Cyril Fitzpatrick's funeral. He even visited the Roman Catholic cathedral to acclimatise himself so that he would be prepared for the popish surroundings. It was to take place a week and a day after Mrs Hartigan's funeral, hardly allowing time to press the black skirt.

Sykes and I sat halfway down the church. There was a good turnout for the Requiem Mass. A couple of sombre-looking chaps took round the collection plate, the task once undertaken by Fitzpatrick himself.

What intrigued me was the hymn singing. One voice soared above all others and this was most marked in the final hymn, *Faith of our Fathers*.

The mystery was solved as we watched mourners file along the aisle behind the coffin. Deirdre walked with her aunts; Uncle Jimmy led a posse of relations. Here came the singer. Alongside faithful Eddie Flanagan, in his well-brushed dark jacket, stepped Joseph Barnard, wearing an impeccably tailored black suit and cravat, carrying a homburg.

I felt a reluctance to attend the interment, in case

of further accidental deaths at the cemetery, but Sykes urged me to see it through, for poor Fitzpatrick's sake. Consequently we made for the motor. Had my new Jowett been black, I would have followed the cortege, but having chosen dark blue I thought it proper to drive separately, which meant that we arrived first and were able to wait by the cemetery gates.

Sykes studied the mourners closely. 'Mr Sykes, you're not on duty.'

'I'm never off duty, any more than you are, Mrs Shackleton.'

'Well I hope I'm not making it so obvious.'

We walked up the path in the direction of Fitzpatrick's family grave. A man in an astrakhan coat sidled up beside me and cleared his throat. 'Mrs Shackleton.'

It was the solicitor who had come to Deirdre's aid. 'Mr Cohen.'

He smiled as affably as one dare on such an occasion. 'Thank you for asking me to represent Mrs Fitzpatrick.'

'It was Mr Brasher, the boxing promoter, who made the suggestion.'

'Yes, but you took Mrs Fitzpatrick to Brasher's gym when you could have acted differently. She is most grateful, and so is her brother. If I can ever be of service, Mrs Shackleton, you only have to ask.' He produced his card and handed it to me.

'Thank you.'

'And I am asked to give you an envelope, from Mr Hartigan.'

It was difficult to refuse as he did a reverse pickpocket action and thrust the envelope into my pocket. I could feel its width and knew its contents would be used notes.

I looked at the nuns in a small group by the foot of the grave and chose one that I would hand it to. It may be that the money was clean as newly fallen snow, or it may be splattered in blood. I would not keep it.

Deirdre stood at the graveside, her friend Rita beside her, linking her arm. It struck me that Rita was one of the few people who knew the nature of Fitzpatrick and Deirdre's marriage. Eddie supported the two aunts, who looked most distressed, despite not being close to Fitzpatrick, or perhaps because of that.

I was glad when it was over. I went to Deirdre and shook her hand, murmuring a few words of sympathy.

Her eyes were red-rimmed, and her nose sore from the friction of too much wiping. She said, 'There's a breakfast at the Lloyds Arms.'

'That's kind of you, but I won't this time.'

That was a silly thing to say, because it hinted that if she laid some future husband to rest, I might come then. But I hope she understood that I meant I would find it awkward to be a stranger amongst the relatives and friends at such a time.

Sykes whispered, 'I'll go. You never know when it might come in handy to have a friendly face on the Bank.' Given the number of nuns and clergy that would be in attendance, it surprised me that Sykes would feel at home at such a repast. He read my look and said, 'The landlord at the Lloyds is a left footer.'

That was my moment to give the money to the Little Sisters' Mother Superior, with a whisper that it was from Anthony Hartigan, for the poor of the parish. Which I suppose included absolutely everyone.

I drove both Sykes and Joseph Barnard into town. After

I dropped Sykes by the Lloyds, Mr Barnard stepped out from the dickey seat and came to sit beside me.

'I read about Mr Fitzpatrick's death in the paper,' he said. 'I wanted to pay my respects to the poor man, and show Deirdre that I care.'

'And do you care?'

'I do indeed. I shall be writing to her and asking if we can see each other again. And if there is ever a show you wish to attend, please let me know and I shall be happy to arrange tickets for you.'

'Thank you.'

Somehow, I did not feel in a hurry to see and hear Mr Barnard singing his heart out. For a long time, Gilbert & Sullivan music would serve to remind me of terrible deaths, and of smoke rising from an overworked Jowett.

'Mr Barnard, what is happening about your divorce? Has it been put in jeopardy by events?'

'Fortunately not.'

I was glad of that, having heard that his solicitor, Mr Lansbury, had escaped with a stern warning.

We were at the station. Barnard thanked me for the lift and hurried to catch his train.

There would be two more funerals for me to attend.

Leonard Diamond was buried in Beckett Street Cemetery. Three of us said our last goodbyes: me, Mr Duffield and young Tom Ashworth, who had taken Diamond's place as newspaper photographer.

By contrast with Diamond's muted funeral, Everett Runcie's last goodbye was exceedingly grand, as befitted a minor member of the aristocracy, the second son of a long-established family of bankers. He was laid to rest in the family vault. The day dawned cold and blustery. Philippa Runcie drew no odd looks for being swathed in a voluminous sable coat. At the funeral breakfast, a cleverly designed black velvet dress concealed her pregnancy. In a few more weeks she would sail for New York, smuggling in her womb the rightful heir to the Runcie name and ancestral home. He would be born on the other side of the Atlantic, and live an altogether freer life.

Marcus had travelled north for the funeral. We exchanged a few words before entering the chapel, and I felt glad that we would always get on with each other.

During the service, he sat with an elderly man who sported a colonial style moustache and carried a cane with a gold horse's head knob.

Aunt Berta whispered, 'I see your old friend Mr Charles is getting to know the right people. Is he chasing a knighthood?'

'I shouldn't think so. Who is the man he is with?'

'My dear, you must get to know your dukes. I'll introduce you later. He owns an immense chunk of the Highlands. Your uncle won't buy anyone else's whisky.'

The pair left the chapel before us. As they walked along the aisle, they glanced in my direction.

Aunt Berta said, 'They are talking about you.'

It was on the walk back to Kirkley Hall for the funeral breakfast that the bewhiskered duke engaged Aunt Berta in conversation.

Marcus fell into step with me. 'Kate, you'll hate me for saying this, but I want to know that I can rely on your discretion regarding that little deal between Hartigan and the distiller.'

The sun had put in an appearance when we left the chapel. But for me, brightness fled from the day.

Marcus did not trust me. He would never completely trust me. As far as he was concerned, he was inside the establishment tent and I was outside, slightly dangerous, a person to watch.

The two women in Runcie's life stayed apart from each other at the funeral, and at the breakfast that followed. Caroline Windham remained in the orbit of Lord and Lady Fotheringham. My aunt spoke to her, but I did not, not until it was almost time to leave.

We were on the veranda, with glasses of sherry. She was standing alone, near a potted plant, and waved to me.

Not a person to take time coming to the point, she said, 'Rupert asked to see me, a condemned man's last request.'

I did not know what to say.

'I broke his shoulder, you know, when I hit him with the poker. I'm not sorry. He said he wished I'd hit him on his skull and killed him.' She took another sip of sherry. 'I don't know how he did it, but he had a will that pre-dated his arrest or something. All his work comes to me.'

It seemed an unusual outcome. I would have expected a condemned man's assets to be seized by the Crown. Perhaps one of the Viking Queen's ancestors had fought alongside the ancestor of an Important Person in probate. Would she try and flog me a sculpture?

Mercifully, not.

'I don't know what to do about any of it,' she said.

'Fotheringham has no idea either. He says no one in England will want Cromer's work for a generation or more. You wouldn't, would you?'

'No.' I thought of the bust of Philippa that she had sent me. It remained in its wrappings. Then I spotted King. A brilliant idea occurred to me. 'Go to Paris, Miss Windham. Sell the work there. You could open a gallery.'

Her eyes widened at the possibility.

Having come up with the idea, I warmed to it. 'I will photograph the work for you, anonymously. That would help make the pieces more widely known. It will give you a fresh start.'

'I should hate to leave England.'

'But you were going to Italy.'

'That's different. I'm not sure about France, but I suppose I might take to Paris.'

'Paris would take to you.'

'Something will have to happen. Otherwise the sculptures stay on Fotheringham's estate and he thinks there's something ghoulish about it all. I would not be surprised if he had them smashed up for gravel. There has always been a philistine streak in that family.'

'Then do it.'

'I could certainly talk about the work, be enthusiastic about it.'

'And knowledgeable.'

'But I'd be hopeless at the business side.'

'Not if you had the right partner. There's someone whom I believe would be very good. He is going to Paris, and with no particular plans that I know of.'

'Who?'

I nodded towards King. 'With your flair and Gideon

King the third's business acumen, you'll go far I should think. Do you get on with him?'

'I've never had much to do with him. He is Philippa's secretary don't forget.'

'Not any more.' I waved to Gideon. 'Go into the maze, Caroline. No one will see you. I'll tell him to follow, and you can talk it over.'

Forty

Since my niece Harriet had let slip that her mother would be asking to stay with me to establish residency for marriage at Leeds Register Office, I had expected to hear from Mary Jane. A brief letter had followed, asking could she stay in my spare room, and that she would visit me soon.

For once, her timing was impeccable. She knocked on the door the day after Everett Runcie's funeral, bringing the children with her.

Never previously having contact with my birth family, I did not know of Mary Jane's existence until the spring of this year. It was then that she sought me out to ask for help, when her husband disappeared. Meeting my new family had come as something of a shock.

She and I sat in the back garden. Harriet and Austin played in the wood, looking for the best trees to climb.

'Don't fall and break anything!' Mary Jane called to them. 'I'm not spending hours sitting in that dispensary.'

'They'll be fine.'

We had made a picnic and brought it outside, taking advantage of the fine day.

'Catherine, you know you said I could stay here for residency until my banns have been called.'

'Yes.'

She glanced towards the house. 'This is a really nice spot, and such a lovely house.'

A chill ran through me. She had relinquished her tied house. She and her children had been camping out with her mother, or I should say 'our mother'. Mary Jane did not like the tongue-wagging that resulted when she and the children moved into the farm with her fiancé. And since the farm was being sold and furniture auctioned off, it was not the most comfortable place to be.

'The children have had such a lot of disruption,' she said.

Their voices floated from the wood. Harriet was shouting, 'Coming, ready or not!'

'Well you know your spare room that you said I could stay in?'

'Yes,' I said cautiously.

'The thing is, Catherine, I know it's a bit soon but the people selling us the newsagent's shop and house in Helmsley want to bring the sale forward. It will suit us down to the ground. Of course it means early mornings for the papers and so on, but Roland is used to that. And Harriet is quite keen on the idea of serving on in the shop.'

'She's a bit young isn't she?'

'Oh only at weekends and after school. But the thing is, we don't want to delay. We want a totally fresh start and to turn up in Helmsley as man and wife, all official.'

'Yes I can see the sense of that.'

'Otherwise, I wouldn't have thought of re-marrying so very soon. I would have let a year go by, out of decency.

'But you'd already set the date for November.'

'And now we're bringing it forward to October.'

'October?' I heard the panic in my voice. Was she planning to move in today?

'Roland is so particular about keeping to the rules. You'd be surprised. So if we could just move in here, quite soon. You won't notice us. Roland has various bits of business to attend to before we can leave Great Applewick, but we're thinking of a date early in October, then I'll be a clear six months widowed and it won't seem so appalling.'

I was glad we were sitting side by side and she could not see my face. Her arithmetic was a little at fault. It would not be six months since her husband's death, it would be five. It amazed me that she could put the past behind her so quickly. What kind of idiot am I, that I stick in this muddy might-have-been world of never quite acknowledging that Gerald is not coming back?

I have turned down Marcus Charles, and am probably destined to live alone forever. But it could be worse. I could have married Marcus.

'Do you all want to move in here?'

'Oh no, just me and Roland. The kids can stay with Mam in Wakefield.'

'What about school?'

'There's no point in them enrolling in a new school until we get to Helmsley. Mam will put them through their paces. She's good at times tables.'

I could have said no, but it seemed mean to deny them hospitality after all they had been through. If they were staying here, I would lock my filing cabinet, hand the key to Sykes for the duration and de-camp. Aunt Berta was still at Kirkley Hall and had asked me to go back to London with her early next week.

I looked at the children, happily climbing trees, and thought of the cramped situation at the house in White Swan Yard.

'Mary Jane, there's a house I sometimes rent in Robin Hood's Bay.'

'Oh we don't want to marry in Robin Hood's Bay. Where is it anyway?'

'It's near Whitby.'

'We don't want to go near Whitby, all fish and wind and Dracula.'

'I was thinking of the children and their grandmother. I have to go to London, but before I go, I could drive them to Robin Hood's Bay, for a holiday by the sea.'

Their grandmother, my birth mother, the woman I call Mrs Whitaker. Now would be our opportunity for us to get to know each other a little, with the buffer of my niece and nephew to smooth out any awkwardness.

Mary Jane waved to Austin who was sitting on the low branch of a tree. 'I think that's a wonderful idea.'

'I'll see what I can do. It'll take a bit of organising at such short notice, but it'll be a good run for my new motor. The luggage could be sent on by train.'

'And I have a favour to ask.'

'Oh yes?' I said lightly, keeping the dread from my voice. What could it be now?

'Will you be my maid of honour, or I suppose it will be witness in a registry office?'

'What about Barbara May?'

Barbara May was her elder and closest sister, and Mary Jane's maid of honour when she married Ethan.

I had said the wrong thing. Her face crumpled into a copy of Disappointment from the Five Boys chocolate advertisement.

'We've fallen out over it. She's telling me it's too soon for me to marry again. Do you think it's too soon?' She did not wait for me to answer. 'It's either marriage, or living over the brush. And I'm thinking of the children, starting again at a new school. I don't want gossip. It'll be bad enough that we're different names, but Harriet is adamant that she won't change her name, little madam.'

'It's not too soon if you don't think it's too soon.'

Mary Jane, who is normally the most self-possessed of women, suddenly burst into tears. 'It will be too soon, and it will be too late. I should have married Roland years ago. And if I marry him now, it will be like turning back the clock and rubbing Ethan out of existence. Ethan swept me off my feet, but it was always Roland who was there, always Roland who was my soul mate.'

'Then marry him. Look forward, not back.'

She nodded miserably.

Polishing off a couple of jam tarts cheered her up.

Mary Jane seemed so relieved and relaxed to have steamrollered me into agreeing that she and Roland could move in that she fell into a sound slumber, snoring gently.

All that remained was for me to break the news to my housekeeper. Mrs Sugden would probably get on well with Mary Jane, and if she did not, then at least she has her own quarters.

I watched the children playing, hiding among the trees. My little wood would have looked quite different with a fine piece of Cromer sculpture at its heart.

Cromer's trial was imminent. I hoped not to be called.

He would plead guilty, Marcus had told me, because he had already confessed, and because he could not bear to have Caroline Windham take the stand against him and point her fine finger at his broken and dastardly heart.

'Mrs Shackleton!'

The man's voice came from behind. I turned, and just for a second could not place him because his appearance was so unexpected. He was smartly turned out, cleanly shaven and had his unruly hair plastered to his head. It was Eddie, the punch-drunk boxer, Deirdre Fitzpatrick's faithful swain.

'Mr Flanagan.'

'I've summat to tell you.'

Mary Jane did not wake, but she might.

Something in Eddie Flanagan's look told me that his words were for my ears only. 'We'll go inside, Mr Flanagan.'

If this was some new concern about the errant Deirdre, he could bark up another tree.

We went through the back door into the kitchen. 'Please sit down.'

He sat down, and put his cap on the table, but made no effort to speak. I would have to start the conversation.

'We didn't get the chance to speak at Mr Fitzpatrick's funeral.'

'I'm not here over that.'

'Oh?'

He took something from his pocket, holding it in his fist. Opening his hand, he revealed a scrap of brown paper. He set it on the table in front of him and unfolded the paper to reveal a small circular piece of glass, its surface dull and scratched. 'I brought you this.' He pushed it towards me.

We both stared at it.

'What is it?'

'I think it's from his camera.'

'Whose camera?'

'The medical officer's camera. Mr Shackleton's camera.'

Something tightened in my chest. 'His camera? Gerald's camera?'

'Aye. I found it. I saw it glinting in the sun, after the explosions, and I thought, I know what that is. I don't know why I picked it up, I just did.'

'When?'

'On that day, the day of the big explosion on the road.'

I pulled the piece of glass towards me and held it between fingers and thumb. It could be a camera lens. It was the right shape and thickness.

Eddie sat very still, hardly breathing, waiting.

All this time I had searched for news of Gerald, among officers and men, written letters and made visits. Now here was this man whose wits had been punched around his skull so many times that you would not want to send him on an errand that required him to read the number on a tramcar.

'Tell me, tell me about it, Mr Flanagan. Please. Take your time.'

'I can't remember the day, but I know it was April, because Deirdre sent me a bar of chocolate for Easter, and she drew a picture of a little yellow chicken and it had come a little bit late, after Easter Sunday had passed. I was in the quarry because I'd had to be bandaged and a lot of them was killed when the shell came, but not the medical officer and not me. We took what we could carry and set off, walking. Only I was a bit behind. I stopped for summat. And up in front of me on the road, it all went off, all sudden like, and smoke and sparks and all the rest. After it, there was not so many of us walking along. He was the one I looked for because you need an MO. I thought, even he won't be taking photographs of this mess. And then this bit of glass glinted. It caught my eye. I picked it up.'

I held the lens in my palm, and then clutched it tight. And I believed him. So this was it. This was the end of my search, a small circular piece of glass, scratched and dull.

Gerald would never come home.

There would be no burial, and no goodbye.

I would cherish this memento.

And I imagined a time to come, when I would be gone. Someone would clear my things. They would pick up this piece of glass. Why did she keep this?

And it would be thrown away.

Epilogue

I had taken my niece and nephew, their grandmother and the dog to the seaside. On the way to Robin Hood's Bay, we called at Scarborough for fish and chips in the Golden Haddock.

As we sat at a table in the window, the dog making itself small in exchange for dropped chips, I watched the world walk by, and the world included Deirdre Fitzpatrick, on the arm of Joseph Barnard, who was playing Scarborough this week.

I would not have minded a break by the sea myself, but I deposited the family at the Robin Hood's Bay cottage, planning to stay just one day, having promised Aunt Berta that I would travel back to London with her and my real mother, the one who adopted me, Ginny Hood.

A person must be hardy indeed to swim in the North Sea in the middle of September. The cold turns your eyes to ice cubes and a snowman would be white hot by comparison with us three, leaping into the waves, screeching with laughter and jumping deeper.

Mrs Whitaker sat in her big coat and felt hat, drying the wet shaggy dog. She had bravely insisted the steep hill to the bay was no impediment for her, but that the dog found it rather trying.

It was the first time the children, and the dog, had seen the sea so there was something quite magical about it. We explored the rock pools with fishing nets and found fossils. Austin insisted they must all be taken home, for the garden of the new house in Helmsley.

The three were happily ensconced in the cottage. Deciding against driving across the moors in darkness, I drove to Whitby and spent a solitary night in a room with a sea view, remembering happier days. This was the place Gerald and I had first met. This was where I said goodbye to him, looking out to sea.

Aunt Berta's house in London seemed a world away. I stayed with her for three weeks. Towards the end of my visit, Mother was upstairs. I was sitting at breakfast with Aunt Berta, looking over the menu for the evening's dinner party. She had invited the mourning Baron Kirkley, Harold Runcie, Everett's elder brother. Once again the baron had taken over ownership of Kirkley Hall, due to Philippa having made good her escape.

Aunt Berta confided in me. 'I asked Harold because he needs taking out of himself after his ordeal. I know it's a little late for him, but he must find a wife, or there'll be no heir for the Kirkley title.'

Alarm bells rang. For a long time, Aunt Berta had tried to match-make on my behalf.

She laughed when she read my look. 'Oh don't worry, Kate dear, not you! I know you've let that policeman go, but you and Harold are not a match. He needs to find a woman with a great deal of money, if he's to keep Kirkley

Hall.' She sighed. 'Though it would be nice to have you titled and in London a great deal.'

The guest list included a commander from Scotland Yard, a widower and old school chum of my uncle. The commander had specially wangled an invitation in order to thank me for my help in solving Everett Runcie's murder.

All in all I was looking forward to the dinner party. It had been a tricky few weeks as everyone wanted to ask me about the investigation, and I would not speak of it. The Everett Runcie and Leonard Diamond cases had certainly made me well known among the kind of people who might bring an interesting puzzle to a private investigator.

And truth to tell, I was glad to be away from the north when Rupert Cromer went to the scaffold for the murders of Everett Runcie and Leonard Diamond.

I hoped that the Scotland Yard commander would be indiscreet about Marcus Charles. The American Ambassador had praised Marcus for his vigilant observation of Anthony Hartigan, and his firm assurance that the man was allowed to do nothing worse, while visiting England, than see his family, pay respects to his dying mother, and arrange her funeral.

The cooperation between Washington and London was highly valued. As a result, Marcus had been invited to Washington to have high-level meetings regarding future cooperation.

I had to laugh, feeling sure that Marcus's reports had included nothing about the importation into the USA of spirits; gin from London, whisky from the Highlands.

Marcus's letter had arrived that morning. Aunt Berta was perusing a letter of her own, and so I read mine.

Dear Kate

Here I am in New York, after a most eventful voyage. I am pleased to say I have good sea legs and found the passage much to my liking. It is a strange experience being between worlds, and yet bringing the past along.

No, I am not becoming poetical or philosophical. That is not in my nature as you know. I am a practical man. It happened that Mrs Runcie was on the same voyage, and we acknowledged each other, politely but distantly. I respected her wishes not to be reminded of all that has just passed. Her private secretary did not travel with her. She told me he has gone to Paris where he intends to deal in art.

I put down the letter. Did Philippa know that King had gone with Caroline Windham? Perhaps she would not mind where her former secretary went, now that she was starting her life anew. I began to read again.

There is something else which I hesitate to mention in case I am being premature, but I do so because you and I have a great respect for each other and have always been honest. (Sometimes you were more honest than my vanity would have wished!) I met a young lady on board and I know that ship's romances are common and do not always last, but I have some hopes that I may have found someone who will want to share my terrible policeman's life. If this turns out to be true, you will be the first to know, dear Kate.

I paused in my reading. Well thank God for that.

The rest of his letter was filled with the sights of New York, the strangeness of the streets, how differently things were done there, and that the next morning he would take a train to Washington DC.

He said nothing more about the woman he had met on board. I wished him well, and hoped she was not an undercover agent for the Mafia who would trip him up before he began.

My mother swept in for breakfast. 'Both of you with letters. Anything interesting?'

Aunt Berta shook her head. 'Another friend trying to wangle an invitation to meet the famous Kate.'

Mother laughed. 'How about your letter, Katie? I might as well be nosey.'

'It's from Marcus. He seems very happy to be in America.'

Mother smiled brightly. 'Good.' She turned to her sister. 'Your guest list for this evening, Berta. I think you said one of the men is very keen to meet Kate.'

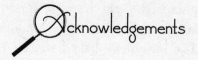

Acknowledgements

Thanks to Ann Hazan, good friend and seasoned racegoer, for her winning tips. My uncle, Peter Brannan, would have been pleased at his resurrection in his old occupation as bookmaker's clerk for Willie Price.

Tom Howley, formerly Father of the Chapel at Yorkshire Post Newspapers, generously shared his knowledge.

Thanks to retired police officer Ralph Lindley and his wife Mary, who kindly discussed the case with me.

Noel Stokoe, editor of the *Jowetteer*, and author of several books on the Jowett (a motor that contained "all the best bits of Yorkshire except the pudding") advised on Kate's change of vehicle.

Stuart Walker helpfully drew on his knowledge of country pursuits to answer my questions regarding grouse shooting.

It is always a pleasure to hear from readers. Eddie Kelly

wondered when Sykes would visit his local, the Chemic, for a pint. Cheers, Eddie.

As lapsed and unlapsed Catholics will know, the Sisters of the Sacred Candle of St Genevieve should have existed but never did. The long-demolished area of Leeds called the Bank was real enough; life there would have been desperate without the dedicated work of the Little Sisters of the Poor.

Shady prodigal, Anthony Hartigan, was inspired by Owney Madden who went from the Bank to New York, via Wigan, and became well known to the FBI. In his highly readable and authoritative *The English Godfather*, Graham Nown gives Madden's place of birth as Somerset Street. A surviving relative places him on Cotton Street, and says that Madden's famous Harlem Cotton Club was named after the street on the Bank. Fact or legend? – no contest.

Very special thanks to my agent, Judith Murdoch, to editor, Lucy Icke, and all at Piatkus.